A Vengeful Longing
A St Petersburg Mystery

R.N. MORRIS

R.N. Morris © 2008.

R.N. Morris has asserted his rights under the Copyright, Design and Patents Act, 1988, to be identified as the author of this work.

First published by Faber and Faber Limited in 2008.

This edition published by Sharpe Books in 2020.

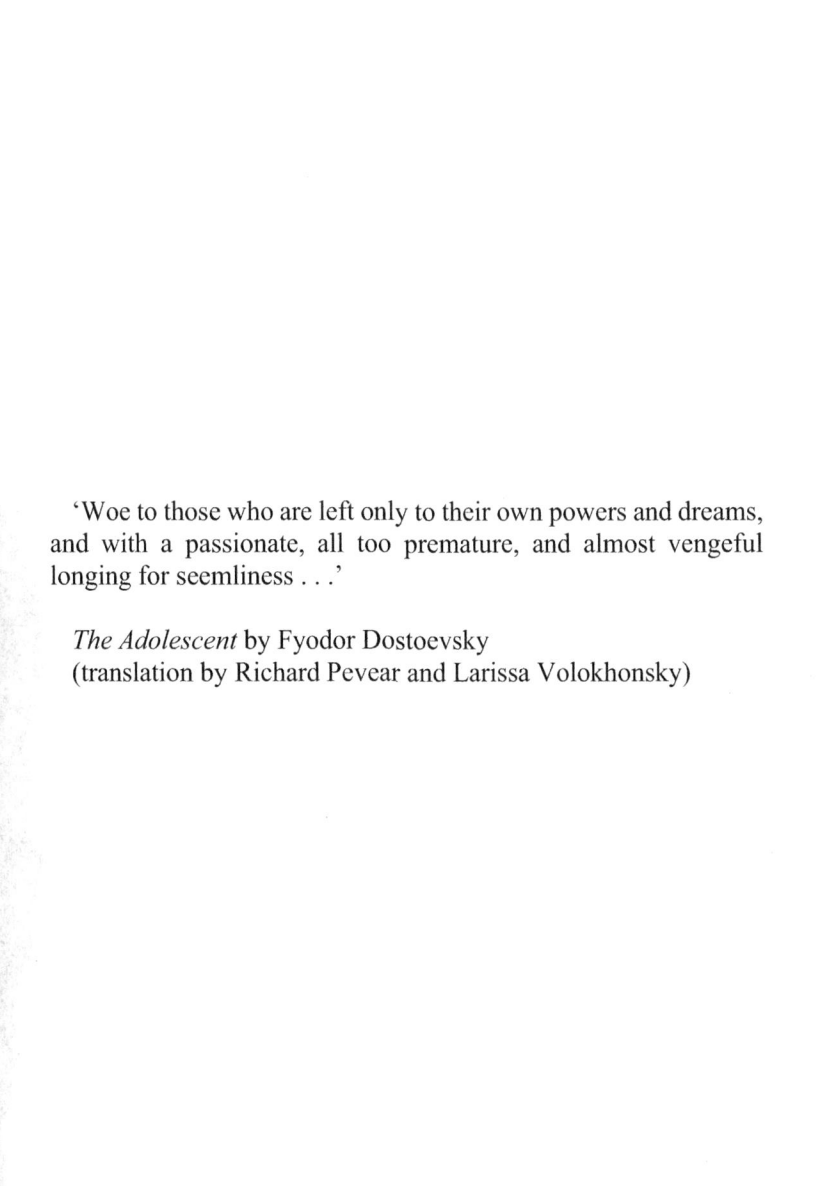

'Woe to those who are left only to their own powers and dreams, and with a passionate, all too premature, and almost vengeful longing for seemliness . . .'

The Adolescent by Fyodor Dostoevsky
(translation by Richard Pevear and Larissa Volokhonsky)

CONTENTS

PART ONE: Poison
1: In an island dacha
2: The new recruit
3: A Russian beauty
4: Examination and elimination
5: At the confectioner's
6: One Bezmygin, a musician
7: Count Akhmakov's orchestra
8: The nasty letter
PART TWO: Pistol
1: 'Gunshot!'
2: Lost and found
3: The girl in the counterpane
4: The bachelor diary
5: The angel (and her daughter)
6: Among the whores
7: The Uninvited One
8: Family obligations
9: Golyadkin's classmates
PART THREE: Poniard
1: The fallen man
2: Nikolai Nobody
3: *Misericorde*
4: The widow Dobroselova
5: The house at the eleventh verst
6: A litigious man
7: Inside the ministry
8: Interview with a madman
9: The diminished man
10: Panic in Stolyarny Lane
11: The vacant rooms
12: Philosophical ideas
13: In the secret heart of the city
Acknowledgements

Summer, 1868

R.N. MORRIS

PART ONE: Poison

1: In an island dacha

Raisa Ivanovna Meyer was sitting on the veranda of a rented dacha, listening to distant music from a pleasure boat as it filtered through successive screens of foliage. The notes that came to her were fragmented, barely music, but they compelled her attention more than the novel she had been drowsing over. She placed the book down on the marble table and looked up.

She was irritated, rather than soothed, by the broken strains. If only she could place the tune, then she could relax, and the music would have fulfilled its promise. But it set her nerves on edge, and the wafts of nostalgia that it carried with it only depressed her. Sometimes it seemed to be getting closer, clarifying into something almost recognisable, but immediately it would again recede and disintegrate. Raisa looked at her son, Grisha, as he leant over the circular table, utterly absorbed in the activity of copying the Daily Events section of *The Voice*. The neatness, indeed the beauty, of Grisha's script provoked a surge of feeling in his mother: something fiercer, more complicated than pride. Pride was something she could never allow herself. But if she could not be wholly proud of Grisha, she would not be ashamed of him either. So they took their place on the front veranda, and Raisa met the questioning gazes of any passers-by with silent defiance.

Grisha's pen moved swiftly, the letters forming with seemingly mechanical perfection. The lines ran true and straight, although the paper was not ruled. It was as if he was painting, not writing, the characters. There was something wonderful in her son's obsession. It struck her at times as a blessing: a gift, truly, despite its pointlessness. The nib of the pen made little noises of contentment, chuckling scratches, as the ink flowed from it onto the surface of the paper. The absorption in his face frightened her. It was something she could never understand. What it said to her was that his devotion to this task was greater than any other feeling he was capable of. She knew that he needed her; that went without saying. And there were moments when only her clinging embrace was capable of calming and containing him. But this activity, the repeated copying of passages from the day's newspaper, was the only thing he went to voluntarily. He chose this over her, and she was jealous of it.

Of course, it was better that he was occupied and quiet than upset in any way, and so most of the time she left him to it. There had been days when she insisted on his laying down his pen to accompany her on a walk along the linden avenue to the orchard. Sometimes he went peaceably, sometimes there were scenes. The greater his agitation, the more determined she would be that he should go with her. Why did she do it? She could not imagine whatever possessed her to initiate these storms. She wondered at her own perversity. Part of it she recognised as a craving for humiliation. But she had no right, really, to parade her son, like the banner of her wickedness. She felt a rush of shame. As it always did, it came down to her shame. Once she had arrived at that, everything fitted into place, and she realised she could have no complaints. Whatever happened, she could not complain.

This was where she belonged, here on the veranda with Grisha. He was her son, the son she deserved, the son she would always accept without question.

She looked out along the dusty road. A slight, stooped figure in a dark green civil service coat and cap was walking towards the dacha, carrying a black bag in one hand and a slim box, wrapped in colourful paper, in the other.

The music from the pleasure boat changed. It became simply the clashing of a cymbal and the boom of a bass drum. There was no hope now of melody.

*

Grisha did not look up, not even at his father's footsteps on the veranda.

Dr Martin Meyer laid the box on the table without looking at his wife. 'Eat them quickly, before they melt.' The wrapping on the box announced *Ballet's Confectioners, Nevsky Prospekt.*

Raisa glanced at her husband as he took off his cap and ran a hand through his damp hair, then pushed the bridge of his wire-rimmed spectacles back up his nose. His face was clean-shaven, but glistened with sweat. He narrowed his eyes as he penetrated the interior of the dacha with an ambiguous gaze, both searching and apprehensive. His mouth was set in a grimace of discomfort.

'Chocolates?'

Dr Meyer appeared still distracted by the interior of his dacha, but he had heard his wife and answered her sharply. 'Don't I bring you chocolates every Saturday? Why should today be any different?'

If she was hurt by his bristling temper, Raisa hardly showed it, although perhaps the movement of her head did have something in common with a flinch. 'It is rather warm today,' she said quietly to the table.

At last Dr Meyer tore his eyes away from the inside of the dacha, and lowered them to consider his son's handiwork. 'Why do you let him do this?' he murmured, though still he did not look at Raisa, so that at first she was not sure the question was addressed to her.

'He enjoys it.'

Dr Meyer frowned self-consciously. It was as if he was waiting for her to see his displeasure, rather than considering what she had said. Raisa Meyer watched her husband closely, though with a detachment that shocked her. His face had once been illuminated by a passionate engagement; at times he had even been capable of impetuosity, as she well knew. Something petty, a kind of wretched, angry unhappiness, had driven out this vitality.

'He *enjoys* it?' Dr Meyer gave the word sarcastic emphasis. 'How can we know what he enjoys or does not enjoy? Besides, this is a compulsion. One does not enjoy a compulsion. We must take steps to break it.'

'Why?'

'Because it is not healthy.'

'Let's not talk of him as if he were not here.'

'Your sentimental . . . interventions . . .' Dr Meyer kept his eyes downcast as he spoke, as though he were scanning his son's writing for the words that he was struggling to produce. 'Are not . . . conducive to . . . progress.'

'Sentimental interventions?'

'Yes.'

'I am his mother.'

'Yes. And so . . . you of all people . . . must . . . should . . . be aware . . .' Dr Meyer broke off, pulling away the sheet that Grisha was working on. 'Just look at this!' The shock of his sudden deprivation showed in the boy's whole body, which recoiled as if charged with a spring. His arms flew up and his head began to bob. A kind of grunting moan rose in his throat.

Raisa watched him with alarm, knowing how this would end. She wanted to smother him in an embrace, to press him into her, for she knew that such complete contact with his mother would be the only thing that would go some way to consoling him for his loss. But she felt oddly constrained in her husband's presence.

Dr Meyer read from the sheet: "'On the eleventh of June on Vasilevsky Island, the partially decomposed body of an unidentified male was discovered by a party of picnickers." And this! "A young woman, thought to be a prostitute, hanged herself from the stairwell of an apartment building on Voznesensky Prospekt." And this! "In Tsarskoe Selo, the retired Collegiate Assessor Zarnitsyn killed his wife with a revolver before turning the weapon on himself . . ."'

'It's your newspaper!' protested Raisa.

'That has nothing to do with it! Such subjects are not suitable for a child of his . . .' For the first time since that afternoon, Dr Meyer looked directly at his son. He did not seem to like what he saw. 'Constitution.'

'It does not matter to him what he copies. It is only important that he copies something.' Raisa snatched the paper back and returned it to Grisha, placing an arm around his shoulder and pulling him to her tightly. Grisha moaned and resumed his copying.

Dr Meyer looked down at his wife and son in disbelief. 'You defy me in this? After everything.' He broke off. 'Of course! What should I expect?' Dr Meyer almost seemed to bow to his wife as he made to go inside. A strange smile settled on his lips. 'At least do me the favour of consuming the chocolates I have bought for you at considerable expense. Perhaps you will find it possible to obey me in that.' He lurched towards the open door, his shoe heels clacking on the boards of the veranda, as he fled the possibility of any response.

A moment later a door slammed inside. She felt the reverberation in the boards beneath her chair.

*

Raisa slipped the ribbon off and pulled away the wrapping. She removed the lid from the box and gazed almost with disgust at the gleaming dark spheres. Yes, she would obey him in this. She wouldn't be able to stop herself. It was this that disgusted her. She was appalled too by the sense that her husband was counting on her greed. She felt little stabs of misery accumulate into a bitter resentment.

Suddenly she knew that it was within her power not to eat the chocolates. She would not, after all, abase herself in his eyes, in the world's eyes.

To gorge on chocolates that were melting unappetisingly, on a day when it was too hot really to eat anything: she would not do it. The sense of rebellion that came from this decision liberated her. She looked down at the spreading bulk of her own body, and felt that she had taken a stand against the enemy that her life had become. She did not smile but she bowed her head, in solemn self-respect.

She heard footsteps approaching from inside, and looked up to see Polina, flushed in the face, carrying the samovar. The girl's youthful, lithe figure mocked her, as did the heedless beauty of her features. Raisa felt her resolve desert her as she looked at her maid. Self-pity took its place. It was hard to believe that she herself had once been just as slim. She even began to feel sorry for Polina, knowing that the day would come when she too would lose her figure and her looks. It was not pleasing to realise that she found this thought oddly consoling.

Polina laid the samovar down heavily. She bowed her head in a kind of curtsy, without meeting her mistress's eyes. The box of chocolates was thrust in front of her.

'Will you not have one, Polina?'

'No thank you, Raisa Ivanovna.'

'You must help us out. We have to eat them all before they melt.'

The girl wrinkled her nose in an expression of distaste. Raisa was mortified. She felt the existence of a different hierarchy from that of social class, one in which the privileges of youth outranked all others. Now all she wanted was for Polina to be gone, taking her haughty disapproval with her.

And so, she pushed the first chocolate whole into her mouth. It liquefied instantly, filling her mouth with the cloying cream of its praline centre.

Raisa kept her eyes on Polina as she worked her mouth around the chocolate. As she swallowed the soft globule of sweetness, she became aware of a slight, bitter aftertaste. Even so, her hand went back to the box. And quickly, the aftertaste gave way to a pleasant and addictive tingle, an eager craving in her mouth. She appeased it with a second chocolate that dissolved as quickly as the first.

'Chocolates, Grisha!' She shook the box at her son.

Grisha looked up from his copying. An immense smile spread over his face when he saw the chocolates. Raisa took it in eagerly.

'*Chocolats!*'

'*Oui, chocolats!*' Raisa was teaching her son French. She had been surprised at how quickly, and delightedly, he had picked it up. To realise that there was another way of referring to the world, that the objects around him could be dressed in different words, seemed to have opened a door in his mind. Her husband had watched with a vague, suspicious disapproval, but so far had said nothing.

'*Chocolat!*' repeated Grisha, the word bubbling through the sweet it named, now reduced to a sticky mush in his mouth. Raisa did not dare look at her maid, knowing the disgust she would find on her face.

'Shall I serve the tea, Raisa Ivanovna?'

Raisa nodded, still without looking at Polina. The slight bitterness that she had noticed before had returned. She looked at the box, as if to confirm that they had indeed come from the usual confectioner's.

Polina passed her a glass of tea. Her heels stomped sternly on the veranda.

'Will there be anything else?'

Raisa shook her head, as she hurried another chocolate into her mouth. Polina took her noisy disapproval back inside.

The maid's departure was liberating. Raisa and Grisha devoured the chocolates in an absorbed frenzy of consumption.

Raisa stared at the box, empty now apart from one remaining chocolate. It shamed and depressed her to look at it. To leave it was almost worse than to eat them all: the solitary chocolate exposed her weakness. But her self-disgust was becoming physical.

All she could taste now was the bitterness. She looked at her son. His expression was uncertain, almost fearful.

'*Ho-cla!*' he said, seemingly unable to form the word correctly.

The tingling had spread from her throat over the whole of her mouth, even numbing her lips and tongue. She felt that if she tried to speak, she wouldn't be able to. She began to be aware of a hot, parched sensation. She sipped her tea, but couldn't taste it.

Raisa noticed the look of panic on her son's face. His hands went to his throat. 'Grisha? Are you all right?'

He gasped harshly, trying to expel his fear, the flesh of his soft palate grating in a desperate hawking.

Raisa felt the tingling intensify into a fire in the flesh of her mouth and throat, as a numbness spread through her chest and out from her stomach. Her heart began to palpitate wildly.

A sudden, sharp cry from Grisha. He jumped up. The wrought-iron chair behind him fell over. The crash of the chair was strangely distant and muffled. He clutched one hand to his mouth. The fist of the other was pummelling his belly.

A thick, dark liquid seeped through his fingers. He took his hand away. His body shook in a violent convulsion that ended in a loud retch. His neat pages were covered in a viscous murky puddle.

Grisha turned a distraught face on his mother. For a moment, there was an edge of outrage to it, as when any child seeks out its parent to explain the unfairness of the world. But that gave way to simple fear.

'Oh, Grisha,' began Raisa, stretching out a consoling hand. But the nausea hit her now. A systemic convulsion took hold of her and her own vomit chased the words out of her mouth.

A high-pitched keening came from somewhere. It seemed to answer the pain Raisa was feeling, but she was not aware of making the sound: it was as though something inside her was being stretched and twisted and squeezed by iron hands.

And where was Grisha now? The table and the chairs on the veranda swam and merged, and somewhere in this swirl of detail was her son. Her eye picked out the discarded ribbon of the chocolates. Then she was aware of a fist beating down upon something solid and smooth.

Raisa's heart now felt as though it had been filled with mercury, her pulse laboured and erratic. Her breathing came unevenly, her lungs no longer certain what was expected of them. She felt a sudden hot weight in her bowels. A liquid gurgling came from Grisha.

'Mama!' Her vision came and went. She saw eyes, his eyes, fearful and imploring.

'It's . . . all . . . right . . . Grisha.' She was amazed how clearly she was able to think as she recognised the panic in her own voice.

Raisa reached out towards where she believed her son's hand

must be. She could see a hand, but it divided into two hands, which circled one another in her failing vision. She grabbed for one of the hands but pulled only air towards her. Her hand went flying. She had no control over any part of herself. She watched her hand smash into the samovar. Strange, she did not feel its heat, or even its hardness. The samovar toppled over and fell apart with a loud clatter.

Raisa sank to her knees. It was as if a heavy weight was pushing down on her shoulders, and her legs were just not up to it. Grisha now was lying on his back, writhing.

'Martin!' It was as if the name was the articulation of her pain. She broke it down and cried it out again, at a higher, fiercer pitch: 'Marrrr-*tin*!'

She was aware of the girl, Polina, at the door, tried hard to focus on her. Horror quickly settled in Polina's face.

'Get my husband,' Raisa managed, gripping the table edge. Then, more sharply, as she felt herself unable to control her bowels: 'Get my husband!'

But Polina did not move. It seemed she could not take her eyes off the spectacle before her. At first she was dumbstruck by it, her mouth gaping idiotically. Then, when finally she stirred herself to act, it was to close her eyes, throw back her head, and scream. She screamed for a long time, a high, steady note, as clear and hard as steel.

2: The new recruit

'I have come to see Porfiry Petrovich.'

Alexander Grigorevich Zamyotov, chief clerk of the Haymarket District Police Bureau in Stolyarny Lane, remained bent over the case notes he was sorting. He was reluctant to lift his face into the full force of the stench that permeated the receiving hall.

There was a light tapping on the counter. Zamyotov froze, but still did not look up.

'My dear sir, respectfully, I request . . .'

'Respectfully?' Zamyotov slowly straightened himself at last, wincing and blinking through the eye-watering smell. He subjected the clean-shaven young man before him to a withering scrutiny. The young man was crisply turned out in a brand-new civil service uniform, with a single-breasted coat of bottle green. Its nine silver buttons shone in admonition of Zamyotov's own dull buttons, one of which hung by a loose thread. 'Is it respectful to hammer thus?' Zamyotov rapped his knuckles angrily on the counter. 'Can you not see that I am engaged in important police duties here? I am not at the beck and call of the likes of you, even if you have come straight from the outfitters.' Zamyotov's face contorted into an impressive sneer, marred only by a slight pursing of his lips.

'Forgive me. I was not sure that you had heard me.'

'I am not deaf.'

'But you did not acknowledge . . .'

'I am not here to acknowledge.'

The young man bowed deeply, and held his bow.

'What are you doing now, you ridiculous individual?'

'I am waiting. For you to finish your task.'

Zamyotov leant forward to hiss: 'Get up! Before someone sees you! Think of your uniform, your rank. When you abase yourself, you abase us all.'

The young man obeyed.

'Name?' demanded Zamyotov.

'Pavel Pavlovich Virginsky.'

Zamyotov started. He looked at the young man with new interest. 'You've put on weight.'

Virginsky nodded.

'And smartened yourself up. Well, well.'

The young man seemed embarrassed by the observation.

'So,' said Zamyotov, with a malicious grin, 'what trouble have you got yourself into this time?'

'I'm not in trouble. I joined the service. I've just graduated from the university.'

'*You* graduated? They are giving degrees to madmen now?'

'Yes, I have a degree in law. I have decided to become an investigating magistrate. My father thought . . .'

'Your father?' Zamyotov smirked sarcastically.

'I thought,' Virginsky corrected himself, 'and my father agreed, that it would be good for me to train under Porfiry Petrovich. There is no doubt that he is one of the best investigating magistrates in St Petersburg.'

'And who is your father? Tsar Alexander the Second?'

'No. He is former Actual State Councillor Pavel Pavlovich Virginsky, a landowner of the Riga province.'

'How was a provincial landowner able to pull strings in order to get you the position you had set your heart upon?'

'It was not a question of pulling strings. Our family has no connections. Or very few.'

'And yet, you decide something and it comes to pass. If only my career had run along such a track.'

'My father wrote a letter.'

'Ah! So that's it!'

'To the office of the *prokuror*.'

'I see.'

'Who passed it on to Porfiry Petrovich himself.'

'I think I remember it now,' said Zamyotov thoughtfully. 'You have me to thank for putting it before him, you know.'

'But it is your duty, surely, to pass on all his mail to him?'

'No, it would be quite wrong of you to think that. If you are to work here you must get such nonsense out of your head. My duty is to exercise my discretion on his behalf. On behalf of them all.'

'I see.'

'Another clerk, remembering the disreputable, one might almost say contemptible, figure that you once cut -- your matted hair, the parlous state of your clothes, indeed your apparent madness -- as I say, another clerk would not have troubled the investigating magistrate with a petition on behalf of such an individual.'

'Then I am grateful to you.'

'*Are* you?' There was a testing petulance to Zamyotov's tone.

'I just said as much.'

'But you have not said "thank you".'

'There's a terrible smell in here,' said Virginsky, sniffing the air.

'Get used to it,' said Zamyotov. 'It is the Ditch. It always stinks in the summer. It's full of excrement.'

'Will you tell Porfiry Petrovich that I am here to see him? He is expecting me, I believe.'

Zamyotov sighed heavily and rolled his eyes. 'If he is expecting you, then what are you waiting for? It is not advisable to keep the investigating magistrate waiting on your first day.'

Virginsky frowned in confusion. Zamyotov, now bent once again over his paperwork, waved him away impatiently, towards the door to Porfiry Petrovich's chambers.

*

Porfiry Petrovich stood at the window, his back to the room. The window was high, narrow and arched, set in the furthest corner, at the very tip of the iron-shaped block. It over-looked the Yekaterininsky Canal, at the spot where the Kokushkin Bridge spanned it. A cloud of cigarette smoke hung around him; despite it, the underlying smell of raw sewage was just as strong in here as it was out in the main hall. The din of building work outside, the clash and rumble of hammers and falling masonry, was barely muted by the dust-coated panes.

The back of the investigating magistrate's coat was stretched taut under the pressure of his squat form, which seemed shorter and fatter, even more like a peasant woman's, than Virginsky remembered it. His head was close-cropped and protruded at the back like a bulbous tuber. His expression, as he turned, was severe, pained even, although there was something comical about the effect of this severity on his round, snub-nosed face. He looked like an angry pug. He was clean-shaven, his skin dark, so that his white eyelashes stood out strikingly, drawing attention to his eyes. If there was a danger of not taking Porfiry Petrovich seriously, it quickly passed when one looked into the penetrating force of those eyes.

For a moment, he seemed not to recognise Virginsky, even to be affronted by his presence, although he had just that moment invited him to enter with a lethargic 'In.' A fat black fly buzzed close to Virginsky's face as he entered. Porfiry Petrovich drew sternly on his cigarette, before his face wrinkled with delight and warmth around the eyes.

'My dear . . . Pavel Pavlovich!' Porfiry crossed the room, his short legs moving quickly. He paused to stub out the cigarette in the crystal ashtray on his desk, then took Virginsky's hand in both of his own. 'You must forgive me. This heat, and the smell . . . it puts me in the foulest of moods. I had forgotten you were coming. But my, let me look at you! You look well. Indeed, you do!'

'Thank you.' Virginsky bowed his head, then lifted it quickly as if remembering himself. He looked Porfiry in the eye almost defiantly.

'Come in! Sit down! Let us chat!' Porfiry winced as he perched on the edge of his desk. It was a difficult manoeuvre for him to pull off without appearing comical again. He seemed precarious there, one leg dangling short of the floor. 'I was delighted to receive the letter from your father, for a number of reasons.'

This was what Virginsky had been waiting for. 'It's not what you think.' He sat stiffly on the sofa -- government-issue, upholstered in brown artificial leather -- and looked beyond Porfiry at the cracked plaster of the wall. The fly, or perhaps it was another one, was climbing at an angle. It took off. Virginsky tried to track it, but it disappeared against the glare from the window.

'And what do I think?' Porfiry crinkled his eyes as if he was going to wink.

'That I have been reconciled with my father.'

'Is that not the case?'

'It may shock you to know, Porfiry Petrovich, that I have become a materialist.'

Porfiry lazily threw up his hands. It was an ironic gesture. 'Please, you will have to do better than that if you want to shock me.'

'An egoist, then.'

'Ah, well . . . *what is to be done?*'

'Exactly! I see that you understand me perfectly. You are referring to the novel by Chernyshevsky. Anyone who has read that book will know that any rational man will always act in accordance with that which is in his own best interests. I have consented to behave as though I am reconciled with my father because it is in my own best interests to do so. My father is in a position to help me achieve my ambition. It would be irrational of me to refuse to allow him to do so.'

'And I'm sure your father is pleased to help you.'

'That may be. But it is nothing to me. I am not interested in my father's pleasure.'

'Ah, but as a materialist, and a rationalist -- and indeed as an exemplary egoist -- if it pleases your father to be of service to you, then surely it is in your interest to increase your father's pleasure.'

'So far as it pertains to his being of service to me, and no further. You will accuse me of hypocrisy, no doubt?'

Porfiry pursed his lips and fluttered his eyelids in a distinctly womanish gesture.

'You may be assured that I have accused myself of the same crime,' continued Virginsky. 'After considering the matter fully, I realised that I cannot be a hypocrite because I am aware of the hypocrisy involved. A genuine hypocrite is blind to his hypocrisy. He believes that he acts in an upright and indeed honourable way at all times, while in reality pursuing his own interests.'

'You have acquitted yourself then? Perhaps you should consider a career as a defence lawyer instead? Was that not once your intention?'

Virginsky half-closed his eyes, acknowledging the jibe. 'What further acquits me of this charge is the fact that I have not entered upon this course, to become an investigating magistrate, for my own pleasure. But rather for the benefit of society as a whole. The occupation will undoubtedly be a burden for me, involving onerous and unpleasant tasks for little recompense. However, I will persevere with it -- have no fear on that front, Porfiry Petrovich. And I will do so, as I say, because of the benefits accruing to society as a whole. In acting in this way I am nevertheless behaving as an egoist. I have realised that the thing that will give me personally the greatest pleasure is for society to be organised along more just lines. Such must be the goal of any sane and rational man. I admit, I do not need a legal background, or a job in the Department of Justice, to assist in bringing this about. I need . . .' Virginsky broke off and considered his words. He saw Porfiry looking at him with amusement. 'I need other materials for that. However, the skills of an investigator will help me, at some future date, when society has begun to be organised in the manner I have indicated, to root out and bring to justice those guilty of the greatest crimes against their fellow men. In the meantime it will satisfy me to prosecute ordinary criminals and to acquire the skills I will need, when . . .' Again Virginsky broke off. 'When the time comes,' he concluded, avoiding Porfiry's eyes now.

'Well,' said Porfiry with a broad smile. 'I hope that it will . . . *satisfy* you.' He stressed the word ironically.

Virginsky bristled. 'You do not take me seriously.'

'Oh but I do.'

'Then you are embarrassed by what I have said? You think I am sincere, but foolish?'

'It is not that either.' Porfiry Petrovich held Virginsky's gaze sternly. 'May I give you a word of advice, my young friend? Do not ever speak in the way you have just spoken to anyone else here. Indeed, I would advise you to give up such a mode of discourse entirely. You are a servant of His Imperial Majesty now, no longer merely his subject -- his *servant*, understand. You are employed in the Department of Justice. Justice here is not an abstract concept. It is the Tsar's justice. It is the Tsar's laws we are upholding. And it is those who break the Tsar's laws -- the Tsar's enemies in effect -- whom we are to hunt down and prosecute. Besides, you are surrounded by policemen. It is most unwise to talk of society being organised along different lines. There are those who would construe it as seditious.'

'Are you one of them, Porfiry Petrovich?'

'What a question! Please, Pavel Pavlovich. You cannot ask me such questions.' Porfiry began to cough. 'Really! The stench in here is insufferable! I cannot open the window, because the smell outside is worse. And there is the noise of the workmen in the street. How am I expected to think?'

'It is the effluence in the canal. Raw sewage flowing in an open drain. A society organised along just lines would not tolerate such a circumstance.'

Porfiry did not take the trouble to remonstrate with him. 'I sent a letter. Nothing has come of it.'

'At any rate,' began Virginsky with a shy, sarcastic smile, 'as loyal subjects and dedicated servants, we should be thankful that the Tsar at least is safely removed from such noxious hazards. Indeed it is gratifying to know that anyone who has sufficient wealth and leisure may take themselves away from the city when such dangers are most prevalent.' Making this final remark, Virginsky couldn't prevent himself from blushing self-consciously.

'At least you had the decency to look abashed,' commented Porfiry. 'However, I must warn you against sarcasm too, Pavel Pavlovich. It is not an endearing habit. Policemen in particular do not like to feel themselves ridiculed. You will find that you will need the cooperation and, indeed, the goodwill of policemen. You would do well to make yourself amenable to them.'

'That will be difficult for me. You forget that I have been manhandled by policemen. I do not have pleasant memories of my period of incarceration.'

'The experience will serve you well. You will understand more than most the need for certainty when constructing a case. You know what it means to be wrongly accused and deprived of your liberty. I am confident that you will not take your responsibilities lightly.'

'May I remind you, Porfiry Petrovich, that it was you who arrested me?'

Porfiry held a hooked forefinger along his mouth. 'It was not too bad. You had time to reflect. You might even have written a novel, had you been so inclined. Wasn't that how Chernyshevsky produced the novel we were talking about, the one that has so influenced you?'

'I am sure he would have preferred to have enjoyed his liberty while writing it. In fact, I imagine he would rather have been spared the necessity of writing it altogether. In a rationally organised society, such a book would be redundant.'

'I see we have returned to the topic of conversation that we must make a strenuous effort to avoid.' Porfiry at last pushed himself off his perch and paced to the centre of the room. He stared up at the ceiling, moving his head in erratic jerks. Virginsky tried to follow his shifting eye-line. 'There is a fly in this room,' said Porfiry abruptly. 'It is at the moment a more pressing problem to me than the future organisation of society. You would be more usefully employed catching the troublesome fly than discussing utopias.'

Virginsky made no move to take up Porfiry's suggestion. 'But again, I say to you, with respect, Porfiry Petrovich -- the fly and the organisation of society are not unconnected. It is the filth in the Ditch that encourages the breeding of flies.'

Porfiry's gaze snapped towards Virginsky. His look was forbidding. 'I will say one more thing on this subject. Then we will never talk of it again. Perhaps you are right. Perhaps too there is an analogy that can be drawn between flies and criminals. You will argue that in a rational and just society, there will be no criminals and no crime, for every citizen will realise that it is not in his best interests to commit crimes. You will probably also argue that it is the irrational and unjust organisation of society -- analogous to the putrid Ditch -- that produces the criminals, who are represented by the flies in our analogy. Eradicate the open sewer and you will diminish the population of flies. Transform society, and there will be no more criminals. That is all very well, but in the meantime, there are flies and there are criminals. We must do what we can, as sane and rational men, to ensure that they do not overrun us.'

'But if . . .'

'Enough!' Then Porfiry added more gently: 'Really, that is enough on the subject. I have said all I want to say and heard all I need to hear. Besides, there is a case . . .'

'A case?'

Porfiry sat down behind his desk. 'I see that there is more to your wishing to join the department than simply a desire to further the *common cause*.'

'I admit that the intellectual challenge appeals to me. I like to solve problems.'

'You need not apologise for that.'

'I was not . . . apologising.'

'It *can* be stimulating. And when it is a question of uncovering the truth, it may even be noble. However, unfortunately, very few of the cases you will be called upon to deal with will challenge your intellect. Even here in the Department of the Investigation of Criminal Causes, as our particular branch of the Justice Department is known. The solutions in most of these cases are all too depressingly obvious. If there is a wife who has been murdered, it is the husband who has done it. A tyrannical father, his son. An oppressive rent collector -- look among the tenants. There is more often than not a connection between the murderer and the victim. Nine times out of ten, it is immediately apparent. It is that tenth instance that is the challenge, and for that the investigator has to be alert. But whether it is the intellect that is the most useful faculty here, or instinct, coupled with an understanding of human nature -- well, my own view inclines towards the latter. These are not abstract puzzles to be unpicked, nor exercises in logic. We are dealing with people's lives. Crimes are the eruptions of human passions, of greed, desire, jealousy. Despair. These are the criminal causes we investigate. An investigator needs to be watchful. But most of all he needs to be capable of looking into his own heart. Do not rely on your intellect, Pavel Pavlovich. Rely on your humanity. Of course, there are very rare instances in which the victim is selected completely at random, when the connection is merely accidental. I am talking about the crimes of the insane. But perhaps even here, if one knew how to look, one would find a connection.'

'But what of the case you mentioned?'

'Ah, yes, good. Good. The case.' Porfiry picked up a telegram that lay on his desk. 'This came in shortly before you arrived. From the Shestaya Street Police Bureau in the Petersburgsky District. I will explain the details on the way. I assume you are ready to start work immediately?'

*

'Where are we going?' Virginsky had to hurry to keep up with Porfiry Petrovich, who was capable of moving at a surprising speed, considering his portly figure. They were racing along a low-ceilinged but narrow corridor on the fourth floor of the building in Stolyarny Lane that housed the Haymarket District Police Bureau.

'Petrovsky Island.'

Virginsky came to a halt. 'That was where . . .'

'Yes. Where it all began the last time you and I met. However, this is a new case.'

Virginsky ran to catch up. 'The place does not have happy associations for me.'

'Nor for me. In fact, there are few places remaining in St Petersburg that I can go to without being reminded of some tragedy.'

'Surely Petrovsky Island is outside the jurisdiction of the Haymarket District?'

'That is so. But the Department for the Investigation of Criminal Causes is at the service of the whole of the St Petersburg police force. There are certain cases that are recognised at the outset to be rather more challenging than the usual. Or possibly it is due to the seriousness of the crime. In this case, a suspected double murder. Earlier today, the wife and son of one Dr Martin Meyer collapsed and died, simultaneously, at the family's dacha.'

'I see. And you suspect the doctor?'

'My dear Pavel Pavlovich! It is assuredly too early to make such pronouncements.'

Virginsky noticed the way ahead was blocked by a man in a civil service uniform, who was holding his ground in the centre of the corridor, instead of stepping to one side as Porfiry rushed towards him. Porfiry had his head down and seemed not to be aware of the other man. The civil servant in question was of average height and build: a nondescript individual. It seemed he would inevitably be knocked down by Porfiry's flying bulk.

'Porfiry Petrovich! Watch out!'

Virginsky uttered his cry just in time. Porfiry teetered forwards and then back on his heels. He looked up at the human obstacle.

'Sir, you will kindly give way.' Porfiry's politeness hardly masked his fury.

'I give way? No sir. *You* will give way,' said the other.

'I have an important case to attend to.'

'Ah! And so my duties are unimportant!'

'It is surely a simple matter for you to step to one side.'

'An equally simple matter for you!'

'You must surely agree that I am the one who is in a hurry, the one running along the corridor, while you were the one who was standing there like a . . . like a . . . like a . . .'

'Like a what, may I enquire?'

'Like a dummy, sir!'

'A dummy! You are calling me a dummy!'

'You pressed me to complete my comparison.'

'Will you take it back?'

'I don't have time to take it back. Simply get out of my way and let's have an end to this nonsense.'

The other man drew himself up. 'Sir, we are coming close to the point where I will be compelled to demand satisfaction.'

'Don't be ridiculous. I am a magistrate. You are in a police station. You cannot possibly challenge me to a duel.'

'Ah! You are admitting that one cannot expect honour from a magistrate!'

'I am simply pointing out that duelling is against the law. Now kindly step to one side. You have made your point. You are my equal. You yield to no one. As far as all that goes, I agree in principle with your position. However, as a matter of practical necessity, I urge you to get out of my way, sir!'

The civil servant seemed momentarily confused by this. He frowned and drew in a deep breath, as if preparing to frame a question. But instead, the back of one hand shot up to his forehead, and a sinuous swoon seemed to come over him. He fell back against the wall.

Porfiry nodded tersely and stormed on, closely followed by Virginsky.

'It is my vertigo!' cried the civil servant. 'I have not given way to you!'

Porfiry shook his head. 'They are always hypochondriacs,' he muttered. They reached the stairs. The soles of his shoes slapped rapidly as he skipped down them.

3: A Russian beauty

They stepped out into a cloud of red dust, their ears assaulted by the clamour of destruction. A wall had just come down, on a site being cleared for building work. The gritty particles revolved in the sunlight, uplifted, celebrated, unstoppable. Porfiry coughed, and instinctively felt for his cigarette case.

'What are they building now, I wonder?'

The city, in summer, was a transitional place. A temporary population of migrant labourers, peasants from the outlying countryside, displaced the regular inhabitants and reshaped the city's fabric with casual vigour. Their indifference was brutal: without a flinch, hardly pausing to wipe the sweat from their eyes, they would tear down a house here, throw up a new one there, or mask familiar landmarks with novelty. There was the sense that there was no one to stop them; that the permanent citizens would return dismayed and disorientated by the changes wrought in their absence. And so, over the years, their city would become unrecognisable, and they would be left strangers in it.

The workmen whistled and shouted through the kerchiefs over their faces. Their eyes never sought to meet the eyes of any residents who were left to witness their vandalism. If accidental eye-contact was ever made, as happened now between Porfiry and one of the hammer-wielding demolition workers, a momentary flicker of defiance or suspicion was all that was exchanged.

Porfiry hailed an empty *drozhki* that was coming over Kokushkin Bridge. There was a flash of welcome and complicity in the driver's sidelong glance as he half-turned to watch them climb in. His eyes were squeezed almost shut from blinking out the sweat and sunlight.

'Petrovsky Island. As quick as you can.'

Porfiry fell back into his seat with a grimace of pain as the cab lurched away, the driver standing to whip and threaten his horse.

'Does it not occur to him that his horse would live longer if he whipped it less?' said Virginsky.

'Be careful,' Porfiry muttered warningly as he shifted his position on the bouncing seat.

'What?' Virginsky stiffened.

Porfiry raised his eyebrows and smiled, but wouldn't be drawn.

It wasn't long before they were driving alongside St Isaac's Cathedral, whose gilded dome blazed in the sun's profligacy. Virginsky turned a sullen gaze towards the church.

'Imposing, isn't it?' commented Porfiry, smiling watchfully.

'What has always struck me about it is its proximity to the War Office.'

'It is just as well to have God on your side before you go into battle.'

Visible now ahead of them, the broad surface of the river glistened and beckoned, alive with teeming craft. A barge hugged the granite embankment, drawn by a team of peasants, who leant and strained and pushed into their harnesses.

As they passed the equestrian statue of Peter the Great, his great bronze horse rearing in the direction of the Neva, the serpent trampled beneath its hooves, Porfiry cast a provoking look at Virginsky, as if to say, 'Well, and what do you have to say about him?'

The *drozhki* thundered on to the temporary pontoon bridge, its boards reverberating under the hooves and turning wheels. Porfiry felt a sudden lightening of his mood, an almost festive impatience. It was summer, and he was crossing the river to the islands. The cool breeze of movement, the water's freshness, lifted him.

*

Two more bridges later, and they were on Petrovsky Island. As they raced through the park, Porfiry was aware of a desire to slow the *drozhki*. The easy, squandered greenness around him had a clinging appeal. He looked with an envious nostalgia at the parties singing folksongs around samovars and smiled at the couples strolling and the children chasing the breeze along the paths. He remembered the island's winter desolation, and it seemed like a duty to make the most of these few green months.

They could tell which dacha it was from a distance: the only one in its group with a cluster of carriages and men around it.

Porfiry tapped the driver. The horse snorted and slowed, released from constant curses and lashes. Its gait became complicated and tripping.

Porfiry took in the details of the house. He saw the crudely rendered horse's head, cut from a plank and projecting from the apex of the eaves. It was there both to celebrate and ward off the unruly forces of nature. To Porfiry's eye, no doubt influenced by his knowledge of the two dead bodies within, the dacha's prettiness was entirely without charm, though he acknowledged that the boards were well maintained.

The dacha creaked in protest as they set foot on it.

The uniformed men on the veranda straightened protectively. Porfiry recognised a kind of jealousy in their faces. The scene, and its contents, belonged to them, and they resented the newcomers' intrusion.

Porfiry noticed the smell immediately. It was that that drew his gaze down to the two bodies on the decking. He turned solicitously to Virginsky. 'Are you all right?'

Virginsky's nod was barely perceptible, a mere bob in the aftermath of closing his eyes. 'You forget. I have seen the dead before.'

Porfiry regarded the young man closely, the face drained of colour, the line of the mouth thin and tight, his eyes held closed. 'That's what concerns me. You may wait outside if you wish. But I must go in.'

Virginsky's eyes now flashed defiance. 'I would not miss it for the world,' Virginsky hissed through clenched teeth. He minutely signalled the other men watching them. Porfiry swivelled his body to follow his glance, then turned back and tilted his head way from Virginsky. His look was assessing, almost disapproving.

'I understand. However. This is a serious business. There is no place for bravado here. We are all men, that is to say, human beings. No one will think any the less of you.'

'It is something I have to do. And besides, if not now, when?'

Porfiry conceded with a nod.

A young *politseisky* whom Porfiry recognised had been following their exchange with interest. His face was open and bright, his eyes sympathetic.

'Ptitsyn, isn't it?' said Porfiry, remembering the officer's name.

'That's right, Your Excellency.' He was all eagerness and energy, a puppy of a man.

'So, who have we here, Ptitsyn?' Porfiry's face became duly solemn, indeed pained, as he looked down at the bodies. His eye in passing took in the pools of vomit.

'The woman is Raisa Ivanovna Meyer. The boy is her son, Grigory.'

Raisa's body lay face down, partially covering Grisha, as if to shield him. The boy's face was staring straight up, orange vomit smeared around the uncomprehending O of his mouth. His pupils were unusually dilated as his eyes held on to their final panic.

'Who discovered them?'

'The maid. Polina Stepanovna Rogozhina.'

'And the husband? Dr Meyer, isn't it? Where was he when this happened?'

'Working in his study, apparently.'

'Was he not able to help them? He is a doctor, after all.'

Ptitsyn shrugged. 'Would you like to ask him yourself?'

'All in good time.' Porfiry continued to survey the veranda. 'Are there any other members of the household?'

'No. The maid does everything for them.'

'This is vomit?'

'Yes. It would seem so.'

'And that smell?'

'They crapped themselves -- begging your pardon, Your Excellency.'

Porfiry bent down and sniffed the one chocolate remaining in the Ballet's box. 'There will have to be a medical examination, of course. But it seems obvious that we are dealing with a case of poisoning here. Whether accidental or deliberate, that is the question we must determine.'

'You have made your mind up already, Porfiry Petrovich?' asked Virginsky with a frown.

'Well, something must have killed them. Some substance has disrupted these organisms to a fatal degree. If it is a case of accidental food poisoning, then it is surely the most virulent and severe incidence that I have ever encountered.'

'You do not think it is accidental then?'

'As I said, there will have to be a medical examination.' Porfiry dropped to the floor and prostrated himself alongside the corpses. Raisa Meyer's cheek lay on her son's shoulder. Porfiry looked into her face. It was a singular intimacy, that between the living and the dead, unreciprocated and presumptuous. This woman in life, only hours ago in fact, would not have suffered such proximity, such a probing gaze, from a strange man. Her eyes looked nowhere, and however much he tried he could not make them meet his. The pupils, he noticed, were dilated in the same way as her son's. He could think -- inappropriately, and with a tingle of shame -- of only one other situation in which a man attends so closely to, and expects so much from, a woman he doesn't know. She was wearing make-up, he noticed. The kohl around her eyes was streaked from tears. Her mouth was stretched out of shape; the orange mess around it made her resemble an infant after feeding. She would not want to have been seen like this, not for the most fleeting of instants, let alone laid out and displayed. He was touched by the pathetic sprawl of her arms, her fists clenched uselessly, her elbows angled with despair and rage. Her whole body was contorted by a fierce but ineffectual determination.

Porfiry stood up. 'She was a beauty. Once. I imagine.'

'Really?' Virginsky's surprise seemed almost insulting.

'Death is always ugly. But I see strength in her. And love. These are qualities I associate with beauty. And remember, a face, a living face, is made up of a succession of fleeting expressions.' Porfiry made a series of faces to illustrate his point, moving through rapid transitions from respectful solemnity to a buffoonish leer. His face then snapped into an expression of deadpan neutrality. 'Even the most beautiful of women is capable of looking ugly, at least for an instant, when taken off her guard. And nothing is more prone to take us off our guard than sudden death.' Porfiry turned his head towards the door leading to the interior of the dacha. 'We will talk to the maid now.'

'She's inside,' said Ptitsyn. 'Do you want me to bring her out?' He was looking down at the havoc on the floor.

Porfiry seemed to consider his question. 'No,' he said at last. 'There's no need for that. Just yet.'

*

Porfiry paused on the threshold to take in the interior of the dacha. He was aware of the two people seated at opposite ends of the room, the man in an armchair, the young woman on a divan, but he did not turn to either of them until he had finished a slow, systematic scan that seemed to search into every corner. It was a familiar enough setting, a dacha in the chalet style: birch-plank walls, covered with folk art, rag rugs on the floor, old and mismatched furniture, draped throws to conceal the ruptured upholstery. There was an upright piano against one wall, lid lifted, an album of Russian folk songs open on the music rest. The whole was suffused with a soft golden light, which completed the ersatz bucolic effect. The heavy tick of a cherry grandfather clock measured out time into stilted units.

He turned his attention decisively to the pale, bespectacled man in the armchair -- an archetypal intellectual, slightly built and high browed. 'Dr Meyer?'

The man looked as though he had just been, or was just about to be, sick. His eyes swam without focus.

'You have my condolences,' continued Porfiry.

At last Dr Meyer's gaze latched on to Porfiry, as if he had only just connected the sounds he had heard with this entity before him. Almost immediately he looked away, it seemed in disappointment: had he expected something more than condolences?

'This must be a difficult time for you.'

Now Meyer's expression became suspicious. 'Who are you?' His voice was high and harsh.

'My name is Porfiry Petrovich. I am the investigating magistrate. This is Pavel Pavlovich. He is assisting me.'

'Why do you offer me your condolences?'

'Because you have today lost your wife and son.'

'What is it to you? What do you care?'

'I am capable of human sympathy.'

'I know why you are here. I know what you really think. I do not believe in your condolences.'

'I have a job to do, Dr Meyer. You must understand that.'

Meyer did not reply. He seemed to have lost interest in Porfiry. His eyes flitted about the room as if it was unfamiliar to him.

Porfiry looked at the girl now. He was taken aback to see her scowling ferociously at Meyer. Glancing at Virginsky to have his surprise confirmed, he saw that the younger man's gaze was locked on her face in bashful appreciation.

Of course! thought Porfiry, *she is pretty!*

Perhaps she was even beautiful; if so, it was a fiery and forceful beauty. Evidently, she was Virginsky's type.

She had a proud face; the pride was there in the dark glower she was directing towards the doctor. A long straight nose, deeply recessed cheeks, full lips, quick to pout -- how haughty they could be, these peasant girls. Porfiry smiled, thinking of Virginsky's democratic principles. Was it these that drew him to her, or their opposite: the vestigial sense of aristocratic privilege?

'You must be Polina?'

Somehow she damped the fire in her eyes. Her expression became shy, self-effacing. *Ah! So she can act, this one!* She bowed her head and barely managed to meet Porfiry's eye. He noticed, however, that she flashed a glance at Virginsky. Was that a little smile that played on her lips?

'It must have been very distressing for you, to find your mistress and the young master like that?'

She nodded tensely, then looked quickly -- was it warningly -- at Dr Meyer.

'Perhaps you would care to step outside with me, on to the veranda. There are some questions I would like to ask you concerning what happened when you found them.'

Again Polina looked towards Meyer, though this time it seemed she wanted reassurance from him. But he was lost to her.

'Outside? Where *they* are?'

'Yes. I'm afraid so. It will help if you can show me how things were.'

She rose warily, smoothed her apron with flattened palms and nodded once more. Porfiry let her lead the way out, noticing another flash of interest pass between her and Virginsky.

Porfiry gestured away the men on the veranda with a single back sweep of his hand. They shuffled and clumped to the periphery.

'So, Polina, could you tell me what happened here today?'

The girl's eye-line dipped down, to the bodies, then swooped away quickly, repelled. She chose to settle her gaze on the comparatively neutral surface of the table. But something troubled her there. The vomit, perhaps, thought Porfiry. Or those sheets of paper, with that strange, tight handwriting on them.

'I brought the samovar out for Raisa Ivanovna.'

'I see. What time was this?'

'Two o'clock. I had not long taken away the lunch things. And Dr Meyer had just come home.'

'Was Dr Meyer out here on the veranda?'

'No. He was in his study.'

'So, Raisa Ivanovna took her tea at two o'clock.'

'I always bring it out to her at two.'

'Yes. Good. I see. And what did they eat today? For breakfast, let's say?'

'Sour cream and caviar. With coffee.'

'I see. And did Dr Meyer eat the same?'

'Yes.'

'And you?'

'Yes.'

'Is there any of this sour cream and caviar left?'

'Do you want some?' she asked, incredulously.

'No!' Porfiry laughed. 'It's just that we will need a sample, to have it analysed.'

'You think I poisoned them?' Her eyes flashed outrage.

Porfiry threw up his hands. 'At this stage, all we are trying to do is eliminate possibilities. What did she and her son eat for lunch? Did you prepare lunch?'

'They had some bread. And pickled mushrooms.'

'Again, I will need samples if there is any left. Did you have the same lunch?'

'Yes.'

'And Dr Meyer?'

'No. He wasn't here.'

'Where was he?'

'At work. He left for work after breakfast.'

'But came back just after lunch, and just before you took the samovar out? I see. What else did Raisa Ivanovna and her son eat today, do you know?'

'The chocolates.'

'These?' Porfiry indicated the near-empty box on the table. 'Where did these come from, do you know?'

'He brought them for her.'

'Dr Meyer?'

The girl nodded.

'They both ate them?'

'Yes.'

'Did you have any?'

'She offered them to me. But no.'

'Did Dr Meyer have any of the chocolates?'

The girl shrugged.

'How long have you been in the Meyers' employ, Polina?'

She thought for a moment, her large dark eyes rolling upwards as she calculated. 'Since just before Christmas last.'

'About six months then.' Porfiry nodded reassuringly, as though she had given the correct answer. 'Can you describe to me exactly what happened? You brought the samovar out and --?'

'Grigory was working away on his copying. He likes to copy from the newspaper. It's something he does. Did, I mean.'

'This is his handiwork here?'

Polina nodded as Porfiry bent over to look more closely at the sheets.

'Interesting.'

'He is . . . was not . . . Not quite right. In the head, Grisha.'

Porfiry looked at her closely as she struggled to make this pronouncement. He detected a certain element of distaste in her expression.

'They had no other children, the Meyers?'

Polina shook her head vehemently. 'He was enough. They didn't want another like him.'

'So. You brought the samovar out. Served tea. Oh, did Grisha and Raisa Ivanovna both have tea?'

'I gave only Raisa Ivanovna tea.'

'Very well. Carry on.'

'I went back inside. There was nothing else for me to do out here.'

'So when did you discover the bodies?'

'Well, she was screaming.'

'She was still alive, therefore?'

Polina nodded nervously. She looked to Virginsky for succour. 'It's all right, my dear. You're doing very well,' he said.

Porfiry compressed his lips. 'So, she called for help? And Grisha? Was he still alive at this point?'

Polina's face rippled with tension. A tight anguished nod came out of the convulsion.

'What did you do?'

'I . . . went to fetch Dr Meyer.'

'Of course,' put in Virginsky. He reached a hand out towards her to comfort her. Porfiry shook his head forbiddingly. Virginsky moved the hand up to his chin, as though he had always intended to make this self-conscious gesture of thoughtfulness.

'And what did Dr Meyer do?'

'Well, you see . . .' Polina bit her bottom lip uncomfortably. 'He wouldn't come.'

'Indeed?'

'Not at first. I was hammering on his door for an age. He wouldn't answer it. I shouted to him as well.'

'You communicated to him the distress of his wife and son?'

'Yes!'

'And he ignored your cries?'

Polina nodded sadly and looked down. Porfiry and Virginsky exchanged significant glances.

'Let me see if I understand you correctly,' continued Porfiry. 'Dr Meyer refused to come to the aid of his wife and child?'

Polina shifted her feet uneasily. 'Well, I don't know. It wasn't exactly that he refused. Sometimes he gets carried away with his work. He doesn't hear. It's quite often difficult to get him to come for meals.'

'To come for meals is one thing. But you were raising the alarm because his wife and child were dying out here. You were hammering on his door. How is it possible he didn't hear you?'

The girl flinched under the force of Porfiry's exasperated disbelief. Her expression became resentful.

Porfiry blinked his eyelids rapidly, in a spasm of self-control. He smiled soothingly at the girl. 'Forgive me if I have frightened you, my dear. I am not such a fearful ogre as I seem.'

Polina smiled, almost sardonically.

'You're doing very well, Polya. Now, please, if you would be so good, tell me in your own words what happened when you knocked on Dr Meyer's door. I would very much like to hear it from you before we talk to Dr Meyer.'

'He came to the door eventually. But . . . he didn't seem to understand what I was saying. He seemed. Ill. In himself. His eyes. He couldn't look at me. His face . . . was blank. There was nothing there.'

'So, his demeanour struck you as out of the ordinary?'

Polina considered the question, or perhaps she was thinking carefully about her answer. Before she was able to give it, they heard footsteps approach the veranda. Meyer was standing in the doorway. 'What's going on here? You can't talk to her without my permission. I forbid you to talk to her.'

'My dear sir, I can. And I have,' said Porfiry. 'You may go inside now, Polina.'

The maid did not look at the master as she pushed past him, although it seemed that there was, in the tension of his body, a desire to reach out and stay her.

'Dr Meyer,' began Porfiry, 'I understand that you bought these chocolates for your wife?'

'I buy my wife chocolates every week.'

'Always from Ballet's?'

'It is a habit we have fallen into. Perhaps it was time we broke it.'

Porfiry widened his eyes at the casual cynicism of the remark. 'Did you eat any of these chocolates yourself?'

'No.'

'And neither did your maid. When did you buy the chocolates?'

'Today.'

'You came directly home with them?'

'Yes, of course.'

'Your maid, Polina, says that she had trouble rousing you from your study.'

'I was working. When I am working I become lost in my thoughts.'

'What work, exactly, are you engaged in?'

'I am a sanitary inspector. The summer is a very busy time. The cholera, you understand.'

'How interesting!' Porfiry's gaze became almost devouring as he looked at Meyer. He nodded thoughtfully a couple of times. 'You know, we have a public health problem at the bureau. The Yekaterininsky Canal is a disgrace. The water is running with human excrement. You can imagine the stench. And the flies. I have been trying to get one of you chaps to come over and inspect it for weeks. I wrote a letter. Nothing was done. I was not even granted the courtesy of a reply.'

'Do you know how many sanitary inspectors there are in St Petersburg?'

Porfiry shook his head and frowned, sensing the gist of what was coming.

'Six. If you arrest me it will be five.'

'What makes you think I want to arrest you?'

'Oh come now. I know the way you policemen's minds work.'

'I'm not a policeman, Dr Meyer. I am a magistrate.'

'Even so.'

'I will not be arresting anyone until I have determined what killed your wife and son. That will require a medical examination of the bodies. I will have this remaining chocolate analysed too, of course. As well as samples of everything else Raisa and Grisha ate today. But tell me, as a doctor, what do you make of their symptoms? The vomiting? I believe there was loss of bowel control too. Did you notice the eyes? The pupils, dilated. And, of course, the sudden and painful death. Do recognise here the pathology of any natural disease?'

Dr Meyer's expression was stripped of hope. He surveyed the veranda with an appalled gaze. 'No.'

'So what, Dr Meyer, in your opinion, could have killed them?'

'A toxic agent of some kind. That is to say, poison. And judging by the violence of their reaction to it, I would have to say a particularly virulent agent. Probably an alkaloid. Aconite, for example.'

'Aconite? An interesting suggestion. As far as I know, there is no reliable test for it.'

'It is impossible to detect. However, its presence can be inferred, if other poisons are ruled out.'

'It is part of your job, as a sanitary inspector, to be well-versed in toxic materials, I imagine?'

'There is some call for expertise in that field.'

'And access to? I am thinking of the control of pests.'

'It is true. I know where to lay my hands on certain substances not generally accessible to the public.'

'Thank you. You have been most helpful.'

'Are you sure? I mean to say, have I incriminated myself enough?' A snarling leer disfigured Meyer's face, from which strained high-pitched laughter was expelled, as if under pressure.

'Is there anything else you would like to add?' asked Porfiry, smiling with uncomfortable amusement.

'Perhaps you would consider it relevant that I took my PhD in toxicology?'

'I shall make a note of it.' Porfiry bowed politely, and began to feel the need for a long-deferred cigarette.

4: Examination and elimination

The room was in the basement of the Shestaya Street police station: whitewashed brick walls, no windows, the light instead provided by a series of oil lamps hanging from a beam across the ceiling. Stacked on a pallet in the corner were barrels of ice hacked from the Neva in the winter, covered in a tarpaulin. The ice was there to keep the temperature down. It is occasionally useful, in a police station, to have a cold room in the height of summer, on hand for certain aspects of investigative work. However, Porfiry had the impression that the air would have been just as chill without the ice.

The bodies were laid out side by side on a broad table in the centre, beneath the lamps. A doctor called in from the Military Hospital in the Vyborg district was stooped over the first of them, that of Raisa Ivanovna. He was absorbed in the task of cutting away the clothing with sheers. The two official witnesses stood to one side, watching with expressions of rebuked awe. Retired civil servants of vertiginous rank, they had entered the room medals first, talking loudly and self-importantly about past glories and mutual acquaintances. But a stern glance from the surgeon, who had been waiting impatiently for their arrival with implements in hand, silenced them. This doctor, one Feurbach, a German like Meyer judging by his name, was a taciturn but efficient technician. The air in the room was chastening, too. Despite the temperature, there was a faecal ripeness to it, which outdid anything the Ditch could muster.

The corset snapped apart. The dead woman's flesh sprang out and absorbed the glare of the oil lamps with a sullen coveting. Porfiry gave a pained wince. He cast an absent-minded glance at Virginsky, as if he regarded the young man as an irksome responsibility he believed he had shaken off. He had a vague sense that he owed him some kind of explanation.

The doctor continued to work away methodically at the clothes. It was when the cadaver was finally stripped bare, the layers of clothing splayed around it, that Porfiry felt the strongest inclination to turn to Virginsky. For now, he resisted.

The skin was smooth and bloated, the colour of grubby linen. He could not help assessing the shape of her body, in a way that appalled him, even as he did it. He tried instead to imagine how she must have felt about her body. She would not have been happy with it, he believed. Or perhaps that was a presumption on his part. Looking down at the amorphous spread of her trunk, the bulges of her abdomen, the two swollen capsules of her thighs, which were smeared with the soiling of her last evacuation, he had more the sense that she did not care about any of it. Her physical form, even perhaps her physical existence, was almost a matter of indifference to her. If this were so, he wondered when and how it had come about. Her face, he felt, had the potential to be counted beautiful. But if happiness and goodness are necessary elements of beauty, he wondered if he would have found them on her living features.

The doctor examined the surface of the body and made notes in silence. His scrutiny was almost unseemly in its scientific rigour. Porfiry knew that it was necessary, but he could not help feeling a proxy outrage at the way the man laid claim to the flesh with probing gaze and fingers. She was exposed, but no longer vulnerable. A doctor who deals in the dead has no need to make his touch gentle, or his manner deferential; the normal proprieties can be dispensed with. Porfiry sensed a shifting of discontent from the others watching. He remembered Virginsky, and at last half-turned in his direction.

He took in the complexity of Virginsky's expression immediately: his mouth rose at one side, as if in a snarl, or in preparation for a cry of protest; but his eyes were rapt. Porfiry recognised the appetite in those eyes. Virginsky was in his early twenties, and yet the knowledge of death and evil was already there in him. Porfiry knew that once that knowledge has been awoken, there is no going back. The witnessing of one horror can produce a taste for more.

There was a relaxation in Virginsky's face. Porfiry looked back to the examination table. The doctor had made the first incision, the right arm of a Y that began at the collarbone.

'It is the contents of the stomach that we are particularly interested in,' Porfiry said, feeling the redundancy of his words. The doctor said nothing, barely nodded an acknowledgement.

And now it began. The final conversion of Raisa Ivanovna Meyer from a human being to an assemblage of matter. It was not enough to strip away her clothes, her skin had to be removed, in an exposure beyond nakedness. There was no howl of pain or protest, just the soft, adhering sounds of a body unravelling.

Porfiry looked again at Virginsky, whose head was now rocking in a compulsive nod. He touched the younger man's shoulder. Virginsky met his eye with startled resentment. He looked down at the hand on his shoulder as if that were more repulsive than the spectacle on the table. Porfiry removed it. Virginsky had stopped nodding.

If Porfiry was only interested in the stomach, Dr Feurbach showed an admirable impartiality towards all the internal organs, each of which he held up as if it was a trophy won from bloody battle, before handing it to his *diener* for weighing. The stench from the body increased with each unpacking.

'Here is your stomach,' he said at last, holding the loose livid sac, its breaches secured with metal clips, towards Porfiry.

Porfiry raised a hand in demurral. 'Would you be so good as to decant the contents into a bottle? And do the same with the other stomach. Then, if you please, have them delivered to Dr Pervoyedov of the Obukhovsky Hospital. He is currently analysing the food samples and vomit taken from the Meyers' dacha.'

Dr Feurbach's brows clenched in a bemused frown, which somehow conveyed that this was the most ridiculous and incomprehensible suggestion he had ever heard. He turned his back on Porfiry with a shrug and barked commands at his *diener* in German.

*

In his laboratory at the Obukhovsky Hospital, Dr Pervoyedov held a magnifying glass to a chocolate. The chocolate, which was by now losing its smooth, spherical perfection, was placed on a circle of filter paper. If he needed to move the sweet, he would handle it only with tongs. For one thing, he didn't want the heat of his fingers to accelerate its melting. He was also aware that certain poisons can be absorbed through the skin. Until he had determined what had killed Raisa Ivanovna Meyer and her son, he would take every precaution.

At the other end of the long table, two dozen white mice huddled and shivered in their cages. Occasionally one would break free to scurry and defecate in the sawdust, the sudden motion causing the bars to rattle and sing.

Through the lens, beads of fatty sweat stood out on a surface of tiny pits and pores. He held the point of a scalpel to each of these imperfections in turn, trying to get some sense of their scale. There was one point in particular where the chocolate dipped sharply, although when he looked at it without the magnifying glass it disappeared. Dr Pervoyedov located it again and pushed his scalpel into it. He then cut in the opposite direction.

The cream of the filling was pale brown, except for one area, now revealed in both sections of the chocolate, where a white powdery deposit, like the tail of a comet, could be seen. It was possible these were un-dissolved sugar particles; it was equally possible they were something else. He scooped some of the substance on to the end of his scalpel, which he dipped into a flask of distilled water. He allowed the extracted sample to dissolve, stirring the water with a glass rod. Finally he drew some of the water off with a pipette and pumped it into a feeding bottle, which he exchanged for the bottle on one of the cages.

The movement of his hand, and the noise of the metal clip as he put the water bottle in place, startled the mice into a mass convulsion. He saw the tiny rodents as bundles of living matter, life reduced to one of its purest and most meaningless forms. *For what does a mouse live?* he thought. *Only for life itself.*

But they were such timid creatures, shivering even in the heat of summer; dropping black slugs of faeces at the slightest disturbance of their precarious and reduced world. Even had these mice been in the wild, they would live out their lives in a narrow pattern of behaviour circumscribed by their habits and instincts, under the constant shadow of fear and more often than not racked by the ache of hunger. They reminded him of those peasants who never leave their village, not because they are forbidden by lack of passport, but because it would never occur to them to do so.

And yet this was life. He would even say it was one of the higher forms of life, compared with the twitching, seething organisms he saw under his microscope.

He did not do so now, but he had handled these mice many times. As he watched them, he cupped his hands and felt the remembered spasms of their weightless bodies, the sharpness of their fine claws against his skin, the nip of their teeth. He would always handle them reverently. He felt himself to be handling particles of life itself. The life force, the only thing he was capable of worshipping, pulsated in their fur and fear.

He watched as one of the mice came to sip at the water bottle. It moved away and cleaned its whiskers in a mechanistic reflex. Almost immediately, it returned to the water bottle for a second drink. No doubt it was the sugar in the water that drew it back. Again, this was followed by a burst of cleaning activity, more energetic and extended than the first, Pervoyedov judged. It was enough of a variation from the norm to pique his interest. Pervoyedov leant forward. As if in response, the mouse reared up on its hind legs and opened its mouth in a silent cry. Its pink eyes stood out wildly as it stretched its neck and rotated its head. He saw its throat go into spasm as the breaths came fast and sharp. Now the animal scrubbed at the side of its snout in what seemed like a desperate effort to remove its own face. It finally tucked its head down under its belly, so extremely that it flipped over on its back. The mouse quickly righted itself and began chasing its tail. Then it ran blindly into the side of the cage. After that it began to gnaw at its own forelimbs, drawing blood almost immediately. The mouse fell on to its side, though its legs continued moving, as if it believed it was still running. Before long, these movements became convulsive. There was a final shudder, then the creature was still.

*

Porfiry let out a small groan of dismay as he entered his chambers. The temperature was perhaps a degree or two higher than previous days, and the stench of sewage was more pungent than ever. The room gave him nothing to breathe. He felt immediately exhausted and nauseous. He swatted a hand vaguely, prompted by the enquiring buzz of a bluebottle circling his head. He saw it fly in an erratic swooping zigzag over to the window, where it rattled uselessly after hitting the glass with an audible pop.

Virginsky followed him in. 'Shall I open a window, Porfiry Petrovich?'

'Yes, yes. See if you can get rid of that fly.' Porfiry took a seat behind his desk, then immediately stood up, pushing the chair away impatiently. In front of him was a large yellow envelope with his name handwritten on it. Porfiry lit a cigarette before turning his attention to it.

Virginsky opened the window to release the fly. The atmosphere in the room worsened perceptibly.

'Close it!' cried Porfiry. He took out a sheaf of official form papers clipped together, which he recognised as a medical examiner's report. A small note, the handwriting matching that of the envelope, fell out with them.

His Excellency, The Honoured and Esteemed Magistrate Porfiry Petrovich,

Allow me to present for your attention my findings regarding the substances that you had delivered to me for analysis. As you will see from the document enclosed, it is impossible to identify with absolute certainty the toxic agent responsible for killing the two bodies examined by my esteemed colleague Dr Feurbach, although a number of candidate substances for which there are currently reliable tests, to wit, arsenic, prussic acid, etc., have been eliminated. However, it has been possible to establish the method of administration of the toxic agent. A small quantity taken from the remaining Ballet's chocolate induced death in a sample of mice; the peculiar symptoms suffered by these mice were replicated in other test groups when distillations taken from the victims' stomach contents were administered. The same results were achieved with distillations from the vomit recovered from the scene of death. In the interests of providing a juridically acceptable identification, by means of experimentation rather than analysis, a number of known poisons were then administered to further samples of mice, and the reactions monitored. One substance produced manifestations which corresponded exactly to the results provided by the remaining Ballet's chocolate, stomach contents and vomit: aconite. It is the opinion, therefore, of this medical examiner that the deaths of Raisa Ivanovna Meyer and Grigory Martinovich Meyer were caused by aconite poisoning, administered by means of a contaminated box of chocolates. The full scientific reasons for this opinion are given in the enclosed report.

I would like, if I may, to add one personal note. I have known Martin Meyer for a number of years, both in a professional and personal capacity. I will only say that I do not believe him capable of murdering his wife and son. This belief, and indeed my declared association with Martin Meyer, is not pertinent to my medical

opinion, and should have no bearing on it.
Your humble servant,
Dr P. P. Pervoyedov.

'The idiot!' Porfiry threw the letter down, disturbing two flies that were crawling on his desk.

Virginsky snatched the note and scanned it.

Still standing over his desk, Porfiry riffled through the pages of the report impatiently. 'This is useless. A clever defence lawyer will argue it is inadmissible, because of Pervoyedov's relationship with Meyer.'

'But I don't understand. His findings incriminate Meyer,' said Virginsky as he finished reading. 'So, as he says, the friendship is irrelevant. It can be disregarded, surely? Or at least separated off. It is perfectly possible, theoretically, that Pervoyedov could appear as an expert witness for the prosecution and a character witness for the defence.'

'And in which capacity do you think he would be more likely to carry the jury?'

'It would have been helpful if he had told you, perhaps,' said Virginsky, returning the note to Porfiry.

'Really, these clever men can sometimes be so . . . naive. Or perhaps it is not naive at all. Perhaps it is a deliberate attempt to undermine his own findings and so help his friend. The connection alone is enough to ruin everything.'

'Can you not simply commission another doctor to repeat his tests?'

'Provided there are enough mice left in St Petersburg, then I suppose it is a possibility, but really it is too aggravating.' Porfiry cast a dismissive glance over the medical report.

'Porfiry Petrovich, what if Pervoyedov the character witness is right?'

'Impossible! These doctors always stick together. There is more than enough evidence to justify bringing in Meyer. Once we have him, and he is away from his sources of comfort, whatever they may be, I feel sure he will crumble. A confession will count for more, as far as a jury is concerned, than confusing scientific evidence. I shall instruct the Shestaya Street Bureau to arrest him.'

'And that's it?'

'What else do you suggest I do?' Porfiry's eyes narrowed as he surveyed Virginsky through a cloud of smoke he had just produced.

'What about the confectioner's? Should we not investigate the possibility that the chocolates were contaminated at source?'

'Do you really think that's likely? What would their motive be?'

'I don't know.'

'It's hard to imagine what motive any shop could have for poisoning its customers.'

'Yes, but surely it is a question of eliminating every possible cause, until only one survives.'

Porfiry met Virginsky's heated insistence with an aggressive flurry of lashes. The younger man blushed. Porfiry expelled more smoke. 'You mean, a question of going through the motions? And in the meantime, a murderer remains at liberty.'

'The converse of that is that you may arrest an innocent man.'

Porfiry slammed Pervoyedov's report down on his desk. 'Another cursed fly! How *are* they getting in here?' He looked up at Virginsky. 'Pavel Pavlovich, as I have had occasion to remark already, you think and argue like a defence advocate. This is useful skill for an investigating magistrate to have, although I should warn you against taking it too far. Experience informs me that by far the likeliest explanation in this case is that Meyer has murdered his wife and child. He is a doctor. He has access to toxic materials. I do not think we will have to look far to find a motive.'

'I am surprised to hear you talk like this, Porfiry Petrovich.'

'However,' Porfiry pressed on, the batting of his eyelids increasing emphatically, 'in order to construct a watertight case against him, we must caulk any chinks. Therefore, I would, as a matter of course, send someone to the confectioner's on Nevsky Prospekt.'

'As a matter of course?'

'Yes.'

'Then why did you not mention it earlier, I wonder.'

'It is all part of your training. Another skill you will find useful to possess is the ability to persuade a sceptical superior of your theories.'

'I see. I thank you, therefore, for the lesson, Porfiry Petrovich.'

'Not at all.'

5: At the confectioner's

Sunlight flashed in the vast window of Ballet's the confectioner's, a white blaze that transformed the glass into a field of living energy. Lieutenant Salytov watched his reflection as it was consumed by the glare, his cockaded hat being the last of him to disappear. Ballet's was on the sunny, even-numbered, side of Nevsky Prospekt. In general, and particularly in summer, Salytov preferred to keep himself to the shady side of the street.

His startled reflection reappeared for an instant. He drew himself up and regarded his ghostly double with a disdain it had the effrontery to reciprocate. For a moment it appeared that he was about to challenge himself to a duel. But then he looked through himself and took in the interior of the shop. Most of the twenty or so tables were empty. Circular, draped in sharp-edged linen, they seemed like miniature suns, with the same relentless brilliance. He spotted only three customers. Sitting on his own at a table by the window was a young man, somewhere in his twenties, of surprisingly impoverished appearance, considering the tariff at Ballet's. He was reading one of the newspapers that Ballet's provided for its customers, with a half-drunk cup of coffee on the table before him. At another table, further into the interior, two men were deep in conversation, their heads inclined conspiratorially. Other than that, he couldn't ascertain anything meaningful about their appearance. The glass flared again, obscuring his view, and he went inside.

As Salytov crossed the floor of the shop, the two men broke off talking and watched him warily. One of the men had a red, pock-marked face and tiny eyes. The other was almost handsome, though his collar was very grubby and he had dark rings around his eyes, as if the grubbiness had spread there.

There was a stout woman serving behind the counter. Her expression, as well as her build, suggested a reluctance to part with the pastries and sweets she was selling.

Salytov looked down at the display of goods in a glass-fronted cabinet, as if he might buy something. 'The chocolates that you sell, they are made here on the premises?'

'That is so, sir.' The woman had a strong German accent; her nationality was possibly significant, it seemed to Salytov.

'Were you serving here in the shop Saturday last?'

'I . . .?' She regarded him uncertainly.

'You must answer my questions.'

'Yes. I was here. I am here every Saturday.'

'You have many customers for your chocolates, I imagine?'

She shrugged and at that moment looked over Salytov's shoulder. Salytov turned round. The two men had risen from their table and were heading for the door. The German woman took up a small pommelled stick and beat angrily on a gong that was on the counter top. The sound of the gong was curiously muted, given the energy she put into striking it. 'You men! You do not leave without paying. This man is policeman. He will arrest you.'

The two men stopped in their tracks. The pock-marked one whispered something to his friend, who glared and was about to say something but ran out of the shop instead. The remaining man turned slowly to show a premeditated smile. 'A simple oversight, Fraulein. You know us. We are friends of Tolya's. We always pay our way. And if we are temporarily embarrassed, for whatever reason, Tolya is usually magnanimous enough to extend us reasonable credit. Is Tolya in today?'

'That is no business of yours. And no business of Tolya's to do this thing. You will pay now. Forty kopeks.'

'Ah! How insignificant a sum for men of enterprise and industry such as ourselves. A mere forty kopeks! Fraulein, shame on you, for presuming that we were unable to pay this paltry sum.'

'Pay it then!'

'Pay it then! Pay it then! she cries, giving voice to my very intention. It is as if you have read my mind. How could I not pay it? I am a man of honour. It is easier for me to throw myself into the raging Neva than to walk out of here without paying.'

'I am waiting.'

'And so am I, Fraulein. I am waiting, indeed, for my associate, Stepan Stepanovich, to return having completed a certain business transaction destined to release the required funds. To be candid, it had been our intention to conduct the necessary dealings prior to coming into your establishment, but we were tempted from the righteous path, as it were, by the sight of your beauteous and, if I may say so, bountiful sweetmeats. Fraulein, you have only yourself to blame. Are we not men? That is to say, mortals? Weak, imperfect. I make no claim to perfection, Fraulein. None whatsoever. Ask Tolya.'

The woman behind the counter made a contemptuous noise, then bluntly declared: 'You are thieves! Criminals!'

'Fraulein! Is it a crime, now, not to be perfect? A mistake, a simple human mistake, Fraulein, that is what we are dealing with here, one which, as we speak, is in the process of rectification.'

The shop door opened and the man with the grubby collar and smudged eyes returned. After some tense and whispered negotiation, which involved the pock-marked man grabbing his collar at one point, he counted out some coins which were then handed over to the unsmiling German woman.

The two men left, the pock-marked one jostling his associate all the way out.

'They are regular customers?' asked Salytov after a strangely empty moment.

'They are friends of Tolya's. They are no good. Tolya is no good.'

'Tolya works here?'

'He is apprentice confectioner. A bad boy.'

'Does he assist with the making of the chocolate?'

'Of course.'

Salytov's left eyebrow shot up. 'I see. That is very interesting. I would like to talk to him. After I have had a chance to ask you a few more questions. We were talking about chocolates, weren't we? I am interested in a man who comes here every Saturday, around lunchtime, to buy a box of Ballet's chocolates. A fellow countryman of yours. A doctor, he would be dressed in a civil service uniform.' Salytov took out a notebook and consulted the notes he had made when Porfiry Petrovich briefed him. 'Clean-shaven. Bespectacled. Thinning, blond hair. Of slight build. Walks with a stoop.'

'Yes, I know him. That is Dr Meyer.'

Salytov snapped the notebook to. 'Good. Now you will fetch this Tolya.' The woman disappeared through a door behind the counter. There was a brief explosion of clattering and clamour in the opening and closing of the door. While she was gone, Salytov looked around at the only remaining customer, who lifted his coffee cup absently, but then replaced it without it reaching his lips. The young man sighed balefully as he turned the page of his newspaper, paying no attention to Salytov.

A lad of about sixteen, with wild hair and staring eyes, burst out through the door to the workshop. He was wearing a white coat, spattered with cocoa dust, which to Salytov's eye looked at first glance like dried bloodstains.

The large German woman followed him through the door, her eye watchful and anxious. It seemed she did not trust the boy, and trusted Salytov less.

'What do you want?' demanded the youth, with a sullen glance.

'What do I want? It is not for you to ask me what I want. It is not for you to ask any questions. I will ask the questions and you will answer them. Is that understood?'

The boy did not answer.

'Is that under*stood*?' roared Salytov.

'Why are you shouting? I have done nothing wrong. I am a law-abiding citizen.' Tolya's own voice was raised in volume and pitch now. 'I am supposed to be working. The master will miss me.'

'You must answer my questions.'

'You haven't *asked* any questions!' Tolya pointed out in exasperation.

Salytov seemed momentarily thrown by this, which gave Tolya the advantage. However, his smirk at the lieutenant's discomfiture was a mistake. 'Get out here now!' barked Salytov.

Tolya groaned and began to move with resistant lethargy.

'Now!'

If Tolya hurried his step, it was done only in a token way, and perhaps even sarcastically. When at last he was out from behind the glass counter, Salytov approached him ominously, regarded him for a moment, like a gymnast poised before a manoeuvre, then threw back his hand and slapped the boy square in the face. Tolya's head was twisted round under the force, and shock, of the blow. A red imprint showed on his cheek when he turned his head back to look at Salytov. His eyes stood out from his face more than ever. With some satisfaction, Salytov noticed these eyes glisten moistly as tears welled in them.

'You are the one they call Tolya?'

'Yes.'

'Full name.'

'Anatoly Denisovich Masloboyev.'

'You associate with scoundrels, Anatoly Denisovich. Isn't that so?'

'I don't know, sir.'

'Do you want another slap, boy?'

'No, sir.'

'Then answer the question.'

'I . . . what was the question, sir?'

'Do you associate with scoundrels?'

'No, sir.'

Without warning, Salytov planted another smack on the same side of the youth's face.

'Try again.'

'Yes, sir.'

'I have seen your friends and they looked like scoundrels to me. Are they scoundrels?'

'Yes, sir.'

'Are you a scoundrel, Anatoly Denisovich?'

'No, sir!'

'You look like a scoundrel to me.'

'No, sir! It's not true.'

'You have the eyes of a scoundrel. Stop blubbering, boy. It will not help you.'

Tolya wiped his eyes on the sleeve of his coat and sniffed loudly.

'Where are you from, Anatoly Denisovich?'

'The village of Ulyanka, Your Honour.'

'Ulyanka?' Salytov's eyes narrowed coldly. 'We all know what Ulyanka is famous for. The house at the eleventh verst.'

'I was never in that place,' said the boy quickly, emphatically.

Salytov looked at Tolya assessingly. He did not seem to like what he saw. His lip curled almost cruelly. 'You're lying.'

'No, sir, Your Honour. Never. Never set foot in it!'

'Your passport?'

'I do not have it with me, Your Honour. It is at my lodgings.'

'No passport? It is all the more likely that you are a refugee from the house at the eleventh verst then.'

'I do have a passport, as I explained, Your Honour. I do not have it on me, that's all. And, believe me, I was never in that place. Not on my own account. It was my mother --'

'Your mother is a lunatic?'

'No, sir, there were lies told about her. My father's family was cruel. She is dead now, Your Honour. They drove her to it.'

'A suicide?'

'They drove her to it!'

'Let me see your hands.' The suddenness of Salytov's request took Tolya off guard. He held out his arms. His hands were surprisingly clean. Salytov slipped the handcuffs on him with the practised deftness of a conjuror. He grasped Tolya firmly under the arm. 'A suicide and a lunatic for a mother. No passport. These are sufficient grounds for taking you in. Now you,' Salytov addressed the stout German woman, 'get your master out here now. I wish to speak to the owner of this place.'

She disappeared back into the workshop, shaking her head and shouting in German.

While he waited, Salytov turned to look at the young man in the window, who had stopped reading his newspaper and was watching events unfold with some trepidation. 'As for you -- you finish your coffee and leave. This place is closing until further notice.'

A moment later, Salytov was sharing this information with the proprietor of Ballet's, whose agitated protestations, and over-groomed moustache, only served to strengthen the police officer's resolve that his decision, taken admittedly without consultation, was nevertheless the right one.

*

Lieutenant Salytov shifted uneasily as he heard the lock turn. The flimsy pamphlets in his hands were damp with sweat. The door to the interview room creaked open. Porfiry Petrovich came out, quickly followed by Virginsky, on whose face Salytov detected a mocking leer. Salytov felt his teeth clench with rage. Really, it was too much to bear. The last time he had seen that insolent puppy, he had been the suspect in a murder investigation. Outraged, Salytov searched Porfiry Petrovich's face. The magistrate's expression was pained. He avoided Salytov's eye.

The *politseisky* who had let them out locked the door behind them.

'Release him,' drawled Porfiry Petrovich wearily.

Salytov bristled. 'Are you serious?'

'We have no grounds on which to hold him. Indeed, I am puzzled as to why you arrested him in the first place, Ilya Petrovich.'

'He had no passport.'

'He says that it is at his lodgings. Did you send anyone round to look for it?'

'Yes.'

'And?'

'We found it.'

'And is it in order?'

'Yes. However, we also found these.' Salytov handed Porfiry Petrovich the pamphlets, crudely printed on thin, almost transparent paper. Porfiry glanced at them with indifference, before passing them on to Virginsky. 'You cannot ignore these,' insisted Salytov hotly.

'Such pamphlets are widely circulated, I believe,' said Porfiry Petrovich. 'Is that not so, Pavel Pavlovich?'

Virginsky didn't answer.

'They are subversive. They express opinions critical of our government. Possession of such material is an offence,' insisted Salytov.

'Then we will confiscate them.' Porfiry made a sweeping gesture with one hand.

'That is no solution. The fact is, the boy is an insurrectionist.'

'The boy,' countered Porfiry Petrovich impatiently, 'is a boy.' He closed his eyes. 'I grant you, we could come down heavily on him, Ilya Petrovich. We could even turn him over to the Third Section. We could grind him under the heel of our boot, so to speak, as a blind man tramples a flower.'

'He is no flower.'

Porfiry opened his eyes to look at Salytov. 'In all respects, he is more than a flower. He is a youth. A Russian youth. Our youth. He is as yet unformed. If we respond to him with brutality, we may very well turn him into an enemy of the state. If we show him tolerance and understanding -- forgiveness, even, of his youthful folly -- is it not then more likely that he will grow up to respect rather than hate the rule of law?'

'The rule of law is not ours to bend as the whim takes us.'

'Not as whim, but as wisdom dictates. It is my job to decide if there is sufficient evidence to warrant a prosecution. I have decided that there is not. However, in the light of the new evidence that you have just now presented, you have my authority to issue him with a stern warning, so that he understands both our leniency in this instance and our determination to prosecute should he ever again be found in possession of such material. And then you may release him.'

'Are you not interested in finding out how he came by the pamphlets?'

'I have a murder case to investigate. As the proverb goes, if you run after two hares, you will catch neither. Good day, Ilya Petrovich.'

Porfiry Petrovich half-bowed and moved away, followed by Virginsky, still clutching the pamphlets. Salytov watched them go then nodded for the door to be opened.

6: One Bezmygin, a musician

Shestaya Street, where Meyer was being held, was on the Petersburgsky side, off Bolshoi Prospekt: across the wide Neva and into a different St Petersburg, one built more of wood than stone. The buildings were lower, flimsier, more provisional, staging posts to a future that might never arrive. The Shestaya Street Bureau itself was one of the exceptions: it dominated its jerry-built neighbours with its precise and ruthless geometry, by the power of masonry.

'He has been asking for you,' said Ptitsyn as he led the way to an interview room. 'He started asking for you this morning. Apparently he has remembered something that can only be divulged to Your Excellency's ears.'

'I thought his memory would improve if we allowed him to stew for a couple of days.' Porfiry turned to Virginsky, who was beside him, and smiled. 'You have kept him alone?' The question was for Ptitsyn, though Porfiry continued to fix Virginsky with a steady gaze.

'As Your Excellency requested.'

'How does he appear to you?'

The young *politseisky* stopped walking. He turned to face the magistrates, his expression one of concern. 'He is in a bad way.'

'How do you mean?' asked Porfiry.

Ptitsyn shook his head gravely. 'Some kind of sickness, I think. In my view, a doctor should have been called. I have made my opinion known, but my superiors have seen fit to ignore it.'

'They are acting under my instructions.'

'But Your Excellency! I fear that he is very ill.'

'I believe it is a disease that will cure itself if we leave him be. You will continue, please.' Porfiry gestured ahead.

Ptitsyn bowed slightly and began walking again, without speaking now, however.

'What have the symptoms been?' asked Virginsky.

'Alternating fits of indolence and raving. Instability of mood. Loss of appetite. The sweats. Fever. Agonising stomach cramps. Constipation.' It was Porfiry who had answered.

'That's correct,' Ptitsyn confirmed over his shoulder, somewhat surprised.

'He is withdrawing from a morphine addiction,' said Porfiry. 'Why else do you think the maid had such trouble rousing him the day his wife and son died?'

*

A pungent smell came off Dr Meyer, which was more than simply the odour of a man who had not washed for a few days. It was as if he had sweated something vile and rotten out from his core, and the rancid exudate had soaked into his clothes. He was sitting at a flimsy painted table, the surface of which was pitted and scratched, in a small room with chipped plaster walls. A batch of brilliant sky, disrupted by silhouetted bars, cast a beam of light on to the back of Meyer's head. When he looked up as the door opened, it seemed that he had aged since they had last seen him, though it was only a little over a week ago. His face was haggard, heavily stubbled, his eyes dazed and adrift.

As soon as he saw them he sprang to his feet, his eyes now blazing with a sudden fervour. 'Thank God you've come! You must let me out. This is all a terrible mistake. I can explain everything. There was a man. How could I have not mentioned it before!' Meyer struck his forehead in a mime of acknowledged stupidity. 'I thought nothing of it at the time. Annoying, yes. But . . . uh . . . my mind . . . you have to understand, I had a lot on my mind.'

'Please sit down, Dr Meyer,' said Porfiry. The manic light in Meyer's eyes died as suddenly as it had sparked. His expression became utterly crestfallen. At those few neutral words from Porfiry, he had lost all hope. He sank back shakily into his seat.

There were two other chairs. Virginsky took one of them; Porfiry ignored the other and instead began to pace the room. Ptitsyn stood by the door. Meyer winced at the sound of the key turning as it was locked from the outside.

'How are you, Dr Meyer?' began Porfiry cheerfully, wrinkling his face into a smile.

'How do you think I am?' Meyer twisted his head to follow Porfiry's restless movement.

'Yes, yes, of course. This is a very bad situation for you. Your wife and son are dead and . . .'

'And I stand accused of their murder.'

Porfiry seemed surprised by the force of Meyer's bitterness. 'I'm afraid so. I presume you maintain that you are not responsible for their deaths?'

'Of course! I'm not a monster.' Meyer stared desperately. 'Anyhow, I can explain it all. I know what happened.'

Porfiry stopped pacing and pulled back the seat next to Virginsky, as if he intended to take it. He did not, however, and by remaining standing he introduced a strange tension into the interview. 'I am very interested to hear what you have to say.' Porfiry continued to stand over the doctor, fixing him with an expectant gaze. At last he let go of the chair and began pacing again. 'Forgive me. At the moment I find it uncomfortable to sit down for long periods. It is better for me to remain on my feet. It makes me rather restless, I confess. I'm sure as a doctor you will understand. Perhaps you will say the exercise is good for me. By the way, you are aware that your friend, Dr Pervoyedov of the Obukhovsky Hospital, has confirmed that Raisa and Grisha were killed by a poison administered via the chocolates you gave her? It was you who gave her the chocolates, was it not? You bought them from Ballet's that day, I believe.'

'Yes, that's true. I-I-I don't deny it,' Meyer stammered in confusion.

'There is no point in denying that which is self-evidently true, my friend.'

Meyer became suddenly excited. 'But here's the thing! I remember now what happened.' He was almost shouting.

'Very well. Tell me what happened. But please, try to calm down.'

'There was a man.'

'A man?'

'At the shop. The confectioner's.'

'Someone who works there?'

'No. Another customer. Although, now that I come to think of it, it was outside the shop. I was coming out. I'd just bought the chocolates. He was going in and . . . he walked into me. Quite deliberately! Don't you see? I didn't think anything of it at the time, but the thing is, you see, I dropped the chocolates. No! I didn't drop them! He knocked them out of my hand! It was quite deliberate. I see that now. At the time, well, you cannot believe such things. You do not trust the evidence of your own eyes. "Why would anyone do such a thing?" you think. No, it can't have been so. He can't have knocked the chocolates out of my hand. I simply refuse to believe that a stranger would do this. And yet . . . he did it! Afterwards he was so apologetic, and made such a fuss of retrieving the chocolates for me. What if, what if -- this is what I'm thinking -- what if he swapped them for another box of chocolates? A poisoned box!'

'Did anyone else see this encounter?'

'Oh yes! There were many people on the pavement. It was on the Nevsky Prospekt. Another fellow even tried to pick up the chocolate box but he -- the man, you understand -- he screamed at him hysterically to leave them be. I thought that most odd, but at the same time, thought nothing of it.' Meyer frowned. 'He was very particular -- jealous you might almost say -- about picking up the box himself.'

'Can you give us the names of any of these witnesses?'

'No! Of course not! They were just people on the street. Passers-by. How could I be expected to know their names?'

'And this man? Was he known to you?'

'That's what's strange about this whole affair! I've never seen him before in my life.'

'Can you describe him?'

'He was a man. I don't know, just some kind of man. I didn't look very closely at him. I found him rather annoying. I do not like to look closely at people who annoy me. I wanted him gone from my sight. I had no idea, at the time.'

'Why would he do this, do you think, this stranger?'

'I don't know! That is to say, I only have one theory.'

'And what is your theory?'

'Bezmygin.'

Porfiry broke off his pacing once more. He stood with his back to Meyer. 'Who is Bezmygin?' Porfiry angled his head as he awaited Meyer's answer.

'A musician.'

'And what does Bezmygin the musician have to do with all this?'

'Why it's obvious, isn't it?'

Porfiry turned and transmitted a blank look to Meyer.

'He put the man up to it.'

'You will have to help me here. I'm afraid I don't understand. Why would he do that?'

'He was in love with Raisa. They played duets together. He even came to visit her sometimes when I was not there. I caught them together once. They denied any impropriety, of course. They were rehearsing for a concert. Ha! But why would he be at the house of a married woman when her husband is absent if not for immoral purposes? I made her break with him completely. In point of fact, she was happy enough to do so. She did not love him. It was all on his side. My wife . . . well, my wife is easily influenced. She is weak. He is a flashy gewgaw of a man. She was a woman. It was only natural that there would be some degree of infatuation. But love? No. Never. But this man, this Bezmygin, he is a vain, arrogant man. You have no idea. He didn't take it well. I believe he has done all this to get even with her, with me. To destroy us. Do you not see?'

'We will naturally want to talk to this Bezmygin,' said Porfiry, beginning to pace once more. 'Do you know where we might find him?'

'He plays in the private orchestra of Count Akhmakov. I believe he is at the count's dacha near Petergof. He is little more than a serf. A performing lackey!'

'But why would he wish to kill your son?'

'He hated Grigory. To him, Grigory was always in the way. He could never be alone with my wife, you see.'

Porfiry stopped pacing to light a cigarette while he considered what Meyer had said. The doctor looked between Porfiry and Virginsky with desperate expectancy, trying to gauge on which of these two magistrates to focus his appeal. Virginsky's expression held more promise of sympathy, but he too watched Porfiry in some expectation. Everything, clearly, hung on what the older magistrate decided. For the moment, however, Porfiry seemed interested only in absorbing and enjoying the smoke from his cigarette. His face gave nothing away. At last he nodded, decisively, and said, 'We will look into it.' Finally, he took the seat next to Virginsky. 'At the dacha we found a number of sheets of paper covered in close, neat handwriting, apparently passages copied from the newspapers. All of them seem to be sensationalised accounts of murders or suicides. Rather singular, I think you will agree. Extraordinary, one might almost say. Dr Meyer, do you have any idea who made these copies?'

'Grigory. It was something he did.'

'If you don't mind me saying so, it seems rather a strange hobby for a boy to have.'

'It was not a hobby. It was a compulsion. Grigory . . . was not . . . he faced particular difficulties.'

'How would you characterise these difficulties, speaking as a doctor?'

'As a doctor?' Meyer seemed surprised by this acknowledgement of his profession. 'As a doctor, I would characterise them as imbecilic.'

'And as a father?'

Meyer said nothing. Anguish writhed on his face.

'He must have been a disappointment to you,' pressed Porfiry softly, grinding his cigarette out into the tin ashtray on the table.

Meyer flashed the briefest, and rawest, of looks at him. 'He was my son.'

'And yet . . . not the son you had hoped for.' Porfiry put this as a statement. 'No one would blame you for feeling this way.'

'I tried to help him, to break these habits. If only we could have ruptured the pattern of compulsion, we might have made progress.'

'But it was hopeless? He did not respond to your treatment.'

'Raisa Ivanovna would not support me in it. Her mollycoddling undermined my efforts.'

'There must have been times' -- Porfiry's voice cracked on the edge of a whisper -- 'when you thought it would have been better for Grigory if he had never been born.'

Meyer took off his spectacles and cleaned them with a handkerchief. He lifted his head as he replaced them, but did not look at Porfiry. 'Better for Grigory? Grigory's condition caused him no suffering. If anything, it was we who suffered more because of it.'

'And you, most of all, I imagine.'

'That does not mean I wished him dead.'

'It must have been hard though, for a man such as you, with a brilliant academic record, a PhD, an intellectual, to have such a son.'

'For all that, sometimes I envied him.'

Porfiry kinked an eyebrow sceptically.

'Grigory was an innocent,' continued Meyer. 'Sometimes I wondered what it must be like to live in such a state of . . . innocence, a state of grace.'

Porfiry smiled. 'I understand. I understand completely. And yet you must have feared for him too? There would come a day when you and Raisa would no longer be able to look after him.'

'I had thought of that, even if Raisa wouldn't. There are provisions one can make. Institutions. As a doctor, one knows a little more about these things than a layman.'

'You visited asylums?'

'I went to Ulyanka. The house at the eleventh verst.'

Virginsky shot a significant, excited glance at Porfiry, who batted it away with three quick blinks.

'When was this?' asked Porfiry, neutrally.

'Is it important?' It seemed Meyer had picked up something from Virginsky's glance.

'It may be.'

Meyer frowned and shook his head, trying to remember. 'I don't know. It was in the summer. It must have been last summer.'

'And what were your impressions?'

'It is run in accordance with the latest scientific thinking.' Meyer's tone was strangely dead.

'And what did Raisa think?'

'She didn't go with me. She wouldn't countenance it. I couldn't talk to her about the future.' Meyer's imploring gaze sought out Virginsky. 'I did not wish my son dead,' he insisted.

'The maid, Polina,' said Porfiry, his tone harsher now, 'she couldn't raise you. She said she knocked on your door and called out for you, but you didn't answer.'

'I was working. I told you that at the dacha.'

'Ah, yes. Your work. It must be very absorbing work.'

'It is.'

'What were you doing, exactly, in your study, when the maid roused you?'

Meyer's expression of shock at this question was almost comical. 'I was looking at a map,' he said at last, his voice surprised, and then defeated. He had been so taken off his guard that he had not thought to lie.

'This was part of your work?'

'I . . . do . . . need to look at maps for my work, yes.' The answer stumbled out, Meyer's brow creased in a frown. He was a bad liar; he was evidently struggling to comprehend his own inconsistencies.

'Had you taken morphine?'

'What?'

'You heard me.'

'It is an outrageous question.'

'Which you haven't answered yet.'

'I am tired now.'

'We will search your study anyhow.'

'And what if you do? And what if you find morphine there? It means nothing. I am a doctor.'

'You are a sanitation inspector. I imagine you are not often called upon to dispense morphine.'

'I am self-medicating. I suffer from neuralgic pain.'

'And you had medicated yourself that afternoon?'

Meyer nodded minutely.

'It is unfortunate,' said Porfiry. 'Perhaps if you hadn't, your wife and child might still be alive.'

'Bezmygin!' shouted Meyer. 'Bezmygin is to blame, not me!' His fingers curled as he clutched the edge of the table. It seemed for a moment that he would hurl the table at them.

Porfiry signalled mutely to Ptitsyn.

*

'So, Pavel Pavlovich. What do you make of all that?' Meyer's rancid aura lingered, even though he had been taken back to his cell. Porfiry, on his feet once more, lit a cigarette, as if to dispel it.

'A connection?' Virginsky made the suggestion tentatively.

'A connection?' Porfiry threw it back with sceptical emphasis.

'With the boy Lieutenant Salytov brought in. Tolya, the apprentice from the confectioner's.'

'Whom we had to release because there were insufficient grounds for holding him. His passport turned out to be perfectly in order. And it is not a crime to have a suicide for a mother. Besides, a search of the workshop -- and the boy's lodging -- turned up nothing.'

'The pamphlets?'

'If we searched your lodgings would we not find the same pamphlets?'

'Lieutenant Salytov is convinced he is a political agitator.' There was something wry and teasing about Virginsky's tone.

'Lieutenant Salytov sees conspiracies everywhere.'

'But what of the Ulyanka connection? The house at the eleventh verst. Did that not strike you?'

'Yes, it struck me as quite possibly a meaningless coincidence. There are such things, you know. They serve to distract the investigator.'

'You said "quite possibly". That means you equally accept that there might be something in it.'

'Tolya's mother was an inmate at the house at the eleventh verst three years ago, in sixty-five. Incarcerated for six months, at the end of which she hanged herself using a knotted sheet tied to a window bar. Meyer visited the place last year. The timings do not fit.'

'But was that the first time he visited there?'

'Ah, my young friend, be careful. Do not go chasing chimeras. Do not be led astray by random correspondences. They beguile the eye, but there is nothing to them, take it from me.'

'Are you testing me again, Porfiry Petrovich? Is this another of your training methods?'

Porfiry smiled ambiguously. 'That's something you will have to work out for yourself.'

Virginsky curled his mouth into half a smile. 'And what of this musician, Bezmygin?'

'Poor Dr Meyer,' said Porfiry. 'In his eagerness to supply us with a suspect, he has provided himself with a motive.' He took out his cigarette case and counted the cigarettes without lighting one.

7: Count Akhmakov's orchestra

They took the train from Petergofsky Station. The morning was bright and warm, the city in the full luminous grip of summer. It felt to Virginsky like they were going on an excursion. Porfiry's cook had even prepared a lunch for them, putting a loaf of black bread, a hock of ham and some gooseberries into a small wicker basket. Porfiry had the basket on the seat next to him, as if it were the third member of their party. Most of the daytrippers to Petergof had taken earlier trains, giving Porfiry and Virginsky the whole of a second-class compartment to themselves.

The train gathered speed as it passed the Mitrofanevsky Cemetery. Virginsky watched the memorials and mausoleums flicker by, the grey palaces of the dead projecting sharply from the all-consuming earth. He remembered this was not an excursion after all.

'Have they buried them yet?'

Porfiry was lost in the enjoyment of a cigarette. He had been looking out of the same window, but without seeing the sombre landscape, it seemed. And by now they had left the cemetery behind. He turned a quizzical face to Virginsky.

'Raisa Ivanovna and Grisha.'

'Yesterday,' said Porfiry. 'We let Meyer out to attend the funeral. There were no other relatives.'

'No one on her side?'

'No one.'

They travelled through the borderland of squalid dwellings that lay at the southern periphery of the city. Roads broke up into dirt tracks; walls crumbled; sheds and shanty houses tumbled into each other. Out of all this arose a new and sinister-seeming presence, that of looming, smoke-grimed manufactories. The train banked away from Virginsky's sight-line, as if turning its back on the pervasive ugliness. Pulled by the direction of movement, Virginsky looked through the opposite window, across the corridor of the carriage. His gaze swooped along the momentous curve of the tracks, carried away by perspective, westward. The landscape here was taken up with a series of garden plots, another manifestation of the human instinct for purpose and production, the force that drew the hurtling train on. He picked out isolated figures, peasants, stooped and barely moving, as though they had grown out of the soil they worked.

Clumps of woodland squatted over the horizon. In the middle distance, Virginsky glimpsed a large ochre and white house, half-concealed by trees. He stirred and sat up, then leant forward and touched Porfiry's knee.

'Ulyanka,' said Virginsky.

Porfiry shrugged. 'So? Ulyanka is on the way to Petergof. This really shouldn't come as news to you.'

'But it is another connection. Now with this Bezmygin fellow.'

Porfiry smiled at Virginsky's excitement. 'Or another meaningless coincidence,' he said.

They were both silent as they watched the building dance in and out of vision behind the veil of birch.

'The house at the eleventh verst,' said Virginsky redundantly. Porfiry screwed his face up into an expression of reproof.

The train stopped at a station on the Ligovaki Canal. The lunatic asylum remained in view, as if to provoke them. Porfiry fidgeted in annoyance. Virginsky felt somehow embarrassed. It was a relief to them both it seemed when the train pulled out.

From Ligovo, the short next stop, the railway climbed and ran through woodland. A green translucent fire blazed around them. As they emerged they scanned the horizon hopefully for a glimpse of the sea. Now the tracks ran parallel with the Petergof Road a couple of versts away to the north, its chain of magnificent dachas spread out along the coast. Beyond it, the edge of the land crumbled into the bay.

*

The summer residence of Count Akhmakov was a grand, neoclassical palace looking out over the Gulf of Finland. To reach it, they took a *drozhki* from New Petergof station one and a half versts back along the Petergof Road. The salted air and the flicker of light through the beech trees rekindled the holiday mood in Virginsky. There was a breeze from the sea; the morning hovered on the edge of coolness. But he felt the sun on his face and that counted for a lot.

Porfiry sat with the basket of food on his lap. There was something fussy and comical about the figure he cut. *It would be easy to underestimate him*, thought Virginsky, looking at the placid, almost animal, expression on his superior's face. Porfiry had his eyes closed, those hyperactive lashes of his still for the moment, as he smiled, basking in the sun. Virginsky remembered the fear and, yes, hatred he had once felt towards this man. But he realised that even when these feelings had been at their most intense, there had been room for others. Porfiry Petrovich had always fascinated him. There had been times when he had even liked the man, and wanted to be liked by him in return. Certainly, he had never made the mistake of not respecting him. Now, in retrospect, the sympathy he had at the time entertained towards his persecutor seemed inexplicable. He wondered whether he would ever entirely trust him.

As the *drozhki* turned into the canopied lane that led winding up to the house, Porfiry opened his eyes and saw Virginsky looking at him. Porfiry's smile was questioning. Virginsky met it with an ironic, slightly mocking face. 'You are quite comfortable?' he asked.

'Yes,' answered Porfiry, bemused.

'I was merely thinking of something you said to Dr Meyer. About sitting down. For long periods. I wondered . . .'

'It comes and goes,' said Porfiry carelessly, looking away.

'I rather imagined it was just something you said. Off the top of your head, as it were. An invention.'

'How could you suspect me of such a thing, Pavel Pavlovich?'

Virginsky shrugged. 'I thought it was part of your technique.'

'Do you really believe me capable of such *deviousness*?' Porfiry's tone was hurt. 'Besides, I am more superstitious than you allow. To lay claim to a malady one does not have seems almost to invite it. I am not so rash as to wish the complaint in question upon myself.'

'What malady?'

'Haemorrhoids.' Porfiry's expression sealed off any further discussion.

*

Catching sight of the gardens, formally landscaped in the 'French' style, with symmetrical lawns and statue-lined avenues, Virginsky was stirred first to delight and then to anger. *Really, these aristocrats!* he thought, *they believe that even nature must do their bidding.* He looked back to Porfiry and saw now that it was he who was being watched with interest. Porfiry smiled and nodded for Virginsky to look at something: a fountain sprayed out from a statue of Neptune, within an arc of columns.

'He has made his own little Petergof,' said Porfiry.

Virginsky allowed himself a collusive smile.

The path curved round and brought them to the front of the house. A gleaming facade of columns faced the sea, as if demanding obeisance of it.

Virginsky, however, was determined not to be cowed, though he was curiously discomfited by Porfiry's basket, which was handed him to hold as the senior investigating magistrate climbed down after him from the cab. He made sure to give it back to Porfiry at the soonest opportunity.

The doors were opened to them by a gaunt-faced butler who affected a superior attitude, despite the fact that he was the one done up in livery. When Porfiry explained who they were and why they were there, the butler turned a contemptuous eye on the basket before admitting them.

They followed his satin-clad back across a marble-floored reception hall towards the muted sounds of an orchestra playing. The hall was dominated by a huge painting of an Arcadian scene. *How typical!* thought Virginsky, hotly. He imagined the declaration he would make when he was brought into the count's presence. *You celebrate the rural idyll, adorn your walls with idealised images of shepherds and shepherdesses, yet the wealth that makes it possible was borne out of the ownership of human souls.* The count will probably protest that he no longer owns any souls. Perhaps he will even claim to be a liberal, saying that he gave his serfs their freedom in advance of the reforms of '61. But Virginsky would not spare him. *You refuse to renounce the crimes of your forefathers! Your life of luxury and idleness is tainted by its source. You are the child of theft and oppression!*

With an unpleasant jolt of awareness, Virginsky recognised the face his imagination had supplied for the count in this self-soothing fantasy: it was his father's.

The flunky opened a door and released a blast of music that was both lush and somehow also ragged. The room they were shown into was a circular hall with a domed ceiling painted with clouds.

The walls were lined with paper in which gold leaf predominated. In the middle of the hall, stretched out on a sofa, was a man of around forty, a Chinese dressing gown draped around his considerable bulk. He wore his hair long and unkempt and had his eyes closed, though he did not seem to be asleep. His expression was somewhere between the pained and the ecstatic. The musicians, who were dressed in the same pale-blue livery as the butler, were seated on a platform in front of their solitary audience. They were about twenty in number, and by the sounds of it, of varying degrees of musicianship. The string section produced a passable, even rich, sound, but one or two of the woodwind were out of tune, as well as out of time. Virginsky couldn't see the face of the conductor who was bringing them more or less to the end of a limping rendition of Beethoven's *Pastoral Symphony*, but his shoulders were rounded and the movements of his arms seemed rather constrained and lacking in conviction.

When the music finished, he turned a face in which fear and hopefulness were combined to pathetic effect towards the lounging aristocrat, who did not deign to open his eyes or acknowledge the end of the piece in any way. Virginsky also discerned in the conductor's meek and suppliant expression a stifled hatred that were it ever to be released would result in an explosion of violent passion.

'Well, Iakov Ilyich,' began Count Akhmakov at last, for it was surely he reclining on the sofa. 'The noise your rabble produces reminds me of the female pudenda, heavenly bliss in close proximity to utter filth and degradation.'

There was a titter of amusement from the players.

'Thank you, Your Excellency.' Iakov Ilyich smiled uneasily.

Count Akhmakov kept his eyes closed, but his arms swept magisterially about him, trailing the loose sleeves of his dressing gown. 'Don't thank me, you fool. I'm insulting you! Don't you even have the wit to know when you are insulted?'

Iakov Ilyich shrugged and mugged for the orchestra. By such small acts of insubordination, he asserted his freedom from the tormentor on the sofa.

The butler who had shown Porfiry and Virginsky in cleared his throat loudly and walked over to Count Akhmakov. After the flunky had whispered something in his ear, Akhmakov sat up sharply and turned a blue imperious gaze on the visitors. 'Magistrates from St Petersburg! For Bezmygin!' he shouted, in mock alarm. 'You cannot arrest Bezmygin. He is a scoundrel and a philanderer, but he is my best player. Arrest one of them instead!' Count Akhmakov pointed to a pair of flautists, little more than boys, who seemed as unhappy to be in his orchestra as he was to have them there. 'In fact, you may arrest the whole of the woodwind section, but not Bezmygin. I am holding a masked ball tonight. I cannot do without my Bezmygin.'

'Your Excellency,' protested Porfiry, mildly, 'we have not come to arrest Bezmygin, merely to talk to him.'

'What is in your basket?'

'Food.'

'You have come to invite him on a picnic?'

'Not exactly, sir.'

Count Akhmakov regarded first Porfiry then Virginsky with open, almost offensive curiosity, like a schoolboy inspecting snails. He seemed particularly interested in Virginsky, perhaps sensing his hostility and wanting to provoke it more.

'Very well, you have my *permission* to talk to him.' Virginsky bristled at that 'permission' and the count allowed himself a small smile of triumph. He rose from the sofa, swishing his sleeves about him. 'I shall retire to the orangery. My auditory senses are worn out. Iakov Ilyich, you will be busy this afternoon, I think. There is much work to be done, but you are the man to do it, of that I have no doubt. Now then, where is that young wife of yours? We must do our best to keep her entertained while you are occupied. It is the least we can do. It would not do for one so pretty to be bored. Though how a booby like you won such a wife, I'll never know.' With that, Akhmakov padded out of the ballroom, his slippers flapping mocking applause as he went.

'Which of you is Bezmygin?' Porfiry called out, when the emotional wake of the departed aristocrat had cleared from the room.

The man who occupied the position of first violin tilted back his head and looked down superciliously. There was arrogance in his posture, but also a kind of sly wariness that undermined it. Perhaps it was this contradiction, the hint of vulnerability in his soft, dark eyes, that made him attractive to women. To Virginsky, he had the look of the Lothario who expects the husband to burst in at any moment. He laid down his instrument and stepped down from the platform. His gait was stiff and self-conscious. He held himself away from Porfiry and Virginsky as he approached them.

'What is this about?' Behind him, the orchestra master tapped his baton on his music stand and called out bars for the woodwind players.

'You are Bezmygin?' demanded Porfiry.

The musician nodded confirmation.

'We have come to talk to you about Raisa Ivanovna Meyer.'

An unpleasant smirk contorted Bezmygin's face. 'What has she done? Murdered that insufferable philistine of a husband of hers?'

'No. In fact, I am afraid to say that she is dead and it seems someone has murdered her.'

The shock of receiving this news seemed to knock some of the stuffing out of Bezmygin's pose. It struck Virginsky as genuine. He remembered his own experience of how Porfiry used such revelations as psychological tools to prise out the truth.

'Poor Raya,' said Bezmygin.

'Dr Meyer seems to think you might have had something to do with it.'

'That's ridiculous!'

'Is it true you were having an affair with Raisa Ivanovna?'

'I deny that.'

'My friend, you may deny it and yet it may also be true,' observed Porfiry. 'Her husband's view is that when she broke off the affair, your pride was wounded and you determined to extract revenge.'

'He's a fool. This would be laughable if it weren't . . .' Bezmygin broke off.

'You were often at her house. Alone with her, when her husband was not there.'

'Yes. We were putting together some pieces for a soirée. She . . . was a gifted accompanist.' Sudden anger flared in Bezmygin's eyes. 'I cannot believe you have come here to ask me these questions. I should have thought it quite obvious that her husband killed her out of jealousy.'

'Did he, then, have grounds to be jealous?'

'No! Except that she was bored with him. The man is a philistine and a morphine eater who had no appreciation of her talents. Besides, he was having an affair with the maid, Polina. Did he tell you about that?'

Porfiry and Virginsky exchanged a glance. 'No, he did not,' said Porfiry.

'Well, it's true. Raisa told me about it.'

'So relations between Dr Meyer and his wife were strained?' asked Porfiry.

'I should say so. He had turned away from her. The man had a heart of ice.'

'As far as you know, was there any specific reason for the deterioration in their relations, other than her friendship with you?'

'Our friendship had nothing to do with it. It was all to do with a letter he received.'

'A letter? Who was it from?'

'It was anonymous, apparently. The thing upset her terribly. Really, there are some quite malicious people in the world. Live and let live, is what I say. But it seems there are those who hold to a different philosophy.'

'Did she tell you what was in the letter?'

'No. She wouldn't go into the details. But it was pretty spiteful stuff, I should think, judging by the effect it had.'

'You think the contents concerned Raisa Ivanovna?'

'All I know is that after he received it, Meyer would have nothing to do with his wife, not in the normal way of married couples, if you take my meaning. If you ask me, he was looking for an excuse. And, anyway, it didn't take long for him to fall into the arms of his wench.'

'When did he receive this letter, can you say?'

'Two or three months ago.' Bezmygin shrugged his shoulders uncertainly. 'I think it was about then that she first spoke to me of it.'

'This is all very interesting,' said Porfiry. 'If true.'

'Of course it's true! You have only to find the letter. He would not destroy it, though she begged him to.'

Porfiry pursed his lips distractedly, then it seemed as though he had remembered something. 'Tell me, what were your feelings towards Grigory, the Meyers' son?'

'Pity, mostly. Why? What has Grigory got to do with this?'

'Whoever killed Raisa, also killed him,' said Virginsky, and he wondered why he had wanted to be the one who broke this news to Bezmygin.

'What a terrible business,' said Bezmygin, and there was something deliberate about the way he made this declaration. He looked back at the platform. The other musicians had stopped practising and all eyes were on him. His look to Porfiry, seeking release, was defiant.

*

'Are you not going to eat that?' said Virginsky, indicating the basket that was once again on Porfiry's lap. They were on the train back to St Petersburg. 'You have taken it all the way to Petergof and now you are taking it all the way back without touching it.'

Porfiry's surprise at discovering the basket seemed a little overdone. 'I have been so preoccupied, I forgot all about it.'

'If you had ever been a starving student, you would have found it impossible to forget about eating.'

'It has been on your mind all the time? Here, have it. Help yourself. I'll perhaps have . . . just a few gooseberries.'

Virginsky took the basket. He broke off a piece of the bread and sliced the ham with a knife that the cook had supplied. 'So? What do you think now?'

'I think we need to find this letter. I would like you to go to the dacha this afternoon to find it. You could meet young Ptitsyn there. He is a good man to have at a crime scene.'

'Very well.'

'Perhaps you could give me a little of the ham, after all,' said Porfiry.

'But what did you think of Bezmygin?'

'Obviously, he had nothing to do with it.'

Virginsky nodded. 'That was my impression too.'

'I don't suppose Zakhar put any wine in there, did he?'

Virginsky shook his head.

'Really, that man. He persecutes me terribly. One's servants always do.'

Virginsky furrowed his brow in distaste at the joke. 'Then don't have servants.'

'In which case, who would I have to persecute me? Or would you have me marry?'

But Virginsky had lost his appetite for the banter, as he had almost for the food. He pretended sudden interest in a somewhat pretentious dacha that was gliding past at that moment.

'Any bread?' said Porfiry. 'I think I must be hungrier than I realised.'

*

They were driving north now on Izmailovsky Prospekt, having just crossed the Fontanka, when Virginsky stood up in the *drozhki* and called the driver to a halt. He leapt down from the cab and ran back some distance along the pavement towards a couple who had just come out of the entrance of an apartment building opposite the Novo-Alexandrovsky Market. A tall, well-to-do middle-aged gentleman was arm-in-arm with a very pretty and fashionably dressed girl about half his age. The gentleman's expression when he saw Virginsky coming towards him was at first one of shock, which gradually gave way to shame-faced contrition.

'Father!' Virginsky called out. 'You did not tell me you were coming to Petersburg.'

'Why it's Pasha!' cried the young woman delightedly. At the same time she broke away from Virginsky's father and threw her arms out towards Virginsky. He slowed his step and ignored the offered embrace.

'Ah, my dear!' Virginsky's father at last began. 'It all happened so quickly. There did not seem time. And besides . . .' His father suddenly seemed to think of something. 'We thought it would be nice to surprise you!' His voice rose brightly, but there was something not entirely trustworthy about his eyes at that moment. Virginsky felt a pang of depression.

'How long have you been here?' he asked leadenly.

'Oh, simply ages,' said the girl, rolling her eyes. 'It feels like a lifetime. Pavel Pavlovich has had all sorts of boring business to attend to with his boring old cronies. It has been the longest week of my life.'

'A week?'

'Now now, Natasha! Don't exaggerate. Not a week, nothing like. A matter of days, that's all. We were intending to pay you a visit once I had sorted out all my business affairs.' Virginsky's father smiled nervously.

Natasha, that is to say, Natalya Ivanovna, Virginsky's young stepmother, placed her hand on his arm and turned him gently away from his father. He was aware of a wild excitement that her touch provoked in him, something closer to hatred than desire.

'Pasha, you must rescue me from your father.' Her eyes were imploring. But again he recognised in them a suspect quality. *Oh, how they deserve each other*, he thought bitterly. 'He has been neglecting me awfully. He prefers to spend all his time with that old lecher Colonel Setochkin.'

'What's that?' said Virginsky, his smile frozen anxiously.

Natasha addressed him over her shoulder. 'You wouldn't object, would you, dearest, if Pasha were to look after me for the next few days, while you sort out your affairs with Setochkin?' Then to Virginsky she confided: 'You wouldn't believe it. I have to sit on my own in a tiny room with only the walls to talk to, while they lock themselves away discussing I know not what.'

'Business matters. It would be even more tiresome for you to have to listen to it all. But yes! Why not? What a capital idea. Pasha, you could show your mother the sights of St Petersburg. The Hermitage, the Summer Garden, the Fortress . . .'

'No,' said Virginsky quickly. He pulled away from the disturbing touch. 'I'm afraid that won't be possible. I have work to do. Now.' He gestured back to the waiting *drozhki*.

'Ah! The magistrate! Of course. Is that the great Porfiry Petrovich?'

'Yes.'

'Will you not introduce us?'

'Another time, perhaps. Right now we are engaged in urgent business. A case. Time is of the essence.'

'I see.' Virginsky's father dropped his gaze to the ground in disappointment. He worked quickly to dispel it. 'Of course. You must devote yourself to your work. I am glad to see you taking so well to it.' And then he remembered: 'The letter! It did the trick then, the letter I wrote?'

Virginsky frowned in annoyance and did not answer.

'But what will I do?' implored Natalya Ivanovna petulantly. 'You men and your business, it is all you ever think about.'

'Sweetest, I will make it up to you, I promise. I shall take you to the opera!'

'Good day to you, sir. And you, madam,' Virginsky cut in,

tersely. He began to walk away without waiting for a response.

'We're at the Hotel Regina,' called his father after him. 'On the Moika Embankment. Charming view of the river. You must come and see us.'

Virginsky shook his head to Porfiry's questioning face as he climbed back into the *drozhki*.

8: The nasty letter

Inside the dacha was hot and oppressively scented with pine. An uncomfortable tension showed in Ptitsyn's face. He seemed wary and eager at the same time: holding back to take his lead from Virginsky, yet more than willing to do whatever was asked of him.

For his part, Virginsky felt hopelessly out of his depth as soon as they stepped inside, their footfalls met by the building's creaking protests. The young *politseisky*'s expectant gaze only served to increase the sensation. Virginsky found himself wishing that Porfiry Petrovich was there with him. Then resentment drove out the wish.

'Where is the girl now?' said Virginsky, unconsciously voicing a thought that came to him, apparently randomly, as he looked around. He was looking at the divan that the maid had been sitting on the first time he had come to the dacha, willing the memory of her to solidify into her person.

'Polina? She is lodging with a relative in the Spasskaya district. We know where she is if we need her.'

Virginsky experienced a pang of unearned jealousy. Ptitsyn had evidently conversed with the maid, from which Virginsky constructed a familiarity that tormented him. Of course, there was the question of class. Ptitsyn would naturally find it easier to talk to the girl, coming from a similar peasant background. There was none of the constraint that he himself would feel. Virginsky found himself envying the young policeman. Not knowing what to say, he nodded once tersely, but felt the gesture belonged more to Porfiry Petrovich than to himself and blushed. Then, quite self-consciously, he blinked his eyelashes rapidly, straightaway shaking his head at his own foolishness.

'What are we looking for, Your Honour?'

'A letter. It will be in the doctor's study.' Virginsky masked his uncertainty with a harsh, decisive tone. Ptitsyn smiled appeasement and led the way into the study, his step quick and untroubled, now that he had a direction to follow.

Ptitsyn made straight for a walnut escritoire and opened it. 'There are letters here.' He began to sift through the papers. 'All sorts of correspondence.'

Virginsky joined him and looked down. He was aware of a frisson of transgression, a sense of himself as a voyeur that was both pleasurable and shaming. And yet, as he reminded himself, he had a right, a duty even, to pry. He tried to will his face into a mask of professional dispassion, as if by so doing he would suppress his inappropriate excitement.

He picked up a sheet at random and read a printed letter in which certain details had been handwritten:

Dear Dr Meyer,

We regret to inform you that your article 'Notes on the Non-Sexual Transmission of Syphilis in Peasant Communes' has not been selected for publication in The Russian Journal of Public Health. We thank you for your consideration in submitting to The Russian Journal of Public Health and return your submission herewith.

The note was unsigned, though a handwritten addendum below -- *Insufficient rigour. Findings not supported. Political.* -- was initialled K.P.N.

The next letter was in German. It extended over several pages and was signed *Deine dich liebende Mutter*.

Virginsky glanced up at Ptitsyn, who was watching him intently, his face open and inquisitive. 'It's from his mother,' explained Virginsky.

'And is that the letter we're looking for?'

'No. The letter we are looking for is anonymous. And malicious. It refers to Raisa Ivanovna, the doctor's wife, in rather nasty terms.' Virginsky now had in his hands a number of bills, some correspondence from Dr Meyer's colleagues and superiors, as well as a letter from the St Petersburg College of Physicians concerning membership details. Also in the escritoire were a number of maps of St Petersburg.

'Perhaps we should take them all in so that the investigating magistrate can decide,' said Ptitsyn.

'We do not need Porfiry Petrovich to tell us that none of these is the letter we are looking for.' Virginsky avoided Ptitsyn's eye. 'However, naturally, it is too early at this stage to say what may or may not turn out to be relevant as the case develops. So, of course, everything here will have to be taken away and analysed at length by myself and . . . uh . . . Porfiry Petrovich.' Virginsky added the name distractedly. He had spread out one of the city maps and was studying it closely. Someone, presumably Dr Meyer, had added to the map a number of markings: clusters of red dots and ruled black lines, connecting buildings with each other and with the city's many waterways.

Ptitsyn seemed to lose interest in the escritoire and its contents. He moved away, nosing the air as if he were a bloodhound. Virginsky watched him out of the corner of his eye, distracted by his purposefulness, competitively anxious. He pulled out the drawer of the escritoire and saw the faces of Meyer and his wife staring back at him in dusky monochrome and miniature. There were a number of studio photographs of each of them and even, at the back of the drawer, an albumen print of the baby that had once been Grigory, so faded that the ghostly infant was almost invisible.

'Apparently, the good doctor was engaged in an illicit sexual relationship with your Polina,' Virginsky felt himself compelled to say, as he picked up a photograph of Raisa Ivanovna. It must have been taken some years ago: the dark dress she was wearing showed off a slim figure. Her face was undeniably handsome, and still youthful, though a complicated unease shadowed her eyes. But perhaps it was just the discomfort of maintaining her pose for the portrait.

Virginsky watched Ptitsyn to see how he was taking the revelation.

'It happens,' was all the young policeman offered. He had dropped to one knee and was running his fingers along the edge of a floorboard.

'What is it?' asked Virginsky, anxious and resentful.

'The board was sticking up on one side. I thought it might be loose. Sometimes, you have to think like them, you know? They don't always hide things in the obvious places.' He followed the jutting board to a skirted chair, which he tilted back. 'Ah now, there's something here.' Ptitsyn pulled out an open cardboard box that had been placed beneath the seat, concealed by the chair's cover. He let the chair drop back down on to its four legs. 'Is this what he did them in with, do you think?' asked Ptitsyn, lifting from the box a small bottle made of dense brown glass.

'I wouldn't touch that,' said Virginsky. 'It may be highly

poisonous.' Ptitsyn put the bottle back hurriedly. Virginsky took the box off him. He looked inside. As well as the bottle, there was a single sheet of white notepaper and a dead woodlouse. He took out the sheet and read what was written on it. When he had finished, he said to Ptitsyn: 'But that was just luck. You thought the board was loose. It wasn't. The board had nothing to do with it. There was no reason why the board should have led you to it.'

'I found it then, did I?' said Ptitsyn, unable to keep the grin from his face.

*

'Well?' asked Virginsky impatiently.

Porfiry's mouth twitched into something that could have been a smile. 'The regularity of the script is striking,' he said at last. 'It is as if it were written by someone who couldn't help but take pride in his writing, whatever the content.'

'It reminds me of the passages copied by Grigory,' commented Virginsky. And this, it seemed, was the source of the impatience in his voice: a desire to have this observation stated.

Porfiry pursed his lips sceptically. He brushed aside a small fly that had settled on the paper, as if it were interested in analysing the letter too. The fly buzzed away and joined two or three others that were frantically circling the ceiling of Porfiry's chambers. 'This is a more mature hand, I would say. For me, it brings to mind more the work of an official copyist. It is a slightly relaxed version of the copperplate calligraphy that we are used to seeing on department communiqués. What is striking to me is that the person who wrote this has made no effort to conceal his -- or indeed her -- skill. There are many people who can write badly, but fewer who could produce a script of this quality. And while it is possible for a good copyist to conceal their ability, a bad one cannot pretend to a greater level of competence than they possess. Is it arrogance or negligence that has prevented our letter-writer from taking pains to disguise his skill, I wonder?' Porfiry folded the letter along its crease. He rose sharply and regarded Virginsky across his desk with a look of keen excitement. 'I think it's time we had another chat with Dr Meyer.'

*

Meyer was brought to the same interview room at the Shestaya Street Police Bureau in which Porfiry and Virginsky had seen him two days ago. His physical and mental deterioration was marked. Sweat plastered his hair to his scalp and showed in patches of dampness through his jacket. His face was as pale as a ghost's, apart from the dark sunken rings around his eyes. There was hardly anything to him, and if it hadn't been for the two *politseisky* holding on to him, it seemed that he would have floated away. They planted him firmly in the seat, releasing him reluctantly, almost fearfully.

When he saw the magistrates across the table, a flicker of energy came to his eyes. He licked his teeth to ask: 'Well? Have you arrested him?'

Porfiry frowned as he lit a cigarette.

'Bezmygin! Did you arrest Bezmygin?' insisted Meyer shrilly.

'We spoke to him.'

'And?'

'He mentioned a letter. An anonymous letter. We searched your study and found this.' Porfiry produced the letter from a pocket and threw it down on the table. Meyer did not need to pick it up to know its significance: a look of surly resentment showed on his face. 'I wonder,' began Porfiry hesitantly, almost apologetically, 'why you did not mention this letter before?'

'I forgot about it. Perhaps I had made a conscious effort to put it out of my mind.'

'Understandable, of course, although I imagine that it would be difficult to forget a letter like this. Shall I read it to you?'

'There is no need. I am aware of its contents.'

'All the same,' said Porfiry, 'I would like to read it to you, if it would not inconvenience you. Just so that we are sure that we are talking about the same letter.'

' "My dear friend Dr Meyer," ' began Meyer, his eyes closed, his voice harsh and mechanical. ' "I feel compelled to inform you that your wife, Raisa Ivanovna, is a whore, and in fact fourteen years ago worked as a common prostitute at a licensed brothel on Sadovaya Street, where I, and many other gentlemen of my acquaintance, had the pleasure of her. If you do not believe me, ask her about her time with Madam Josephine. That was the name of the proprietress of the establishment, who, I believe, has since died from a disease associated with her profession, which if your wife has escaped it is a miracle. She was one of the filthiest whores I have ever known. Yours respectfully, a well-wisher.'"

'That *is* the same letter,' said Porfiry. 'It seems you were not entirely successful in casting it from your mind.'

Dr Meyer gave a rueful snort.

'Have you any idea who sent it?'

'None.'

'It is a horrible letter. I am sorry to bring it up. I am sure there is no truth in what it alleges. I dare say you did not deign to discuss it with your wife.'

Dr Meyer turned his head deliberately from Porfiry.

'You confronted her with it?' Porfiry gave the impression of being thoroughly astonished.

'Yes.'

'And?'

'She did not deny it.'

'I see. It must have come as a terrible shock to you.'

Meyer said nothing.

Porfiry considered the letter in his hands, shaking his head over it woefully. 'The period to which it alludes,' he began delicately, 'I take it that was before you met Raisa?'

'No. That is not entirely a correct assumption. I have known her almost all my life. We grew up together.'

'Oh? And where was this?'

'In Pskov. Her father was a well-to-do shopkeeper. He owned the town's main store. My father was a prominent doctor. Mind you, it is easy to be prominent in a small town. Raisa and I were friends from childhood. But we grew apart. Her beauty was the barrier between us. A beauty beyond my aspiration. I was content to admire her from afar. And besides, I had my studies. When the time came for me to come to Petersburg to follow my calling, I allowed myself the indulgence of writing her a letter. A declaration of sorts. I took myself off, without waiting for a reply, knowing what the reply would be, of course. I was not the sort to win the heart of the town beauty, not with my studious ways, and reserved manner. I did not have any further contact with her, though I heard about her through my parents' letters. I heard that she quarrelled with her father. He kept her on a tight rein, you see, not trusting to her goodness. My mother seemed to think there was a cavalry officer involved, but my mother could not always be relied upon in these matters. At any rate, I refused to believe it. And when she ran away from home, I persuaded myself that she was fleeing the injustice of gossip and calumny. And then, some time later, when I was working on my PhD --'

'The one on toxicology?'

'That is correct. I ran into her again, in Petersburg. She was in a bad way. I could tell something was wrong from her eyes, the way they latched on to me. Such desperate hope, and it would have been inconceivable, once, for her to look at me with anything akin to hope. To look at me at all, even, is what I mean. I think I also saw some kind of calculation take place within her. She looked at me and calculated, then hoped. However, it goes without saying that I did not consciously register that at the time. I was overcome. Perhaps it was pity. Whatever it was, a tremendous emotion swept over me at the sight of her. I immediately, and rather insanely, blurted out a marriage proposal. I think I sensed that she was at the weakest and most vulnerable moment of her life. And if I ever stood a chance of winning her, it was then. And indeed, she accepted me, with tears. Tears I chose to believe were of joy. But really they were tears of gratitude, or so I now believe. I did not ask her any questions about how she had spent her time since leaving Pskov. She declared herself unworthy of me. I forgave her unconditionally for whatever was on her conscience. I could not imagine -- how could I imagine? -- what her life had been. I knew she was poor. It was obvious from the state of her clothes. I knew she was afraid and on the run -- from someone, or something. The cavalry officer, I assumed. I was willing to forgive her the cavalry officer. I did not want to know the details. She wanted to say things to me, and I forbade her. And so we were married, quickly, and settled down to a life together. I abandoned purely academic pursuits and took up a medical practice. I had a wife to support now, and a baby on the way. It seemed we had wasted no time. I was . . . I knew happiness. And then Grisha was born. At first, everything seemed normal. He was only a baby, after all. And then, as he grew up, it became clear that all was not right.'

'And you blamed Raisa for his condition?'

'I certainly could not blame myself.'

'No.' Porfiry's agreement was automatic. After a moment's pause, his face clouded in puzzlement: 'I'm sorry. I don't understand. I'm feeling rather dull-witted this morning. How do you mean?'

'At first, I pretended I couldn't count. And it was close enough for there to be a possibility. I proposed to her on the day I met her in St Petersburg. It was the first time I'd seen her in five years. He was born seven months and six days after that. I could not have been the father, even though we consummated our marriage in advance on that first day. I took her eagerness as a sign of love, or trust, or some such romantic nonsense. In addition, I was a young man, eager for a particular kind of sensation.'

'You know of course that some babies are born before full term.'

'That's what I told myself for thirteen years. I thought that might explain his simple-mindedness.'

'But when the letter arrived . . .'

'Yes. Besides, he was seven pounds and nine lots at birth. Physically he did not seem to be in the least premature. However, in time everything became clear. It is her degeneracy -- or the degeneracy of the father, which ultimately amounts to the same thing -- it is their degeneracy that is to blame.'

'Just to clarify -- these things are sometimes important -- when did you receive the letter?'

'Does it really matter?'

'It might do.'

'The strange thing is that when it came, it was as if I had been expecting it. It did not surprise me, somehow. And now I feel as though I have had it in my possession all my life.'

'According to Bezmygin, you received it about two months ago.'

'Why do you ask a question to which you already know the answer?'

'That is the way of investigators.' Porfiry smiled apologetically. 'It is rather distasteful, I know, but it is a habit we fall into. Sometimes I am quite ashamed of myself. Of course, with a man of your intelligence such crude methods will not work. I do apologise. From now on I will conduct myself in a more straightforward manner. So -- where were we? I believe that talking to that fellow Bezmygin has rather confused me. I have to say, I found him an unsympathetic type. Rather unsavoury, in many ways. I can understand how uncomfortable it must have been for you to witness his friendship with your wife. I find that such people have a habit of making vulgar insinuations that -- regrettably -- one cannot get out of one's mind. According to Bezmygin, the letter provides you with a motive. Your sense of betrayal. You stewed on it for a couple of months. All the time, the poison of this spiteful missive was festering away in your mind. And then you could bear it no longer. You killed her.'

'It is rather a weak motive, is it not? What did I stand to gain from it?'

'Of course, one really shouldn't pay any attention to what that type of man says, but according to Bezmygin -- how I hate to say those words -- you wanted her out of the way so that you could continue your affair with Polina.'

Meyer narrowed his eyes, then shook his head slowly, without surprise or vehemence. 'No,' was all he said. He spoke the denial calmly, almost questioningly, with a strange detachment, as though he were examining the contents of his heart through a microscope before deciding.

'I'm afraid that's how it will look to a jury.'

'That's how you will make it look.'

Porfiry stubbed out his cigarette. 'So, there is nothing in it? This fairy tale of Bezmygin's, about you and the girl? That will teach me. Really I should have known better than to listen to such an obviously self-seeking individual.' Porfiry paused for a moment before continuing: 'However, unfortunately, once something has been said, no matter how unreliable the person saying it, it is difficult to discount it utterly. Do you not find? One has to follow these things up. And so, we will have to talk to Polina, I'm afraid. It is just a formality, you understand, merely to confirm that which we know already. It is always better, when countering these slurs, if one can point to a number of consistent rebuttals.'

'There is some . . .' The sentence trailed off. Meyer looked down. 'Truth,' he said abruptly, as if it was something he had just spotted on the table. He looked up forlornly at Porfiry. 'I did make advances to Polina.'

'I . . . see.'

'A kind of temporary insanity came over me. It was absurd. I could do nothing. Her beauty. I was possessed.'

'And how did Polina react to your advances?'

Meyer's wan face crimsoned.

'They can be very cruel, these girls,' said Porfiry sympathetically.

'It is humiliating sometimes to be a man. Is there really any need to talk to her though? It is a tawdry and quite ordinary story. Nothing came of it. Except . . . she used her power over me in ways you can probably imagine. Promise me you won't bother her with this.'

'Let us talk of it no more,' said Porfiry. 'I think you loved Raisa very much, once. In the same way. You must have done. You were prepared to overlook her condition when you met her. You must have known she was not a virgin. You are a doctor, after all.'

'Yes, I knew. And I overlooked it. To do so was consistent with my ideas at the time. And, yes, you're right. I did love her. At least I deluded myself into believing so. That is to say, I fell victim to the insanity of romantic longings and was fool enough to find happiness in their fulfilment. It is a sickness, nothing more, this whole business of love. A mental disorder. And the act. The truth of it is quite disgusting. A question of physical needs, to which the male and the female are both subject. But because we cannot bear to confront the truth of our animal natures, we cover it in the trappings of romance. Or we reduce it to a commercial transaction. No doubt we are very *civilised* in doing this.'

'I take it from your tone that you do not think much of being civilised.'

'It is all hypocrisy. And I am the greatest hypocrite of them all.'

'You are perhaps too hard on yourself.'

Meyer laughed thinly. 'Please! I am only accusing myself of hypocrisy. *You* are accusing me of murder.' The laughter went from his eyes. A slight tremor flickered across his face and a mantle of loneliness seemed to settle on him.

PART TWO: Pistol

1: 'Gunshot!'

'What is it now?' muttered Yegor as he shuffled along the hallway of Colonel Setochkin's apartment towards the relentless pounding that threatened the integrity of their door. It had been a morning of interruptions. That busybody from the department of whatever it was, with his constant comings and goings, had driven him almost to distraction. So the drains stank -- didn't the drains stink every summer? What did the fellow hope to achieve going in and out of people's homes and sniffing the air? If this was him again, come to fill up more of his bottles with their water, the water Yegor himself had drawn from the Neva -- if so, he'd get more than he bargained for this time.

'All right! All right!' Yegor shouted. 'I've heard you. Give me a chance. I'm not as young as I used to be.' This overlooked the fact that even in his youth Yegor had not been one to hurry in the fulfilment of his duties. In those days he had been Colonel Setochkin's batman, when they had served together in the Izmailovsky regiment. What a fool the colonel had been to resign his commission. There wasn't a day went by when Yegor didn't have cause to bemoan the change in their fortunes. Look at them now, stuck in this stifling apartment over the summer when the cream of society had long since left for the country. But the invitations ceased to come soon after Setochkin left the regiment. At the time there had been some suggestion of the old dog having no choice in the matter, scandalous rumours about missing regimental funds, a gambling debt, and the major's daughter. There was always somebody's daughter -- or even wife -- mixed up in things. But the master had always managed to worm his way out of such predicaments in the past. Ah well, there was never a dull moment with Setochkin. He had to give the rascal that.

Yegor smiled in begrudging admiration as he threw back the bolts. No sooner had he turned the handle than the door was pushed back into his face.

'Where is he? Where is that villain?' A middle-aged man with a cane in one hand bustled past Yegor. His silvered whiskers gleamed against the pink flush of his complexion. His eyes stood out in indignation.

'Be careful who you are calling a villain!' For all his master's foibles, Yegor felt instinctively drawn to his defence.

'Let there be no mistake about it. It is Setochkin I am calling a villain. And I will do so to his face.' By now the irate gentleman was some way down the corridor. He struck each door he passed with his cane as if to beat Setochkin out of cover. 'Let him come out! Let the coward show himself!'

'By God!' cried Yegor. 'You cannot come here buffeting our walls and calling out names. Who do you think you are?'

'I will tell you who I am. I am Ruslan Vladimirovich Vakhramev.'

At this point one of the doors that Vakhramev had struck opened and a man of about forty-five, still in his dressing gown, appeared, blinking, bleary-eyed.

'What the devil is this all about?'

'*This* is Setochkin?' cried Vakhramev incredulously. 'My God, I had expected a golden Adonis, not this washed-up, bloated monkfish of a man.'

Yegor couldn't help smirking. There was some accuracy to the description; he had to admit his master had seen better days.

'What on earth was Tatyana thinking?' said Vakhramev.

'Ah!' said Colonel Setochkin, a look of shame-faced understanding descending on his features. 'So that's what this is all about. You are --?'

'I am Vakhramev!'

'Tanya's father?'

'How dare you let my daughter's name pass your lips?'

'I fear that it will be very difficult to resolve this matter if I am not permitted to say her name. Perhaps, though, it would be better if you were to come with me into my study. I find it is preferable not to discuss these matters in front of one's servants.'

'I don't give a damn about your servants.'

'All the same, sir, if you will be so good as to accompany me, I believe we may settle the affair satisfactorily.'

'You talk of satisfaction?'

'No no no! You are mistaken. I didn't mean that at all.'

'It is for me to demand satisfaction, not you. Do you understand that?'

'I was not --' Setochkin forced a smile. 'Sir, I very much fear that we are getting off on the wrong foot.'

'I cannot be held responsible for that.'

'I was not suggesting that you should be.'

'It was you who began to talk of satisfaction. You cannot pretend to be a man of honour with me.'

Setochkin's expression darkened. 'Be careful, sir. I am a reasonable man. Above all, I pride myself on that. Nevertheless --'

'There is no nevertheless, sir. You have forfeited all right to a nevertheless. You did so the day you seduced my daughter.'

Setochkin was about to say something, but an unfortunate coughing fit from Yegor just at that moment seemed to put him off his stride. Yegor felt his master's attention on him and regretted his incontinence. 'I must insist that we continue this discussion in my study, sir. If only for Tatyana's sake.'

Now Yegor felt himself the object of Vakhramev's disapproving scowl. 'Very well. Perhaps it would be better, after all.'

Setochkin held out one arm, allowing Vakhramev to go first. The other man shook his head contemptuously as he walked past.

Yegor sought his master's eye again but was refused it. The study door was closed to him. He heard the visitor's voice rise immediately to a shout. Setochkin was compelled to raise his voice in response. In the resultant clamour, it was difficult to make out any details of the recriminations levelled against Setochkin, or of his rebuttals, however much Yegor strained to listen. But the general drift was clear enough from what he had been privy to already; so when he heard the clump of footsteps coming back towards the door, he relinquished the thrill of eavesdropping and hurried off towards the kitchen.

*

He found Dunya with her hands in a bowl of flour and butter. Yegor watched her naked elbows pump, fascinated by the deep T-shaped clefts in her bulbous upper arms, and was for the moment distracted from his purpose. Reflections on the weakness of human flesh imposed themselves upon him and an unexpected sympathy for his master's predicament almost took the pleasure out of sharing what he knew. He blinked and looked away from those fascinating elbows.

'He's been up to his old tricks again,' he said dourly.

Dunya grunted. It was neither encouragement nor forbiddance.

'Some gentleman's daughter,' continued Yegor. 'It will end badly, no question. They're working themselves up to a duel.'

The wattle at her throat shook as a register of her contempt.

'It's a question of honour. That's what it comes down to.'

Dunya clicked her tongue in disdain.

'It's that haughty-looking one. Tatyana. I knew she was trouble as soon as I clapped eyes on her. My, she's a beauty though. You have to give her that.'

Dunya snorted, as if she would give her no such thing.

'That's all very well, Dunya, but you're not a man. Not a man like the colonel.'

'As he cooked the porridge, so must he eat it,' said Dunya at last, with great deliberation.

Yegor nodded at the truth of this. He even opened his mouth to comment on it. But any words he might have produced were taken from him, as was his breath, by a sharp explosive crack in the air. Having once served in the Izmailovsky regiment, he was in doubt as to what it was. 'Gunshot!'

Dunya lifted her hands from the bowl, causing the loose skin on her forearms to quiver. Cook and butler looked into each other's faces, then all at once, Yegor turned towards the door. By the time he reached it, he was running.

*

He found Vakhramev with the pistol in his hand. Colonel Setochkin lay face up on the rug, into which he was seeping a dark and prodigal colour. The angles of his arms were like those of a running man, frozen mid-bound. His features were set in a frown of puzzlement.

'You'd better get the police,' said Vakhramev calmly.

'You've killed him!'

'You'd better get the police,' repeated Vakhramev, rather less calmly. He looked sharply down at the weapon he was holding and mirrored the expression of the dead man, frowning as if at some gross impertinence.

2: Lost and found

'Ah, Polya, my dear, how delightful to see you again.' Porfiry rose to his feet and gestured to the empty chair in front of his desk. 'So good of you to pay us this visit. You have met Pavel Pavlovich, I believe.'

Polina wrinkled her brows and regarded Porfiry suspiciously out of the corner of her eye as she sat down. She barely glanced towards Virginsky, who had just risen from the sofa. He sank back into it, withered by her disregard. 'But I was presented with a summons. I had to come. That's what the man said.'

'Oh? Did they do that? I am so sorry. I expressed a wish to see you -- just to clear up one or two things, you understand -- and one of my subordinates' -- Porfiry glanced reproachfully at Virginsky, although in fact he had had nothing to do with issuing the summons -- 'was rather too zealous in executing it.'

'It doesn't matter. I wished to see you too.'

'You did?'

'Yes.' Some kind of turmoil rippled in the girl's brow. Porfiry could not shake off the impression that it was affected. 'Something has been on my conscience.'

'I see.' Porfiry sat down slowly, not taking his eyes off Polina.

'The master, Dr Meyer . . .'

'Exactly!' broke in Porfiry, rising to his feet excitedly. 'That is exactly what I wished to talk to you about! How extraordinary! We were thinking along the same lines. It's all right. He has told us everything. You are blameless.'

'No. Not blameless. I . . .'

Porfiry sat down again, smiling and blinking his face into a childlike openness.

'Please do not look at me like that. I cannot bear it. You look so trusting. I do not deserve that look.'

Porfiry pursed his lips and frowned. Polina burst into giggling laughter. She angled her head coquettishly as she looked at Porfiry.

'And now you are making me laugh,' she said in mock rebuke.

'Perhaps it would be better if you looked at Pavel Pavlovich?'

Polina cast a desultory glance at Virginsky. 'No.'

Virginsky shifted awkwardly between resentment and

devastation.

'My dear,' said Porfiry. 'I shall try to help you. Dr Meyer confessed that he made advances to you. He led us to believe that you rejected those advances. From his discomfiture, I rather imagined that your rejection was laced with a wholly understandable scorn. You humiliated him. Perhaps you blame yourself for that, but I do not. He tried to take advantage of your relative positions. It was an abuse. Your behaviour was entirely proper.'

'But what if I had encouraged him?'

'In what way might you have?'

'Oh, surely you know how it is? There are looks . . . and sighs. Surely even you have had experience of such things?'

'Of looks and sighs? Perhaps.' Porfiry's became became solicitous. 'Did you really encourage him?'

'I cannot explain it. I did not like him. I did not like any of them.'

'Sometimes, when one is unhappy, the only thing one can do, the only thing one wants to do, is make others unhappy. It was all the power you had.'

'You are not how I imagined you would be. I thought you would shout at me and bully me. You are not at all like that. You are nicer than that.'

'I am nice, Pavel Pavlovich!'

There was a growl from the sofa.

'But did he really kill them?' asked Polina, her face struck with sudden horror.

'I don't know. What do you think?' Porfiry gave every indication of being sincerely interested in her view.

'*I* don't know. Why would he?'

'To . . . get them out of the way,' suggested Porfiry, tentatively.

'Yes, but why would he want them out of the way?'

'So that he . . . and you . . .'

'No!'

'Ah, you see. I'm afraid that's the way it might look. Did you ever, you and he, discuss . . .?'

'What?'

'Getting them out of the way.'

'No.' Polina shook her head emphatically. 'No, no -- never.'

'Of course. I am sorry. One is forced to ask these questions.'

'If he did it, he did it on his own. I had nothing to do with it.'

'Do you think him capable of doing it, Polya?'

'No,' said Polina flatly. 'Besides, he did not need to kill her. She would not have stood in his way, whatever he had wanted to do. If I *had* consented, she would have turned a blind eye.'

Porfiry nodded. 'What can you tell me about Mr Bezmygin? Did you ever observe Raisa Ivanovna with her friend Mr Bezmygin?'

'Yes.'

'Were there grounds, do you think, for Dr Meyer to be jealous of their relationship?'

'There were grounds, but he was not jealous.'

'Really? How can you say that with such certainty!'

'Because he did not love her.' Polina narrowed her eyes and looked into Porfiry's. 'I do not believe he killed her. Why would he kill her? She was already dead to him.'

Porfiry mirrored her expression, screwing his eyes up thoughtfully as he met her gaze. A knock at the door interrupted their silent consideration of each other. Zamyotov came in, breathless with excitement. 'You are to go to Izmailovsky Prospekt. There has been a murder. A retired colonel has been shot. It is a terrible scandal. A respectable gentleman did it. Lieutenant Salytov is already there.'

'Good heavens, if they know who did it and Lieutenant Salytov is there, why on earth am I required?' Porfiry still had his eyes on Polina, for whom he wrinkled his eyes and winked. 'Thank you, my dear. You have given me much to think about. Now, if you will forgive me, it seems that another case demands my attention.'

*

'A strange coincidence, is it not?' said Porfiry, affecting a casualness that he did not quite pull off. 'Is this not the very building from which emerged the couple you spoke to? You remember, we were coming back from interviewing Bezmygin. You stopped the driver and ran back. An older gentleman and a young, rather pretty, lady.'

Virginsky looked up at the apartment building they were about to enter. 'Mmm, it may have been,' he said dubiously.

'Who were they?'

Virginsky hesitated, his mouth open, a protest frozen on his lips. 'My father,' he said with dull finality. 'And his wife.'

'Ah! I wondered if it were so. There was a certain resemblance, you see, between you and the gentleman.' Porfiry thought for a moment and then added: 'I wonder if they knew our dead man?'

Virginsky shrugged, as if he were trying to shake off the suggestion. 'Is it always like this? You have not finished one case and you must begin another?'

'I'm afraid the criminals of St Petersburg have all together too little regard for those who must investigate them. They do not adhere to any almanac. Nor do they wait for all pending crimes to be solved before perpetrating their own. They are very bad.' Porfiry held the door for Virginsky, his face deadpan.

*

They climbed the stairs in silence. A *politseisky* guarding one of the doors on the fourth-storey landing indicated their destination.

The door was opened by Lieutenant Salytov. The summer did not suit Salytov. With fiery-hair and whiskers, as well as being fair-skinned, the slightest increase in temperature turned his face as red and steaming as a bowl of borshcht. He turned his back on them without a word of welcome.

'So Ilya Petrovich,' Porfiry called after him. 'What do we have?'

'It seems a clear-cut case.' Salytov shouted out the words with his usual antagonism. He was used to Porfiry's habit of overturning all obvious assumptions, and resented it, just as he seemed to resent his role in having to state them. 'One Vakhramev was admitted earlier this afternoon -- no precise time given, but the butler thinks somewhere around three. He was seen to argue with Colonel Setochkin. There was talk of a duel, according to the butler. Vakhramev was demanding satisfaction. Called Setochkin a villain. Threatened him with forfeiture of rights, or some such, according to the butler. Something to do with Vakhramev's daughter. The two men went alone into Setochkin's study. About ten minutes later, a shot was heard. Setochkin dead, Vakhramev holding the gun. The local doctor has had a look at him. He has given the cause of death as a single gunshot wound to the heart, subject to a full medical examination, of course.'

'Whose gun?'

'The gun has been identified as belonging to Colonel Setochkin. One of a pair of duelling pistols. The other was still in the case.'

'Where was the case kept?'

'In the same room, Setochkin's study.'

'In open view?'

'The case was on the colonel's desk.'

'So Vakhramev could easily have taken the pistol from it. What is Vakhramev's version of events?'

'You can ask him yourself. I'm sure you will. He's in here.' Salytov had his hand on the handle of a door.

'But for now I am asking you.'

Salytov sighed heavily. 'He says he didn't do it.'

'Well, he would, wouldn't he?' said Porfiry.

Salytov seemed taken aback by the response, and then annoyed, as though he felt he had let Porfiry get the better of him once again.

*

Vakhramev was being held in the study, where Setochkin's body still lay on the rug, a large stain, with a dark flowering of matter at its centre, on his chest. Porfiry's quick scan of the room took in its inhabitant's tastes.

The walls were hung with Caucasian rugs over *chinois* wallpaper, the latter influence echoed in the Chinese peasant figures on the three-panelled *shirmochka* screen; two Moorish busts, one male, one female, confronted one another from opposite walls, across a Turkish ottoman, an Empire chaise longue and a number of wicker chairs. An interest in Old Muscovy and a fondness for folk art was apparent in a number of the decorations. There was a cluster of icons mounted in the holy corner. A large canvas-covered trunk with wooden ribbing increased the sense of clutter. The lid was thrown open. A melee of random objects -- books, map rolls, bundled correspondence, a cavalry officer's cap, a sabre in its scabbard, a number of stuffed birds -- seemed to be frozen in the act of clambering to get out. Porfiry was affected by a strong desire to close the lid on this glimpse of a disordered life.

Porfiry's impression, to which the presence of a dead body only contributed, was that the room was over-furnished for its size. At Colonel Setochkin's feet, a large baize-covered desk crowded in beneath the window in the far wall. A glass-panelled door next to the window suggested a balcony.

Vakhramev was seated in one of the wicker armchairs, a *politseisky* positioned next to him. He looked up as Porfiry and Virginsky came in with Salytov. His expression was naturally pensive, although he seemed to will defiance into his features.

'Good afternoon,' said Porfiry, taking one of the other chairs. He braced himself as he settled but, seeming to experience no discomfort, breathed out his relief. 'I have to be careful,' he said by way of explanation to Vakhramev. 'You will understand, I think. A gentleman of your age.' Porfiry cast an accusatory glance at Virginsky. 'These young ones do not.' He nodded for Virginsky to sit down too. 'You are Vakhramev?'

'Ruslan Vladimirovich Vakhramev.' Vakhramev's expression was slightly startled. His chair creaked as he drew himself up proudly.

Porfiry bowed. 'I am Porfiry Petrovich, the investigating magistrate. I would be grateful to you, sir, if you could tell me what happened here this afternoon. Please take your time. Try not to overlook any detail. It may turn out to be significant.'

'I have already given a statement.'

'Yes, yes, I know. It's tiresome. But it's important to me that I hear it directly from you. You may think of something that you missed last time. Of course, I apologise for any inconvenience to *you*.' Porfiry looked down at the corpse distractedly. He then turned a startled face on Vakhramev, as if the sight of the dead body had reminded him why he was there.

Vakhramev nodded. 'The mood I was in, I would not have been very surprised if I had killed him. But I did not. You have my word, as a gentleman.'

Porfiry raised a questioning eyebrow. He offered Vakhramev a cigarette, which was declined. Lighting one for himself, he said: 'Forgive me for asking such a blunt question -- sometimes I find it is easier for all concerned if one gets straight to the point -- but what was your intention in coming here?' Porfiry's face tensed into a smile.

Vakhramev was flustered by the question. 'I had a right to confront him. I wanted him to know what I thought of him.'

'And what did you think of him?'

Vakhramev considered his words. 'I did not think much of him.'

'So it wasn't your intention to challenge him to a duel?'

'The thought had crossed my mind.'

'Of course. I find all sorts of thoughts cross my mind. Some of them most unwelcome. One cannot control one's thoughts. But, tell me, please, just to clear things up, did you act on this particular thought?'

'In the event, I saw that he was not worth it.'

Porfiry nodded in satisfaction. 'The butler admitted you, I believe. And were you shown here, directly to the study?'

'No, Setochkin came out of another room. We . . . talked in the hall. Then we came here.'

'And what happened then?'

'I showed him the letter.'

'Excuse me. What letter is this?'

'I received a letter informing me of Setochkin's behaviour.'

Porfiry flashed a glance in Virginsky's direction. 'Good heavens. Who was it from?'

'I don't know. It wasn't signed. But the contents seem to have been well informed. He didn't deny it.'

'And where is it now, this letter? I would very much like to see it.'

'I gave it to him. Or rather, I threw it at him. Screwed it up and threw it in his face. It landed on the floor somewhere.'

All eyes shot downwards at the same time.

'We have searched the room. There was no sign of any such letter,' said Salytov.

'How strange. But we will come back to that later,' said Porfiry. 'Please, Ruslan Vladimirovich, would you tell me what happened after you confronted Colonel Setochkin with the letter.'

'If there ever was a letter,' put in Salytov.

Vakhramev gave him a stern glance. 'I left. That is to say, I went out of the room with the intention of leaving the apartment. However, I had taken but three paces when I heard the gun discharge. I ran back immediately. He was lying where you see him now. The gun was on the floor nearby. For some reason I cannot explain, I picked it up. A moment later, Setochkin's man came in.'

'It would, you know, be helpful if you could explain why you picked it up.'

'I couldn't help myself. I hated him. And, yes, wished him dead. But now that he was, I couldn't quite believe it. I needed to handle the gun to believe it. I can see it would have been so much better if I hadn't picked it up.'

'I wouldn't be so sure about that,' said Porfiry, with a thin smile. He blew out smoke and stood up, beginning to search around the room distractedly. 'There is always this problem of ashtrays.'

'Filthy habit,' said Vakhramev.

'Ah, but I find it essential to thought,' said Porfiry, stepping over the body to find an ashtray at last on the desk. He took the opportunity to try the door to the balcony. It was locked, the key still in the lock on the inside. 'And I must think.' He said the words to himself, gazing deep in thought out of the window, one pane of which was open. The view was of an empty courtyard. He wrinkled his nose at the pungent stink of the soil barrels. After a moment his gaze dropped down to the desk and settled on a nondescript birch-wood case. 'What happened to the pistol that was fired?'

'We have it,' said Salytov.

Porfiry opened the wooden box and looked down at the one remaining pistol, surrounded by the polished accoutrements of charge and discharge, two ramrods, a wooden mallet, bullet mould, brass powder flask, various screws and implements, including an elaborate pair of pincers, all compartmentalised in velvet. Lead spheres, the bullets themselves, nestled like eggs of death. The gun had a rounded walnut butt with a carved grip and damascened trimmings, from which the barrel, with its severely hexagonal cross-section, projected brutally. The inscription inside the hinged lid announced the maker as Alexei Babyakin of Tula. Porfiry thought of this Babyakin, and of the evident care -- the craftsman's love of his craft -- that had gone into the making of this handsome and highly covetable object. He wondered if any thought of its ultimate purpose had distracted Babyakin, or whether he had looked upon it purely as a beautiful mechanism. Porfiry closed the box again and turned back to Vakhramev. 'And so, who shot him, if not you? I imagine you have given it some thought.'

'Why, I should have thought that was obvious,' said Vakhramev. 'He shot himself. Our conversation, and the letter, the irrefutable evidence of his worthlessness, provoked feelings of shame and remorse that overwhelmed him.'

'Hmm, it is possible, I suppose,' said Porfiry. 'Certainly, if you did kill him, it is strange that you did not make any effort to escape. Of course that would have been incriminating in itself. Only a guilty man runs. Or perhaps not. Someone who believes that he might be thought guilty may run too. Conversely, someone who wants to be thought innocent may decide not to run.' Porfiry gave a little chuckle, seemingly of embarrassment. 'And as for your holding on to the gun, perhaps that indicates innocence rather than guilt -- indeed a touching naivety, if anything. Or . . . again . . .' Porfiry smiled almost regretfully as he made the suggestion: 'It could be the strategy of a man who wants to create the impression of innocence. Or, more simply, you were paralysed by the enormity of what you had done. You had been carried away by wrath. You are a civilised man. It is difficult for you to accept that you gave in to passion so completely. Perhaps your mind has obliterated all memory of the deed. If so, a jury would go easy on you. We would not press for a charge of murder. Manslaughter at worst. A good lawyer would be able to make a case for diminished responsibility. Temporary insanity. There have been many such cases. There are lawyers who specialise in this type of plea. You would be acquitted. I have no doubt. So much so that it is debatable we would even bring a case against you, though of course we must go through the motions. Justice must be seen to be done.'

'I did not kill him.'

'I was rather afraid you might say that. You see, it does complicate things for us your saying that.'

'I cannot help that.'

'Unfortunately, the position of the wound does not incline me to accept your theory of suicide.' Porfiry looked down at the body on the floor. 'We can see that the flesh and material have been pushed inwards, indicating that the bullet entered from the front.' Porfiry looked at the window and frowned. 'Nevertheless,' he continued thoughtfully, 'I have never yet come across the case of a suicide attempting to shoot himself through the heart. In my experience, those who elect for the pistol as a means of self-annihilation invariably choose to blow their brains out, either by holding the gun to the temple, or inserting the barrel into the mouth. This is the preferred method of the disgraced cavalry officer. I take it you would have informed us had there been anyone else in the room with you during your interview with Colonel Setochkin?'

'We were alone.'

Porfiry peered tentatively around the back of the screen; then, finally, closed the lid on the trunk, as if he expected to find someone crouched in its lee. Discovering no one there, he looked at Salytov meekly, though he continued to address Vakhramev. 'Could anyone have entered the study in between the moment you left it and the moment you heard the gunshot? Without your noticing?'

'I do not believe it would have been possible. It was only a matter of minutes, and I was in the hall the whole time.'

'But were you watching the door?'

'No, admittedly, I had my back to it.'

'Tell me, was the windowpane open at the time of your interview with Colonel Setochkin?'

'I didn't notice.'

'And the door? Closed as it is now? Locked?'

'I really have no idea.'

'But did anyone come into the room afterwards, besides Colonel Setochkin's manservant -- and the police, of course?'

'No. I was in here all the time. I saw no one else.'

'You did not see the servant open the window at any time?'

'No,' said Vakhramev decisively. 'So I think it must have been already open.'

'What about the door to the balcony? Did you see him lock the door?'

'No.'

'And you did not lock it yourself?'

'No.'

'So we may assume that the windowpane was open and the door was locked at the time of the colonel's . . . demise?'

'I think it's a reasonable assumption,' agreed Vakhramev.

'And to go back to our mysterious letter, is it possible that the servant removed it?'

'I didn't see him do so,' said Vakhramev. 'I suppose it's possible. My mind was not entirely focused.'

'Of course . . .' Porfiry smiled and batted his eyelids to compensate for what was coming. 'We have only your word that this letter existed.'

'And that isn't enough for you?'

'I personally would be content to accept your word on it. But now we have juries. And there is this new emphasis on evidence.' Porfiry's smile became apologetic.

Vakhramev puffed out his cheeks as if he had never heard anything quite so preposterous. Porfiry nodded with sudden grim finality to Virginsky, who frowned back uncertainly.

'And so, am I to consider myself under arrest?'

'Not at all, not at all,' said Porfiry brightly. 'That is to say, not for the moment. We have yet to speak to the butler.'

*

The kitchen welcomed Porfiry and Virginsky with a freshly baked aroma that for an instant took all thought of anything apart from bread and meat pies out of their minds. Porfiry paused at the threshold to lose himself in it, his eyelids fluttering with pleasure.

At last he looked at the two people who were gazing up at him with some bewilderment from the kitchen table.

'Forgive me. Such smells always take us back to our childhood, do they not? I was somewhere else entirely for a moment. Colonel Setochkin was a fortunate man indeed to have such a cook as you in his household.'

The cook, a large woman with muscular forearms from a lifetime of stirring, beating and folding, wrinkled her face suspiciously. Her eyes gave nothing away.

The butler's head shook in an unceasing gesture of denial. 'But who will eat them now?' he said. 'There was to have been a party tonight.' His eyes, beneath bristling eyebrows, were bloodshot and moist. He looked at Porfiry without comprehension.

'We are the investigating magistrates,' explained Porfiry. 'You are?'

'Yegor.'

'Colonel Setochkin's servant?'

Yegor gave a dignified, though trembling, nod. 'I have been with his honour for twenty-six years. We served together in the Izmailovsky regiment. I was his batman. When he resigned his commission, I followed him and entered into service as his butler.'

'Can you tell me what happened today?'

Yegor glared in outrage. 'He was shot down in cold blood.' His outrage intensified into fury: 'By Vakhramev.'

'You witnessed this?'

'Witnessed?' Yegor frowned impatiently. 'I heard the gun. He had the gun when I got to him.'

'Where were you when the gun was discharged?'

'Here in the kitchen, with Dunya.'

'You are Dunya?'

The woman nodded confirmation, without taking her eyes off Porfiry for one moment, as if he were some exotic creature at the zoo.

Somewhat disconcerted by her gaze, Porfiry continued questioning Yegor. 'And how long did it take you, after hearing the gun, to get to the study?'

'Why, it's only just across the hall. It would have taken me no time at all.'

'Provided you went immediately.' Porfiry pointed a finger at nothing in particular, one of his courtroom tics.

'Of course I went immediately. What else would I do?'

'You might have hesitated. It would have been reasonable to proceed with caution.'

'Are you suggesting I was afraid?'

'Caution is not the same as fear. This Vakhramev . . .' began Porfiry.

'He is the murderer.' Yegor thumped the table. 'He said he would kill the colonel and he did.'

'I see. What exactly did he say?'

'He demanded satisfaction. He was going to fight a duel with the colonel. Obviously, he couldn't wait. He shot him in cold blood instead. In the back, I shouldn't wonder.'

'No. Not in the back, as a matter of fact. So they argued?'

Yegor's eyes bulged. 'I should say so.'

'What was it about?'

'Vakhramev accused my master of seducing his daughter. But if you knew this Tatyana, you would know it was she who had him wrapped around her little finger. She is not as innocent as her father would believe. She is a one. A Russian minx.'

'When you went into the room after hearing the gunshot, did you see a letter lying on the floor?'

Yegor frowned as he thought back, then shook his head. 'No. No letter.'

'You are sure about this? You did not tidy it up, thinking it a piece of litter?'

The cook guffawed, prompting a wounded look from Yegor. He shook his head dejectedly.

'I see. And you did not take it for any other reason?'

'I saw no letter.'

'And did you lock the door to the balcony at that point? To prevent Vakhramev from escaping perhaps?'

'No. I didn't think to.'

'Then the door was already locked. Did you see anybody else enter or leave the room by the other door?'

'No.'

'Could there have been anyone, hiding behind the screen say, who slipped out while you weren't looking?'

'Impossible.'

'Yes. I am inclined to agree with you. Here is the mystery. If there was a letter, how was it transported from the room? And if it wasn't Vakhramev who discharged the gun, who then was it and how indeed did they effect their escape? Surely not through the single small pane that was left open.'

'There! You see! It *must* be him,' cried Yegor.

'There is one other thing I would like to ask you. Could you tell me of anything else out of the ordinary that has happened here today? However trivial.'

'You mean apart from his honour being murdered? Is that not unusual enough for you?' Inexplicably, Yegor was shouting. Dunya placed a hand on one of his agitating arms and whispered something soothing. Yegor began to sob.

'He loved the colonel,' said Dunya to Porfiry. She squinted as if into the sun.

'Yes,' said Porfiry.

'What will he do now?' Dunya asked the question flatly, almost without any emotion at all.

'Please, any small detail that you can remember may prove crucial,' insisted Porfiry. 'For example, were there any other visitors today?'

Dunya whispered something to Yegor again. The butler grew calmer and dabbed his eyes with a large grey handkerchief. 'The colonel had no visitors before that man. He was abed all the morning. There was some fellow, a public health inspector, who came to look into the quality of our water. It is something to do with the cholera epidemic. Not that we have had any cases here, I hasten to add. But he has been going in and out of all the apartments for the last few days.'

'And he came to the apartment?'

'Yes, but that was hours ago. Long before the colonel was up and about.'

'I congratulate you,' said Porfiry. 'We have been trying to induce a sanitary inspector to look into a similar problem we are having at the bureau. We too have had no cases of cholera yet, just an almighty stink. So far, despite a strongly worded letter signed by myself, we have been unsuccessful.'

'You do not need to be a sanitary inspector to discover the problem,' put in Virginsky, the force of his sudden contribution taking Porfiry by surprise. 'At Stolyarny Lane, it is caused by the proximity of a canal that is used as an open drain for raw sewage. I imagine that the stench here is the result of the widespread practice of storing barrels of human excrement in yards in the height of summer. Such a practice is fine in the winter, when the waste matter freezes, but in the summer? The wonder is that there are not more cases of disease.' Virginsky's little speech was met with silence. He himself pinched the bridge of his nose and winced in embarrassment. He did not seem to know where to put himself.

Porfiry placed his palms together and rested his nose on the tips of his forefingers. It was a conscious effort to refocus. His thoughts were interrupted, however, by a commotion in the hall. He could make out Lieutenant Salytov's raised voice but there was another voice, raised even higher, that he did not recognise. Before he had the opportunity to speculate further, the door opened and Salytov burst in, pushing before him a young woman, who appeared to be naked apart from the counterpane she held about her with both hands.

'I found her in Setochkin's bed,' said Salytov gleefully. 'She doesn't speak a word of Russian.'

3: The girl in the counterpane

Her hair was dark and loosely suggested the coiffeured rings that had shaped it the night before. Traces of cosmetic showed on her face, which appeared pale. She pouted and glared at Salytov.

'Ilya Petrovich, kindly escort the young lady back to the bedroom and allow her the opportunity to make herself decent.'

'I fear that is something she will never be able to do,' said Salytov. This provoked a torrent of French: apparently the girl in the throw's understanding of Russian was greater than she had led Salytov to believe. Porfiry understood her to insist that she was a good girl.

Porfiry reassured her, also in French, that he believed her. He invited her to join him in the drawing room as soon as she was dressed. *'Je dois vous demander quelques questions.'*

Salytov led her out, though she refused his offered hand. Porfiry looked back at the couple at the kitchen table. The stupefaction on their faces seemed genuine. *So*, he thought, *they did not know she was there either.*

*

An hour later, freshly perfumed and newly made-up, a necklace of pearls at her throat, her hair restored to a fragile magnificence, the unidentified French woman swept into Setochkin's tiny drawing room almost filling it with the layers of lace and pink satin of her décolleté gown. She held a Chinese fan, decorated with peacocks, which she agitated constantly, as if it were a living thing that depended on this movement to keep it alive. She was utterly unabashed; in fact, her gait was stiff with outraged dignity. Porfiry found himself in the extraordinary position of admiring her.

With its pretty figurines, floral drapes and delicate watercolours on lilac-papered walls, the room revealed an unexpectedly feminine side to Setochkin's taste, unless he had surrendered the furnishing of it to someone else, a sister perhaps, or his mother, or even -- and more probably -- a mistress. The young woman seemed perfectly at home there. Doubtless she had sat in similar rooms in similar apartments, and had possibly even advised on the furnishing of them.

'What is this about?' she demanded in French, as she snapped the fan shut with callous finality. It seemed she needed both hands to scoop her skirts to sit.

Porfiry answered her in French. 'We are investigating the death of Colonel Setochkin.' Virginsky winced at the bluntness of the statement, which was not softened by the filter of another language.

'Alyosha? Alyosha is dead?' The pearls at her throat rose and fell. The fan snapped open again. And now the impression was that it was the fan that caused her hand to move, and that without her holding on to it, it would flutter up to the ceiling. She controlled it enough to bring it close to the fresh flush of her throat. She showed no other sign of emotion; the powder on her face was perhaps too thick to allow it.

'Are you sure? He was perfectly alive the last time I saw him.'

'And when was that, mademoiselle?'

'Really, monsieur, when do you think?'

'Do you always sleep so late?' Somehow, this was not the question Porfiry had meant to ask.

'It had been an exhausting night. As I said, Alyosha was full of life. How did he die?'

'He sustained a gunshot wound. It seems likely that that was the cause of his death.'

'Ah, poor Alyosha. What a tragedy.' The French woman rose from her seat and took two or three paces forwards, as though to the front of an imagined stage.

'What is your name, mademoiselle? And how did you come to be in Colonel Setochkin's . . . apartment?'

'My name is Alphonsine Lambert. I am here because Alyosha brought me here. We came by cab. How did you get here?'

'It is really for me to ask the questions.' Porfiry bowed and fluttered his eyelids in gentle remonstration. He angled his head to look at her, smiling indulgently. 'Mademoiselle Alphonsine, my dear . . . this may prove to be quite painful for you. Perhaps more so than you are prepared to admit. How long have you known Colonel Setochkin?'

'He is an old friend.' The fan swept wildly around her, almost escaping her grasp.

'I see. And were you in the habit of returning with him to spend the night in his apartment?'

'Please. You are not my mother. And even if you were, you would not take that tone.' Alphonsine's laughter was deep and disquieting. Porfiry took a cigarette from his brightly enamelled case and lit it. He was about to put the case away when Alphonsine said: 'Don't be a brute, darling. Won't you let me have one?'

He offered the case without a word and lit her cigarette for her.

'How did you meet Alyosha?'

'The usual way. He came to see me.' At Porfiry's puzzled frown, she explained: 'At the theatre.'

'You're an actress?'

'Hardly, darling. How would I manage the lines?' More deep laughter rippled the pearls on her necklace. 'Unless it were Racine, of course,' she added seriously. 'Or Molière.' Her naked shoulders shook in an inexplicable convulsion. 'No. I'm a dancer. There's no need to look like that. But, yes, there comes a point in a girl's career when she must start to think about retirement.'

'And Alyosha was your future, after retirement?'

'He was one possible future, I suppose.' Alphonsine seemed to regard Porfiry with a deeply thoughtful gaze. 'Do you like the dance, darling?'

'We are not here to talk about me,' said Porfiry, managing somehow not to look at Virginsky.

'I used to do many dances for Alyosha alone.'

'Do you know a friend of Colonel Setochkin's by the name of Tatyana Vakhrameva?'

Alphonsine clicked her tongue distastefully. 'Did she kill him? I would not be at all surprised. She was very jealous.'

Now Porfiry allowed himself to look at Virginsky, who nodded slightly back.

'And such a temper on the girl!' Alphonsine was evidently encouraged by the effect of her words on the two men.

'I see. And did you ever witness any scenes between Colonel Setochkin and Tatyana?'

'There were always scenes. Last night, for example. After the show, Alyosha and I were dining in a private room at a restaurant.'

'Which restaurant?'

'The Cubat on Morskaya Street.'

'And what happened?'

'It was all too ridiculous.' Alphonsine became fascinated by her cigarette.

'Please.'

She blinked irritably and at last met Porfiry's eye. 'Somehow she found out where we were. She burst in and . . . it is sufficient to say, the waiters had to be called to remove her.'

'She became violent?'

'Not violent. Just ridiculous.' After a beat, she added, 'Which is far worse.' She hid her smile in her colluding fan.

*

'Good God!' said Virginsky, inflating his cheeks. He flinched away from the source of the stench that assailed them, the three leaking barrels standing against one wall of the courtyard. The well was filled with intoxicated flies that buzzed angrily at them, jealous and protective.

'What a rare privilege,' said Porfiry, 'to have a balcony overlooking this.' He looked up at the back of Setochkin's apartment building, at the one wall from which a few rickety-looking wrought-iron balconies projected. Streaks of rust marked the masonry beneath them. 'It is something in which we specialise in Petersburg, concealing decaying yards behind splendid facades. Perhaps it stands as a metaphor for something peculiarly Russian.' He pointed up at a fourth-floor balconied window in which one pane was open. 'That must be his.' There was a balcony on the window next to it, and balconies on the two windows above them, but none beneath.

'What are we looking for?'

'It is important to get the lie of the land, to consider every means of access to and from a murder scene.'

'But the balcony door was locked from the inside. Surely that rules out the possibility of the murderer escaping through it?'

Porfiry did not answer immediately. 'Oh, incontestably,' he replied at last. He shook his head despondently when he turned back to Virginsky. 'We have no choice but to take him in. Of all the imaginable explanations, it is the least impossible.'

4: The bachelor diary

'Congratulations!' Chief Superintendent Nikodim Fomich gave his face an ironic smile as he poked it around the door to Porfiry's chambers.

'For what?' Porfiry looked up from behind his desk with an expression of genuine confusion.

'For solving two murder cases in as many days.'

'For one thing, it has been longer than two days. And for another, I am not convinced they are solved.'

Nikodim Fomich's ironic smile widened into a beaming grin. 'I knew I could count on you.'

'What *are* you implying, Nikodim Fomich?'

The policeman looked over his shoulder gleefully then came into the room, closing the door behind him. His open, amiable face registered good-natured surprise when he saw Virginsky on Porfiry's fake leather sofa. 'Good morning to you, Pavel Pavlovich. I heard you had joined the service. A case of poacher turned gamekeeper, is it?'

'I cannot imagine what you mean. Your jest makes it sound as if I was once a criminal. I was never charged with any crime, merely suspected. And wrongly arrested.'

'Of course, of course. A very important distinction, I'm sure,' said Nikodim Fomich, winking at Porfiry. 'One can always count on you, Porfiry Petrovich, to eschew the obvious in preference for the obscure.'

'On the contrary, as I have explained to my young colleague here, the obvious should never be overlooked. I would be perfectly happy to accept both Dr Meyer and Ruslan Vladimirovich Vakhramev as the culprits in their respective cases were it not for a rather singular coincidence. As you know, I do not believe in coincidence. That which appears to be a coincidence very often turns out to be a connection.'

'And what is the coincidence linking these two cases?'

'Each of the suspects was sent an anonymous letter maligning their victim.'

'But you found no such letter in Setochkin's study,' Nikodim Fomich pointed out. His tone was blithe, untouched by any real perplexity. 'Are we not forced to conclude that Vakhramev invented this detail?'

'Why should he?' objected Porfiry. 'And besides, even if it is invented, it is still a coincidence -- that he should choose to invent the existence of an anonymous letter.'

'But if there was a letter, how was it removed from the room? That is the heart of the mystery, is it not?'

'I have no theory as to that,' Porfiry answered forlornly. 'I expect that there will turn out to be some perfectly simple and even prosaic explanation. Of course, it could still be in the room. It is simply that your officers have not found it.'

'If it is there, I feel sure Lieutenant Salytov would uncover it. Whatever else one may say about the Firecracker, he is a first-rate man to have on a crime scene.'

'I grant you that. However, sometimes, the hardest objects to find are those that are hidden in the open.'

'Did you not look for it yourself?' Nikodim Fomich asked disingenuously.

'I preferred to leave it to the police officers on the scene. There were enough of them, after all.'

'Someone took it then. That is the obvious inference. But who? The manservant?'

'It is possible,' conceded Porfiry doubtfully. 'If *he* killed Setochkin, he would naturally want to incriminate Vakhramev. The removal of the letter casts doubt on Vakhramev's testimony. He cannot be believed about the letter, because there plainly is no letter. Therefore he cannot be believed about anything, including his denial of murder.'

'So it was the manservant?'

'I sincerely doubt it. He was in the kitchen with the cook when the gun was fired.'

'Ah, but there could be a conspiracy here.' Nikodim Fomich's eyes narrowed with cunning.

'I agree, they do seem rather close. However, I am not convinced.'

'Well, at least you found a letter at the Meyers',' said Nikodim Fomich brightly. 'Or rather, young Ptitsyn found it.'

'He was lucky,' said Virginsky.

'I hear he is very often lucky. It is a useful talent for a policeman

-- or an investigating magistrate -- to cultivate. Any news on the substance that was found with it?'

'According to Dr Pervoyedov, the bottle contained morphine. It was as I thought,' said Porfiry.

'Pity. It would have been more helpful had it turned out to be aconite.' Nikodim Fomich's expression remained cheerful as he expressed his disappointment.

'There was never any aconite in the doctor's study,' said Porfiry forcefully. 'I do not believe Dr Meyer needed to kill his wife. He had already shut his marriage up in a drawer. I am not sure his wife existed for him any more. Perhaps the same could also be said for his son.'

'You and your psychology, Porfiry Petrovich. So it was that Bezmygin fellow who killed them?'

'No!' cried Porfiry in despair. 'That is to say, I don't know. We must probe the connections.'

Nikodim Fomich was no longer paying attention. A new thought was distracting him. 'Ah, but what about that French woman? Naked, I hear, apart from a counterpane. That will provide a colourful detail for your memoirs, Porfiry Petrovich.'

'I will not be writing any memoirs.'

'I wish I had seen old Firecracker's face,' said Nikodim Fomich delightedly. 'What a picture that must have made.'

Porfiry let out a heavy, despondent sigh.

'Well, my friend, I'm sure you will work it all out. There's nothing you like so much as an impenetrable mystery. I have every faith in you.'

Porfiry said nothing. Instead he startled the room by bringing his open palm down heavily on his desk. He turned his hand over slowly, peering into the widening gap. At last he lifted his hand and held it suspended in front of his face, studying the empty palm for a further minute or two. He gave Nikodim Fomich and Virginsky a challenging look but offered no explanation.

*

Ruslan Vladimirovich Vakhramev sat up straight in the chair. His clothes were remarkably unruffled for a man who had spent the night in a police cell, as were his hair and beard, both freshly and deeply combed. Porfiry noticed the cleanliness of his hands, particularly his fingernails. He seemed to have slept well.

Porfiry laid a bulging file on the deal table of the interview room and sat down opposite Vakhramev. He lit a cigarette as Virginsky took the seat next to him. Porfiry smoked in silence, watching Vakhramev closely all the time. Vakhramev met his gaze with a variety of expressions, as older people often respond to inquisitive but silent children. But when this produced no effect, Vakhramev allowed himself the one face that expressed his genuine sentiment, a deep and devastating rage. His face flushed with colour. He stared at Porfiry with hatred, for what he had brought him to.

'Have you ever visited prostitutes?' said Porfiry at last, keeping his tone neutral. He did not look at Vaharamyev as he asked the question, but at the cigarette that he was grinding into the tin ashtray.

Vakhramev's rage shot him to his feet, the chair scraping back on the floor. 'What kind of despicable question is that?'

'It is a question that could gain you your liberty,' said Porfiry. 'Please sit down.' He looked up at Vakhramev with a steady gaze.

Now Vakhramev's expression was utterly bewildered. He seemed lost. There was no pretence left to him. He took his seat again, slowly. 'I do not see what you are getting at, or why you feel the need to ask these insulting and quite filthy questions. I am a respectable man. Besides, this line of enquiry can have nothing to do with Setochkin.'

'On the contrary, it may turn out to be highly relevant.' Porfiry took out a handkerchief and folded it precisely into a neat square. He then used it to dab his face, particularly around his eyes. 'Allow me to be frank with you, Ruslan Vladimirovich. The case against you is strong, at least as far as the circumstantial evidence is concerned. Your testimony simply does not add up. There are those who would say that you are trying to bamboozle us with this story of the letter.' Porfiry put the handkerchief away. 'That your intention is to whip up a mystery to confuse the jury. You are feeding them a doubt, by which you aim to wriggle off the hook. And yet, the fact remains that the simplest, and therefore most likely explanation, is that you shot Setochkin. That you went to his apartment with the intention of shooting him, and indeed of killing him. That you are his murderer.'

'If you are convinced of this then why are you tormenting me with these questions of brothels?'

Porfiry placed the heel of his right hand into his corresponding eye socket and twisted it. When he took the hand away, he blinked ferociously. Vakhramev watched him uncertainly.

'Don't you see? It's precisely because I am *not* convinced that I'm asking you this. If I were convinced I would not even be here talking to you. The letter, that mysterious, phantom letter -- I believe in it. I am probably the only one who does, apart from yourself. Not only that, I believe it could provide the key to the whole mystery. Who was it from? I know, you cannot say. Can you at least enlighten us as to its content?'

'It concerned Setochkin. And my daughter, Tatyana. More than that I will not say. A gentleman would not ask.'

'You don't understand, do you? You must forget all this business of what a gentleman would or would not ask. I am afraid the rules of gentlemanly conduct no longer apply. We have gone beyond all that. Now we must deal in evidence. The content of the letter constitutes evidence. We cannot see the letter, so we must rely on your account of it. Was it to protect Tatyana that you spirited it away?'

'I did not . . . spirit it away, as you put it. I hate to think whose hands it has fallen into.'

'Was it something like this?' Porfiry partially raised the cover of the folder and took out the sheet of white notepaper found in the box under the chair in Dr Meyer's study.

Vakhramev took the letter. Bewilderment changed to amazement. 'How extraordinary! It could have been written by the same hand.'

'Very likely it was,' said Porfiry. 'What about the content? Would you say it is broadly similar in tenor?'

'Well, it was equally nasty, if that's what you mean.'

'As you can see, the letter I have shown you makes reference to a licensed brothel on Sadovaya Street. Madam Josephine's. In an attempt to establish a further connection between the two letters, I am desirous to know whether you ever visited that establishment.'

'But sir, I am a respectable married man.'

'Before you were married, perhaps?'

'Well, before one was married, one did many things.'

'Exactly.' Porfiry smiled encouragingly.

'Are you married, sir?'

The smile died on Porfiry's lips. 'No.'

'Then how do you solve the problem of needs? I presume you are subject to them. You are a man, after all. You *are* human?'

'Indeed.'

'So?'

Porfiry sensed an anticipatory shifting from Virginsky beside him. He did not deign to turn towards it. 'We are not here to talk about me,' he said at last.

'Humbug. I will not be judged by a hypocritical prig.'

'I'm not here to judge you,' said Porfiry. He kept his eyes closed, tensely, as he turned in Vakhramev's direction. Finally his eyelids fluttered open and he met Vakhramev's gaze. 'I have visited an establishment similar to that mentioned in the letter. It is also on Sadovaya Street as it happens, beneath a milliner's shop. The madam is a German woman, Fraulein Keller. Perhaps you know it?'

'No sir, I do not,' Vakhramev answered crisply.

'Well, then. I have made my confession to you. We are men of the world. We are subject to needs. We can talk openly about these things.'

Porfiry thought that he detected disappointment in Virginsky's restlessness now.

'It will go no further?' Vakhramev leant in.

'I see no reason why it should. That is to say, I cannot promise. But I will do my best.'

'It was all a long time ago, you understand.'

'Of course.'

'I have mended my ways.'

'Yes.'

'That man, the man who visited these places, is a stranger to me now. I do not recognise him. I pity those who still have need of such a recourse.' Vakhramev looked at Porfiry pointedly.

'Please, all this is understood.'

'No, I'm not sure that you do understand, sir. I have repented, my God, how I have repented. I have atoned. It has not been something trivial, this atoning. It has not been something I put on like a cloak. It has been an upheaval, sir, a veritable upheaval of the soul. I bared my face to my God. I lay prostrate, my face in the dirt. I told my wife everything too. Everything. I kept a journal, you see, when I was a bachelor. A journal in which every sordid encounter was inscribed. I gave it to her to read -- no, I insisted she read it. Before we were married, you understand. To give her one final chance . . . to walk away. So that she could know the beast, the unworthy, worthless monster that I was, and escape from me. She was repelled. Disgusted. She hated me. But she -- *angel!* -- forgave me. Can you imagine such magnanimity of soul? Can your understanding encompass it? You have never married. I am sorry for you. How can you know of what I speak? *She forgave me!* But, there was one condition. We were never to speak of it again. I promised, I swore, to destroy the diary. And I would never mention it to another living soul.'

'Ah, I see. Pity -- that you destroyed it.'

Vakhramev looked down at the table, his face quivering with emotion.

'And you were married . . . when?'

Vakhramev lifted his gaze proudly. 'Nastasya Petrovna and I were married on March the twenty-first, eighteen forty-eight.'

'So we are twenty years too late to read it.' Porfiry smiled but watched Vakhramev closely, who once again looked down. 'My interest in the diary has nothing to do with prurience, you understand,' continued Porfiry. 'It's just that it might have contained a significant name or two. This Madam Josephine, for instance.'

'I believe I did go there once,' said Vakhramev quickly, still not looking at Porfiry.

Porfiry lifted the cover of the folder again and took out the photograph of Raisa Ivanovna Meyer from many years ago that Virginsky had recovered from the dacha. He passed it across the table to Vakhramev. 'Do you remember ever seeing this woman there?'

Vakhramev studied the photograph. His lips pursed slightly as he did so. And then the hand holding the photograph began to shake. 'It was a long time ago. I only went there once.'

'Really?'

'I swear.'

'But did you see her there?'

'I cannot be expected to remember their faces,' said Vakhramev. His own face became sealed off from further enquiry, as he laid the photograph face down on the table.

*

'Is there, do you think, a specifically Russian type of hypocrite? And if so, who would stand as our *exemplum* of it?' Porfiry was again looking out of the window, down at the Yekaterininsky Canal, as he had been the morning Virginsky first presented himself at his chambers twelve days ago. He was smoking now, as then.

Virginsky did not answer. It was clear that the questions were asked rhetorically.

'Ruslan Vladimirovich Vakhramev?' Porfiry's voice seemed to come from far away. He turned to face Virginsky, as if he did want an answer after all. He had finished his cigarette.

'But Vakhramev has confessed to visiting prostitutes. A true hypocrite would not be able to do that, I feel,' said Virginsky.

'Yes. He even wrote it all down in a diary for his wife to read. What a charming wedding present that must have made.'

'I admire him for doing that.'

'Do not admire him too much. You see, he did not destroy his bachelor diary as he promised her.'

'How can you know that?'

Porfiry shrugged. 'How could he have borne to do so? He would have been destroying part of himself.'

'But what if it was a part of himself he wished to destroy?'

'Hmm. That is certainly the impression he wished to give to his angelic wife.'

'I am beginning to wonder, Porfiry Petrovich, whether the only qualification one needs to be an investigating magistrate is a mind as filthy as your hated Ditch out there. That and an ability to suspect everyone of the vilest acts.'

Porfiry half-turned, almost wistfully, back towards the window. 'Perhaps you're right. Perhaps the only reason I don't like the Ditch is because it reminds me of myself.'

'You certainly spend long enough staring at it. But why can't you take Vakhramev's word that he destroyed the diary?'

'Because he did not give me his word. He did not say that he had destroyed it at all. He merely said that he had promised his fiancée that he would destroy it. And when I deliberately chose to assume that this meant the diary was destroyed, he became quite embarrassed, and yet did not correct the misapprehension.'

Virginsky angled his head, almost conceding the point, but allowing himself to retain some scepticism. 'But perhaps there was no misapprehension?'

'No, no, no,' said Porfiry shortly. 'When you have worked in this job as long as I have you will learn to pay especial regard to the precise form of words people choose, particularly suspects.'

'So you do suspect him of killing Setochkin?'

'I suspect him of something. I suspect him of lying to his wife. I suspect him of not destroying the diary. I suspect him of continuing to visit prostitutes after his marriage. Despite his deep atonement and repentance. Yes, he continued in that -- how shall I describe it? -- *practice* for at least six and possibly seven years after he had abased himself with his face in the mud.'

'Again, how can you know that?'

'Because he recognised the photograph of Raisa Ivanovna. From what Meyer said of Raisa Ivanovna's history, she cannot have worked at Madam Josephine's for long. A year, possibly two at most. Raisa Ivanovna was already pregnant with Grigory when Martin Meyer married her. Grigory was thirteen at the time of his death. Let us say, then, that Raisa Ivanovna was at Madam Josephine's fourteen years ago -- which is indeed the timescale given in the malicious letter sent to Meyer. The photograph I showed Vakhramev must have been taken soon after then. And yet Vakhramev has been married to his angel for twenty years.'

Virginsky was silent for some time, during which Porfiry lit and began smoking another cigarette. 'Do they help, the cigarettes, really?'

Porfiry held the case out towards Virginsky, who nodded once and took one. He coughed three times as Porfiry lit it for him, then held the cigarette away from his face and studied the burning tip. 'You said you were not here to judge him, but that is what you have done. Despite the fact that you yourself have confessed to identical peccadilloes.'

'What peccadilloes have I confessed to?' Porfiry narrowed his eyes.

'To visiting brothels. You said that you have visited brothels.'

'I said that I had visited one establishment. Fraulein Keller's. I went there once -- no, actually, twice I think it was -- in the course of the investigation during which you and I first became acquainted, Pavel Pavlovich.'

Virginsky gingerly attempted another inhalation. 'So how do you?'

Porfiry met the question with an innocent blink.

'Deal with the issue of needs?'

Porfiry looked at Virginsky thoughtfully but did not seem inclined to provide an answer. At any rate, there was a knock at the door and Zamyotov came in, as usual without waiting to be admitted.

'There are some *females* here . . .' His emphasis was one of disapproval, outrage almost. 'They claim to be connected with that individual Vakhramev.'

In his wake, was the sense of a commotion nearing.

5: The angel (and her daughter)

'Ruffians! Ruffians and rogues!'

Bursting in like a cannonade of silk, the woman came to a halt before Porfiry, her eyes wrathful and seeking. 'Where is he? Where is our Vakhramev? What have you done with him?'

She was compact, almost compressed, a little shorter than Porfiry and somewhat stouter. She moved with a top-heavy momentum. Porfiry was relieved that she had stopped short of charging him. Her mouth was pinched with determined indignation.

Following her into the room was a drifting, aloof girl of about nineteen or twenty, who looked around her from the vantage point of a long neck, seemingly without seeing, as if she did not want her vision to be demeaned by the objects it might fall upon. If she believed herself visible to those around her (for example, to Virginsky, who could not take his eyes off her) she certainly gave no indication that they were visible to her.

'We are holding him,' said Porfiry, 'in a cell.'

'Ruslan Vladimirovich Vakhramev? In a cell?'

'I'm afraid so, madam.'

This provoked a disdainful jerk of the head from the drifting girl. Her gaze, though, refused to come anywhere near Porfiry.

'Who, may I ask, are you?' ventured Porfiry to the indignant woman.

'What business is it of yours?'

'I am Porfiry Petrovich, investigating magistrate. I am dealing with the case in which Vakhramev is implicated.'

'*Implicated?* How dare you!'

'Are you, by any chance, his wife?'

'I am Nastasya Petrovna Vakhrameva and I have the honour to be the wife of Ruslan Vladimirovich Vakhramev. I command you to release him this instant.'

'I'm afraid that will not be possible. A man has been murdered. Until we have eliminated Ruslan Vladimirovich from our investigations, it will be necessary to hold him in a secure place.'

'I have never heard of anything so ridiculous in my life. You take him away without a word to his family. He is a gentleman. We have friends, you know. Friends who could crush you like a beetle.' The woman pulled on Porfiry's shoulder and hissed into his ear: 'Yaroslav Nikolayevich Liputin.' When she pulled back, Porfiry saw that she had a gleeful smile on her face. 'There! That's scared him. That's right. Yaroslav Nikolayevich Liputin. So, what are you waiting for? Release Vakhramev.'

'I'm not sure I understand,' said Porfiry. 'You are friends with the *prokuror*?'

The woman nodded. 'And he is not happy about Vakhramev's arrest, let me tell you. He is on his way here now. So, if you want to avoid trouble, little man, you would do well to release Ruslan Vladimirovich immediately.'

'As I have explained, that will not be possible. As a matter of course, Yaroslav Nikolayevich would be informed of the details of the case. He frequently visits the department.'

'He is furious. When Vakhramev failed to come home, I naturally went straight to my good friend Yaroslav Nikolayevich. Good friend that he is, he made enquiries on our behalf. That is how we discovered that you had brought Vakhramev here. I would not like to be in your shoes when Yaroslav Nikolayevich arrives.'

'It is always a pleasure to receive a visit from Yaroslav Nikolayevich. I'm sure today will be no exception,' said Porfiry with a tense smile.

'Whom did he murder?' The question came, unexpectedly, from the drifting girl, who angled her head in the direction of the ceiling, while regarding Porfiry out of the corner of her eye.

'The victim, I believe is known to you, if I am correct in assuming that you are Tatyana Ruslanovna. It is Colonel Alexei Setochkin.'

'Alyosha!' There was a moment in which her disconnected gaze latched on to Porfiry hungrily. She even turned her head to face him. But then she rolled her eyes upwards in a gesture of dismissal. 'He had no need to do that. I had finished with Alyosha.'

'Tatyana,' said Nastasya Petrovna darkly. 'What is the meaning of this? Who is this Alyosha?'

'A nobody. I'm glad he's dead. I will congratulate Daddy.' For the first time, the girl seemed to notice Virginsky. She looked at him with a glance that invited complicity.

'Good grief! What has got into you?' To Porfiry, Nastasya Petrovna added: 'See what you have done? Yaroslav Nikolayevich will sort this out. We will do nothing until Yaroslav Nikolayevich arrives.'

'I am afraid that will not be possible. At least not as far as I am concerned. I have my duties to attend to. I will have to ask you to wait outside, Nastasya Petrovna.'

'Really!'

'There are seats provided for your comfort.'

'You expect me to rub shoulders with common criminals?'

'Of course not.' Porfiry turned to Zamyotov. 'Alexander Grigorevich, would you kindly see to it that no criminals are seated next to this lady.'

'But it is so difficult to tell these days,' said Zamyotov airily. 'Anyone may turn out to be a murderer.' He fixed Virginsky with a pointed look as he said this.

'Your sarcasm has not gone unnoticed,' said Nastasya Petrovna to Porfiry. 'Yaroslav Nikolayevich will be made aware of it when he arrives, rest assured. Come, Tatyana.'

'If you please,' put in Porfiry quickly, 'Tatyana Ruslanovna will stay. I have a few questions I wish to put to her alone.'

'Alone? But she is a child. I will not have you intimidating her.'

'I am *not* a child. You're worse than Daddy. He's always treating me as a child and now look what's happened.'

Nastasya Petrovna's eyes enlarged significantly at this outburst.

Tatyana softened her tone to her mother. 'It's better we do what they want. Better for Daddy.'

'But Yaroslav Nikolayevich --'

'Yaroslav Nikolayevich is not coming. Yaroslav Nikolayevich thinks you are a tiresome old woman. He barely remembered you. And didn't remember Daddy at all. He only agreed to help us to be rid of us. We were disturbing his breakfast and he wanted us out of his sight. So he sent a man to find out what had happened. It does not greatly inconvenience Yaroslav Nikolayevich to have his man running to the police headquarters. There were probably papers that he needed picking up. Didn't he make us wait in a shabby drawing room while he finished his breakfast? And he did not even have the grace to say goodbye in person. He left that honour to his pimply servant, who as good as escorted us off the premises. Do you not know what it is to be insulted, Mother?'

'How can you say such things? In front of them?'

'It is the truth. Why will you never face up to the truth? You have deluded yourself about Yaroslav Nikolayevich. You have deluded yourself about Daddy. You delude yourself about everything.'

Nastasya Petrovna put her hands over her ears and began screaming. 'Cruel, ungrateful child! I will not listen to another word!'

'Then wait outside, Mother. You need not concern yourself on my behalf. I'm not afraid of these men.' Tatyana's gaze swooped imperiously over Porfiry and Virginsky. She angled her face upwards imperiously.

*

'Please sit down.' Porfiry gestured with both hands to the fake-leather sofa. Tatyana Ruslanovna viewed it suspiciously, but at last deigned to lower herself into it. 'Please be assured', continued Porfiry, 'that I earnestly desire to eliminate your father from my investigation and that I will do everything in my power to bring that about as soon as possible.'

'Don't trouble yourself on my account. I'm sure you had your reasons for arresting Daddy.'

Porfiry froze on his way to his desk, turning his head sharply back towards her. 'But do you really think your father capable of murder?'

'It's like that other man said, isn't it? Anyone may turn out to be a murderer.'

'I wonder, do you include yourself in that philosophy?'

'Certainly. I have come close to it many times. I would not be surprised if one day I find myself in one of your cells.'

'I sincerely hope not.' Porfiry at last took his seat.

'Me too. I'll be very clever and escape your detection.' Tatyana gave a glassy little laugh.

'I rather think a better course of action would be to avoid murdering anyone in the first place.'

'Well, of course, I will try. But I *am* only human.'

Porfiry flickered his eyelids in an attempt to gather his thoughts. 'What did you mean when you said that your mother had deluded herself about your father?'

'There are things that I am not supposed to know. For example, Daddy has a bookcase in his library. It is kept locked. But I know where the key is. And I have read the books that he keeps in there.'

'Novels?'

'I think there is another word for the type of books they are.'

'I understand. I know the kind of books you are referring to.'

'I expect you do. I expect you like to read them too.'

'I have encountered them in a professional capacity.'

Her brittle laughter rang out again. There was something broken and cynical to the sound which, given her youthfulness, disturbed Porfiry. 'You men can never own up to your natures, can you? Well at least Alyosha was honest in that respect. He knew what he wanted and was not ashamed to ask for it.' She looked at Virginsky, who was standing by the window. Her smile was a fragment of the same laughter. He was not able to return her look.

'Were you aware that your father received an anonymous letter concerning your relations with Colonel Setochkin?' asked Porfiry.

'Oh yes! He was furious about it.'

'Did he show you the letter?'

'Of course. He thought it would shame me into mending my ways, or some such nonsense.'

'I see. I take it that it did not have the effect he desired?'

'I will not be lectured to by a hypocrite. All his sanctimonious bowing down before the icons, and he was no better than me.' Once more she tilted her head upwards, a gesture of contempt.

Porfiry flexed his brows thoughtfully. A small, almost pained smile flickered briefly. 'Strange. Those were almost the same words he used to me.'

'My mother has fallen for his act, but not I. She hasn't seen what I have seen.'

'You are referring to the books in the locked bookcase?'

'Yes, the books. And the diaries. He keeps dirty little diaries, you know, of all his dirty little antics.'

'Diaries? You mean there's more than one?' said Porfiry.

'Oh yes. Five or six.'

'And you have read them?'

'Oh yes.'

'That must have been hard for you.'

'Oh yes. He has a terrible style.'

Porfiry head trembled towards a bow. 'And does your father know that you have read them?'

'Oh no.' Tatyana smiled her self-satisfaction.

'These diaries are in the locked bookcase in your father's library?'

Tatyana nodded.

'Where is the key to the bookcase?'

Tatyana laughed, the same broken laugh as before. 'You'd like to read them, would you?'

'They may have some bearing on the case.'

'Of course,' said Tatyana. Porfiry was beginning to find her knowing irony tiresome.

'Young lady. A man is dead. This man, I believe, was once someone close to you. Although your father is necessarily a suspect, I am not absolutely convinced that he is the perpetrator. What happened yesterday in Setochkin's study remains a mystery. It could be argued that you yourself have a motive for killing Setochkin. Therefore, you are a suspect too. I urge you to take this seriously. You may very well find yourself in one of my cells sooner than you thought.'

Tatyana clicked her tongue and turned her face away from him in a dismissive shrug. 'The key is at the back of one of the drawers in his desk. The right-hand drawer.'

'Thank you.'

'However, that drawer is locked.'

'I see,' said Porfiry rather stiffly. 'And where is the key for that drawer?'

'That is in the left-hand drawer of the desk.'

'And is that drawer locked?'

'Oh yes.'

'And the key?'

Tatyana turned on him a face brimming with mischief and excitement. 'Where do you think? You're a detective, aren't you? Where would you look for it?'

Porfiry gave it only a moment's thought. 'Knowing your father as I do, knowing the tensions that his soul is subject to, the very real conflicts that torment him, and for which I pity him, as a man . . .' He looked steadily at Tatyana Ruslanovna. 'I would not be surprised if you found the key hidden in the pages of his Bible. In the New Testament. If I were to offer a more precise opinion, I would say somewhere among the verses of the Book of Revelation, perhaps in proximity to chapter two, where Jezebel is mentioned, or, more likely, chapter seventeen, which as you know refers to the Whore of Babylon.'

Tatyana's mouth dropped open, and her sense of her own cleverness seemed to fall out of it.

At that point, however, the interview was interrupted by another commotion outside, in which the voice of Nastasya Petrovna once again dominated. A moment later, the door to Porfiry's chambers opened and a tall, severely impeccable man wearing the buttons of a high-ranking civil servant entered. In addition, he was decorated with the medal of the order of St Stanislav.

Nastasya Petrovna's bustling form was visible behind him, protruding on either side. 'He is here! Our saviour!' Nastasya Petrovna peered around the man's elbow, her mouth now pinched with vindication. She glared at her daughter. 'You said he would not come but he has. You were wrong. Cruel and wrong.' To Porfiry, she added, 'You must not believe a word she says. She speaks only out of spite. What did we do to deserve such an ungrateful child?' Nastasya Petrovna threw up her hands.

Porfiry rose from his seat. 'Yaroslav Nikolayevich, good-day to you.'

'Porfiry Petrovich.' His name sounded like a summoning to account.

'You are in trouble now, little man,' cried Nastasya Petrovna triumphantly. 'It is not for the likes of you to lock Ruslan Vladimirovich Vakhramev in a cell.'

The *prokuror* turned stiffly to Nastasya Petrovna. 'Madam, kindly wait outside.' It looked for the moment as if further protest would erupt from her, but she remembered herself in time and instead smiled simperingly. 'And take your daughter with you.'

'Tatyana!'

The girl rose slowly with a final tilt of her head and sauntered after her mother's sweeping bulk. Virginsky's magnetised gaze tracked her.

'Thank God she is gone,' said Prokuror Liputin as the door was closed behind them. The usual impervious dignity of his expression for the moment gave way to an almost hounded, certainly human, vulnerability. 'She is the most annoying woman I know,' continued Liputin, 'but she is a friend of my wife's.' A spasm of regret tensed the muscles of his face. He then noticed

Virginsky and his expression became guarded. He turned quizzically to Porfiry.

'Allow me to introduce Pavel Pavlovich. A new recruit to our department. His appointment was approved by your office, naturally.'

'Ah yes, I think I remember the letter now. But were you not once . . .?'

'Pavel Pavlovich recently graduated from the university with great honours,' said Porfiry quickly.

'Your face looks somehow familiar.' Liputin frowned at Virginsky, then shook his head slowly. 'Now, what is this all about, Porfiry Petrovich? I was about to leave for Pavlovsk today. I do not appreciate this delay.'

'I am sorry that it has inconvenienced you, Yaroslav Nikolayevich. That was not my intention. It is not a straightforward case, however. A man, a former officer of the Izmailovsky regiment, one Colonel Setochkin, has been shot dead. That lady's husband, Ruslan Vladimirovich Vakhramev, was discovered minutes after with the gun in his hand. The *prima facie* evidence is incriminating, I am afraid. No one else was seen to go into the room -- or out of it, for that matter. There is no question of suicide.'

Yaroslav Nikolayevich murmured distractedly. 'If I were to act as guarantor for Vakhramev, if I were to take him with me to Pavlovsk . . .? Believe me, Porfiry Petrovich, this is not something I undertake lightly. For one thing, I will have to endure that woman's company for the duration of the train journey.'

'Pavlovsk? That would not be very convenient if we need to speak to him again, as I feel sure we will.'

'No, no, you are quite right. Here, I have a better solution. I will stay with Vakhramev in St Petersburg and we will pack the woman and her daughter off to Pavlovsk to be with my wife. How would that suit you?'

Porfiry could not conceal his surprise at the *prokuror*'s conspiratorial familiarity. 'He would be, in a manner of speaking, under house arrest with you?'

'If you wish to put it like that.'

Porfiry thought for a moment. 'Very well. There will have to be police officers in attendance. We will need Nikodim Fomich's consent.'

'You may leave Nikodim Fomich to me,' said Yaroslav Nikolayevich, drawing himself up with a sigh.

A mirroring movement from Virginsky drew the attention of the two other men. Liputin considered him sternly. 'If I remember rightly, Porfiry Petrovich, there was a moment when it seemed very probable that this young man was a murderer.'

'Yes, indeed, Yaroslav Nikolayevich.'

'Let us hope that we have a similar outcome to look forward to in the case of Vakhramev.' Liputin's look to Porfiry as he said this was one of command rather than hope.

Porfiry smiled and nodded automatically as the *prokuror* left to meet the importuning cries of Nastasya Petrovna.

6: Among the whores

Salytov looked up at the glowing sky, away from the voices and the snatches of raucous music thrown out from basement taverns. In this nocturnal softening of the sun, some strange wildness was unbound, a spirit of recklessness and licence. The flowing waterways, the Moika, Fontanka, all the branches of the Neva, even the stinking Yekaterininsky Canal, shimmered. Everything was stirred and intoxicated. Salytov felt it too. Who could sleep at night in the summer in St Petersburg, without first exhausting themselves on the streets, wandering the embankments, pacing squares as wide as the days, in search of the promise of a passing scent or danger?

And it was now that they came out, in all their shameless glee. The Haymarket crawled with whores. Some of them, almost certainly the illegal ones, backed off at the sight of his uniform, though among this group were those too diseased or drunk to care. The yellow ticket carriers were undeterred by his appearance. They either ignored him and carried on their business or, seeing through the uniform to the man, approached him with brazen, beckoning eyes and coaxing words. *Even a policeman has to fuck*, was evidently their reasoning, as well as their experience.

He wanted to let them know that they disgusted him; that he saw through their daubs of face paint and tawdry dresses, even through their soft flesh to the soulless bones beneath. Without doubt, he wanted to punish them, even the legals, for the humiliation that their glances and their words inflicted. For is it not humiliating to be reminded of the things that are beyond our power, the forces that control us? At the very least, he wanted to inconvenience them, to take them in, shake them up, scare them, if necessary hurt them. Then perhaps, when he had made his position and his power clear, he would consent to their proposals.

But tonight, as he consciously had to remind himself, he was on official business. 'Do not antagonise them,' Porfiry Petrovich had said to him, as he handed over the photograph of Raisa Ivanovna Meyer. 'You need to win them over.' As always it galled him to receive advice from -- to be patronised by -- the investigating magistrate, especially when his own suggestions as to the management of the case were so flagrantly ignored. *They had let the boy from the confectioner's go! Unbelievable!* It was not even clear that Porfiry Petrovich had informed the Third Section of the pamphlets found at the boy's lodgings.

No. Salytov's views had not been appreciated. And instead of following a genuine lead, he was sent to chase loathsome chimeras around the Haymarket.

The first girl that approached him was too young to remember Raisa Ivanovna in her working days, even allowing for the young ages at which most of them began their careers. He declined her mocking proposition with a shake of the head.

He made for a group of older women, who seemed to have given up any real expectation of trade, certainly at this early stage of the night, while there were still younger, prettier girls about. Instead, they were absorbed by their own hilarity, passing a vodka bottle around and cackling. At his approach, they began to preen and pout. Salytov felt a flinch of tension quiver in his face as he suppressed his disgust and allowed them their advances. God only knew with what diseases they were riddled. Their vile and filthy fingers came out towards him. Even in the soft whiteness of the night, the sores and pockmarks of their faces were discernible beneath the layers of make-up. Porfiry Petrovich's words came back to him: 'You need to win them over.' But at what cost?

'Aren't you ashamed of yourselves? Some of you are old enough to be grandmothers.' He could not help himself. It was the only way he knew.

Their responses to his reproach were good-natured, or perhaps their renewed laughter was simply a reflex. 'Whores are like fine wines, dearie, they get better with age,' came from one of them. Her wink seemed not to be for Salytov, but for her companions. She clung to the necks of two of them. There was a round of appreciative laughter.

'So you admit to being whores? But what use is there in denying the obvious. I hope your yellow tickets are all in order?'

'If it's our yellow tickets you want to see, you know where to look for them!' The voluble one unhooked her arms from her friends and spun around to present Salytov with a view of her backside, which she stuck out and wiggled.

'Enough of that. Show more respect, woman. Here now. You

must all look at this picture. That's right, pass it around. Do any of you recognise her? She worked as a whore many years ago at a brothel run by one Madam Josephine. Our records show that this brothel no longer exists, or at any rate is no longer legally licensed. It is believed that Madam Josephine is dead. God knows how it is that any of you are still alive. The name of the woman in the picture is Raisa. She may have worked under a different name, however. Cast your minds back, if you have anything left of your minds. Come now, do any of you recognise her?'

There were murmurs of distrust now, heads were shaken, and the women began to back away. Some of them tried unsuccessfully to recapture their former mood, which this intrusion of the past, a reminder of the youth they no longer possessed, had muted. In particular, Salytov's mention of Madam Josephine seemed to have had a sobering effect. And it was almost as if the picture of Raisa acted with a repulsive force on them.

The woman who had done most of the talking was the first to go, making a beeline for a solitary man whose drunken swerve marked him out as easy pickings. She paused only to cross herself as she passed the Church of the Assumption.

Soon only one of them remained. She was left holding the photograph of Raisa, her head bowed over it.

'I remember her,' she said. When at last she lifted her face, Salytov saw that her eyes were moist with tears.

*

'Raisa. That was her name. She came from a good family, didn't she? Yes, she was a nice girl, a good girl, really she was. I can see the way you're looking at me, but believe me, it's true. It happens, you know. Girls fall on hard times. Their families forsake them. What else are they to do?'

'Nonsense. They have many options. They could enter service. If she was from a good family, and educated, why could she not have become a governess? Are you telling me that because she was too proud to find work as a seamstress, she became a whore instead? Only the lazy and the wicked go down your path.'

'But there are many small steps on to it. Sometimes a girl finds herself friendless, that's somehow worse than penniless and homeless. You have to imagine the depths of despair.'

'Depravity!'

'No. Despair. Then, at last, she finds a friend, or so it seems. She is taken in by a kindly soul who understands everything. She is given a bed, food, warmth, and nothing is asked of her in return. At least not at first. More and more she finds herself in the debt of this kindly soul, whose name may be Madam Josephine, or Fraulein Keller, or some such. She is reassured daily not to give the mounting debt another thought. Perhaps there are practical measures, not to mention expenses, that the girl needs help with. There is a way of getting into trouble that only girls have. These kindly souls know all the remedies. Then the day comes when the poor lost girl no longer feels herself poor or lost. She feels herself strong and ready to go out into the world again. But now she is reminded of the debt. Her ingratitude is thrown back at her. "But what can I do?" she asks. "I have no way to repay you. I have no money." "There is a way," says the kindly soul. And so begins her education. There will be tears, no doubt. But no one will hear them. In the meantime, the debt increases. It always increases, no matter how hard the girl works. And she begins to see herself as a spoiled, worthless creature with no way out, no life of her own, and more alone than she has ever been.

'That was Raisa's story, but not the whole of it. It did not end for her as it did for so many others. As it will for me. She got out. She met a man. A gentleman. He came to Madam Josephine's and saw something in her eyes that moved him. He got her to tell him her story and was moved by that too. He slept with her, of course. He was not such a saint as to forgo that privilege. He promised her money to buy off Madam Josephine. It was not such a large sum as all that, though any sum is large when you have nothing. He gave her more. His address and the promise of another life. She left to find him. And the day she left was the last time I ever saw her. Tell me, is she happy now, do you know?'

'She's dead. It's thought her husband killed her.'

*

The Vakhramevs' apartment was in a respectably solid building on Bolshaya Konyushennaya Street, around the corner from 22 Nevsky Prospekt. Porfiry and Virginsky exchanged a startled look as they walked past that address, though neither felt inclined to comment.

'These nights are deceiving,' said Porfiry, looking at his pocket watch. 'I always think it is earlier than it is. There is no need for you to come with me, you know. It is long past the hour when you are required to attend me.' Porfiry's tone became solicitous: 'You may go home, Pavel Pavlovich.'

'No,' said Virginsky. 'There is nothing for me there.'

'But isn't your father still in Petersburg? Would not he and your stepmother appreciate a visit from you?'

'That can wait.'

'As you wish.'

They walked in silence along Bolshaya Konyushennaya Street.

'Will there be anyone in the apartment?' asked Virginsky at last.

'No. The household, apart from Vakhramev himself, have removed to Pavlovsk. Vakhramev, as you know, is the guest of our esteemed superior, the Prokuror Liputin.'

'Is it right, do you think, the way that between you, you drove a coach and horses through the justice system? Simply because he is a friend of the *prokuror*, he is allowed to go free. It is a pity that I did not have such friends when I was in a similar predicament.'

'I am confident that Ruslan Vladimirovich will not abscond.'

'That has not answered my question.'

'Very well. Let me say that it *is* right, it is very right and proper that a friend of the *porokuror*, or to be more accurate, the husband of a friend of the *prokuror*'s wife, should receive preferential treatment in this way. It is right because it is necessary. What is necessary is always right. Is that not so?'

'But it isn't fair.'

'Ah, Pavel Pavlovich, how are we to cure you of this morbid preoccupation with fairness?' Porfiry looked up at the precise geometric facade of the street, following the upward lines of the windows to the pale sky. 'This is the one, I think.'

*

They climbed to the first landing. A brass plaque on the wall beside the white double panelled door announced *Ruslan Vladimirovich Vakhramev*. Porfiry Petrovich placed the key in the lock and looked at Virginsky, who felt again the thrill of transgression that he had experienced reading the letters in Meyer's study.

'Where did you get the key?' he asked as Porfiry opened the door.

'Vakhramev supplied it. He had little choice.'

'But does he know what we are looking for?'

Porfiry shook his head as he closed the door. 'Neither is he aware that we know where to find it.'

There was an air of stagnant domesticity about the flat. The aroma of a recent meal, or possibly the accumulation of many such aromas, lingered in the entrance hall. A stand by the door was fully charged with canes and umbrellas. The floor was of soft painted boards and the walls were papered with a dull geometric design, reminiscent of masonry. The entrance hall was L-shaped and doors led off from every side.

Porfiry opened one door to the left. 'Kitchen and washroom through there. And servants' quarters beyond, presumably. So . . . let us try this one.'

They entered a drawing room. The same wallpaper continued in here. A broad metal stovepipe running almost the full height of the room cut into the wall. There was a sofa with a table pushed up against it. The table had a cloth over it and an oil lamp in the centre. Virginsky had the sense of the social gatherings that had taken place around it, and imagined the ghost-like faces of the family turning in surprise as they entered. The shadowless dusk of a summer night lay like a soft filter over everything. It seemed to be a third presence in the room with them, and Virginsky felt the need to speak to dispel it.

'We are like thieves in the night.'

Porfiry seemed surprised by the remark. 'It is a necessary part of the job, I am afraid. This is what we deal in. People's lives. In the course of your work, you will discover far more about people than you wish you knew. If this makes you uncomfortable, then I fear that the role of an investigator may not be suited to you, after all.'

'Are you not uncomfortable?'

Porfiry gave the impression of being even more taken aback.

'Or do you, perhaps, relish it?'

'Relish? No. I do not believe there is any prurient element to my constitution, if that is what you're implying. It is merely necessary, as I said.'

'And what is necessary is right.'

Porfiry blinked in a self-conscious display of patience. 'One must overcome one's misgivings. Besides, what we may find may prove Ruslan Vladimirovich's innocence, or at least support it. If that is the case, then I am sure he will forgive us this . . . intrusion.'

Virginsky raised his eyebrows sceptically.

Another door led off from the drawing room, which Porfiry tried now. 'Ah! This I imagine is Tatyana Ruslanovna's room,' said Porfiry, stepping through the doorway.

'What are you doing?' cried Virginsky. 'There is no need to go in there, surely?' But Porfiry did not hear him, or at least did not acknowledge him, so he had no alternative but to follow.

Virginsky was somehow surprised to see the omnipresent wallpaper here too, as if he expected Tatyana Ruslanovna to impose her personality more forcefully on her living space. Indeed, at first he was at a loss to understand why Porfiry had assumed this was the daughter's room, unless it was the subtly invasive perfume. But then he saw the toys, the large doll on the bed, the doll's house on the floor, the rocking horse in one corner.

'And she wonders why they treat her like a child,' said Porfiry. 'She is a strange, contradictory creature, do you not agree? Fascinating, but dangerous. Is she really as worldly as she would have us believe? And why does she cling to these relics of her childhood? Perhaps she grieves the passing of it more than she acknowledges.'

'She is neither child nor woman,' said Virginsky, absent-mindedly running one hand over the smooth surface of the room's stovepipe. It was as if by this touch he believed he could possess her life.

Now Porfiry was opening another door, that faced the one they had entered by. 'And here it is. Her father's study. Everything is connected. Room connected to room. Life connected to life. That is the way in St Petersburg.'

Virginsky felt a sudden firmness in the beating of his heart at their proximity to their object. Something too disturbed him about the juxtaposition of rooms.

Now the insistent wallpaper struck Virginsky as an infestation. He was repelled by it. He saw its straight lines and unvarying angles as the imposition of an unfeeling authority, of which the study was undoubtedly the source. *No wonder she rebelled against him*, he thought.

One corner was clustered with icons.

On the desk was a large leather-bound Slavonic Bible. Porfiry moved briskly to it, crossed himself, and heaved it open. He turned the rough-edged, thick pages eagerly. At last he held up a small key. His smile was triumphant. 'It *was* chapter seventeen.'

Virginsky was beset by a strange dread.

Porfiry sat down at the desk to try the key in the left-hand drawer.

'Do you really want to see what is written in those diaries?' asked Virginsky, voicing his dread.

Porfiry hesitated and looked at him questioningly. 'We have no choice.'

'But think of her reading them. I cannot help feel that it is these diaries that have made her the way she is. That have corrupted her.'

Porfiry nodded thoughtfully. 'Yes. They may have played a part.'

'I find myself exceedingly reluctant to know what is written there,' confessed Virginsky.

'Sometimes one must be forced to do what one most desires,' said Porfiry, looking up at him with a strange expression.

'What do you mean?' demanded Virginsky. He felt the heat of his rage in his face.

Porfiry didn't answer immediately. He turned back to the Bible and flicked through the pages, looking for a passage. 'Here we are. Paul's first letter to the Thessalonians. Chapter five, verse two. *Sami bo vy izvestno vestye, yako den Gospoden, yakozhe tat v noshchi, tako priidet.* Which, if my understanding of Church Slavonic is correct, can be translated as "For you know perfectly well that the word of the Lord comes as a thief in the night".'

'Your point?'

'My point is that even subterfuge may result in good.'

'But this feels . . . despicable.'

'It is not just the perpetrators of crimes that we must pit ourselves against. Sometimes those who are wholly innocent present us with our greatest obstacles -- and challenge. We must use every means -- stealth, cunning, even deceit -- against them. For you may be assured that they will use the same against us.' Porfiry Petrovich pulled open the drawer sharply. 'Even the innocent. For though they may be innocent of the crimes we are investigating, they know themselves to be guilty of others, which in their own hearts they may feel to be far worse.'

'How can you know this?'

'Because I am human myself.' Porfiry's hand probed the back of the drawer and produced another small key, seemingly identical to the first. With this he unlocked the right-hand drawer. 'These secrets that Ruslan Vladimirovich has locked away with three keys . . .' Porfiry pulled out the third key now, a long, fine-shafted object cast in brass. 'What a burden they must place upon his soul.'

'But why not destroy the journals? Isn't he laying himself open always to their discovery?'

'Because they *are* his soul. How could a man bear to destroy a part of his soul? However base, however humiliating, he must find a way to acknowledge it, if only to himself. Have you ever had the dream of standing before a crowded room of people, as though to deliver a lecture, only to look down and discover yourself naked? I wonder if this dream does not represent some deep-seated wish, not for literal humiliation in this way, but for our true natures to be revealed. Of course, it can never be.' Porfiry's tone as he said this was almost regretful.

'You think Vakhramev will welcome this discovery?'

'It will be very painful to him, for sure. Particularly when he realises that his daughter has been exposed to the details of his immorality.'

Virginsky's face opened in the shock of realisation. 'Unless . . . unless he wanted her to find it.'

Porfiry's brows shot up. He pursed his lips approvingly. 'We'll make an investigator of you yet, Pavel Pavlovich.'

*

There were two bookcases in the room. One was glass-fronted, but turned out to be unlocked. At first glance, the books it contained seemed to be innocuous. There were few novels, various works of history, including Shcherbatov's six volume *History of Russia*. Pushkin was in evidence, as well as Levshin's *Russian Tales* and the fables of Krylov. Virginsky also noticed Bishop Rudneyev's *Russian Library*. By far the majority of the books it contained were homilies and saints' lives and other books of a religious bent.

The second bookcase appeared to be entirely open, without even glass doors. But when Porfiry tried to extract one of the many identical and unmarked books, his fingers slipped uselessly over the unmoving spines. Porfiry's face lit up appreciatively. 'Ah! They are false! She could have mentioned that detail. Now, let me see. It must be here somewhere.' His probing fingers discovered one spine near the centre that swung out as though on a hinge, revealing a keyhole. Porfiry smiled to Virginsky as he fitted the key.

The spine-covered doors swung open on rows of genuine spines, almost all in the same maroon cloth binding. 'I see Vakhramev is a collector of Priapos editions,' said Porfiry, shaking his head.

Six kid-bound notebooks on the bottom shelf broke the uniformity. Porfiry crouched down and pulled them out.

Virginsky watched the magistrate scan the pages devouringly. 'Yes. Journals. All thoughtfully dated.' Porfiry handed the first notebook to Virginsky as he finished it. Virginsky gave one shake of the head, like a horse troubled by flies, and stared, appalled, back at Porfiry. Then he opened the book that had somehow found its way into his hands.

Picked up a little whore on Sadovaya Street. Not much older than eleven.

'Oh my God,' said Virginsky, dropping the book. He bent to retrieve it.

'Don't worry about that. There's no need to read it. It pre-dates the period in which we are interested. As do these.' Porfiry handed over all but one of the other notebooks. 'This one is the last. The year is given as 1854. Fourteen years ago. That would be around the time that Raisa was at Madam Josephine's. I wonder.' Porfiry flicked through the pages rapidly. 'Just as I thought. The very last entry. Raisa. And it is at Madam Josephine's. This is very interesting. He says that he went there with some other men. Old schoolfriends. Two of them are named. Golyadkin and Devushkin. A third man is referred to only as "the Uninvited One". It is he who goes with Raisa.' Porfiry read on in silence for a moment, then looked up at Virginsky. 'I confess to feeling a terrible apprehension concerning this uninvited one. I would not be surprised if we had found our murderer.' He closed the book. 'All we have to discover now is his identity.' Porfiry clutched the notebook to his chest. 'And how he was able to do it, of course.'

7: The Uninvited One

The morning light through Yaroslav Nikolayevich's drawing-room window was clear and uncompromising. The *prokuror* himself was pacing the room, in a manner that somehow combined anxiety with authority. He was anxious, clearly, for the whole sorry business to be over. His guest, Ruslan Vladimirovich, was seated at a sofa. Porfiry noted that Vakhramev's remarkable imperturbability had abandoned him. His eyes stared, wild and distraught now, at the six kid-bound notebooks on the table before him.

'How did you get them?'

Porfiry weighed his choices for a moment, in which he exchanged a glance with Virginsky. 'Your daughter alerted us to their existence.'

'Tanyushka knew about them?'

'I'm afraid so. She found the key to your concealed bookcase.'

'No!'

Porfiry studied the pattern in the tablecloth.

'Has she, do you know, read them?'

Porfiry nodded. Vakhramev placed his hands over his face so that the high, broken sounds of his distress snagged in his fingers.

'What is left for me now?' he said at last. Still he did not take his hands from his face.

Porfiry looked at Yaroslav Nikolayevich, who shook his head in disapproval.

'I am sorry for you,' said Porfiry to Vakhramev, in conscious response to the *prokuror*'s severity.

'Are you?' As Vakhramev dropped his hands, he seemed to release a blast of bitter fury. 'You have brought this on me. Was it really necessary to go looking for these?'

Porfiry place a crooked forefinger to his lips. The touch was comforting. 'Yes. It was necessary. Besides, Ruslan Vladimirovich, you must realise that Tatyana had already read them. That was nothing to do with me. All that has changed is that you now know that she has.'

'All that has changed! All that has changed is that I have nothing left to live for! She can have no respect for me. And if she has no respect for her father, how can she respect herself? I have destroyed her.'

'These were not the only books we found in your study,' said Porfiry gently.

Vakhramev closed his eyes. His mouth stretched taut, like a child's the moment before tears. A huge spasm worked its way through his body.

'She saw those too!'

'I was not referring to those books. I meant, there was a copy of the Holy Bible on your desk. You have practised the forms of religion, perhaps the time has come to open your heart to its message. The word of the Lord comes like a thief in the night.' Porfiry shot a stealthy glance to Virginsky.

Vakhramev opened his eyes and looked at Porfiry wildly. A sound escaped him that could have been laughter, though it was a mirthless sound, and barely human. 'Do not mock me! I do not believe. I have never been able to believe. At least, not since I was a child. I may wish I did, but I cannot. I am a vile worm. I cannot escape my nature. The only escape' -- Vakhramev's face seemed to sink in on itself, as if it masked a vacuum -- 'is death.'

'Pull yourself together,' said Porfiry firmly. 'You are alive. You must carry on living. That is your duty. You will find a way to believe.' Porfiry looked down at the notebooks. 'You have brought this on yourself. In some part of you, you have desired this. At any rate, you always knew this day would come. Certainly, you did less than you could have to prevent it. You say you are a worm. No. That's not the case. All this' -- he gestured at the books -- 'are the actions of a man. Face up to them. Face up to yourself. And draw a line.'

'I cannot draw a line,' Vakhramev got out desperately.

'How do you think Tatyana knew where to find the key? After all, you had taken great pains to conceal it.'

'I have no idea.'

'Really? Her room adjoins your study, does it not?'

'What are you suggesting?'

Porfiry glanced again at Virginsky. 'Could it ever have been possible that the door to her room was left ajar, allowing her to spy on you as you went to the hidden bookcase?'

Vakhramev's flinching glance away contradicted his words:

'No. I was always careful. I think.'

'You think?'

Vakhramev bowed his head. 'Is it really possible?'

Porfiry did not take his eyes from him. 'I believe so.'

'Am I so depraved?' The question from Vakhramev was barely audible.

'Please understand,' said Porfiry crisply, almost impatiently now. 'I'm not interested in moral judgements. I am only interested in the truth. Possibly that is what motivated you, too. It was not a question of wanting to corrupt Tatyana. It was rather that you wanted the hypocrisy to end.'

'What good has it done me?'

'I believe it was necessary.' Again Porfiry looked at Virginsky. 'And what is necessary is always right. Now, we must clear up a few things regarding Colonel Setochkin's death. You know that Tatyana considers you perfectly capable of being his murderer. We must show her that you are not.'

'I may as well be. To take the life of a Setochkin is a lesser crime than those she knows me guilty of.'

'Nonsense. This will be painful to you, I'm sure. But we are all men here. We must talk about a certain incident related in one of your journals. The last entry, in fact, in the last book.' Porfiry picked up the relevant notebook and found the page. 'It is here where you mention a prostitute called Raisa. Was this the woman whose photograph I showed you?'

'It was all so long ago.'

'Come now. Please. No pretence. We have gone past that point.'

'No. You don't understand. I really can't remember. That was why I wrote it all down. So that I could forget. I was tormented by my actions. I could not get them out of my mind. And I found that as I wrote something down, my memory was cleared of it. I was able to divide that part of me from the rest of me, from the respectable Ruslan Vladimirovich Vakhramev, who was able to go about his respectable business untroubled by these . . . disreputable memories. Until of course he sinned again.'

'I do understand that. But this is the last entry, dated fourteen years ago. I cannot help but feel there must have been something significant about it. I mean to say, why did you stop here?'

'Because I stopped. Believe me, I have not been with a prostitute since that day. I have found other outlets.'

'The Priapos books?'

Vakhramev nodded.

'What enabled you to break with prostitutes?' pressed Porfiry.

'Give me the book,' said Vakhramev. He turned to the last entry. 'I do not remember in all honesty whether this Raisa is the woman you showed me in that photograph. Her face did seem familiar, I confess. It awoke some memory. But there were so many of them, you know. It gives me no pleasure to say that. However . . .' Vakhramev tapped the page decisively. 'I do remember the night in question. There had been a dinner in honour of Devushkin, who was leaving St Petersburg the following day for the Caucasus. Myself and Golyadkin were invited, but Golyadkin turned up with this other fellow. An old schoolfriend of his.'

'The Uninvited One?'

'Yes.'

'What was his real name?'

'I don't remember. Or rather, I'm not sure I ever knew. He called himself the "Uninvited One", you see, out of a perverse pride. "You don't want me here," he said. "But here I am." He did his best to insult us all. Particularly Devushkin, whose party it was. After the dinner, in the course of which, if I remember rightly, he as good as challenged Devushkin to a duel -- Devushkin laughed it off, of course, which only infuriated him the more -- yes, after the dinner, we tried to shake him off. We pretended that the party was breaking up but we met again and took a cab to Madam Josephine's. I had never been to that particular brothel before. It was a favourite haunt of Devushkin's, in whose honour the party was. Well, somehow, he, the Uninvited One, got wind of our plot and followed us there. He had the effrontery to demand we pay his cabdriver. Strange how all the details do come back to one. Well, he was drunk. We were all drunk and getting drunker. There was a terrible scene. Madam Josephine tried to calm things down. She offered him a new girl. Or at least Madam Josephine said she was a new girl. Can one ever believe what they say? I wonder, do you have that photograph still?'

Porfiry reached a hand into a pocket and produced Raisa's picture.

'I do believe that was her, you know. Yes, I'm almost certain of it. You have to realise that the light in those places was never very bright. But I remember how I felt looking at her -- I feel the same thing now. I remember, you see, thinking at the time, "That girl is from a good family. That girl is afraid. How on earth did she end up here?" And I thought of my own daughter, Tatyana, who must have been five or six at the time. Do you know you can buy girls that young, perfectly legally, in the Haymarket?'

'Please continue,' said Porfiry.

'Well, I looked at her and I looked at *him*, and I saw something horrible in his eyes, something that I knew was in my own eyes too. And that was when it ended. I swear to you that was when it ended.'

'Do you remember if this man promised her money to buy her way out of the brothel? If he promised her a better life?'

'Yes! That was it! He was determined to show himself better than us. It was a way of insulting us, that was all. He had no intention of going through with it.'

'We picked up a report that this is what happened to Raisa. It would rather suggest that we are talking about the same woman.' Porfiry's hand delved into another pocket. He held out a photograph of Martin Meyer recovered from the escritoire in the dacha. 'Was this the man? Is he the Uninvited One?'

Vakhramev frowned at the picture. 'No. Not him. I am sure of it.'

Porfiry nodded. 'Good. I did not think it would be, but I had to confirm it. This man is Raisa's husband. In the event, it was he who gave Raisa the better life that the Uninvited One promised her. However, he himself claims not to have known until recently that Raisa ever worked as a prostitute. It would not fit with his story if he had in fact slept with her at Madam Josephine's.' Porfiry took back the photograph of Meyer. 'Now then, your friend, Golyadkin, the schoolfriend of this mysterious individual -- he must surely know the identity of the Uninvited One. Where may we find Golyadkin?'

'In the Mitrofanevsky Cemetery,' said Vakhramev. 'He died in a boating accident three months ago.'

Porfiry let out a sigh, in which there was more than simple disappointment. 'I doubt very much that it was an accident. Perhaps you remember which school it was they were at together?'

'It was a private boarding school in Moscow. Golyadkin talked of it often. He had a miserable time there. I don't remember the name.'

'I have only one other question. Do you happen to know what age Golyadkin was at his death?'

'He had recently celebrated his forty-seventh birthday.'

'Thank you,' said Porfiry, looking Vakhramev in the eye. 'You have helped us very much. This has provided the first real breakthrough of the case and I realise that it has been hard for you to talk of these things. Allow me to shake your hand.' Porfiry stood and held out his hand.

A sob of gratitude shook Vakhramev. The tears sprang to his eyes as he took Porfiry's hand.

8: Family obligations

Salytov stood at the entrance to the yard, in full view, watching the boy on stilts. Every now and then Tolya would lose his balance and jump off. He would regard the lieutenant defiantly before climbing back on and resuming his strange stiff-gaited walk. Gradually, the periods between his falls lengthened, and at last he was able to totter over to Salytov. He held on to the trembling handles grimly as he looked down on the police officer.

'You're not a very good spy.'

'I want you to know that I have my eye on you.'

'I was released. Without charge. You have no right.'

'What do you know about rights?' said Salytov.

Without warning, Salytov swung back his boot and launched it at Tolya's stilts. The boy fell heavily. When he picked himself up, there was horse ordure over his clothes. His hands were bleeding.

'You should be more careful,' observed Salytov.

Tolya glared back at Salytov. 'I have told Monsieur Ballet about this. He intends to lodge a complaint.'

'Let him. I have closed his shop down once. I can do it again.'

'Leave me be.'

'What was that? A command? Surely you have learnt the dangers that ensue when you raise yourself above your station.' The boy's stilts lay one on top of the other on the ground. Salytov jumped on them, snapping one over the pivot of the other.

'One day . . .' Tolya began.

But Salytov's mocking, questioning leer discouraged him from saying more.

*

'How nice that you have come to visit us,' said Natalya Ivanovna, holding Virginsky by both hands. Her smile uplifted him. He felt it pour into him.

'At last!' added Virginsky's father warmly.

Virginsky chose to take offence. 'You could have come to see me at any time.' He let go of his stepmother's hands.

'Please. Let's not argue. The important thing is that you are here. And we are glad of it.' Natalya Ivanovna's smile now was anxious, straining to hold on to a moment already gone.

'What do you think of the suite?' said Virginsky's father with a satisfied smile, as the sweep of his arm offered the sitting room to Virginsky. 'A good set of rooms, is it not? And the view, of course. Natasha had to have her view of the river. It is an extra expense. But I am not the man to begrudge a beautiful woman that which she has set her heart upon.'

Virginsky looked about without commenting on the quality or size of the accommodation. At last he said: 'I'm surprised you have requested a room overlooking one of the city's stinking waterways. However, you must dispose of your money in whatever way you deem appropriate, father. It matters not to me. Please be assured that I expect nothing from you in that respect.'

The elder Virginsky's lips twitched apprehensively. 'There is no need to talk like this. Your inheritance is secure, you must know that.'

'Then let us talk no more of it,' said Virginsky, with some attempt at magnanimity. 'Well, I have some news for you,' he resumed briskly, but immediately regretted his tone and dampened it. 'It concerns your friend, the gentleman you were visiting the day I met you. Colonel Setochkin.'

'You know Setochkin?'

'No. I don't know him. Not personally, at least.' One side of Virginsky's mouth contracted. 'I am afraid to have to tell you that Colonel Setochkin is dead.' Virginsky looked immediately down.

'No!' cried his father. Out of the corner of his eye, Virginsky noticed his father's arm float uselessly.

'I am sorry,' said Virginsky. He had the sense that he had unleashed something he could not control. To that extent, his apology was sincere. He thought of Porfiry Petrovich, of the power he seemed to draw from such disclosures: it repelled him, and he judged himself loathsome for having coveted it. 'I had no idea you were such good friends. I have never heard you talk of him.'

'It is just the shock of it, that's all,' said his father. 'My dear, if you are to deliver such messages in future, it would be as well to adopt a more appropriate demeanour. So, Setochkin is dead. It was his heart, I suppose. But he was still a relatively young man, and he seemed quite healthy the last time we saw him.'

'He was shot,' said Virginsky. 'Murdered. It is one of the cases I am working on with Porfiry Petrovich.'

'How extraordinary.' Virginsky senior found a chair and sank into it. His expression clouded, then he looked at his son wonderingly. 'But this unfortunate event, it is not the reason for your visit, surely?'

'You are my father, I am your son. Is it not natural that I should visit you? I recollect that you invited me.' Virginsky looked away, abashed. 'I merely mentioned Setochkin's death because I believe you were coming from visiting him that day when I met you. It is just one of those connections that the mind makes.'

'I see.' His father's tone was guarded. 'Then it is not the case that you suspect me of somehow being involved in Setochkin's death?'

Virginsky waited perhaps too long before replying. 'No.' After a further pause, he added, rather self-consciously, 'It is merely that it is a striking coincidence. As an investigator, one learns to distrust coincidence.'

'As an investigator?' His father seemed to grow in his chair as he loomed forward threateningly. 'What about as a son?'

Virginsky looked at Natalya Ivanovna. Her beauty was indisputable; his need to confirm it was a compulsion that he felt destroying him. 'What was your business with Setochkin?' Virginsky's voice was cold. He did not look at his father as he asked the question.

'Has he sent you here to interrogate me, this Porfiry Petrovich of yours?'

'Porfiry Petrovich does not know I am here. He does not even know of your connection with Setochkin. I have kept that from him. There are other things I have kept from him too. This visit is not part of the official investigation. As you see, I am not in my uniform. I am here as your son. I ask you these questions as your son. Please answer me candidly as my father.'

'Then I *am* suspected. By you, at least.'

'I am trying to keep you out of it. For that reason I must learn as much as possible about your association with this man. If you knew the full details of the case, you would understand why.'

'Then enlighten me.'

'I cannot.'

'I have always been too lenient with you. I listened too much to your mother. And this is how I am repaid.'

'I would ask you not to speak of my mother in that way. Not here.' Virginsky's glance towards Natalya Ivanovna was sullen and pointed.

A related anger held father and son to silence. Natalya Ivanovna's mediating smile was sweetly pained. 'This breaks my heart,' she said, 'to see the two men I love most dearly at war.'

Virginsky heard his father say: 'You are right, my dear. Let us talk of other things.'

But it seemed there were no other things left for them to talk of. Virginsky stared, absurdly, at an insignificant point on the floor, as if the fixity of his gaze was holding the room together. In a way it was: he knew that if he looked away from that point there would be nothing left for him to do but leave. Without releasing his gaze, he addressed the floor, his voice charged with aggressive reasonableness: 'What my father must realise is that my filial loyalty alone will not be enough to protect him from the enquiries that must inevitably ensue once it is discovered that he is an associate of the dead man, and that he visited him the day before his death. He insists that I, as his son, consider him above all suspicion. Very well. I do and I will. However, there are others, more powerful than I, who will be moved by no such familial obligation. I know myself, from bitter experience, what it is to be suspected by them. It is because I wish to preserve him from a similar experience that I have asked a question on my own account. To be under suspicion is indeed unpleasant. To be incarcerated is far worse. I fear that my father, due to his age and habits, would be ill equipped to survive the latter. My belief was that he would prefer the enquiries of a dutiful son to those of an indifferent authority. I am sorry if I was mistaken in this. Good day.'

Virginsky bowed to the point on the floor and began to turn.

'Sta-ay,' called Virginsky senior. He managed to charge the elongated word with both contrition and mockery. Virginsky heard his father's groan as he rose from his chair. 'Where has it come from, this constraint between us?'

Virginsky's brows rose and dipped sharply. He allowed the question to remain rhetorical.

'You speak of your duty,' continued his father. 'You speak of your loyalty. But what of your love?'

Virginsky at last looked up from the floor and it was towards

Natalya Ivanovna that his gaze directed itself. Her face was horror-struck as she recoiled from him.

'Father, I cannot answer such a question, other than by my actions. I am able to be of service to you in this current matter. But you must trust me and demonstrate in return that which you demand from me. If you love me, answer my question: what was your business with Setochkin?' Now Virginsky sought his father's eyes, only to find them flitting away from him.

'He had undertaken to act as agent on my behalf in a certain transaction.'

'What transaction?'

'A sale.'

'A sale of what?'

'A sale of land.'

'What land?'

'There's a small birch coppice that's getting difficult to manage. The returns are ever-diminishing. Now seemed the right time to sell. And Setochkin said that he knew a potential buyer. So. Why would I kill him? He was acting on my behalf. You could say I needed him.'

Virginsky did not answer.

'Now may we talk of other things?' asked his father.

'Who is this buyer for the birch coppice that Setochkin had found?'

'Are we back to Setochkin then?'

'Was a price agreed?' Virginsky fired out the question, though he had not yet received an answer to his previous one.

'We were in negotiations.'

'I understand, of course, that you are in need of funds to support your new life with Natalya Ivanovna.'

'You have not yet come into your inheritance, Pavel Pavlovich. Therefore I am still in charge of the management of the estate. I am not required to explain my decisions to you, nor to seek your approval for them.'

'As I think I have made clear, it is no concern of mine how you manage your affairs.'

'But no, you are right to be interested.'

'You misunderstand me,' said Virginsky. 'I have no interest. Not in the way you imagine. I am merely trying to understand your connection with Setochkin. Perhaps there was a quarrel over the price? Perhaps Setochkin was cheating you?'

'You think I killed him over the sale of a birch coppice?'

'These are the questions my superiors will ask.'

'But why should they? How will they ever know that I visited Setochkin? Unless you tell them?'

'Are you suggesting that I suppress information which may prove relevant to the case?'

Virginsky's father smiled. His tone became silky. 'But isn't that what you have already done? You haven't told them yet. Why need you ever?'

'I may find that I have a duty to do so.'

Now his father put on a wounded air. 'That could only be if you suspected me of some involvement.'

'There are other details.'

'So you have hinted. Perhaps if you shared these details with me, I could set your mind at rest regarding them too.'

'They cannot be divulged. The case is at a critical point.'

'Then you have me at a disadvantage. Will you at least inform me what you intend to do?'

'Regarding?'

'Regarding my connection with Setochkin.'

'I fear that I may have no choice but to notify Porfiry Petrovich of it. I advise you, Father, not to leave St Petersburg.'

Virginsky's father said nothing. Instead, he waved his son from the room, with a sharp, upward flick of his hand, and averted his gaze to the window where the blithe summer light streamed in.

*

Porfiry held one hand over his nose and mouth as he hurried over Kokushkin Bridge towards Stolyarny Lane, dipping his head into the noxious air of the canal. He felt the foulness against his eyes and blinked away the moisture that sprang to meet it. The rising arch of the bridge seemed to be shaped by a repulsion for what passed beneath. The pink-hued granite embankments that it spanned were streaked with dark stains, pointed fingers of filth around a slovenly tidemark. In the stone's permeability he saw the city's weakness. Here the stone was subtly, but inescapably, breached and into it seeped the water's malign influence, the turgid darkness Porfiry glimpsed and flinched from.

The thought came to him: *Everything is connected.*

Embankments linked by bridges, canals connecting rivers, rivers encompassing islands, islands coupled by bridges . . . and over this matrix was superimposed the network of buildings and courtyards, connected by passageways. You could cross the city on foot through the courtyards of apartment buildings.

As he stepped off the bridge, his head still stooped, eyes half-closed, he felt his shoulder hit the weighted momentum of another human being coming in the opposite direction. Half-turned by the impact, his pardon already begged, he looked up to see Dr Meyer, buffeted and dazed.

'It's you,' said Meyer.

'Yes.'

'They let me go.'

'I know. I ordered it.'

'But you were the one who had me arrested.'

'Yes. I am afraid that is sometimes necessary. Before we can apprehend the guilty, we must process the innocent.'

'Process. That is an interesting euphemism.'

'What will you do now, Dr Meyer?'

'I don't know. Work. There is always work.'

'Yes. I find that is the case.'

'You know,' said Meyer. 'I loved her once.'

'I know.'

'I mean, she was everything to me. It is true that recently . . .' Meyer frowned at the dirty canal. 'It is difficult to talk of these things.'

'Yes,' said Porfiry.

'And Grigory.' Meyer looked up at the investigator in puzzlement. 'They were all I had. And now they are gone.'

'What about . . . Polina?'

'No,' said Meyer, simply and sharply.

Porfiry nodded. 'You have your work. Your work is important.'

'Yes,' said Dr Meyer. His tone was strange and distant, as if he were thinking of something else entirely, some new thought that had suddenly captivated him. 'My work is important.'

*

A residue of despondency from his encounter with Dr Meyer dogged Porfiry as he climbed the stairs to the Haymarket District

Police Bureau. As he opened the door to the bureau itself, the din of human crisis and confusion, of people pushed to the edges of tolerance, was released, and other smells and other despondencies mingled with those he had brought with him. Of course, there were those who held themselves aloof from this, who remained silent and impassive and unmoving, who simply waited, with either meek or cunning eyes, as they calculated their fate.

The voice of one man cut through it all.

Lieutenant Salytov's reflex rage against the daily intrusion of humanity was part of the rhythm of the bureau, especially in the summer. They would come, in all their untidy, unruly variety, the wicked, the indigent, the worthless, victims and villains alike, and he, outraged at their presence, indignant at his own inability to hold them back, would produce from somewhere deep inside himself his snarling, half-strangled commands. And the more he shouted, the less attention they paid him. He may as well have issued orders to the flies that competed for air in the sweltering hall. Of course, this was a lesson that Salytov never learnt.

Porfiry knew from weary experience the difficulty of trying to conduct his own work, which amounted to nothing more or less than thinking, during one of Salytov's summer storms. This was not to say that he required, or even desired, absolute silence: the answering voice of another, whether an imagined other in his head or, preferably, a physical other in the room with him, was the vehicle by which his thought progressed, stoked of course by the endless supply of cigarette smoke. But now Porfiry felt the looming of a blank despair. He felt it pointless even to go into his chambers, where only the ripening stench from the Ditch and an insidious plague of flies awaited him. He even experienced a sympathetic intimation of Salytov's anger, and looked about him for an object on which to vent it.

Zamyotov was at his counter, sorting files, his face set in its habitual expression of detached superiority.

'Alexander Grigorevich.' Porfiry dispensed with his usual efforts to win over the head clerk. He felt a sense of liberation at the brusqueness of his tone. 'Have we received a reply to my letter about the Yekaterininsky Canal yet?'

Zamyotov looked up slowly, his startled disdain suggesting that all the impertinence was on Porfiry's side. He said nothing.

'I cannot be expected to work in these conditions,' continued Porfiry, unwisely, he knew.

'And I cannot be expected to do anything about it.' Zamyotov looked down dismissively.

'I merely asked you whether you were in receipt of a response from the authorities concerning my complaint.'

'Correct me if I am wrong, Porfiry Petrovich, but is it not the case that you make the same complaint every year? You know as well as I do how long it takes for the department responsible to process such complaints. If previous years are anything to go by, I am confident that we will receive a response, but not before the Yekaterininsky Canal has frozen over. By which time, of course, it will no longer be a problem.'

'You will inform me as soon as the official response comes in.'

'My my, it seems this weather is affecting everyone's --'

Just at this point, there was a blazing outburst from Salytov. 'Something must be done about that man,' said Porfiry, turning his back on Zamyotov.

*

'Nikodim Fomich, what on earth is the matter?'

It almost seemed as though another man was sitting in the chief superintendent's place. The features of this double bore some superficial resemblance to those of the good-natured, almost buffoonish man Porfiry knew. He had always considered Nikodim Fomich to be handsome, and yet a wrathful, snarling ugliness was deep-etched into the face before him now. Porfiry couldn't help wondering if this was the true Nikodim Fomich. In the shock of seeing his friend like this, his own ill temper was forgotten.

'He's done it again.'

'He?'

'Who else? Salytov.'

'Ah! It is Salytov that I have come to speak to you about. Have you heard the uproar that he is creating in the receiving hall?'

'Not again? He is quite incorrigible. After this other trouble, I might have thought he would prefer to exercise a little restraint.'

'What other trouble?'

'The boy from the confectioner's,' said Nikodim Fomich with heavy distaste. 'Salytov will not let go of the idea that he is in some way responsible for the Meyer poisonings. He persists in the idea that he is a political agitator. For whatever reason, he has been persecuting the boy. Without my authorisation, of course. We have received a complaint from the boy's employer. You know that Ballet's supplies confectionery to the Imperial Court? Salytov is threatening to close down the shop again. Imagine!'

'The man is a loose cannon,' exclaimed Porfiry, 'as I have had occasion to remark on numerous occasions.'

'Indeed. And one day he will go off in our faces.' Nikodim Fomich shook his head gravely.

'What will you do?'

'I have already reprimanded him, but it seems to make no difference. He shows no contrition, rather almost open defiance, bordering on insubordination. I am intending to put it all in a report. It will go before the disciplinary board.'

'They say you needn't be afraid of a barking dog,' said Porfiry. 'But I'm not so sure. Let's hope that the board views the matter with sufficient gravity.'

'I fear this may be the extinguishing of old Firecracker.'

'It is not as if he hasn't been warned,' said Porfiry, rather primly. He took out a cigarette and lit it. He welcomed the stimulative effects of the smoke, familiar and manageable when compared to the formless agitation of the day that he hoped to banish. He studied the end of his cigarette, then flashed a sly, almost shamefaced look at Nikodim Fomich. 'However . . .' he began, then broke off. 'No, no, it's too ridiculous.'

'What?' snapped Nikodim Fomich.

'What if there is something in it, though?' said Porfiry. He gave every impression of being appalled by the suggestion he had just made.

'Are you mad?' Nikodim Fomich's expression darkened even more. 'Or is this another of your pranks, Porfiry Petrovich?'

'I'm quite serious, and, as far as I am able to say, sane. I rejected Ilya Petrovich's idea previously because the simpler explanation seemed to be that Dr Meyer was responsible for the deaths of his wife and son. Now, as you know, that does not seem likely. The investigation has opened out. We cannot afford to rule out any line of enquiry.'

'But surely it is preposterous! A revolutionary cell at a confectioner's!'

'You're right. I'm sorry I mentioned it.' Porfiry continued smoking. He licked his upper lip apprehensively. 'But what if this Tolya and his associates were, at some time in the future, able to poison the chocolates of the Imperial household?'

'I have to warn you, Porfiry Petrovich, that I am in no mood for such jokes.'

'And what if that happened and we were found to have ignored Salytov's warnings?' Porfiry insisted.

'But I thought you were pursuing the possibility of a connection between the Meyer poisoning and the Setochkin case?' Nikodim Fomich's voice was strained with exasperation. 'Were you not interested in the link provided by this mysterious guest? I rather thought you believed him to be the murderer in both cases. Is he then linked to the confectioner's too? Is he a political agitator? How do the deaths of Raisa and Grigory Meyer and Colonel Setochkin further his cause?'

'I don't know. At present we know nothing about him. He is as unquantifiable as the X on one side of an algebraic equation. I feel very strongly that this figure is significant. But I cannot prove it. Therefore, it is reasonable to consider every possibility.'

'And yet you have ruled out Meyer.'

'Dr Meyer did not murder his wife and child. I can tell you that from having talked to the man. On the other hand, I can tell you nothing about the Uninvited One, other than the fact that he visited a brothel fourteen years ago in the company of Ruslan Vladimirovich Vakhramev, on which occasion he had sex with Raisa Meyer. But I have not looked into his eyes. I have not listened to the timbre of his voice. I do not even know his name, though I know where to look for it.'

'And where is that?'

'I have received from the Ministry of Education a list of the private boarding schools in Moscow. We have sent for their records from the years at which Golyadkin would have been of high-school age. Given that his age when he died this year was forty-seven, I have asked for the records for the years between 1833 and 1845.'

'But that will be like looking for a needle in a haystack. And how will you know the name when you see it?'

'I am not sure that I will. Unless the name occurs in some other context related to one or other of these cases.'

'And if you find such a recurrence, you will have found your murderer?'

'Possibly. At the very least, I will have found another connection.'

'Or another meaningless coincidence. Allow me to remind you of something, Porfiry Petrovich. One usually solves algebraic equations through the exercise of logic, not wild guesswork.'

'But, in criminal investigations, logic is only one of the tools that we may use.'

'Surely you are not advocating the use of guesswork too?'

'Not guesswork,' said Porfiry, placing the cigarette to his lips. After exhaling, he continued: 'I would not call it that. But sometimes one is drawn towards certain irrational ideas. One must explore them.'

'What other random coincidences are you investigating?'

'None, for the moment. And I am not sure that I agree quite with your designation of coincidences as random. I have often found that when such an individual as the Uninvited One begins his work, connections, correspondences and, yes, coincidences, begin to occur. They are merely the outward manifestations -- the symptoms, if you will -- of a murderous pathology visiting itself on the social organism. Of course, the danger is that one sees a pattern where there is none. How is one to distinguish the significant from the contingent? For example, Dr Meyer visited a lunatic asylum at which Tolya's mother was once an inmate. Perhaps, as Pavel Pavlovich would have me believe, that is the connection I should be pursuing. However, one must be methodical. Investigate one possibility, rule it out, then move on to the next.'

'In other words, this is all you have to go on.' The chief superintendent's shoulders began to shake in mirthless laughter.

'I'm glad to see that your humour has improved, Nikodim Fomich.'

'There is nothing like the misfortune of others to cheer one up.'

Porfiry frowned, as if hurt by his friend's easy callousness. 'Regarding Lieutenant Salytov, perhaps we should assign resources to investigate the confectioner's on an authorised basis? A round-the-clock surveillance of the suspect individuals might be advisable.'

'He acted without my authorisation! That would be to reward him. Really you are quite impossible, Porfiry Petrovich. You come in here up in arms against him, and now here you are taking his side.'

'One must be flexible. Of course, we could simply communicate his suspicions to the Third Section and allow them to take over.'

'Do you really wish to involve those snakes?'

'If there is a secret plot against the state, they are the correct office to deal with it.'

'I don't like them. They make me nervous.'

'Why, Nikodim Fomich? Surely you have nothing to fear from them?'

'No more than you, Porfiry Petrovich.' Nikodim Fomich gave his friend a wounded look. 'I disapprove of their methods. There is too much reliance on dirty tricks.'

'They would claim that their methods are necessary, especially since the assassination attempt on our beloved Tsar. They are fighting the enemies of our way of life, men -- and women -- who have shown themselves prepared to stop at nothing.'

'Yes, yes, I understand all that. Even so . . .'

'Perhaps you will find that you have no choice. Once this goes before the disciplinary board, they may well decide that Salytov's suspicions require further investigation. Indeed it could possibly end in a commendation for him.'

'You cannot be serious, Porfiry Petrovich?'

Porfiry shrugged. 'Who knows what view they will take of the matter.'

'Then what do you suggest I do?'

'You must do whatever you feel is necessary.'

'I do so hate it when you say that, Porfiry Petrovich.' Nikodim Fomich seemed once again to have been possessed by his bad-tempered double. He resolutely avoided Porfiry's eye.

9: Golyadkin's classmates

As Martin Meyer's foot pressed down on the first board of the veranda, the empty dacha groaned in protest. The veranda had been cleaned, the wrought-iron chairs set right and replaced around the marble-topped table. *Polina*. Meyer's glance skimmed across the table towards the door, as if expecting it to open, wife and son coming out to meet him. But, of course, he had to cross the devastated space himself and place his own hand on the door to open it.

As he entered the interior of the dacha, an alien silence confronted him. It was as if the house had stopped breathing. The silence unsettled him; he felt it as something malign and unfathomable. He cast his gaze about as if looking for it. And then, he saw it -- or rather the source of it: the grandfather clock, which stood, unwound, untended, a film of dust dulling its cherry wood surface; dumbstruck, emanating the silence that judged him.

He stood unmoving in the centre of the room, listening. At last, he began to hear the small sounds that possessed the dacha in the absence of humanity, the scratching of mice, the scuttling of insects, the clicks and creaks of the timbers adjusting to the sun's transit through the day. The wooden cottage acted like a sounding box, picking up and amplifying these sounds until he, in the centre of it, shook with their reverberations.

The convulsion released him from his fearful immobility. He walked the length of the room, each footfall a hammerblow on the past, irreversible. His steps took him only to the piano, the lid still lifted, the album of folk songs open on the music rest. The keyboard seemed to possess a strange resilience; he had the feeling that the keys would not yield to his touch were he to lay his fingers on them. But a kind of horror prevented him from trying. The instrument had always been hers, and so much represented her that it had taken on the significance of her remains. To press a key would have felt like a desecration. He did not have the right, no one had, he least of all. Besides, he couldn't play, had no feeling for music at all.

He stood over the keyboard, looking down at it, willing it to sound of its own accord. Then, unexpectedly, his hand reached out and he pressed a key in the centre of the keyboard. His touch was gentle. The note it produced, faltering and awed. He pressed again, more firmly, on the same key. The inhuman brightness of the note this time appalled him. A terrible pressure welled inside him, an expanding force in his chest. Then the tears came. They fell on to the piano keys. It was almost as if he expected them to depress the keys and cause the hammers to strike, with such a heavy, laden force did he imagine his tears falling. But, of course, this remained a sentimental fantasy. The tiny puddles spread, weightless, noiseless, on the ivory.

With the clock's ticking suspended, it seemed that he existed outside time. There was a strange sense too of squaring up to the future. How long it was before he turned his back on the piano, he could not say. Nor how long it took him to cross the room and enter his study. It seemed that he was moving through a more viscous element than he was used to, one charged with hostility.

He could tell immediately that the room had been interfered with. They had been there, rifling through his papers. The lid of the escritoire was open, the drawer pulled out. He pulled it further and it fell out of his hands on to the floor with a hooligan clatter. Meyer's hands shot up to cover his ears. His body writhed in an evasive flinch. But there was nothing to evade, except the noise and its aftermath. When that had finally died, he sank to a crouch to sort the debris. With the new slowness that characterised all his movements now, the infinite patience of a man without purpose, he put the scattered papers back into the drawer. The realisation came upon him gradually: they had taken all the photographs. The blank that was his marriage, his family, his life, was complete. They had even, he discovered, taken the one recourse left to him, the small bottle that would allow him to cover one blankness, agonising and self-aware, with another, blissful and oblivious.

They had left him with nothing.

*

'Yes, come in, Pavel Pavlovich,' said Porfiry, looking up from behind his desk. He winced a perfunctory smile. 'I have a task for you.' He shook a thick sheaf of papers for Virginsky to take. 'These have just come in from Moscow. They are the lists of relevant pupils from all the private boarding schools in Moscow.'

Virginsky took the sheets almost reluctantly. There was

something self-conscious about his movements as he scanned them. He said nothing.

'I wish you to look for the name Golyadkin on the lists,' continued Porfiry. 'And to draw up a secondary list of all the boys who were ever in the same class as him. It should not be so difficult. There will be a certain amount of re-duplication as the pupils move up the years.'

'Of course.'

'An investigation may progress in a number of ways. There will always be times when our work is more laborious than otherwise. A crime is often solved when a connection is made between the victim and the perpetrator. Very rarely do these connections leap out at us. We must go looking for them.'

Virginsky nodded but seemed reluctant to move away and begin the task. 'Porfiry Petrovich,' he said at last, tentatively.

'Yes? What is it?'

'My father knew Setochkin.'

'I see.' Porfiry Petrovich sat up sharply. 'Why did you not tell me this before?'

Virginsky could not answer, except by colouring deeply.

'Or let me put it another way, why are you telling me now?'

'I felt sure there was nothing in it. I wished to protect my father from unnecessary inconvenience.'

'How very thoughtful of you. However, something has changed your mind?'

'There is another connection you should be aware of. One that may make the first seem less coincidental.'

Porfiry inclined his head, waiting, his expression severe.

'My father went to school in Moscow. He was a pupil at a private boarding school, the Chermak Private High School. His age is such that his name will be on these lists.'

'I see.' Porfiry nodded thoughtfully. 'Perhaps you should start with this Chermak School. You will then set your mind at rest straightaway.'

'And what if I find the name Golyadkin there? In the same class as my father, even?'

'That would be interesting. At any rate, I would very much like to meet your father, if you do not think it would inconvenience him too much.'

'Porfiry Petrovich, I am very much aware that in attempting to fulfil my duties as a son, I may well have neglected those of my office. I have done wrong. I would prefer to receive your reprimand than your sarcasm.'

'Pavel Pavlovich, I do not blame you. After all, there are some coincidences that are simply coincidences. I suspect this is one of them. There are so many connections now in the cases before us that I fear we have created a veritable net of them. If we are not careful, it will entrap us.' Porfiry looked around him, with a vaguely menacing air.

'Is it not supposed to entrap the murderer?'

'That is the intention.' Porfiry's smile was conciliatory. His tone softened. 'Work on the lists. As for your father, it would be best if I met him informally. We really have no grounds for issuing a summons. Perhaps you could invite him here to see your place of work. I am sure he would welcome the opportunity to discuss your prospects with your superior.'

'My father is not as interested in my career as you might suppose. I am not sure that he would respond to any invitation from me. We parted on bad terms. He did not appreciate my efforts on his behalf. I was trying to ascertain for myself the nature of his involvement with Colonel Setochkin. As it turned out, it was a business transaction, the sale of some land. My father chose to consider himself under suspicion and took umbrage.'

'I command you to be reconciled with him.'

It seemed that Virginsky was not attuned to the nuances of Porfiry's irony.

'I understand. It is for the good of the investigation.'

'Foolish boy, I was not thinking of the investigation, but of your own good.'

Virginsky looked down, abashed. 'I shall work through these lists,' he said.

*

Porfiry studied the list of names Virginsky had drawn up:
BOTKIN, P. P
DOLGORUKY, F. D.
KALGONOV, P. P.
KARAMAZOV, P. P.
KIRILLOV, Z. R.

KRASOTKIN, B. P.
KRAFT, M. M.
LEBEZYANTIKOV, I. A.
MAKAROV, M. S.
MAXIMOV, N. F.
MUSOV, O. A.
MUSSYALOVICH, Y. S.
NELYADOV, L. T.
NIKIFOROV, N. N.
OSTAFYN, S. S.
PERKHOTIN, G. O.
POTAPYCH, M. M.
PRALINSKY, R. D.
PSEDONIMOV, I. I.
RAKITIN, S. A.
ROGOZHIN, K. R.
SAMSONOV, M. Y.
SHATOV, K. L.
SHIPULENKO, O. O.
SMERDYAKOV, P. P.
SNEGINYOV, A. A.
STAVROGIN, M. T.
SVIDRIGAILOV, V. V.
TERENTEV, B. K.
TIKHON, E. D.
TOTSKY, T. E.
VALKOVSKY, D. I.
VARVINSKY, G. S.
VERKHOVERSKY, A. A.
VERKHOVSEV, T. G.
VRUBLEVSKY, F. M.
YEFIMOV, M. I.

'I found the name Golyadkin,' explained Virginsky. 'B. B. Golyadkin attended the Chermak High School from eighteen thirty-four to forty. These are the names of all the boys who were ever in the same class as him.'

Porfiry laid the list down on his desk and smiled reassuringly. 'I do not see the name Virginsky here.'

'My father was in the year above Golyadkin.'

'I wonder if he remembers him.' Porfiry made the comment casually, almost as if it had no importance.

'You know, Porfiry Petrovich,' began Virginsky hesitantly, 'with respect, it may be that the Uninvited One, though a schoolfriend of Golyadkin's, was not in fact in his class.'

'You speak as if you almost wish to discover your father to be the murderer.'

'Not at all. However, it is simply that I fear we may do better to cast our net a little wider. Why limit the list to those who were in Golyadkin's class?'

'Because we have to start somewhere.' Porfiry pushed across his desk a leather-bound ledger book. 'This is the order book from Ballet's. Your next task is to look here for occurrences of the names you have picked out. If you find any, good. We will investigate them. If not, then we shall, as you say, cast our net wider, and look for names from the other classes in Golyadkin's year, and then from the years on either side of him, and so on. To narrow the search initially, is simply a practical measure.'

Virginsky picked up the book. 'But could not these correspondences, if there are any, lead us away from the murderer just as easily as towards him? If they are simply coincidences, I mean. Besides, there may be many men with the same surnames and initials. It does not necessarily indicate the same individual. You will notice the name Maximov, N. F. Do you suppose that may be our esteemed Chief Superindendent Nikodim Fomich Maximov?'

'That would indeed be a remarkable coincidence,' said Porfiry, smiling to himself.

Virginsky flicked through the pages of the book. 'I see it only goes back to April this year.'

'Don't worry,' said Porfiry. 'I have ten others for you to look at when you have finished with that.'

*

He couldn't say how long he had been looking at the maps. It was something he always used to do: look at the maps and wander in his mind along the avenues, across the squares, through the courtyards of St Petersburg. When the opium took hold of him there was nowhere he couldn't go. Even the rooftops were his; he would swoop over them like the all-possessing gaze of an angel on St Isaac's Cathedral. But without the operation of that balm, in which time and space unfolded like the petals of a complex and beautiful flower, the maps remained simply maps, ink imprinted on paper. He could hardly make sense of them. He pored over them, knowing that they held some meaning, but not quite grasping what it was. Yet somehow they held him, until his hunger began to twist.

Flies of all sizes possessed the pantry, buzzing greedily around the last mould-infested crust of bread, the collapsed fruit and seething meat.

Meyer fled the dacha, and the rotten remnants of a life that it contained.

Music from somewhere -- a pleasure boat? -- came at him in a cloud of gnats. He swatted at it uselessly and lurched away from the dacha with blundering step, tripped by the weight of a sudden exhaustion.

The music put an idea into his head: Bezmygin. He would confront the hated Bezmygin. He could hear the man's pernicious influence, the grating bow-scrape over strings, in the strains that reached him.

Meyer walked blindly, not even following the music, or not consciously so. His hunger pangs returned, almost to console him, reminding him of his humanity. From somewhere came the thought: *One should not contemplate such things on an empty stomach.* And yet he would not articulate what he was contemplating, indeed had not realised he was until that moment.

He came to the river, a brooding expanse that seemed to absorb the dusky light without giving anything back. Flecks of movement bobbed briefly on its surface before sinking into the darkness beneath. Pools of light and laughter from the lantern-decked boats hovered above it. They poured out music, and all other sounds of enjoyment. In the need to keep the music coming, he saw a fatal desperation. If the music stopped, all that would be left would be the dark abyss of the river and the blank sky above. The boats and the people on them would be absorbed.

In the distance, the flames of the rostral towers flickered uncertainly. They held nothing for him, nor was he drawn to them.

Beyond them, the city awaited his coming like a spider's web. But he was already footsore and exhausted. He hungered but had no appetite. There was nowhere for him to go, only a dead and empty dacha to flee from.

He stepped on to a big, stone-built bridge spanning the river's full width. There were no names any more, not for the island he was quitting, nor even for the city that lay across the nameless river.

At the mid-point of the bridge, he climbed the balustrade and stood for a moment poised against the pull of the turning earth. One step forward would take him away from the swirling clash of music, into silence. He closed his eyes and imagined taking that step. He imagined his fall. How long would he have to flail his limbs in the air? In his mind, the fall took for ever; the slam of the water never came. He opened his eyes and looked down into the lapping darkness.

His body swayed forwards, giving in to the allure of gravity. He looked up, away from the river, tears blurring his vision, and continued to lean into the empty air. A sickening internal shift carried his body with it. He passed the point of control. The lean became a lurch. He felt his legs buckle.

There were voices behind him. Someone called out the words of a psalm.

His arms thrashed out, winging the air. He bent his knees and lowered his centre of gravity to recover his balance.

It was not that he wanted to live. It was just that he could not bring himself to die. He allowed the hands on his legs and waist to pull him back. He surrendered himself to the grip of strangers.

PART THREE: Poniard

1: The fallen man

'The Lord is my shepherd: I shall not want!'
Yemelyan Antonovich Ferfichkin shouted the words at the man swaying on the balustrade. He crossed himself twice and moved away from the commotion on the Tuchkov Bridge, away from the memory of the man's face as he tottered on the railings, balanced for a moment between life and death. He did not wait to see the outcome. The face had seemed familiar. The more Ferfichkin thought about it, the more convinced he became that he recognised the wretch. It was, without doubt, one of his enemies.

'A suicide is no good to anyone,' he muttered scornfully. 'Especially one who throws himself in the Neva.' He pointed into the air emphatically as he spoke. It was a habit that came from living alone, this talking aloud to himself -- or rather to an imagined audience. He had seen children, and even those old enough to know better, laugh at him to his face, not even bothering to hide their mockery behind their hands.

An unaccountable sense of guilt, as if he were to blame for the man's predicament, hounded him as he moved south. 'R-r-ridiculous!' he called out with a defiant laugh. The glances he attracted were wary. He scowled back and even bared his teeth. It was simply a bizarre coincidence that he should see this man, whose name he couldn't even remember -- 'German, wasn't he? That was it!' -- but with whom he had almost certainly quarrelled at some point in the past; that he should see him tonight, on midsummer's night of all nights, for the first time in God knows how many years, at possibly the ultimate moment of the scoundrel's life. For, whoever the fellow was, whatever his name, Yemelyan Antonovich Ferfichkin was certain that he had to be a scoundrel. None but scoundrels and sinners took their own lives.

Naturally, it unsettled him. Coming on top of the day's events, the rather nasty scene with Gorshkov, it was no wonder that it got to him. His nerves were frayed. 'Understandable,' he cried.

He had braced himself for the inevitable splash but it had not come and he had moved too far away to hear it now. It hung over him like the sense of unfinished business.

He was tempted to return home. There was work waiting for him there, always work to be done, money to be earned by the plying of the needle, or the weaving of words. There was another one to be buried tomorrow. Ferfichkin would need to spend some time beforehand browsing the Good Book, letting the words enter him, joining the words that were already there, so that he could call on them when he needed them: by the graveside. He needn't worry, he knew. The right words always came to him.

Again he felt a strange nagging guilt. He was thinking of the Bible in his room and his conscience was not entirely easy. 'What do you want with me?' The question was not for the faces that turned to him, faces lit by the promise and excitement of the night. He realised that it was the Bible that had driven him out, that and the terrible, aching loneliness that always came upon him at night, especially in the brilliant, restless nights of summer.

Once it had been his friend. 'My salvation,' he even declared, the emotion in his eyes. Had he not taught himself Church Slavonic, in order to accept more wholly the word of the Lord, to take it upon himself and to give it to others? Had it turned against him, or was the fault his own? He could not understand where it had come from, this sense of reproach that he experienced now whenever he was alone with the Bible.

'A man's first duty is to himself,' he pleaded. The silence that answered him held a devastating rebuke.

No, he could not go back home, to the emptiness of his room, and the Bible's sullen presence.

It was all Gorshkov's fault, no doubt. The words that man had said to him. 'How dare he?' Who did he think he was? Could Ferfichkin be blamed for the other's improvidence? These people would bleed him dry if he let them.

'I have to live!' he called out.

The image of the man who had thrown himself off the Tuchkov Bridge came back to him. He too was probably some feckless wastrel like Gorshkov, a fool who blamed others for the consequences of his own sinful ways. Ferfichkin was not ready to follow him into the Neva, not yet at least.

As he rounded the tip of Vasilevsky Island he repeated the words of the twenty-third Psalm: 'The Lord is my shepherd: I shall not want.'

Without pausing in his stride along the University Embankment, he took out a battered pewter flask from the inside of his frock coat. The squeak of the cork released a whiff of harsh spirit. He lifted it quickly to his lips, eager for the fierce communion, but also not wishing to spill any of the vodka through the jog of his step.

'He restores my soul!' Although his eye was eager now, and his voice aggravated by bravado, there was an edge of desperation to the words. It was more a plea than an assertion.

*

He was stitching his way across the city, west to east to west again, moving south all the time, and quaffing from the flask with almost every step.

There were tavern doors along his way, with steps leading down to them, but he resisted their beckoning wafts. He had no need of them, not while he had vodka of his own. Besides, he could hide from his enemies in a dark cellar but not from the eyes of the Lord.

He remembered, and recited in Church Slavonic, the words of the twenty- sixth Psalm. He believed he saw wonder in the eyes of those he passed. 'Yes! I have the word of God within me!' He shouted a Russian equivalent of the text after them as they fled his excitement: 'I have not sat down with the vain, neither will I go in with those who dissemble. I have hated the company of evildoers; I will not sit with the wicked.'

He found himself crossing a great sea of paving stones, blue whorls that swam beneath his staggering feet. He thought of Jesus walking on the water. The blasphemy of the connection, to compare himself in a state of inebriation to the Son of God performing a miracle, both frightened and liberated him.

He looked up and saw the angel on top of the towering Alexander Column. 'Come down from there if you have something to say to me,' shouted Ferfichkin. But the heaven-distracted figure ignored him.

Ferfichkin stumbled on; the stone waters of the Palace Square grew turbulent and treacherous. The Winter Palace, recently painted red ochre, shimmered like a distant shore; the sky's soft glow seemed to draw the substance from it and from everything around it. He looked again at the angel, almost fearfully now, as if he expected the statue to take flight, drawn by the weightless night. A leaden feeling gripped his heart, halfway between the dread of belief and the terrible loneliness of atheism.

The only thing left to him was the vodka. But it wasn't long before he had drained that. A misery, a grief worse than the loss of his God, voided him.

His listing trajectory took him into the arms of passing strangers, who pushed him away in disgust. 'Have I never believed, then?' he demanded of them.

From one to the other he was passed, in a wilder mazurka than any danced inside the palace ballrooms.

'In that case, what was it all for?' But at the same time as he formed the question, the answer came to him, an answer he struggled to suppress, overlaying protestations of his piety: 'No one, not even the holy brothers who clothe themselves in the Scriptures, the monks of Optina Pustyn, no one has immersed themselves in the word of God more than I. The hours of my life I have given to that book! And why? If I did not believe? You cannot tell me I do not believe,' he shouted into the face of a cavalry officer who evidently had no such intention.

He hurried from the square on to Millionnaya. Between the gaudy millionaires' palaces and the stinking Moika, a pack of wild dogs roamed. The dogs were of all sizes, the products of unimaginable miscegenations, absurdly mismatched as a group, and yet bound together by some instinct of canine community. Restless and excitable, they sniffed the air and each others' arses, nipping, yelping, circling, the smallest ones somehow seeming to be the most aggressive. No doubt they were animated by hunger. However, their banding together against it, their ragged solidarity, amazed him. He almost envied them. Ferfichkin had known hunger. But it had never occurred to him to seek its alleviation by associating with others in the same plight. 'It's every man for himself,' he shouted at the dogs, as if remonstrating with them. 'Dog eat dog!' It was a command, or at least an encouragement.

Ferfichkin stood and swayed. The pack of dogs paid him no regard but ran howling up Millionnaya towards the Field of Mars. He felt an instant nostalgia at their departure and realised in that moment how alone he was. He hungered after company, even though the whole basis of his life was self-sufficiency.

'No man is my master,' he shouted up the empty street, after the baying dogs. 'God is my master.' But the words rang hollow.

He set off at a run after the dogs; somehow it seemed important not to let them out of his sight. He was chasing not a pack of wild dogs, but the idea of kinship.

The idea took him across the empty parade ground, where the unseen ghosts of dead battalions were marshalled, into the Summer Garden.

As he entered the enclosure he had the sense of crossing over into a place of magic and awe, a grotto. The dumbstruck, sightless men and women that lined the criss-crossing avenues slowed his step and cowed him. Naked allegories, fabulous pagan beings, they inspired an irrational dread in him. He had a sense of them moving behind his back, but whenever he turned, they were frozen in their original position, the lyre unplucked, the sweep of concealing drapery still miraculously in place.

In amongst the statuary, people of flesh and blood moved, a congregation of sinners, for the most part eschewing the formal paths, the women undoubtedly whores, the men drunks. Ferfichkin slurringly repeated the words of the Psalm: 'I have hated the company of evildoers.' There was laughter from the trees. He threw out a hand towards it and stumbled on, his step unsteady as much from exhaustion as from the drink now.

He lurched from statue to statue, passed now between a different set of strangers, who showed their disgust by keeping their stony heads averted from him.

He could no longer see the dogs but the din of their hunt was louder than ever.

He staggered into one of the sinners who had wandered on to the path.

Ferfichkin looked into this man's face. 'You!' he cried.

The man pushed him away, with the same disgust that those on Millionnaya had shown. Ferfichkin fell to the ground. The man stepped over him and went on his way.

Ferfichkin did not stir. No one troubled themselves about the drunk fallen to the ground. No doubt they had themselves slept in places just as strange.

*

Morning came more stealthily than usual. With infinite gradation, the soft etiolated light became emboldened. The old drunk was still there. He had not changed his position. The *politseisky* who found him couldn't rouse him and when he turned the man over, he saw why.

The fine, long handle of a bladed weapon protruded from a circle of blood on the man's chest, exactly where you might estimate his heart to be.

2: Nikolai Nobody

The day grew heavy with the humidity of a storm held back. The sweltering pressure affected the flies in Porfiry's room badly. They became reckless, crazed, hurling themselves at the panes of the window and into the faces of the men who came and went. As for the men, a short-tempered impatience characterised their dealings as they awaited barometric release. The morning was a series of obstacles they had to move through.

Virginsky, for whom a desk had been installed in the corner by the window, continued to sort through the records of the confectioner's, comparing the names there to those he had gleaned from the school lists. But it was hard to concentrate, not just because of the heat and the intrusive buzz of the flies around his head. Frequently he would look up from his task, peering out of the window in anxious expectation. Whenever there was a knock at the door of the chambers, he would start in his seat, turning a drained and apprehensive face to see who entered. Invariably, it was one of the clerks with correspondence for Porfiry; Virginsky would bow his head once more over the ledger book, relieved for the moment, only to nourish his apprehension for a while longer.

'How are you getting on?' The sound of Porfiry's voice suddenly so close startled him.

'Nothing so far,' said Virginsky, his voice unexpectedly tremulous. He waited for Porfiry to go but the magistrate remained silently at his shoulder. Virginsky turned his head and looked up. The other man's expression was mildly distracted.

'Porfiry Petrovich?'

Porfiry seemed taken aback by the brusqueness of Virginsky's tone. He creased his brow.

'May I make an observation?'

Porfiry nodded.

'This method strikes me as inherently flawed.'

'Indeed?'

'I would go so far as to say that it is a waste of my time. A fruitless exercise.'

'I regret that you find it so.'

'For one thing, can we really suppose that the murderer was so foolish as to give his real name to the shop from which he bought the chocolates he intended to poison? For another, not every customer who shops at Ballet's will have his name entered here. These books only record those who have accounts, or place orders. The casual transaction, paid for in cash, will leave no trace. Is that not the case?'

Porfiry's eyelashes batted away Virginsky's objections. 'We can make no assumptions. We must investigate every possibility, however remote. This search may turn up a name, or it may not. One thing is certain though: if we do not look, we will not find. A criminal investigation does not proceed by guesswork, but by painstaking, methodical examination of all available evidence.'

'But even if I find a name, it could mean nothing.'

'That is perfectly true. However, it could, on the other hand, mean something. I'm afraid, Pavel Pavlovich, that there will be times when you will have almost nothing to go on. And that almost nothing may be so close to nothing as to be mistaken for it.'

'But . . .'

Porfiry raised an eyebrow forbiddingly. Virginsky shook his head and turned away in disappointment. He did not see Porfiry's relenting smile.

'Pavel Pavlovich, is there something else you wish to say to me?'

Virginsky turned quickly in his seat. 'I had thought that your methods were more subtle than this. I believed that you used psychology and the exercise of intellect to solve your cases. I had hoped to learn the art of deductive reasoning from you. But I see that you repeatedly have recourse to the bluntest of tools, trial and error. And more frequently the latter than the former, if I am honest.'

'Please do be honest. Indeed, I would not have you be otherwise.'

Virginsky paused briefly as he weighed Porfiry's smile. 'I have said too much.'

'Not at all.'

'It is not for me to criticise you. You are my superior. I must obey you without challenging your commands, however nonsensical they appear.'

'I do not want that kind of obedience. I . . . I welcome your challenging comments.'

'I find that hard to believe.'

'But it's true, I assure you. So much so that I command you to continue your observations.'

Virginsky regarded Porfiry sceptically for a moment. But he found that there was so much he wished to say that he did not allow his doubts to restrain him. 'Very well, if you insist. You have so far arrested two men, both of whom you have since been forced to release, as you once arrested and released me. Would it not have been better to have first made sure of the evidence against these individuals? You allowed, it seems to me, your prejudices to influence your actions. Most poisonings are committed by doctors, therefore the doctor must have done it. Vakhramev was found with the pistol in his hand, therefore he must have shot Setochkin. This simplistic reasoning has led to elementary mistakes, has it not?'

Porfiry smiled, though the colour at his cheeks revealed his pique. 'One can always release an innocent man whom one has detained. It is less easy to bring back to life the victim of a murderer one has allowed to go free. Now if I may make an observation of my own. You seem to be out of sorts this morning, Pavel Pavlovich. Your present ill mood would not be occasioned by the imminent arrival of your father and stepmother, would it?'

Virginsky turned sharply away from Porfiry.

'It's natural that you should experience a feeling of tension at the prospect; equally understandable that you should transfer your complicated, but largely negative feelings towards your father on to me. It could be said that I stand *in loco parentis* to you here at the bureau.' Now it was Virginsky who felt the heat rise in his face; he was thankful he was looking away from Porfiry. A sky laden with hostile energy pressed at the window. 'You are in a difficult position as far as your father is concerned,' continued Porfiry. 'You entertain an unhealthy resentment towards him, which derives from your inadmissible feelings for your stepmother. In the exercise of your official duty, you have brought your father into our investigation. In all conscience, you could not have done otherwise, and I commend you. And yet, you cannot dispel from your heart the suspicion that you are acting out of revenge. This in its turn generates powerful feelings of unworthiness, disloyalty and guilt. You cannot forget that, whatever he has done to you, indeed whatever crime at all he may be guilty of, he is still your father and you are still his son. Naturally, you do not wish your father to be found a murderer, or even a man of reduced honour. You have already discovered that he is not the hero you once imagined him to be. You can never put him back on the pedestal. All that is left for you to do, it seems, is to witness his further degradation, each step of which you experience as if it were your own. In his fall from grace, your father takes you down with him. In addition to that, the day is oppressively humid.'

Still without turning, Virginsky stiffened in his seat. 'So you do not accept any of my criticisms. You dismiss them with this psychology?'

'I accept that there is some truth in everything you have said. And yet you must accept too that I had no choice but to act in the way that I did. Necessity guided my steps. A criminal investigation is like a journey to an unknown destination. We have neither map nor itinerary. The only determination we are allowed is that of choosing a direction when we come to a fork in the road. Perhaps there will be signs along the way, but we must never forget that they may be pointing in the wrong direction and may even have been positioned deliberately to mislead us. All we can do is set out and continue upon our way. If we take a wrong turning, we must simply retrace our steps. In any event, one must remain calm and decisive.'

'I distrust fanciful analogies,' said Virginsky.

'Really?' answered Porfiry. 'I have to confess I am rather fond of them.'

The door opened with barely a warning rap. Virginsky looked round at last. 'There are some people here,' said Zamyotov. 'Will you see them?'

Virginsky and Porfiry exchanged a colluding smile. 'Would it be possible for you to give me more information than that upon which to base my decision?' asked Porfiry.

'They appear to be related to him.' Zamyotov gave the most minimal of glances in Virginsky's direction.

Virginsky's apprehension solidified into a sickening weight above his stomach. It appalled him to see Porfiry's chipper step as he turned in welcome. 'Of course! Show them in. We are expecting them.'

Natalya Ivanovna came into the room first. Her step was brisk and possessing; her face lit up with a simple -- Virginsky might even have said natural -- eagerness. There was no hint from her of the tensions that had arisen during the last family meeting. And yet it was certainly significant that she led the way while Virginsky's father hung back as if hiding behind her beauty, or rather sending it before him as a peace offering. Virginsky had no eye for, or understanding of, fashion. Even so, he judged her dress to be startlingly advanced in style, as well as exquisitely cut from emerald-green shot silk. Its curves were fuller and more indicative of the body beneath than he was used to seeing; the white muslin underskirt, more revealed. The hoops of the crinoline, if indeed it could be called a crinoline, projected only at the back. As agitatingly novel as all this struck him, there was also an undeniable rightness to it, a perfect, unbrookable inevitability. It was a dress designed to set everything right, and it very nearly did. She brought with her too a freshness which alleviated the day.

Virginsky had to acknowledge that his father's reticence was mirrored by his own: although he had by now risen from his desk, he positioned himself behind Porfiry, using him as shield and proxy in the same way that his father used his young wife.

We are more alike than we know. Virginsky dismissed the thought immediately and refused to look directly at his father. He felt a kind of anticipatory disgust at the idea of his father's face. Knowing the man, knowing what he was capable of, it amazed him that he could walk into a room with his head held high, without any trace of contrition or shame on his features. Brazenly, in other words, for that was how Virginsky felt sure his father would choose to present himself now. Then it occurred to him that the true reason for the bitterness of his feelings lay in the similarity of those features to his own. Just as he resembled his father physically, he was inevitably drawn to the conclusion that he must take after him in other respects, morally for example. How could he be any better than his father? Did he really have the right to set himself above the man? He had in the past pinned his hopes on the admixture of qualities from his mother. But now he was not so sure that he had received anything from her other than a fatal weakness of character, which merely compounded the vicious tendencies he must have inherited from his other parent. All at once, his cherished ideals struck him as alien to his true nature, as much a posture as his father's self-righteous assumption of integrity. All this was, of course, more reason to hate the man.

At last his fascination became too much for him. He sought his father's eye and found its glance at once more complicated and more human than he had allowed for. He saw that his father was seeking him out, and seeking something from him too. But whether it was forgiveness or complicity, he could not tell. His only option was to shake his head and look away.

Porfiry's greetings carried them over the moment: 'Ah, welcome to you, madam . . . sir. I am Porfiry Petrovich.'

'Pavel Pavlovich the elder,' said Virginsky's father with a dignified bow. 'Allow me to introduce my wife, Natalya Ivanovna.'

'It is a pleasure to be able to extend the hand of friendship to the parents of my own dear Pavel Pavlovich the younger.'

Virginsky wanted to correct the misunderstanding, or misrepresentation, in this. 'She is not my parent,' he said, but his father spoke at the same time and it was his words that were attended to.

'I am delighted to receive it. The hand of friendship, that is. I had been led to believe by my son that it would be the finger of suspicion that you would be extending towards us.'

This, Virginsky thought, was typical of his father: to defuse the issue by making a joke of it, as if he could extricate himself from any difficulty by the exercise of affability. How could such a charming fellow be guilty of involvement in a crime? The very idea was ridiculous, it seemed.

Porfiry smiled. 'Yes, your son has informed me of your acquaintance with Colonel Setochkin.'

'A terrible business,' said Virginsky's father, suddenly solemn, as if his earlier witticism had been about something entirely different.

'Indeed. Was he a good friend of yours?'

'More of a business associate.' Virginsky's father nodded, as if this helped to make his meaning clearer.

'So I understand,' said Porfiry, unconsciously mirroring the nodding motion.

'Still, it is a shock,' said Virginsky's father. His eyes widened emphatically, as if he were experiencing the shock at that moment.

'Had you known him long?' Porfiry's tone was casual.

'Not long, really,' answered Virginsky's father vaguely. He assumed a carefully judged expression of mild sadness. There was a moment of respectful quiet, which left nowhere else for Porfiry's enquiries to go, without belying the pretence of conversation.

'Shall we have some tea?' said Porfiry, it seemed to everyone's relief, even Virginsky's. He discovered that he had little appetite for his father's cross-examination and potential incrimination after all.

Natalya Ivanovna and Virginsky's father bowed and smiled their assent. Porfiry opened the door that led to his private apartment and called out for Zakhar. He turned and smiled reassuringly to the room as they waited for the servant to appear. A kind of embarrassment descended on them. They seemed suspended, unable to move or speak until the business of the tea had been settled. Even Natalya Ivanovna's smile appeared strained.

At last Zakhar appeared at the door. It was the first time Virginsky had seen Porfiry's manservant in person, although he had known of his existence through the services he performed for Porfiry. The man's advanced age shocked him and provoked a quickening of indignation. Zakhar had that habit, which Virginsky had often observed in older people, of continually wincing and grimacing, apparently for no reason, though undoubtedly at the private agonies of longevity.

'Zakhar, would you be so good as to bring out some tea?' Dressed in politeness, disguised as a question, this was nevertheless a command from Porfiry.

The old man's eyes were barely open, as though he had just been roused from a nap, as well he might have been. To dispel any impression that he was too old for his duties, he gave a rather overdone spring to his step as he set off on his return. He had to grab the doorframe to steady himself.

They watched him go in some trepidation.

'Should someone not --?' began Natalya Ivanovna anxiously.

'No. He would take it as an insult.' Porfiry smiled tensely. 'Please, do sit down.'

Virginsky's father and stepmother took the brown sofa. Virginsky, taking his cue from Porfiry, remained standing.

'So tell me,' began Porfiry, the tension in his smile easing. 'How much longer are you staying in St Petersburg?'

A VENGEFUL LONGING

'Well, my son tells me I mustn't consider leaving,' said Virginsky's father quickly, again with pointed humour. 'Which is all very well, although he does not also tell me how I am to meet the continued expense of the hotel.'

'Perhaps if you had chosen a less expensive hotel in the first place,' muttered Virginsky.

'What was that?'

Natalya Ivanovna reached out a hand to soothe her husband.

'I am sure there will be no need to detain you longer than is necessary. It is unfortunate that you have been tangled in this messy business. If you wish, we could clear up a few things now?' Porfiry's face registered surprise, as if the thought had only just occurred to him.

'I would be glad to.'

'Your son tells me that you were a pupil at the Chermak High School in Moscow.'

'What? What has that got to do with Setochkin?'

Porfiry ignored the question. 'How did you meet Setochkin? It was not at Chermak High School.'

'Of course not. I told you, he was a . . . business associate of mine.'

'A business associate, yes. But if you will forgive me, that doesn't tell me where or how you met him, only in what relationship he stood to you.'

'Does it matter where I met him? One meets people. One is introduced. One becomes acquainted. It is a normal enough occurrence, I would have thought.' The elder Virginsky's tone was pleading rather than recalcitrant.

Porfiry bowed slightly with fluttering eyelids. 'Do you remember a boy at Chermak School called Golyadkin?'

'Golyadkin? Gol-*yadkin*?' Virginsky's father frowned doubtfully.

'He was in the year below you,' put in Virginsky flatly.

'What? How do you know that?' Startled, Virginsky's father swivelled his gaze between his son and the magistrate.

Porfiry picked up the question: 'The name Golyadkin came up in an interview with another . . . gentleman, one Vakhramev. Do you know him?'

'No.'

'Or his daughter, Tatyana Ruslanovna?'

'No.'

'But Golyadkin? Do you remember Golyadkin?'

'Perhaps I do remember the name. That's all. It was such a long time ago.'

'You have not seen Golyadkin more recently, since leaving Chermak School?'

'Certainly not. I hardly remember him at all.'

Porfiry nodded thoughtfully. 'It would help us greatly if you could try to remember him a little.'

'Of course, I wish to help you as much as I am able. Golyadkin, you say? You must understand that my memories of my schooldays are not happy. I have tried as much as I might to put them behind me. There was a certain brutality of mind amongst the masters, which transmitted itself to some of the boys. I was myself guilty of it at times, much to my shame. It is far worse, in later life, to look back on one's self as the perpetrator rather than the victim of injustice. It was a school of bullies and the older boys had little to do with the younger ones except to terrorise them. Naturally, there were those, either lacking in the necessary stature or malevolence, or possibly simply intelligence, who were inevitably and eternally the recipients of such attentions. Golyadkin, I do not think was one of those. I would have remembered him if that were the case. I find I have the faces of the unhappy ones etched upon my conscience and I do not associate that name with any of those.'

His narrative faltered. Natalya Ivanovna laid her hand consolingly on his arm. He patted it appreciatively and smiled to her alone.

'There was one boy in particular. Yes, he was from the year below, a quite unfortunate boy, sallow-faced, weakly, he was always sickening for something, or pretending to. I imagine that it was nothing other than misery that he was suffering from. He sought escape from his tormentors in the infirmary. He had a particular terror of heights, I remember. And one day a few of his classmates blindfolded him and took him to an attic window from which they forced him to climb out on to the roof -- there was a flat roof adjacent to this particular window I remember. They walked him to the edge of the flat roof and removed his blindfold. Then left him there. His screams filled the school grounds and stay with me even now. Of course, he was punished severely for his misdemeanour.' Natalya Ivanovna shifted uneasily. Her husband avoided her eyes; his smile trembled into weakness, unable to console or explain. 'That was not Golyadkin, though, I am sure of that. I cannot remember the boy's real name but it was not Golyadkin. Everyone called him "Nobody".'

'Nobody?' Porfiry shot a glance at Virginsky.

'Yes. Nikolai Nobody. The son of No One. I wonder whatever became of him.'

'Is it possible, do you think, that Golyadkin was one of his abusers?'

'Golyadkin, Golyadkin . . . it really is so hard to remember, but I suppose it's possible. You see, what you have to bear in mind is that each of us was known by a particular nickname, not always a flattering one, I have to say. My own was "Vomit". I once had the misfortune to vomit in a corridor when I was coming down with a bout of fever, you see.' There was a small sympathetic sound from Natalya Ivanovna. 'It only happened once, quite early on in my time at the school, but I was never allowed to forget it in all the years I was there. The chief tormentor of this Nobody was known by the name of "Worms", I seem to remember.'

'Worms? How disgusting,' said Natalya Ivanovna.

'I think it was in reference to angling. It was his passion.' Virginsky's father narrowed his eyes as if looking into the distance, and spoke as if he dimly saw the boy in question approach. 'It was all he ever talked about. His parents had a dacha by a lake, and apparently he would spend the whole of the summer holidays in a boat on that lake with only his worms for company. Hence the nickname.'

He paused. The hiatus in his narrative was filled by a light metallic rattle. There was a heavy clank against the inner door, then silence. Porfiry sprang to the door and opened it. Zakhar staggered forward, surprised by his release. He was bearing a tray with the metal teapot from the samovar and china, which he came dangerously close to losing.

'Thank you, Zakhar. You may put it on my desk. I will serve us.'

This last information was received with a wince, as if it pained him greatly to be denied the pleasure of serving which was after all his due. He shook his head as he withdrew into the apartment.

'Dear Zakhar, what would I do without him?'

'Do you not find it humiliating to be waited on by another human being?' asked Virginsky with unexpected ferocity. 'Besides which, there is the question of his age. He seems rather past it to me.'

'As to the former question, I confess that I do not. The demands of my office make it rather a necessity. And that which is necessary . . .'

'Yes, yes -- is always right,' said Virginsky impatiently.

Porfiry hesitated and gave Virginsky a slow questioning gaze. 'Quite. But yes, his advanced age is a great concern to me. It has come upon him with alarming rapidity, it seems to us all. I have tried to talk to him of retirement but he broke down in tears.'

'Perhaps they were tears of joy,' said Virginsky drily.

'I think not. His position means everything to such a man. It is his purpose as well as place in life. Take it away and he is left with nothing.'

'Such a man!' Virginsky spat out contemptuously.

'Yes, such a man,' Porfiry insisted with an indulgent smile as he handed a teacup to Natalya Ivanovna. She and her husband were watching the exchange with startled fascination, like spectators at a scandalous play.

'How is *such a man* different from you or me?'

'He is not different at all. That is precisely my point. I include myself in the category of *such men*. I am a public servant. I live to serve. I cannot contemplate a future beyond service.'

'You will move to the country and live out a long and happy retirement,' said Virginsky's father, with childlike optimism. 'Away from all these sordid concerns,' he added, with a note of rebuke.

Porfiry bowed acknowledgement of the wish.

'Do people not murder one another in the country?' asked Virginsky.

'Well, yes. But it is usually a simple matter. A quarrel between peasants.' Virginsky's father looked to Porfiry for support as he took his tea from him.

'Wherever there are human beings there is criminality,' said Porfiry. 'Even amongst gentlefolk.'

'But surely not?' protested Natalya Ivanovna.

'I'm afraid so.' Porfiry offered her the sugar bowl, which she regarded for a moment in horror. She recovered herself enough to place a large crystal on her saucer with the tongs, before transferring it between her teeth by hand. 'I have encountered criminals with every distinction of rank, every privilege of wealth, every advantage of education,' continued Porfiry. 'Indeed, all that they have lacked is moral compunction.'

Virginsky could not help looking at his father, who met his gaze then looked down sharply.

Natalya Ivanovna drank her tea through her teeth that held the sugar crystal. It seemed she sensed the tension and meaning of the silent exchange between her husband and stepson. She swallowed hurriedly and said, 'You are referring to this fellow Golyadkin, are you not?' She cast solicitous glances at her husband. 'You believe he may be Colonel Setochkin's murderer?'

'Golyadkin cannot be Colonel Setochkin's murderer, I am afraid. He himself died in a boating accident some years ago.' Porfiry sipped from his tea. He closed his eyes for a moment, complacently almost, then suddenly stared over his cup, which he held to his mouth without drinking from it.

'What is it?' said Virginsky.

Porfiry lowered the cup slowly. He smiled but said nothing, basking in the speed of his eyelids' oscillation. Instead he directed a mildly enquiring glance to Virginsky's father.

He appeared discomfited by the magistrate's attention. 'But I don't understand what all this has to do with Setochkin,' he complained. 'There is really nothing connecting Setochkin with Chermak School.'

'Nothing?' challenged Porfiry. 'Apart from the fact that his murderer may have attended there?' Porfiry sucked his tea up noisily and continued to watch Virginsky's father with a greedy eye.

A distant rumble of thunder at first startled, then relieved, and, finally, depressed them.

3: *Misericorde*

The savagery of the storm cowed them. Hurled from a booming sky, the rain pelted the windowpanes in an angry fusillade. They could hear it hammering on the roof too, as if its rage was directed against them personally. The air was chill now; a stealthy gloom had taken away every memory of the sun.

Porfiry joined Virginsky at the window and watched the rain streak through the charged darkness. A flash of brilliance lit up the devastated patch of the city before them. Across the Yekaterininsky Canal, its surface frantic with motion, the tenement buildings behind the Haymarket seemed to shiver and flinch in the glare. Hunched figures on the embankments were momentarily frozen in their dash towards doorways. Another flash, a second later, and they had disappeared.

'If this keeps up, the Ditch will flood,' said Virginsky, as if he took pleasure from the prospect.

Virginsky's father's voice behind him reminded Porfiry of his guests. 'It will be impossible to get a cab, of course.'

'Oh, but you mustn't think of going in this,' said Porfiry turning, though in truth he was ready for them to go. He craved a cigarette and there was work to be done. In effect, it amounted to the same thing.

Virginsky's father smiled weakly and cast an eye at the hostile weather. It seemed that he had merely been voicing a wish, the unattainability of which he well understood. There was resignation in his face and posture. 'So . . . it seems we are imprisoned by the storm.'

'I for one am glad of the rain,' said Natalya Ivanovna firmly. 'It will lighten the oppression in the air. I hope it will freshen the generally noxious atmosphere of the city too.'

'Indeed,' said Porfiry. 'If I may say so, you have not chosen to visit St Petersburg in its pleasantest season. Most people in fact choose to vacate the city in the summer.'

'Those who can afford to,' said Virginsky.

'We had little choice in the matter,' admitted Virginsky's father. 'The business that brought us here was pressing.'

'Your business with Colonel Setochkin, you mean?' said Porfiry.

Virginsky's father's eyes stood out with distaste. 'So, we are back to that, are we?'

'Will you be pursuing the sale of the land through another agent, now that Colonel Setochkin is dead?' Porfiry tried to make the enquiry sound casual.

'He was not my agent in any formal sense. He was merely an individual who was facilitating a transaction. But no, to answer your question. The need for the sale is no longer pressing.'

'How fortunate!' said Porfiry warmly. 'That *is* good news.' A moment later Porfiry's expression clouded. 'This change in circumstances, it would not have anything to do with Colonel Setochkin's death, would it?'

'Really!' cried Virginsky's father, rising to his feet. 'That is the most despicable suggestion I have ever heard. Storm or no storm, I will not remain here to be subjected to this innuendo. Come along, Natalya Ivanovna.' He took his wife's teacup and placed it with his own on the tray. 'Unless, sir, you are intending to formally arrest me?'

'Not at all,' said Porfiry, who gave every impression of being baffled by the outburst. 'But really, I cannot let you go out into that storm. At the very least, allow me to give you some umbrellas. You would be amazed how many get left here.'

'He once gave me a dead man's boots,' remarked Virginsky as Porfiry fussed to fetch two umbrellas from a stand by the door.

Virginsky's father took his with a look of indignation, as if this represented the final insult. Perhaps his son's comment had prejudiced him against any gift from the magistrate. 'And may we consider ourselves free to leave St Petersburg?'

'You may consider yourselves free to do whatever you wish,' said Porfiry with a slight bow.

*

'This came.'

Porfiry watched the receding figures of Virginsky Senior and Natalya Ivanovna. They crossed the floor with stiffened gait, carrying umbrellas tightly furled like grudges. Other figures cut across them, some steaming from the drenchings they had just received. Then the couple was lost to him, absorbed by the loose congress of the receiving hall.

He looked down at the letter Zamyotov had thrust at him. He

took it uncertainly. It bore the crest of the Ministry of Internal Affairs, Department of Public Health. He looked into Zamyotov's face in amazement. 'We've had a reply!'

'Contain your excitement,' said Zamyotov.

The brief, though beautifully scripted, note was signed by one A. I. Rostanev.

Re: Yekaterininsky Canal adjacent to Stolyarny Lane.

Your letter regarding the above has been investigated. No action was deemed necessary.

Porfiry read the lines again. An astonished rage rushed through him, rising quickly to his face. 'No action necessary!'

'I told you it was a waste of time,' said Zamyotov, attending to a thread on the cuff of his frock coat.

'This is outrageous.' Porfiry rapped the paper with the nails of one hand. 'Investigated? What do they mean? Nobody has been here. No one has talked to me.'

'Ah,' said Zamyotov, becoming uncharacteristically shame-faced. 'I believe an official from that department did come here. But you were out.'

'But that's no good. He needed to talk to me. He should have come back. He should have made an appointment.'

'It was the day young Virginsky started,' Zamyotov offered, almost as an excuse. Virginsky shifted awkwardly, as if he felt himself implicated in the failure. 'Word had just come in of that double poisoning,' continued Zamyotov. 'The German woman and her son. You dashed off and missed him by a matter of minutes.'

'She was not German,' said Porfiry studying the official letter as if he believed some meaning other than the obvious would make itself apparent. 'She was married to a German.'

'I let him into your chambers. He sniffed around a bit and then left.'

'Good grief! Surely he must have noticed the stink? What did he say?'

'Not much. Nothing actually. He just made some notes and was gone.'

'No action necessary,' repeated Porfiry. 'This is an outrage. We will have to write another letter. We will take it higher up. Who is this Rostanev? He does not even give a rank.'

'Porfiry Petrovich?'

Porfiry looked up to see Lieutenant Salytov frowning impatiently at him.

'Yes, Ivan Petrovich, what is it?'

'Could I ask you, please, to moderate your fury as I am trying to take a statement from a witness and your outburst is proving to be rather distracting?'

'Y --'

'Thank you.' Salytov clicked his heels and bowed.

'But --!'

'Furthermore, Nikodim Fomich has requested me to notify you of the details of the case as he feels a criminal investigation may be necessary.'

'I see.' Porfiry passed the letter back to Zamyotov. 'Of course.' He angled his face away from the attention of the others as he took out and lit a cigarette with shaking hands. 'I hope it is understood that I am not normally given to such shows of passion. However, the communication I have just received would be enough to try the patience of a saint.'

'The case,' insisted Salytov, with a note of censure in his voice, 'as it stands is one of a missing person. The witness I am interviewing, one Lara Olsufevna Mikheyeva of Demidov Lane, came into the bureau to report the disappearance of her tenant, Yemelyan Antonovich Ferfichkin.'

'I see.'

'This Ferfichkin, according to Mikheyeva, has many enemies. In particular, a man called Gorshkov, a former factory worker, now an indigent drunk, was heard to threaten the life of Ferfichkin. It is Mikheyeva's view that he has made good on the threat.'

'Ah.'

'Mikheyeva's description of Ferfichkin matches that of a body discovered this morning in the Summer Garden, according to a bulletin released by the Eastern Admiralty District Police Bureau.'

'Very well. Then the thing to do is to take the woman to identify the body. Do we know how the man died?'

'He was stabbed through the heart. The weapon, a poniard, was discovered still in place.'

'That is very interesting.'

'Nikodim Fomich was of the view that you would like to talk to the Mikheyeva woman.'

Porfiry gave a wincing smile and sighed. 'It is something of a distraction from the cases I am working on at the moment. It is not enough that I am chasing two hares.' He drew deeply on his cigarette. 'I feel it would be better to wait until she has positively identified the body as Ferfichkin.'

'But what if she is right? That would give this fellow Gorshkov time to disappear,' protested Salytov.

'We cannot arrest people merely on hearsay. At the very least, we need to be sure that a crime has taken place. Ferfichkin may have returned home while she has been giving her statement.'

'But somebody is dead and somebody has killed him,' said Virginsky. 'Do you not count it significant that she should report her tenant's disappearance at precisely the moment a body is found answering his description?'

Porfiry rubbed a hand over his face and sniffed the air. 'I had hoped that the rainfall would alleviate the fetid atmosphere. It seems merely to have added an unwelcome rankness to it.'

A distant cannon boom signalled a flood warning.

'The Ditch is rising,' said Virginsky.

'The woman?' pressed Salytov.

'Very well, bring her to my chambers.' Porfiry shook his head in weary defeat. 'If I talk to her now it may save time later,' he added over his shoulder as he made for his door.

*

Lara Olsufevna Mikheyeva inhaled the air in Porfiry's chambers with her head angled back sharply. She regarded Porfiry down the bridge of a long straight nose, upon which a pince-nez was precariously imposed. It seemed she suspected him of being responsible for the smell that pervaded the room. Lara Olsufevna was self-evidently a respectable woman, somewhere in her fifties. The set of her mouth inclined Porfiry to believe her a spinster. She kept her eyes narrowed, in an expression of permanent distrust.

The thunder grumbled morosely now, the storm's ferocity spent. The rain lashed the windows with an erratic beat, falling hard and sharp like cast gravel. The day's light had not yet fully returned. But something else, a kind of cold glow, had taken its place.

Porfiry scanned Salytov's transcript of her statement. 'So, Lara Olsufevna . . . You became aware of your tenant's disappearance this morning.'

'That's right.'

'We do not normally open a missing person file so soon after a disappearance is first reported.'

'Ferfichkin is not missing. He is murdered.'

'By Gorshkov?' said Porfiry, checking the statement.

'Yes.'

'And why do you suspect Gorshkov of this crime?'

'He said that he would kill him.'

'I see.'

'Gorshkov is not a bad man.' Lara Olsufevna sat as self-contained as her pronouncements. She lowered her head to look at Porfiry more carefully, but other than that she held herself quite immobile. She seemed uncannily at one with her stiff, charcoal dress. There was something of the schoolmistress about her, Porfiry decided. 'He has that fatal weakness for drink that so many of our Russian menfolk share. But we have to allow that he has suffered terribly. Ferfichkin's behaviour was the last straw. You can push a man only so far. Then, like the proverbial camel's back, he will snap.'

'How has Gorshkov suffered?'

'He has buried six children, all girls. The last, a babe of three months, not long ago.'

'And what has Ferfichkin to do with Gorshkov?'

'Ferfichkin said the Psalms at his last daughter's funeral. Like so many of the poor folk of this district, Gorshkov could not afford a proper priest.'

'I don't understand. Why would this lead Gorshkov to murder Ferfichkin?'

Lara Olsufevna treated Porfiry to a disappointed stare. 'He could no more afford the services of a self-appointed Psalm reader than he could an Orthodox priest. Ferfichkin was pressing him mercilessly for the settlement of his debt. He began to make his demands on the very day of the funeral. At the graveside, no less. The tiny coffin had not long been laid in the ground. I was there. I saw it with my own eyes. Ferfichkin's behaviour was shameful. He pricked and needled the poor grieving father, pushed him to breaking point. Gorshkov's neighbours had to hold him back. If not, I think he would have killed him there and then, and ripped the cold heart from his breast. I remember saying to a gentleman who was there, "This will end badly".'

'What gentleman was this? We will need to take a statement from him, if possible.'

'I don't know. I didn't recognise him. He was not one of the family, or one of the Gorshkovs' friends or neighbours. I believe he had been just passing and had stopped to watch out of compassion. Certainly he was very interested in the family. He asked many questions and was most sympathetic to their plight.'

'Can you describe him?'

'Isn't that strange? I find his face has gone completely from my memory. I dare say I would know him if I saw him again. I am usually very good at faces.'

'I imagine you are,' said Porfiry with a smile. 'Please, you were telling me about Ferfichkin's prosecution of Gorshkov's debt.'

'With every day that passed he added interest. Really, he was a monster. If Gorshkov hadn't killed him, there would have been others who would have done the deed, I'm sure. He has a history of such usury. One would have thought him a Jew, were it not for his religion.'

'You sound almost as if you have sympathy for Gorshkov.'

'Who would not have sympathy for the sufferings of a fellow human? And his poor wife, to have borne so many, only to bury them, one after the other. She herself was too ill to come to her baby's funeral.'

'And yet you have come here to report him,' observed Porfiry.

Lara Olsufevna's brows shot up. 'However much sympathy one may have, the law must be obeyed. I would expect you, as a magistrate, to understand that. He has taken the life of another. We cannot have people doing such things, not in a civilised society. Besides, I am afraid for Gorshkov. The balance of his mind is disturbed. There is no saying what he might do next. He may take his own life. Or that of his wife. I would not be surprised if he were to go on a destructive rampage. When I last saw him, there was a wildness in his eyes that frightened me.' Lara Olsufevna paused. Her breathing became short and laboured. It was some time before she was able to speak again. 'I hope to prevent such a thing happening.'

Porfiry said nothing for a moment. 'You are aware that the body of a man has been found?'

'Yes. The truculent one told me.'

'I'm afraid I am going to ask you to undertake an unpleasant duty.'

'You want me to look at it.' Lara Olsufevna pinched her mouth minimally.

Porfiry bowed solemnly.

Lara Olsufevna was already on her feet.

Outside, the day flickered with electricity, and a final, vast reverberation shook the sky.

*

The dark capsule of the police brougham hurtled through the rain, the horses' necks slanting against the onslaught, their hooves kicking through the hissing spray. The weather snuffed the driver's whip, as if brooking no rivals to its own immense voice. Huddled in oilskins, he, the driver, raged equally at his team and the heavy drops that hit his face. A muted glow was concentrated in the buildings, the colours of which were strangely intensified.

Inside the carriage, the rain rapped like a thousand fingers on the roof. Lara Olsufevna was seated on her own facing the direction of travel. She looked out of the misted window with a mixture of apprehension and excitement. No doubt she was thinking of the task that lay ahead of her. Porfiry and Virginsky sat opposite, riding the buffetings of the carriage's suspension, watching her with mild curiosity.

'Tell me more about Ferfichkin,' said Porfiry to Lara Olsufevna. 'You say that he has many enemies.'

'Oh yes.' Lara Olsufevna's impatience suggested this were something any fool knew. 'It's true. He *had*.' The last word was given pointed emphasis.

'We don't know that he is dead yet,' said Porfiry. 'I suggest that until that is confirmed we refer to him in the present tense, as one still extant.'

Lara Olsufevna's shrug was amplified by the jouncing seat.

'So he lives with you as a tenant? How do you get on with him?'

'We get along well enough by having nothing whatsoever to do with one another, other than that which cannot be avoided.'

'But your dealings with him are rather different to most other people's, are they not?'

'How do you mean?'

'Well, he is regularly in your debt rather than the other way round.'

'He has always paid his rent on time. I have had no complaints on that front.'

'It's just as well for you, perhaps, that he is so meticulous in recovering the debts owing to him.'

'I do not believe it is quite necessary for him to do so with such unfeeling brutality.'

Porfiry nodded. 'I cannot imagine he makes much of a living reading the psalter at pauper's funerals.'

'It was not his only source of income. He took in tailoring repairs, though I myself would never have entrusted a garment to him.'

They rode the rest of the way in silence, feeling the sun's tentative return uplift the day.

*

Seagulls over the Neva pierced the air with their shrieks as the brougham pulled up at 2 Gorokhovaya Street. The building, indistinguishable from its neighbours in its geometric monotony, was the home of the main police administrative headquarters for the whole of St Petersburg, and also housed the Admiralty District Police Bureau, station number 1.

Patches of clear sky were appearing now amongst the clouds. All that was left of the storm ran in muddy rivulets along the road. Leaves and refuse were scattered over the glistening pavements. Lara Olsufevna lifted her crinolined skirts to high step over puddles.

They followed a *politseisky* to a room at the rear of the building on the ground floor. The windows were shuttered. With the light from the open door, it had the air of a lumber room, provisional, a space of temporary storage and transition. The objects it stored were elongated mounds beneath sheets, laid out on tables.

'Would it be possible to have more light?' asked Porfiry.

The *politseisky* struck a match, at the third attempt, and lit an oil lamp. The flare from the lamp chased the shadows to the edge of the room. 'We never open the shutters,' he explained. 'Now, which one was it you were wanting to see?'

'The body found in the Summer Garden this morning. An adult

male,' said Porfiry.

'Ah yes, he's easy enough to find.'

The *politseisky* approached a mound which had a curious projection in its sheet towards one end. It was from this end that he drew back the sheet.

The face that was revealed, though immobile, was not in repose. The eyes bulged and the mouth formed a small circle as if articulating an accusation or abuse. The hair and beard were long, grey and matted.

'That's him,' said Lara Olsufevna with the primness that she said everything. She continued looking at the face. 'Ferfichkin.'

Porfiry too was staring thoughtfully at the dead man's face. 'He has one of those faces, does he not? The sort that you are convinced you have seen before. Of course, it is entirely possible that he has crossed my path in the past. It would be as well to check the records.'

'What is that?' asked Virginsky, pointing at the tent-like projection in the sheet. His face registered an uneasy determination.

The *politseisky* lifted the sheet and pulled it down even further. The dead man's shirt was drenched in blood. The hilt of the weapon that was sunk into his chest stood proud, an inverted crucifix of tempered steel. It appeared mediaeval, in design at least, made up of simple agglomerations of bossed, banded and cubic forms. Even so, it made an elegant and evocative shape, slender yet solid, modelled after the Christian symbol, but murderous. Ferfichkin's body lay awkwardly on the table, raised on the side that the dagger was plunged into.

'It went straight through him,' observed Porfiry.

The *politseisky* nodded. 'There's not much to him. He's as skinny as a boy.'

'The *misericorde*, or mercy poniard.' Porfiry tensed a hand towards the weapon, though stopping short of touching it. 'Undoubtedly a replica. Even so, an expensive item.' He looked significantly at Lara Olsufevna. She returned his glance without expression. 'If I understood you correctly, Gorshkov was not a wealthy man?'

'He could have stolen it,' answered Lara Olsufevna.

'Pavel Pavlovich, your thoughts?'

Virginsky seemed startled. 'It's possible, I suppose.'

'But really, why would he bother, though?' asked Porfiry, wonderingly. 'He does not need this particular weapon to kill him. He may kill him just as easily by plunging a kitchen knife into his heart. Why risk detection and prosecution for an unnecessary theft, before he has carried out the greater and for him more necessary crime of murdering his enemy?'

'I don't know,' admitted Virginsky, staring at the dagger hilt crossly.

Porfiry raised an eyebrow at Lara Olsufevna but she declined to comment.

'The choice of weapon is significant, I think,' said Porfiry at last. 'Here is a man who earns his living by plying a needle and it seems that his dying came about as the result of a fatal stitch. He was also a religious man, at least outwardly. But really he was a man who could be said to have profited from the word of the Lord, to have exploited the Christian message for venal gain. Perhaps the cruciform handle that stands out from his heart may be seen as some kind of judgement on that. It is suggestive, is it not?'

'I suppose so,' said Virginsky glumly.

'Of course, it may still be Gorshkov who has passed this judgement on him and you may yet be proven right, Lara Olsufevna. He may indeed have stolen the dagger. We shall have to speak to him, that much is certain. Where may we find him, do you know?'

'Pokrovsky's tenement. The Gorshkovs have the corner of a room there. They live with the widow Dobroselova.'

'Pokrovsky's tenement? Where is that, if you please?'

'You will find it where Yekateringofsky Prospekt meets Voznesensky Prospekt, close to the Yekaterininsky Canal. But I would not go there if I were you.'

'And why not, pray?'

'There is cholera there.'

Porfiry nodded slowly as he watched the *politseisky* cover Ferfichkin's face.

4: The widow Dobroselova

The morning's storm, now spent, had swelled the waters of the Yekaterininsky Canal, but contrary to Virginsky's prediction the Ditch had not yet flooded. Churned by the heavy downpour, the murky darkness of its depths had risen to the surface. The stench that haunted the canal's twisting course was given fresh virulence.

Virginsky snarled in distaste as he closed the door of the police brougham. Lara Olsufevna looked out at him, self-contained, watchful and vindicated. He shouted to the driver and she was borne away with a jolt. She seemed to shake her head disapprovingly, or warningly perhaps, as he watched her go.

Porfiry looked up at the high dark mass shouldering out the sun. Pokrovsky's tenement was home to countless souls and yet there was nothing welcoming about it. It seemed more like a prison than a place of refuge. The fabric of the building was decayed and dirty; it was impossible to say how many summers ago it had last been repaired. There were gaps in the masonry around the windows wide enough to slide a hand into. The windows themselves were filthy and broken, in places boarded up. The woodwork had the soft, lustreless look of rotten timber.

'It has the air of defeat to it, does it not?' said Porfiry.

'Of disease, more like.'

'Well yes. That we know.' Porfiry glanced briefly at his companion. 'It troubles you to go inside?'

Virginsky considered Porfiry's question. 'No, sir. It angers me. Shall I tell you what is a crime, Porfiry Petrovich? That people in this city are dying of the cholera when the cause of the disease has been understood for over ten years. I'm not afraid of going into this building. I know perfectly well that I can't contract the disease unless I drink the same water as these poor wretches must. Water that is contaminated with faecal matter. Just as the cause is understood, so too is the means of prevention.'

Porfiry listened with a distracted air. 'That is . . . interesting,' he said after a moment, but without conviction.

'You did not hear a word I said!'

'On the contrary,' said Porfiry, gazing searchingly into Virginsky's face. 'Your words have made a very great impression on me indeed.'

*

They entered the dim passageway that led to the courtyard of the building. With each step the stink grew stronger. Both men involuntarily held their breath but felt the teeming air work on their eyes. A door set in one wall of the passageway bore a crudely painted cross.

Porfiry reached out towards the door, hesitating for a moment as he sought Virginsky's eye.

'Can we wonder that those who are forced to live in these conditions are driven to criminality?' pressed Virginsky.

Porfiry waited in silence with his hand hovering near the door.

'Porfiry Petrovich, have you nothing to say?'

Porfiry finally allowed his hand to touch the door and pull it open. The door's whine of complaint stood for his answer.

There was no relief from the foul atmosphere inside. They waited for a moment, listening, tensed in expectation. It was unnaturally quiet, given the many lives that the building must have housed. But there was something audible, or perceptible in some way, a kind of pulse to the air. As they strained to attune their senses to it, the coarser sound of footsteps lapping on the stairs above intruded. The two men looked up. The footsteps were erratic: at times slow and laboured, at other times progressing in hurried bursts. Occasionally, there would be a break altogether, usually accompanied by a heavy metallic clank. Then a second, lighter clank would precede the continuation of the footsteps.

At last the person on the stairs came into view, a girl who appeared to be about eleven, although her head seemed as large as an adult's. Her clothes were little better than rags. Her scrawny arms were bent back on themselves by the weight of a tin pail. The girl halted on the landing above Porfiry and Virginsky and let the bucket drop on to the boards, releasing the handle. Even in her oversized head, her eyes appeared enormous. They swivelled to take in the two men looking up at her. She wiped her brow with the side of her wrist, then patiently picked up the bucket again and resumed her descent.

They knew the contents of the bucket before they saw them.

'Dear God,' cried Porfiry, lifting a hand to his face. He tried to avert his eyes but the fascination of that dark swill proved too great.

Almost too late he flinched away, swallowing back the quickly rising gorge. The two men parted to let the girl through. Porfiry heard a fast trickle of liquid on the floor. He looked down to see the thin, filthy trail marking where she had been.

'Where are you going with that, daughter?' said Virginsky.

'To the canal.'

'Are there no closets here?' asked Porfiry.

'In the yard.'

'Then why don't people use them?'

'They are too sick, sir. They cannot manage the stairs and it comes on them sudden. They use chamber pots. We empty the chamber pots into the bucket. And when the bucket is full we take it to the canal.'

'It makes no difference anyhow,' said Virginsky. 'The owners of these buildings construct waste pipes straight into the canals.'

'How many sick do you have here?' asked Porfiry.

'I don't know, sir. In my family, there are three.'

'I am sorry.' Porfiry held the door open for her and waited for her to return. Her step was shuffling and weary now. She held the empty bucket in one hand; fortunately for Porfiry, it was the hand furthest from him. He expected her to avert her gaze too, out of embarrassment, or even shame. But she stared straight at him. Her expression was dulled, however: not unabashed, just empty. He felt that if he had struck that face or cradled it, it would have been all the same to her.

'My child.'

She halted and absorbed his gaze.

'We are looking for the Gorshkovs. They live with the widow Dobroselova. Do you know where that is?'

The girl nodded. 'Widow Dobroselova lives in the basement.'

'The basement? I see. Thank you.' Porfiry's slow nod released her.

*

'It is no wonder they lost six children,' said Virginsky, his feet splashing in water. He had reached the bottom of the steps to the cellar, which were at the front of the building, outside.

Porfiry felt the water rise above his shoes and lap his ankles. Looking down he saw a cloudy pool about two inches deep. It seemed the daylight hung back, unwilling to penetrate the surface of the water.

'The cesspit has overflowed.' Virginsky turned his grimace away from Porfiry.

'It would seem so.' Porfiry's eye skimmed along the murky water. Black tide-marks on the walls indicated that there had been deeper floods. The door to the basement stood open.

'Through there?' asked Virginsky.

'There is nowhere else to go,' answered Porfiry, bemused; however, he understood the reluctance that Virginsky's question expressed.

They entered a long open room. Light seeped weakly through high windows, and where it did not reach there was a shadowed gloom, unrelieved by any candle flame or lantern. Arched slabs of darkness were dimly discernible, suggesting that the basement extended into labyrinthine depths beyond. A sound, the amplification of the pulse they had noticed when they first entered the building, echoed somewhere in the unseen periphery, together with the steady dripping, and occasional stirring, of moisture. As their eyes adapted, it was a shock to make out first the odd pieces of broken furniture and then the people positioned among them, lives discarded and consigned to this cellar.

An old woman, dressed in black, stared up at them with clouded, unblinking eyes. Her skirts were soaked in the water that surrounded her seat. She was motionless. Her face possessed a strangely beatific expression.

'Good day, Grandmother,' said Porfiry. His voice reverberated, as if it were startled by itself. She did not react to his greeting. So fixed was her stare that he thought for a moment that she was dead, but a girlish giggle warbled unexpectedly in her throat. 'Are you the widow Dobroselova, by any chance?'

This time the girlish giggle came out strangled and distorted. It could have been intended to express amusement, but there was a mechanical emptiness to it that horrified.

'She may be deaf,' said Virginsky. 'As well as blind.'

'Widow Dobroselova?' shouted Porfiry. The whole cellar rang with his voice.

The old woman's mouth stretched open revealing a few cherished remnants of teeth. 'Is that you, Dobroselov?'

'My name is Porfiry Petrovich.'

'Oh, Dobroselov!' She chuckled indulgently. Her misty eyes opened wide on nothing. 'You and your games.'

'I assure you, madam, I am Porfiry Petrovich and I am a magistrate. We are looking for the factory worker, Gorshkov. It is our understanding that he lives in the basement here.'

'Get away with you, Dobroselov!' The old woman gave a flick of the wrist.

Porfiry straightened up and looked at Virginsky.

'She is . . . mad?' asked the younger man tentatively.

'Can you blame her?' murmured Porfiry. He surveyed the rest of the room and the other human figures in it, bodies curled around their misery on bare mattresses, or sitting slumped over empty tables. He estimated that there were about twenty people visible, though he sensed the presence of many more hidden in the shadows at the edges, beyond the arches. Undoubtedly, only the oldest and most infirm would remain in the flooded cellar when the day outside was dry and warm.

The pulsating sound continued, identifiable now as weeping. It seemed to be all around them.

An old man sitting at a table lifted his head from sprawled arms and looked at them. His face was gaunt and sallow, but his gaze was firm, hostile even. Dressed in the overalls of a labourer, he seemed worn out by the effort of sitting up. His head was massive on puny shoulders. 'What do you want with Gorshkov?' The voice that addressed them was harsh-edged, as if every word was dredged from a corrosive pool of bitterness.

'We are magistrates,' said Porfiry. 'If you know where Gorshkov is, it is your duty to tell us.'

'Oh, I know where he is,' said the old man, wheezing out a dry, empty laughter.

'Where then?'

'You just missed him. They came for him this morning.'

'Who came for him?'

'Your lot. The police. And a doctor.'

'I see. And why was that?'

'He was raving. Worse than raving. He had a knife. Threatened to kill anyone who came near. He had his wife, Nadezhda, by the throat. We all thought he was going to kill her. Then at the last minute he turned the knife on himself. Slashed his own neck. They carted him off then.'

'Was he dead?'

'The doctor patched him up. Mind you, he fell bleeding in the water here, so he might die yet.'

'Where did they take him?'

'Where do they take all the mad ones?'

'To the house at the eleventh verst,' said Virginsky, in something like wonder.

The old man nodded.

'I presume it was the loss of his children that drove him mad?' said Porfiry.

'His moods were never good.'

'Where is his wife now?'

The old man gestured towards the arched darkness. 'She's not long for this world,' he said. 'It was out of mercy that Gorshkov meant to kill her.' He then allowed his head to slump down on his arms once more.

They made their way kicking through the water in the direction he had indicated. The sound of weeping became more focused and it seemed that they were moving towards its source.

Porfiry's hand reached up and touched the brickwork of the arch as he stooped to pass beneath it. He felt a repulsive cold clamminess and withdrew his hand immediately, wondering what had possessed him to touch it in the first place.

In the thickened gloom he could just make out a bundled form on the bed, from which the jagged sobs emanated. The smell in this part of the basement was particularly foul.

'Nadezhda?'

The bundle stirred. A tremulous moan came from it.

'Is there no light in here?' asked Porfiry gently.

There was a more agitated movement from the bed; limbs broke away from the bundle and thrashed about.

'Not even a candle?'

The moan became a wail. 'No candle for my baby!'

'There there, Nadezhda. I will light a candle for your baby. I will go to St Isaac's Cathedral and light a candle for her soul. What was she called?' As he spoke, Porfiry reached into a pocket with one hand.

'Anastasya.'

'A beautiful name.' A match flared in Porfiry's hand. 'There. For Anastasya.' In the fragile glow he saw the woman's agonised face, her mouth locked in a grimace of pain. He saw her body crumple and fold as she drew her legs up around the pain. The dark cast of her flesh, as though bruised from a lifetime of beatings, was clearly visible. He held the dying match to his own face, allowing her to see the smile which he hoped was reassuring. He believed he saw her face relax, if only for a moment.

'Anastasya Filippovna,' said Nadezhda.

'Your husband is Filipp Gorshkov?'

'Filya!' The name was uttered as a cry of despair as the match expired. 'Filya is gone. I am alone. I have been left to die alone.'

'You're not alone, Nadya. I am here with you.' Porfiry bent down and reached into the darkness. He found a hand, in which was clasped an object made of soft, padded fabric. He searched for the other hand. It was as damp as the wall he had touched, but feverishly hot. He wondered if it was the same impulse in operation: the need to know, rather than the desire to console.

'She should be in a hospital,' said Virginsky at his back.

'No!' cried Nadezhda.

'It's all right, Nadya,' said Porfiry, squeezing her hand gently.

She murmured something, the words inaudible. Her eyes closed and she drifted away from them, the tension falling out of her body. Porfiry continued holding her hand. 'I wonder, has any doctor been in here?'

'I very much doubt it,' said Virginsky.

'The thought of hospital inspires terror in her. In her mind, it is not a place one returns from.'

'One thing's for certain. She will not last long here.'

Porfiry leant forward decisively. 'You will help me. We will take her to the Obukhovsky Hospital. Dr Pervoyedov will see her.'

'And what of all the others who are dying in this building, Porfiry Petrovich? And those dying in other buildings? How will your sentimental gesture help them?'

'But to do nothing in the face of her suffering -- is that what you advocate?'

'Far from it, as you well know. I advocate action, urgent and comprehensive action. Coming here, seeing this, you must surely see that it is necessary. And as you have said yourself, Porfiry

Petrovich, that which is necessary can only be right.'

'But the action you advocate will not save her.'

'Porfiry Petrovich, I fear nothing may save her.'

Porfiry was silent for a moment. 'Come, help me lift her,' he said at last. He could not interpret Virginsky's silence in the darkness.

They lifted her by the armpits. As they peeled her body from the bed, there was a sound like a wheel turning in a bog. They raised her to a seated position and swung her arms around their shoulders.

'On the count of three,' said Porfiry. They braced themselves as they reached the final number, only to discover that the woman had barely any weight at all. She almost flew from the bed. She moaned and tossed her head.

'It's all right, Nadya,' soothed Porfiry.

They bent to walk her through the arch, dragging her feet in the flood water. In the comparative light of the open room, Porfiry saw that her feet were bare. He also saw that the object she clutched was an ancient and grubby rag doll.

The old man at the table raised his head to watch them, then lowered it again without comment, overwhelmed by passivity. Nadezhda Gorshkova's body tensed between them. A moment later it was limp. Her head lolled. Her hand opened, dropping the rag doll into the mired water. Virginsky and Porfiry halted and looked at the woman's face. Her mouth and eyes were open. She was no longer weeping or moaning. She made no sound at all.

5: The house at the eleventh verst

It was not really a house, more a low sprawl of buildings, partially concealed from the road by a stand of ragged birch and a decaying fence topped with rusted nails. Glimpsed from a distance it gave the impression, gleaming pale in the new day, of having no substance. Its presence on the ground seemed accidental, owing nothing to the operation of gravity. It might almost have been tethered there, such was its weightless, dreamlike quality. Seeing the turquoise roofs and walls of ochre and white over the fence, Porfiry was reminded of the time that Virginsky had pointed the building out to him that morning they had taken the train to Petergof. He acknowledged a sense of resentment as he approached it now, for it felt like an idea that had been forced upon him. He found himself startled by a detail of the architecture: the windows and doors were arched, as were the passageways through to the courtyards. The motif brought back the memory of the flooded basement and of the arch through which he and Virginsky had carried Nadezhda Gorshkova. The correspondence irritated him. He refused to see anything portentous in the fact that by stepping through another arch he would encounter the dead woman's husband.

The gatekeeper was dressed in a grubby *kosovorotka*. He had deep-set eyes that turned with torpid cunning towards Porfiry and Virginsky. His face maintained a deliberate blankness at their approach, though the abrupt shift in his posture, from indolence to wariness, suggested visitors were rare and unwelcome. He sat on a high stool in a three-sided hut behind a chained gate. Weeds grew all around him; in amongst them could be seen items of discarded rubbish: a rusted bedstead, broken bottles, bundles of clothes and an odd shoe. The gatekeeper's face seemed to absorb all this ugliness and reflect it back at them. His expression was a strange mixture of shame and defiance.

'I am Porfiry Petrovich, investigating magistrate from the Department of the Investigation of Criminal Causes.' Porfiry did not look directly at the man as he made this announcement, almost as if he could not bear to. 'You will please let us in.'

'I can't do that,' said the gatekeeper with a sly smile. 'I don't have the key.'

'Then kindly fetch the key.'

'Do you think they will trust me with it?' The man leered. 'Look!' He lifted his shirt, revealing a striped uniform, equally grubby, underneath. 'They think it looks better if they dress me in a *kosovorotka*.'

'I see. Is there someone you can notify of our presence who would be authorised to admit us?'

'That would be Dr Zverkov.'

'Very well. Please inform Dr Zverkov that magistrates from St Petersburg are here to see him.'

It was a moment before the gatekeeper descended from his stool, a moment in which he kept his eyes fixed firmly on Porfiry. Only with reluctance did he finally turn away from the magistrate. Then, unexpectedly, he broke into a run which carried him across the burdock-infested grounds towards the main house, a central two-storey block winged by long single-storey extensions.

'Is this a hospital or a prison?' said Virginsky.

'Something of both,' answered Porfiry. He looked at the long weeds growing through the wires of the old bedstead. 'A place of abandonment,' he added.

'And they have set one of the inmates to guard it,' said Virginsky.

Now a plump and florid-faced man was striding towards them, at the same time fastening on a black frock coat. He wore his beard neatly trimmed and they could see where the stiff collar of his shirt had rubbed his neck raw. His face wrinkled distastefully as he passed the strewn rubbish, as if it had long been on his mind to do something about it. The gatekeeper followed at some distance, his head averted in a kind of flinch.

The plump man took a key from his pocket and unlocked the chain that bound the gate. 'Gentlemen, welcome to the Ulyanka Asylum. I am Dr Zverkov. How may I assist you?' His voice was a feeble, high tenor, at odds with his bulk.

Porfiry saw that Dr Zverkov's face was bathed in sweat as he pushed the creaking gate open.

'You admitted an inmate yesterday, one Gorshkov, a factory worker.'

'Ah yes, there was an admission yesterday. That is correct.'

'We wish to speak to him.'

'You won't get much sense out of him,' said Zverkov, squaring up to Porfiry as if to block his way, despite the fact that he had gone to the trouble of opening the gate for him. He manufactured a thin smile, but his eyes were hostile, the set of his body pugnacious. 'He was raving when we admitted him and he's raving now.'

'Of course,' said Porfiry. 'Nevertheless.'

'What has he done?' asked the gatekeeper from behind Zverkov.

'Be quiet, Nikita,' snapped the doctor. However, he narrowed his eyes as he looked at Porfiry, as if waiting for an answer to the question.

Porfiry said nothing.

Dr Zverkov at last stepped aside and waved in the two magistrates. He then closed and re-chained the gate.

'Follow me, please.' He led the way briskly towards the right-hand wing. Porfiry could see that the fabric of the building was by no means as pristine as it had seemed from a distance, when the sun had coated it with a sheen that evened out all imperfections. The cracks and stains in the stucco were visible now. He could also see that the windows were barred. 'Back to your post, Nikita,' Dr Zverkov commanded irritably, as if seeking to distract from the shabbiness. He too, it seemed, could not bear to look at the man when he addressed him. 'As magistrates, you will be used to dealing with the criminally insane.' He angled his head back towards Porfiry and Virginsky, who were in step behind him. 'It will not surprise you that we have had to restrain him.'

'Why do you say that he is criminally insane?' asked Virginsky sharply. 'What crime has he committed?'

'He menaced his cohabitants, including his wife, with a knife. And then attempted to murder himself. Suicide is a crime, I believe, as well as being against the laws of God and nature. Anyone attempting suicide is by definition insane.'

'You are aware of the background to his case? The loss of his children?' Virginsky insisted.

'Of course. However, such suffering is by no means unique. Many people suffer far worse and do not become violent. We must find a way to overcome our sufferings, not be overcome by them. That is the rational way. When you consider the age of the earth, and the many ages of man, what really do the sorrows of one lifetime amount to? The Romans, I think, had the right attitude.'

'You are talking of the stoics? It is hard for a parent who has lost six children to be stoical, I think.' Virginsky cast a glance towards Porfiry, soliciting his support.

'Is this how you treat your patients, by reasoning with them?' said Porfiry with a smile.

'Of course not. One cannot reason with the mad.' Dr Zverkov turned sharply into an arched passageway that led through the wing of the building into an inner courtyard. The same long weeds grew unchallenged here. The air thickened with that summer courtyard stench, which here, somehow, made Porfiry think of captive beasts. They crossed the courtyard and followed Dr Zverkov through a door, inevitably arched, into an utterly dilapidated annexe. A man in striped uniform, the same as Nikita had worn beneath his *kosovorotka*, was sitting on a chair smoking a pipe. Behind him, an open doorway led to a ward.

Dr Zverkov turned to Porfiry and Virginsky. 'Gorshkov is in there.'

The animal smell intensified as they entered the ward. There were six or so men, of different ages and physical types. Most seemed to be of the artisan class and all wore grubby dressing gowns, but no trousers or shoes.

A number of men shuffled about the ward. All seemed melancholic rather than raving. They did not meet each other's eyes, or acknowledge anyone else's existence in any way. A couple of them mouthed, or muttered, their grievances to themselves.

One man seemed to hold himself apart. He was sitting on his bed reading. He looked up when Porfiry and Virginsky came into the ward. He seemed to make a decision in that instant and rose from his bed, approaching Virginsky without hesitation. He spoke in a soft, educated voice and looked Virginsky in the eye naturally and easily, without either condescension or insolence; as an equal, in other words. 'I should not be here, you know,' he began calmly. 'I'm not mad at all. There has been a terrible mistake. It was my mistake, I admit that. I was in error. I have said as much. I have begged forgiveness. I have placed myself at the mercy of the Tsar. I wrote a letter, you see, in which were stated certain opinions. It was not meant for public circulation. However, it fell into the hands of a certain journalist. "Dynamite", he described it as. And I suppose I was flattered by the importance he attached to it. I am a weak, vain man, but I am not mad. He urged me to publish it. He promised me help in doing so. He said that my friends would protect me. I have friends in the very highest circles. That was why he believed the letter was so explosive. My social standing, my background, my position -- I was a professor at the university. He said -- the journalist, and I believed him -- that the Tsar would read my words in the spirit in which they were intended; that he would understand my patriotic intentions. I am a noble, I will make no bones of that. I am not like the other men here. These men are all factory workers or former serfs. I do not belong here at all.' The professor looked into Virginsky's eyes, searching for hope. His face suddenly clouded. 'However, he was wrong. I was wrong. I made a mistake. I misjudged the mood at court. I went too far. Of course, I confined myself to generalities. I made no specific criticisms. However, I made the mistake, the terrible mistake, of suggesting that Russia, our Russia, is a backward country. That there are further improvements the Tsar could make, in the name of humanity. Yes, to that extent, in as much as it is true that I did write such things, it is true -- it can only be true -- that they are evidence of a temporary insanity. But I have recanted. I have admitted I was in error. Therefore, the insanity has passed -- it can fairly be said to have passed. You see that, don't you? You are an intelligent young man. Surely you can see that?'

'But you were not in error. What you said is true,' answered Virginsky with a sympathetic passion.

The other man backed away from him in sudden terror. 'No! No! You are the devil! You have come to tempt me! Either that, or you are one of the Tsar's spies. You will not trick me. You must tell the Tsar that I stand by my recantation. He must see that I am sincere in that. You must communicate this to him.'

'Now now, Prince,' said Dr Zverkov, menacingly. 'You must not shout at our guests. Is it time for your bromide? I will get Dima to bring it for you.'

'No -- I will be good. I will be quiet. There is no need. I will behave. Only tell the Tsar I have recanted.' His eyes implored Virginsky as he backed away, in the moment before turning.

Another man, gaunt-faced and skeletally thin, was standing next to his bed, to which he was manacled by a chain to one ankle. The top of his head was bald; the hair at the sides was long and greasy and stuck out wildly. His throat was dressed with a patch of blood-soaked gauze. The beard around it appeared damp and matted together, presumably from blood. There was a pool of dark urine at his feet. His eyes stared starkly and he barked out strange noises as he tested the chain that held him. The bed appeared to be fixed to the floor.

'There he is,' said Zverkov.

'Cannot someone clean up his mess?' said Porfiry, holding back, repelled.

'Of course.' It was as if Zverkov had not noticed the filth on the floor. He seemed startled by it, or perhaps by Porfiry's request. 'Dima!'

The pipe-smoking man in the striped uniform appeared, walking with a stoop as if from a severe backache.

'Get the bucket and mop and clean up Gorshkov,' commanded Dr Zverkov.

Dima nodded and hurried away, reappearing a moment later with the requested items. He scuttled over to Gorshkov and immediately began beating the other man with the handle of the mop. Gorshkov doubled over and pulled up his arms to protect his face and Dima laid into his back. 'You filthy beast! Look what you've done! We won't have that here, you know!'

Both Porfiry and Virginsky flashed outrage towards Dr Zverkov, who said nothing, and indeed looked on with equanimity.

'Will you not stop him? This is monstrous!' protested Virginsky.

Zverkov regarded Virginsky with surprise. 'That will do, Dima,' he said slowly, after a moment's consideration. To Virginsky, he added: 'But he will beat him when we are not here, so what difference does it make to stop him now?'

'Why do you allow it at all? Why do you put him in a position whereby he can terrorise the others?'

'Dima is one of our trusted inmates. He has responded well to treatment. We find that to give men like him responsibilities is beneficial. It is therapeutic for them, and it helps us in the smooth running of the hospital. You see.' Zverkov gestured towards Dima as he mopped the floor.

'But surely he cannot be allowed to abuse the other patients?'

Dr Zverkov sighed deeply. 'But really, in the grand scheme of things, so to speak, is it so terrible? A few blows with a broom handle. There will always be men who bully other men. Outside an establishment such as this, as well as inside it. Besides, how else do you get through to such a man? If it stops him fouling himself where he stands, then perhaps it will be worthwhile.'

Dima carried away the bucket and mop with a self-satisfied nod to Dr Zverkov. The floor around Gorshkov was no cleaner, but the mess had at least been spread more evenly. Gorshkov himself stood up straight once again and bellowed after his persecutor. The sound more closely resembled the cry of a tormented ox than a man.

'Well, gentlemen,' said Dr Zverkov with a mocking smile. 'The man you came to talk to awaits your questions.'

For a moment Porfiry blinked in agitation as he studied the emaciated figure before him. Then it was as if an enchantment was broken. He strode towards Gorshkov with his hand extended: 'Filya. My name is Porfiry Petrovich.' Porfiry sensed Dr Zverkov bristle behind him, as though disapproving of this irregular approach on professional grounds. Gorshkov himself seemed overwhelmed, almost terrified, by the gesture. He would not take the hand, but merely gazed at it in wonder. Then tears broke from his eyes and he began to sob.

'There there, my friend,' said Porfiry, now offering his open cigarette case.

'No!' came sharply from Zverkov. 'We do not allow the inmates to smoke.'

'That villain at the door was smoking a pipe.'

'Dima has earnt his privileges through good behaviour. This one has given us nothing but trouble from the moment he arrived. We have our rules for a reason, you know. You cannot come here interfering with the management of things about which you understand nothing.'

Porfiry gazed steadily into Gorshkov's frightened eyes. *That's all it is*, he thought, *his madness -- fear*. 'Take one,' he said. 'It's all right.' Porfiry lit the cigarette as it quivered between the other man's lips. 'My dear fellow, let us sit down.'

Gorshkov sat down first and the bed hardly seemed to dip under his weight. His dressing gown fell open, revealing damp and grubby linen. Porfiry mimed for him to close it. In some confusion, he obeyed.

'Who are you?' asked Gorshkov in wonder, as Porfiry sat on the bed next to him. His voice had startling depth.

'I am a magistrate. I have come to ask you some questions.'

'They have asked me questions. "What day is it? What year is it? What is the Tsar's name? What is your name?" And I told them, "I care nothing for such questions." The Tsar? Who is the Tsar to me? As for the day, let it be any day you like, so long as it is the day I die. That's all I ask.' Gorshkov drew on his cigarette hungrily, as if it renewed the energy he had lost through speaking.

'Do you know of a man called Ferfichkin?'

'Ferfichkin! Ferfichkin sent you?' Gorshkov drew away from Porfiry in fear. The chain at his ankle rattled angrily.

Porfiry reached out a hand to calm Gorshkov. 'Ferfichkin did not send me. Ferfichkin is dead.'

Gorshkov put a hand at his mouth, covering something like a smile that had broken out in his face. 'What's that you say? The miser is dead?'

'Yes.'

Sounds like laughter, tentative, bewildered blasts, came from Gorshkov. His body began to convulse, setting the bed rattling. But the laughter was so hard-won and wrenched from so deep within him that it did not remain laughter for long. The tears streamed his face. His mouth was stretched in an anguished gape. 'I curse him. I curse his mean miserable soul. May he rot in Hell! I pray to God that he will know the pain that he has inflicted on others. I implore God to show him no mercy in death as *he* showed no mercy in life. Dead! Can it really be true? Dead, you say?'

'It is true.'

'Have you seen him? Did you set eyes on his cold corpse?'

'Yes.'

'How did he die?'

'He was murdered. Stabbed through the heart.'

'Miracle!'

'It is known that you argued with Ferfichkin, over the money for your daughter's funeral.'

'Anya!' The sorrow crashed over him like a wave.

'You were heard to threaten his life.'

'Yes!'

'Did you kill him, Filya? You need not be afraid to tell me.'

'Kill him?' Gorshkov held out his hands in front of him and seemed to tighten them around an invisible neck. 'Of course I killed him. I strangled the life out of him with my own hands.'

'But as I have already said, Ferfichkin was stabbed to death.'

'Yes!' Gorshkov's eyes widened gleefully. 'After I had strangled him, I stabbed him. I took the kitchen knife and stuck it through his neck. I twisted the knife till the blade snapped off.' He mimed this action too.

'He was stabbed in the heart, Filya. I have told you that already too.'

'In the heart, yes! That's what I said!'

'You said the neck.'

'Are you trying to trick me? Perhaps you'll tell me now Ferfichkin isn't dead at all, when I killed him with my own hands.'

'Ferfichkin is dead. He was stabbed through the heart with a poniard. If you really killed him, you should be able to describe the weapon to me.'

'A poniard, you say?'

'Yes.'

'It was a short dagger with a flat blade. The handle was made . . . of ivory . . . carved in the shape of entwined serpents.'

'You didn't kill Ferfichkin, did you, Filya?'

A weight of disappointment seemed to settle on him. 'I would have done, had someone else not beaten me to it.' His mood changed again, to one of intense excitement. 'What a man! I would like to shake him by the hand! Was it you?'

'No, it wasn't me.'

'Of course not. You are a magistrate. Magistrates do not commit murder.'

'It is hoped not.' Porfiry smiled. His tone then became serious. 'Filya, do you remember receiving a letter, an anonymous letter about Ferfichkin?'

'A letter, you say?'

Porfiry nodded.

'What does it say?'

'No, Filya. I want to know if you ever received such a letter.'

'There were letters.'

'About Ferfichkin?'

Gorshkov shrugged. 'There was no one to read them. We used to get Andrey Petrovich to read the letters. But he died. Of the cholera.'

'What happened to the letters, do you know?'

'We have no use for letters.' He stared fierce-eyed at Porfiry. 'You cannot *eat* letters.' He made this statement with surprised force, in the manner of one revealing a profound, but only recently discovered truth. Almost immediately, he became morose, his expression disappointed, his gaze sealed off.

'Filya?'

Gorshkov's eyes darted briefly to the top of Porfiry's head. 'Where is your hat?' he asked sullenly, as if this was a source of great bitterness to him.

'I don't have a hat. Not today.'

Gorshkov sighed heavily. 'You're a gentleman. You should wear a hat.'

Porfiry smiled gently. 'Filya, why did you take the knife to your own throat?'

Gorshkov's gaze locked on to Porfiry's. 'I needed more pain.' After a moment he added: 'They will not let me have a knife now.'

'No. That is perhaps wise.'

'Why? What difference does it make to them?'

Porfiry looked at Dr Zverkov, who was watching the interview with interest. 'Perhaps none. Although I am sure the doctors here do not wish you to suffer any more than can be helped.'

'I want to suffer!' cried Gorshkov. 'I have suffered all my life! I have nothing if they take away my pain.'

'I must leave you now, Filya.'

'Let him come back.'

'Who?'

'The one who beat me. I want him to come back. I will foul myself again so that he beats me.'

'Oh, Filya.'

Gorshkov jumped up from the bed again. 'I must go to work. They cannot keep me here. They are expecting me at the factory. The foreman is a brute.'

'You don't have to go to work any more, Filya. You may rest now.'

Gorshkov's eyes grew large with panic. He sank back on to the bed. For a moment he continued to stare at Porfiry, then his gaze drifted off to an unknowable place. His hands began to move, seemingly with precision and purpose, as if he were miming some task. He brought them together, then drew them apart. Next, he held his left hand still as he described a straight line past it with his right, which was clenched as if holding something. Further lines and arcs were drawn in the air. Then the hands came together and rose sharply, as an imaginary thing was lifted. Without pause, he began repeating the same actions exactly, like a clockwork automaton.

Porfiry rose from the bed and indicated his readiness to go with a sharp and yet evasive bow.

6: A litigious man

'Porfiry Petrovich?' Virginsky said the name quietly, though with breathless urgency and a questioning intonation. He looked over the edge of his desk at Porfiry who was stooping beneath the window in front of him, his attention focused on a saucer he was holding in both hands. The saucer contained a viscous golden liquid.

At that moment, Nikodim Fomich came into the room. He took in the situation with an ironic smile, winking at Virginsky. 'I say, what have you there, Porfiry Petrovich?'

Porfiry met his good-natured enquiry with a preoccupied scowl. 'Honey.' He rose to his feet and stood over the saucer, watching it with fixed determination.

'Honey?'

'For the flies.'

'You're feeding the flies? I should have thought they are flourishing well enough without your encouragement.'

'The honey is laced with *kvas*.'

'I . . . see,' said Nikodim Fomich. He nodded his head and pursed his lips thoughtfully.

'The flies will eat the honey and become intoxicated. They will then become sleepy and erratic. This will make them easier to catch. And kill.'

'But why not simply lace the honey with poison?'

'Ah!' said Porfiry with a flutter of his eyelids. 'Where is the sport in that?' He broke off from his vigil and took his seat behind his desk with a grimace.

Nikodim Fomich settled into the sofa. 'I am surprised you do not use your psychology on them,' he said with another wink to Virginsky, who was watching their exchange with an acutely anguished expression.

'You always say that, Nikodim Fomich, but it is not *my* psychology,' said Porfiry. 'And in a way I am. The psychology of a fly is surely very simple. It is dominated by hunger.'

'So, it's true what they're saying.'

'And what are they saying?'

'That you have lost your wits, Porfiry Petrovich. That the heat and the flies have finally got to you.'

'What?'

'That and the pressure of work. Three murder cases running concurrently, and not a whiff of a solution in any one. Finally, the great Porfiry Petrovich has come face to face with the prospect of failure.'

'Who is saying this?'

'No one in particular. It is just a thing one hears. They say you are going round in circles, that you have no leads, that you have wasted valuable time arresting the wrong men, or that you have let the murderers go. Or even that you are more concerned with the drainage provisions of the city of St Petersburg.'

'No one is saying these things. Apart from you, that is.'

'I? No. I have . . .' Nikodim Fomich cast about for the appropriate word: '*Defended* you. I say to your critics that you will surprise us all, that you will amaze us, in fact, with your powers of deduction and your . . . psychology. Yes. It is always the psychology that does it in the end. You will produce solutions from thin air, like rabbits from a hat. Is that not so?'

Porfiry did not answer.

'I'm confident of it. Indeed, I have good money riding on it.'

'You mean there are wagers on the likelihood of my solving these cases?'

'One can get very good odds at the moment. You'd better not let me down, my friend.'

'But this is appalling. And hardly appropriate behaviour for a man in your position, Nikodim Fomich.'

The chief inspector pouted contritely. 'I merely brought it up to show my absolute confidence in you.'

'Even so.' Porfiry gave his friend an admonishing stare. After a moment's consideration, he added: 'How much did you bet?'

Nikodim Fomich waved the question away. 'Please. Let's not talk about that. I wouldn't want to put you under any more pressure than you are already. But tell me that you are close to a solution in at least one of the cases. The Meyer case, for instance. You have been working on that the longest.'

'I have my theories.'

'I knew it! You are the man for theories.'

'To begin with, I now believe all three cases are connected.'

'What? The latest as well? I knew you had connected the first two -- the letters and all, even though there was no letter found in the case of Setochkin. So is there an anonymous letter involved in this latest case too?'

'Not as far as we know. A search of the Gorshkovs' corner in their rotting basement has turned up nothing. No, it is not the presence of a letter that inclines me to this view but a number of other factors. To begin with, the murder weapon.'

'But the murder weapon is different in each case.'

'Exactly!'

Nikodim Fomich's expression clouded. 'My friend, I fear you have been pushing yourself too far. You cannot connect cases simply because they are different. Why, you'd have all the murders on our books pieced together like a jigsaw puzzle, if that were so. And our entire casebook solved by the arrest of one man! It's madness, you must see that.'

'They are superficially different, but fundamentally the same. Each weapon, I feel, has been deliberately chosen because of its significance to the murder victim.'

'How so?'

'The chocolates, poisoned. A tarnished sweetness. It seems appropriate, does it not, for a woman who once made her living as a prostitute? Setochkin, a dissolute retired officer, a gentleman of little honour, shot with his own duelling pistol, a weapon of honour. Suggestive, is it not? And Ferfichkin, the tailor who exploited the Bible for gain, stitched through the heart with a cruciform dagger. It is all, quite clearly, indicative of a consistent psychology at work.'

'There! You see!' cried Nikodim Fomich to Virginsky. 'I told you there would be psychology in it.'

'Furthermore, I have now had a chance to read the witness statements compiled by the Eastern Admiralty District Police Bureau. On the night before Ferfichkin's body was found, a man answering his description was seen to bump into a number of people. He was evidently drunk. It was after one such collision -- with a man who has not yet come forward -- that he fell to the ground; it was assumed in a drunken stupor. Now, if you remember, according to Dr Meyer's testimony, someone bumped into him coming out of the confectioner's, at which point he believes the poisoned chocolates were substituted for those he had bought.'

'What are you saying? That this bumping-into is important?'

'It is the beginnings of a pattern.'

'But there was no bumping-into in the Setochkin case,' protested Nikodim Fomich.

'No, not that we know of,' admitted Porfiry.

'It is all very . . .' Nikodim Fomich brought his clenched hands together in the air, then wiggled his fingers as his hands drifted apart. 'Tenuous.'

'I can see how it would seem so to you, but to me these patterns are quite as concrete as any piece of physical evidence. Vakhramev's journal provides a link between the Setochkin and the Meyer cases -- the visit to the brothel. There are two instances of collisions between pedestrians, which in turn link the Ferfichkin and the Meyer case. So indirectly, Ferfichkin is also linked to Setochkin. When you add to these correspondencies the significant weapon choices, we begin to discern a presence, and to suspect a definite personality at work.'

'Yes, but who? That is the question.'

'I -- I think I may be able to shed some light on that.' It was Virginsky, his voice tremulous with the import of what he was saying. He blushed as the eyes of the older men turned on him. 'I was trying to tell you, Porfiry Petrovich, when Nikodim Fomich came into the room.'

'Very well,' said Porfiry. 'You may tell us now.'

'As you suggested, I paid a visit to Archives.' Virginsky spoke quickly, breathlessly. 'It was you who said you recognised the dead man's face. There was indeed a case file with Ferfichkin's name on it. It seems that Yemelyan Antonovich was a highly litigious man. He has sought to bring a host of private suits against many individuals. It started when he was in domestic service. It is an interesting case in itself. He accused his master of slander, it seems, because the gentleman complained, as masters are wont to do I believe . . .' Virginsky gave Porfiry an abashed look before continuing: '. . . that Ferfichkin was torturing him. And so Ferfichkin claimed that he was being slandered as a torturer. A report was made, but no proceedings were made. The gentleman's name was struck from the record at his request. However, for

Ferfichkin, it was the beginning of a career of litigation, mostly for perceived slander, or the recovery of debt.'

'This is all very interesting,' said Nikodim Fomich. 'But could you hurry up and get to the point.'

'Well, the point is, I found a name, one of Ferfichkin's recent debtors, a man for whom he had sewn a fur collar on to an overcoat.'

'Yes, yes. And what is the name, dear boy?' urged the chief inspector.

'Rostanev,' said Virginsky. 'Axenty Ivanovich Rostanev.'

'Rostanev?' Porfiry frowned. Then his face lit up with realisation. 'Rostanev! No, I don't believe it! Surely not?'

'Who is Rostanev?' asked Nikodim Fomich.

'My nemesis!' said Porfiry, rising from his desk and rushing over to Virginsky.

'He is described in the record as a civil servant,' added Virginsky, the excitement rising in his voice.

'So! Do you have the letter?'

'Of course,' said Virginsky, sorting through the papers on his desk. 'I retrieved it from Alexander Grigorevich. When I saw the name, I thought I would check the handwriting. You will see.' He handed Porfiry the terse note that had come from the Ministry of Internal Affairs, Department of Public Health.

'I could be, it *could* be,' Porfiry repeated, as if seeking to convince himself of something he doubted.

'What is it?' Nikodim Fomich heaved himself from the sofa to join them. He read the note that Porfiry thrust in his hand. '"Re: Yekaterininsky Canal adjacent to Stolyarny Lane. Your letter regarding the above has been investigated. No action was deemed necessary." I see that it is signed A. I. Rostanev. But what of it?'

'Now the letter that was sent to Dr Meyer,' said Porfiry, impatiently. 'Do you have it, Pavel Pavlovich?'

Virginsky handed him this document.

Porfiry snatched the other letter back from Nikodim Fomich and compared the two. 'There are similarities, definite similarities. But I dare say there are many clerks who could produce an identical hand. Nevertheless, it certainly makes our Mr Rostanev a candidate.'

'There is one other thing,' said Virginsky, 'which I have only now discovered. In fact, it was this that I was checking when Nikodim Fomich . . .'

'Yes, yes, you have already mentioned that I am responsible for delaying your interesting disclosures. There is no need to delay them further yourself.'

'I checked the pupil lists of the Chermak Private High School. If you remember, we were interested in classmates of the individual mentioned in Vakhramev's journal, a certain Golyadkin. We were hoping to identify the mysterious individual who went with Golyadkin, Vakhramev and Devushkin to the brothel where Raisa Meyer worked. There was no Rostanev in Golyadkin's class; however, the name did occur in the list of pupils five years junior to Golyadkin. Rostanev, A. I.' Virginsky pointed to the name on the relevant list. 'And just now,' he continued breathlessly, 'I happened upon an instance of the name in Ballet's order book. The address is given as "care of the Ministry of Internal Affairs, Chernyshov Square".'

Porfiry's hands snapped together in a single loud clap. 'Got one!' he cried. He met Virginsky and Nikodim Fomich's bemusement with a smile of serene satisfaction. 'A fly. The *kvas* worked. They are drowsy now.' His smile solidified as he looked down at his clasped hands.

7: Inside the ministry

Three men were squeezed into the back of the *drozhki* speeding along the northern embankment of the Fontanka. The play of light over the water's surface drew Porfiry's gaze; his eye was baffled by the luminous networks that formed and folded in the instants of their passing. The tide flowed away behind them, provoking a feeling of uncertainty in the magistrate, the sense almost that he was making a mistake, such was the strength of the river's beckoning. He turned away from it. His companions, Virginsky to his left, Salytov to his right, were lost in their own thoughts. Both men stared straight ahead, past the standing, shouting, whip-happy driver, to the next bridge, the Chernyshov, which marked their destination.

As they traversed the riverside facade of the Ministry of Internal Affairs, Porfiry was put in mind of a prison cell. The white columns that masked the upper two storeys looked like a grille of bars, through which the recessed windows peeped. The building as a whole imposed itself on its stretch of the embankment with a squat and brutish authority. Its juxtaposition to the fugitive Fontanka emphasised its own solid immovability. Unlike the river, the building wasn't going anywhere.

Again there were arches, Porfiry noticed, feeling the same twinge of annoyance as when he had looked upon the arches of the house at the eleventh verst. A common enough architectural motif, especially on the neoclassical buildings in which St Petersburg abounded -- it was surely a mark of desperation to place any significance on its recurrence?

Perhaps those voices of doubt that Nikodim Fomich had reported to him were right. Could it be that he was losing his way in this case -- or rather, *these cases*? Was it not perversity that made him view the murders as related? Each of the connections taken alone was far from conclusive, an assumption that could easily turn out to be an error; which meant that the trail he had been following was nothing more than a series of false steps.

The light-coloured plaster and brickwork of the ministry building gave it a harsh, impenetrable lustre that reflected his doubts back at him. For relief his gaze settled on Virginsky's face.

Porfiry wondered if all along he had not allowed himself, despite his better judgement, to be swayed by the young man's persuasive fervour. Dismissing the thought, he looked quickly at Lieutenant Salytov, who, seeming to sense his attention, stiffened in his seat, lifting his head, although self-consciously refusing to face him. Porfiry knew -- and had dismissed -- Salytov's view of the Meyer case, that the chocolates had been poisoned by a revolutionary cell centred around Ballet's the confectioner's. He knew that the policeman had been led to his theory by prejudice. But really, was it not Porfiry's own prejudice that had led him to suspect an anonymous official of being capable of the worst of crimes, simply because of his own frustrations over an open drain?

The *drozhki* took the corner into Chernyshov Square recklessly, causing the driver to topple back on to his seat, and abuse his horse all the more. And then it came to an abrupt halt, whipping the passengers backwards and forwards like shaken dolls.

Virginsky and Salytov sprang out of the *drozhki* simultaneously, leaving Porfiry rooted to the centre of the seat.

The square was congested with carriages, ready to bear the orders of the central administration to the furthest reaches of the empire. Waves of men in civil service uniforms flowed in and out of the entrance. Some hurried into waiting carriages that then became snarled in the throng of unmoving vehicles.

Porfiry sensed the impatience of the other two as they looked up at him from either side. The driver too turned round to cast him a quizzical glance. Porfiry, however, felt no inclination to move.

'This has always struck me as the most premeditated part of our premeditated city,' he said, looking across the square and along the Teatralnaya, the straight and strangely symmetrical street that led to the Alexandrine Theatre. 'The vision of one man imposed on a whole zone. The architect as autocrat, although it is true to say that the architect's vision can only ever be realised with the help of the true autocrat's will, to say nothing of the latter's power and money.'

'What are you talking about, Porfiry Petrovich?'

Porfiry seemed to wink at Salytov's brusque demand. 'I rather think that a murderer is like an architect of destruction, don't you? The crimes he shapes are analogous with the structures an architect imposes on the landscape. A critic of murder -- that is to say a detective -- becomes adept at recognising and interpreting the stylistic devices and motifs in play.' Porfiry turned his head slowly to glance down at the policeman. 'The architect, working in partnership with the true autocrat, creates and constructs a new reality consistent with his fantasy, in his case a harmonious and ordered fantasy, which we deign to call his vision. In the case of a murderer, he is the sole autocrat of his own universe. It occurs to me that the fantasy that guides him may be equally as harmonious and ordered as the architect's, or at least so it appears to him. Indeed, perhaps it is his desire to impose order that compels him to murder.' Now Porfiry turned his head, with the same slow movement, to face Virginsky. 'If that is the case then it may well be that our murderer is indeed a minor civil servant, a petty functionary whose actual power falls far short of his ambition and his egoism. A man who has felt himself thwarted and frustrated -- slighted, insulted, overlooked -- throughout his life. Equally, that same description would apply to one who overtly sets himself up against the state, one who would seek to overthrow the state and replace it with something else of his own design. A revolutionary, for every murder is an act of revolution against God and nature.' Porfiry broke off.

'And so?' prompted Virginsky.

'And so,' said Porfiry, his voice weary as he hauled himself out of the *drozhki*, 'we must proceed with caution.'

At that moment a closed black wagon marked *Politsiya* drew up beside them. Porfiry raised a questioning eyebrow to Salytov who nodded grimly.

'Very well,' said Porfiry, mirroring Salytov's nod. 'The wagon is here. Let us talk to Rostanev.'

*

Echoes of murmured conversations filled the high, marbled lobby. Both urgent and muted, they rose from the shuffling men who crossed the polished floor, to drift like dust into the niches of the walls, before settling on the blank-eyed, stone-deaf busts. The air was stifling, clogged with spinning particles. A desiccated heat drew the breath from Porfiry. Even so, he felt the longing for a cigarette. A large double-headed eagle, emblem of the imperial house, was moulded on to the wall that faced them, picked out in gold leaf. The strange beast looked with inevitably divided attention, left and right, into the corridors that led off from the hall. The new civil flag, that is to say the flag that had been adopted a decade earlier, but which Porfiry still could not bring himself to regard as Russian, hung limply from a staff above the heraldic form, its bands of black, gold and white crumpled into each other. Porfiry saw Salytov's snarl at the sight of it: 'Germans!'

The word reverberated clearly above the hubbub, like a hard ball of sound tossed carelessly against the walls. Heads turned in outrage.

'Be careful, Ilya Petrovich,' said Porfiry, smiling mischievously. 'Such an outburst might be construed as treasonable.'

'Nonsense.' Salytov glared. 'I am a loyal subject of the Tsar.'

'Even when he listens to German counsel, and foists on us an alien flag?' goaded Virginsky.

'It was the Germans who made him do it.'

'But he took up their suggestion readily enough, did he not? That was one reform he was not slow to implement in full -- to put the Romanov family colours on the Russian nation's flag. It shows quite clearly how he regards the country. As his personal fiefdom.'

'I thought you liberals liked this Tsar,' said Salytov. 'He can hardly be described as lacking in reformist zeal.'

'That is enough,' interrupted Porfiry, regretting the attention that the hissed debate was drawing.

'What makes you think I am a liberal?' Virginsky had to get in.

'Enough!' Porfiry's cry provoked a bubbling of shocked reaction around them. 'May I remind you gentlemen that we are here on official business? Furthermore, this hardly is the place to engage in such discussions.'

Porfiry frowned distractedly as he looked about. Two staircases led up from the lobby. Numerous unmarked doors were visible in the corridors that fed into the hall. 'Which way do you suppose it is to the Department of Public Health? In a building this size one would expect there to be signposts.'

'Now it is you who are criticising the way our Tsar has ordered things.'

Ignoring Virginsky's observation, Porfiry accosted one of the clerks hurrying head-down towards the door, a youngish man with a splenetic face. 'Excuse me, sir.' The clerk did not seem to have heard him. Just as the man was about to collide into him, Porfiry stepped sharply to one side. 'Sir!' he shouted. The clerk stopped in his steps and drew himself up. He glanced sharply towards Porfiry, his face crimped in displeasure.

'Do you mind? I have a very important commission to dispatch.'

'If you could only tell us where to find the Department of Public Health.'

The man's eyes bulged. 'There is a saying in the ministry that if you don't know where an office is you really have no business going there.' He brushed past Porfiry and was gone.

'Really!' said Porfiry, gazing in astonishment at the fellow's wake. 'These people.'

Now another one of the bottle-green uniformed men was coming towards him from the other direction. A stooped, grey-whiskered relic, whose coat was nonetheless immaculately brushed, his buttons gleaming. He had the order of St Vladimir hanging from a ribbon around his neck. The old man looked straight through Porfiry, and though he moved with slow, small steps, it seemed that he too was determined to collide.

'Sir!' cried Porfiry. 'If you please!'

The other man tottered to a halt as if he had been hurtling towards Porfiry at breakneck speed. His eyebrows bristled menacingly, with sinister abundance. He glared at Porfiry as if he believed him to be a dangerous lunatic.

'What is it?' His voice was edged with a panicked impatience.

'Could you direct us to the Department of Public Health?'

'The Department of Public Health?'

'Yes.'

'I'll take you there.' The old man began his tortuously slow step again, a gait in which neither foot ever once completely extended beyond the other. They waited for him to get ahead of them before following, at a funeral pace.

'It really is not necessary,' said Porfiry. 'If you could simply give us the directions . . .'

'It's no trouble.' The old man began to wheeze heavily.

'We are in rather a hurry.'

'Yes,' said the old man. 'This way is quicker.'

Porfiry sighed. The old man had led them to the first flight of stairs; he paused for a moment at the bottom before ascending to the first step. Not before he had both feet planted on it did he attempt to scale the second.

*

He led them down a corridor, lined on both sides with mountains of files. These seemed to have grown out like crystal formations from the rooms along the corridor. Moving at their guide's pace, Porfiry had ample opportunity to peer into some of these rooms, at least before the occupants, noticing his attention, closed a door in his face. They were all of different sizes, some as dark and cramped as a cupboard, others extending beyond the reach of his gaze into shadowed edges. Sometimes he glimpsed rows of men sitting on high stools at ledger desks. In other rooms he saw no one clearly, but had the sense of a presence in there: perhaps he saw a vague shape move or heard the fall of footstep, the riffle of paper or something scuttling out of sight; the door would inevitably close by an unseen hand.

The old man led them at last to a pair of closed double doors. He pointed with a crooked finger at the words 'Department of Public Health' etched on a small brass plaque, then continued on his way without a word, almost without pausing. Porfiry widened his eyes, ironically mysterious, as he put a hand on the door handle.

The doors opened on to a large room, which even so felt cramped and stuffy. Piles of papers laid out in rows acted as screens, dividing it into smaller cells. In these, men -- either individually or in groups of two, three or four -- sat stooped over desks. Porfiry, Virginsky and Salytov were presented with a sea of rounded backs, which seemed to be bent under the oppressive menace of the room's disproportionately low ceiling. There was a soft sound, a susurration mixed with an amplified scratching, the accumulated mouthings and pen pushings of this army of copyists and clerks. A hundred quills swished the air at once in a hypnotic dance that quivered with promised meaning. One man was moving between the desks. He looked across the room towards them as they came in and after a moment's frowning hesitation approached them with an armful of files.

Porfiry had the vaguest sense that he recognised the man. *One sees a thousand such faces in St Petersburg*, he thought.

The man placed his burden of files on top of an already teetering paper tower and came up to them. 'Yes?'

'How do they do it?' asked Porfiry, looking past the man at the seated clerks behind him. 'How do they remain seated all day -- every day? I know that I for one could not.' Porfiry looked the other up and down significantly. 'I imagine it is an occupational hazard here too? Haemorrhoids, I mean.'

'I . . . that is to say . . . '

'You need say no more. I understand. You have my sympathy. And now, to the matter in hand. We are looking for one Rostanev, Axenty Ivanovich. The writer of this letter.' Porfiry handed the civil servant the letter about the Ditch.

'But this is highly irregular.' He scowled at the paper and shook his head. 'I shall have to have a word with Rostanev about this. Thank you for bringing it to my attention.' His tone was curt, however, and devoid of any real gratitude.

'You misunderstand,' said Porfiry. 'I am Porfiry Petrovich, an investigating magistrate. This gentleman' -- Porfiry indicated Salytov -- 'is a police lieutenant. We are here to interview Rostanev on police business.'

The man touched the back of one hand to his forehead, a gesture that provoked an elusive sense of déjà vu, and a keen impatience, in Porfiry. 'Is it really necessary?' The man's tone was whining. 'I agree that he should not have written the letter. He has no authority to sign letters from the Department of Public Health. He is a mere scribe. However, I dare say that the details of the letter are correct. It is one I would have signed myself had it been put in front of me. Surely it will suffice if he is subjected to internal disciplinary procedures? Knowing Rostanev as I do, I feel that an official reprimand will certainly have the desired effect of discouraging him from ever committing such a foolish act again.'

'It is not to do with the letter -- not this letter at any rate. We wish to talk to Rostanev in connection with a murder investigation. I wonder, however, could you tell me to whom I have the honour of speaking?'

'I am . . . Yefimov.' The man's startled diffidence, followed by the defiance with which he finally offered his name, betrayed an inner tension. The superficial hostility that was his shield against the world seemed to change into something more particular, directed at Porfiry alone. 'Collegiate Registrar Yefimov.'

'You are Rostanev's superior?'

'Yes.' The answer was given emphatically.

'Your face seems familiar to me. And indeed your name.' Porfiry smiled with vague and hopeful affability. Seeming to remember himself, he handed Yefimov the anonymous letter sent to Dr Meyer. 'We have reasons to believe that he is the author of this letter also.'

'Yes, quite possibly. I would not be surprised.' He handed the letter back. An unexpected sympathy showed in his expression. 'You have to understand that Axenty Ivanovich... how to put this? He is not quite right in the head, poor fellow. I myself once received a letter not dissimilar to this. The handwriting was the same. I knew it was from Rostanev. I did nothing about it, because, well, really -- one cannot hold a man like Rostanev accountable. It seems strange to say this, but Rostanev himself is not malicious. He means no harm. He acts out of a compulsion. It is a disease. He deserves our pity, I would think.'

'Yes, yes, I quite agree. And ordinarily I would be happy to leave it to you, as his superior, to exercise your discretion in disciplining him. However, I regret to say that the recipient of this letter was accused of murdering his wife because of its contents. And another man who received a similar letter was suspected of murdering his daughter's seducer.'

'That is unfortunate.'

'I wonder, do you have the letter that you were sent?'

'I destroyed it and thought no more of it. Until today, that is. He never sent me another.'

'A pity. Nevertheless, what's done is done. I don't suppose you can remember the content of it?'

'It was nonsense. The ramblings, frankly, of a madman. That is why I assumed that Rostanev had sent it.'

'Is Rostanev in the department today?'

'Yes.'

'We would be grateful if you could point him out to us.'

Yefimov nodded distractedly and gnawed a thumbnail. 'Of course. Please, come this way.'

They threaded their way between the desks. At one point, Salytov brushed one of the columns of files, causing it to totter precariously. All the heads in the room turned towards the swaying paperwork. The collective sigh of relief as it settled without toppling sounded like the wind passing through a forest. The copyists bowed once again over their work.

Yefimov took them deep into the warren of desks and stopped next to that of a short, barrel-shaped man with a squashed face and a sharply angled forehead. His civil service coat was frayed and grubby. He had very black lank hair, which he wore long. Unusually for a civil servant, he was bearded. His thick black beard was twisted into four points, giving it the appearance of a dark fuzzy star. The man worked with great concentration, with his tongue stuck out and twisted to one side. The childish habit gave his expression a trusting simplicity.

'Axenty Ivanovich,' said Yefimov.

Rostanev looked up, mildly curious. He inspected Porfiry, Virginsky and Salytov with detached and unsuspecting interest.

'These gentlemen wish to talk to you.'

Confusion rather than concern clouded his face.

'You are Axenty Ivanovich Rostanev?' said Porfiry.

Rostanev nodded. One hand moved to tighten the points of his beard.

'I have a letter here that I would like you to look at.' Porfiry handed him the letter sent to Meyer. 'Do you recognise it?'

Rostanev read it through and nodded. 'Oh yes. I do. I wrote it, you see.' His smile appeared almost facetious. But Porfiry decided it most closely resembled the smile of a child who is surprised by the silliness of adults.

'You admit that you wrote it?'

'Yes.'

'And that you sent it to gentleman called Dr Meyer?'

'Yes.'

'Did you also send a similar letter to Ruslan Vladimirovich Vakhramev?'

Rostanev thought for a moment, his face becoming momentarily serious. It then lit up with pleasure, as if he believed himself to be playing a game, and doing unexpectedly well at it. 'Yes!' The same hand went back to maintaining his whiskery prongs. He held a quill in the other hand.

'Did you also send another letter to this gentleman, your superior, Collegiate Registrar Yefimov?'

'Yes!'

'But why did you write these letters?'

'The voices told me to.'

'I beg your pardon? The voices, did you say?'

'Yes. At night the voices speak to me. They tell me to write the letters. If I write the letters the voices go away. But they always come back, eventually.'

'Good heavens, how perplexing for you! Tell me though, were you once a pupil at the Chermak Private High School in Moscow?'

Rostanev let out a chuckle like a repeated high note on a muted trumpet. 'Yes!'

Porfiry's gaze softened and became almost pitying. 'I must ask you to come with us, sir, to the police bureau. There are further questions I wish to ask you and it will be better if we conduct the rest of the interview in private.'

For the first time Rostanev's expression grew anxious. His beard-tightening fingers quickened. The quill in the other hand trembled. 'But I have work to do.' He looked to Yefimov for confirmation.

'You must go with them,' said Yefimov.

'If your hand offends you, cut it off.' Rostanev's tone was despairing.

'Now now, don't worry. Everything will be all right.' To Porfiry, Yefimov added: 'He can't possibly be held responsible. The new courts will find him insane. You can see for yourself. And this talk of voices . . .'

Porfiry said nothing.

Yefimov nodded commandingly to Rostanev. The copyist laid down his quill and slipped off his high stool. Standing on the floor, he turned out to be even shorter and more rotund than Porfiry. He looked up at them all with untroubled innocence. Now he used both hands to sharpen the points of his beard.

Salytov grasped him firmly by the arm, pulling that hand away from its task. A look of shock and bewilderment descended on Rostanev, and -- suddenly -- fear.

'It's all right, Axenty Ivanovich,' insisted Yefimov. 'Go with the gentlemen.' He spoke slowly, with precise enunciation. His eyes stared steadily into Rostanev's in a way that was perhaps meant to be reassuring.

Rostanev nodded and obeyed.

As they walked Rostanev out of the office, Salytov's shoulder again clipped a tower of papers, this one even more precariously assembled than the first. As before, all heads turned. The room held its breath; there was a sense of inevitable disaster this time. It was a strangely gradual catastrophe when it came, one which they felt ought to be preventable, but of course was not. The momentum of the collapse built and flowed along the twisting rows of paper, as the originally disturbed column took with it those around it, and they in turn transmitted instability to their neighbours. The sound of the whole event, which left only a few half-towers standing in the room, was like a wave crashing over rocks. All around, sheets flew up and floated in the hot, dusty air, before drifting erratically and ostentatiously to the floor.

It was impossible for Porfiry to resist looking at the faces of men who had just witnessed an unimaginable upheaval of their world and not to feel, seeing the extent and depth of their open-mouthed horror, a sense almost of privilege. Even so, he had no wish to linger. They swept Rostanev from the silenced room.

8: Interview with a madman

'Empty your pockets!'

The first item Rostanev took out was a small ebony-handled penknife. The police lieutenant snatched it from him and examined it closely, opening and closing each of the blades in turn. While he was doing so, Rostanev cast his unconcerned gaze around the Haymarket District Police Bureau. His face opened up with wonder, as if he were watching the events of a dream unfold. Both hands were at his beard again.

'Nasty,' said Salytov, laying the knife on the clerk Zamyotov's counter. 'You could do someone a deal of harm with that. Note it down, Alexander Grigorevich. One knife.'

Zamyotov sighed and raised his eyebrows as he was compelled to record the knife's existence.

'It's for the quills,' explained Rostanev, with a slight smirk that was no doubt involuntary. Its effect on Salytov was unfortunate.

'Quills?' Salytov leant down to bark the question in Rostanev's face.

Perhaps unwisely, Rostanev failed to flinch. 'For sharpening them.'

Salytov straightened slowly, keeping his narrowed eyes fixed on Rostanev, on whom the menacing glare was wasted: he now enthusiastically produced a bundle of quills from inside his coat. He beamed triumphantly, as if he believed this would be enough to win the officer's approval. Sensing Salytov's obduracy, he placed the quills -- about six in number -- on the counter next to the knife, then plunged a hand into the other side of his coat. A dozen or so more quills were added to those already on the counter. After further searches in unexpected places, the total number of quills reached twenty-five, laboriously and ironically counted off by Zamyotov. So far Porfiry had been content to stand back and watch as Salytov processed the suspect but now he felt moved to intervene. 'You will be given a receipt for everything. This is normal procedure. There is no need to be alarmed.'

'I am not alarmed,' said Rostanev with disarming simplicity, whiskers rotating under his grinding thumbs.

Porfiry smiled. 'Good. Now, when you have finished giving

Alexander Grigorevich your details, perhaps you would be so good as to join me in my chambers for a little chat.'

Porfiry drew Salytov to one side. 'I want a search done of his lodgings.'

Salytov nodded without looking at the magistrate.

'I also want Dr Meyer and Vakhramev brought in. And the old woman, Mikheyeva.'

Salytov could not now prevent himself from meeting Porfiry's eye. He held the gaze for a moment, before his head twisted away, as though repelled.

*

'There is a terrible smell in here,' said Rostanev as he took the seat opposite Porfiry.

It was several moments before Porfiry was able to speak. He flashed his astonishment at Virginsky, who could not suppress a wry grin. 'Yes. Quite,' said Porfiry at last. 'If you remember, I sent a letter saying as much to your department. And received the reply, signed by you, that I have already shown you. No action was deemed necessary.'

The small smirk that seemed to be Rostanev's stock reaction to difficulty twisted his lips again. 'That was the correct response. There was nothing that could be done. That is to say, no action was deemed possible. We are not required to do the impossible. The impossible is by definition unnecessary. One must take no action when no action can be taken.'

Porfiry's eyes widened as he tried to unravel Rostanev's argument. 'My friend, you might have surprised yourselves.'

Rostanev's stifled brass chuckle sounded again. 'It is not the policy of the department, of any department, to surprise itself. The ministry could not function if departments engaged in surprising themselves.'

'But, the ministry does *not* function,' Porfiry spluttered.

'It is just that you do not understand what its function is.'

Porfiry realised that he had been blinking to excess because he saw the action mirrored in Rostanev's face. He made a conscious effort to stop.

'There are a lot of flies in here,' observed Rostanev.

Porfiry glanced around distractedly. 'Yes, that problem is not unconnected with the original problem.'

'They seem rather lethargic.'

'They are intoxicated,' said Porfiry.

'How did they get into that state?' There was a note of disapproval in Rostanev's question.

'I fed them honey laced with *kvas*,' said Porfiry. It was galling to be on the receiving end of the look that came from Rostanev. 'However, we are not here to talk about flies.'

'My lips are sealed,' said Rostanev, with a wink.

'No,' said Porfiry, momentarily bewildered. 'Let us talk about Raisa Meyer instead.'

'Who is Raisa Meyer?'

'Are you serious? Do you really not remember? Earlier, I showed you another letter, this one. It concerns a woman called Raisa Meyer. You sent it to her husband.'

'Did I?'

'That's what you said.'

'I send so many, you see.'

'How did you come to know Raisa Meyer?'

'I don't know her. I've never met her. Who is she?'

'She is dead.' Porfiry watched Rostanev closely. The information seemed not to permeate his consciousness at all. 'You must have known her. How could you write such things about her if you didn't know her? *Why* would you?'

'The voices.'

'Did the voices tell you to kill her?'

'No,' said Rostanev flatly.

'Then why did you kill her?'

'I didn't kill her.' He made the statement calmly, without any of the defensive force that Porfiry would have expected; as one disputing a minor point of detail, in fact.

'In this letter, you said that you had slept with Raisa Meyer when she was a prostitute.'

Rostanev stared open-mouthed at Porfiry. He then turned his incredulous glare on Virginsky and cried: 'Prostitute! Prostitute!'

'Please,' said Porfiry. 'Try to concentrate. Raisa Meyer was indeed once a prostitute. How could you have known that if you had never met her?'

'The voices?' A note of uncertainty had crept into Rostanev's tone.

'The voices will not help you. You cannot blame it all on the voices. Is it not true that you once visited a brothel with a former schoolfriend called Golyadkin? There were two other men in your party, one of whom was Vakhramev, to whom you sent another anonymous letter concerning his daughter and a man called Setochkin. It was in the course of that visit that you first made the acquaintance of Raisa Meyer.'

Rostanev became agitated. 'No! It is most emphatically not true. I admit to sending the letters, but I have never visited one of those places. I am an official in the Department of Public Health. Am I likely to expose myself to the risk of contracting a filthy disease? Would I defile myself with women?'

'A man may act under any number of compulsions,' said Porfiry. 'He may even be driven to do things that are not in his own or others' interests. That is what it means to be human.'

'Then I would rather be a fly,' said Rostanev hotly.

'Do you think that flies are any less subject to compulsion?'

Rostanev's head bobbed and oscillated as he followed a drunken fly's plummeting trajectory.

'Who is Nikolai Nobody?' demanded Porfiry.

Rostanev turned his gaze slowly on the magistrate. 'No one?' It seemed like a guess.

'Are you Nikolai Nobody?'

'Am I?' Rostanev looked about the room conspiratorially. 'My lips are sealed,' he added, at last.

'Have you ever bought chocolates from Ballet's the confectioner's?'

'On Nevsky Prospekt? I know it well.'

'That's right.'

'No.' Rostanev shook his head forlornly, as though he were sorry to disappoint. 'I cannot afford to shop there.'

'And yet the name Rostanev shows up in one of their order books.'

Rostanev chuckled. 'That is a striking coincidence.'

'The address of this Rostanev is given as care of the Ministry of Internal Affairs, Chernyshov Square.'

'Even more striking!'

'And outside Ballet's you contrived to bump into Dr Meyer,' pressed Porfiry. 'Switching the box of chocolates he purchased for one contaminated with poison.'

'Who has said this? Who accuses me of this?'

'Did you also send an anonymous letter to Gorshkov the factory worker?'

'I don't know. Did I? I suppose I must have. I have sent a lot of letters. I confess to sending the letters. That I know I did. But I never bumped into anyone. I am not the sort who bumps into people. I would always far rather step to one side. I am a stepper-to-the-side. Not a bumper-into.'

'What?'

'The world is divided into three types of men. Steppers-to-the-side, unbudgeables and bumpers-into. I am a stepper-to-the-side.'

'I see. I confess I have never viewed the world in that light before.'

'I can see that you are an unbudgeable.'

'What about Ferfichkin? The tailor who sewed a fur collar on a coat for you. Into which category would you place him?'

'Unbudgeable.'

'So you do admit that you know Ferfichkin?' pressed Porfiry.

'As you say, he sewed a collar on to a coat.'

'Yes. A fur collar. It is strange that you could afford a fur collar and yet you say you cannot afford to shop at Ballet's.'

'To pay for the collar I was forced to secure an advance on my salary. The necessity of paying that back led to a degree of embarrassment that precluded the, uh, aforementioned, herewith, withal, uh, etcetera etcetera, your obedient servant, Rostanev, A. I.'

'You purchased the collar but could not afford to pay for it to be sewn on to your coat. You owed Ferfichkin money, did you not?'

'And he owed me a coat.'

'I see. Ferfichkin is dead. He was murdered. Stabbed through the heart by a man he bumped into.'

'No? He was a bumper-into, after all?'

'We can connect you with all three murders. Indeed, I would say that there are enough prima facie connections to make a case.'

'Then it must be true,' said Rostanev. 'I must have done it.' He scratched his lank-haired head in some perplexity. 'Goodness knows what I was thinking.'

*

The following morning, the Thursday of the third week after Raisa and Grigory's deaths, Porfiry was turning the pages of the latest issue of the *Periodical*. He smoked, with a languid and almost nostalgic sensuousness. From time to time he emitted a heavy sigh, as if overcome by ennui. Whether he was more absorbed in the act of smoking, or that of reading, was hard to say. At any rate, his countenance discouraged interruption.

Virginsky sat at his station by the window and sorted through the case files, trying to bring some order to the clutter he had accumulated. Occasionally, he would be drawn by one of Porfiry's sighs to look up wonderingly, only to find the magistrate sealed off from all enquiry. However, after one particularly prolonged sigh, he met Porfiry's eye at last.

'He is either an innocent lunatic or a very clever dissembler,' said Porfiry. Prompted by Virginsky's quizzical frown, he added, 'I believe we will soon be able to tell for certain which.'

Porfiry lit another cigarette and went back to scanning the journal. After a few moments, he broke off with a jerk of his head and looked down at a number of flies lurching across his desk. Without taking his eyes off them, as though he wished to misdirect them, he rolled up his copy of the *Periodical*. Then he began to beat the desk furiously with it. He did not seem to be aiming at specific flies, but rather striking at random, with the intention of getting in as many blows as possible over the widest area, in the shortest possible time.

Virginsky watched open-mouthed.

When the frenzied swatting was over, the desk was strewn with insect corpses, as well as a few twitching, mutilated, but still living specimens. Porfiry turned a smile of triumph towards Virginsky. Not meeting with the validation he had hoped for, Porfiry turned up the underside of the rolled journal to discover a few squashed flies stuck there. He frowned and then dropped the journal into the waste-paper bin by his chair.

Virginsky shuddered out his incredulity. 'But aren't the connections overwhelming? He admits to writing the letters. He went to Chermak High School. His name is in the Ballet's order book.'

'And he is conveniently mad, of course. Do not forget that.'

Virginsky frowned thoughtfully. 'What do you intend to do

now?'

Porfiry didn't answer. He looked down at the dead flies on his desk.

There was a knock at the door.

'Yes,' called Porfiry.

Lieutenant Salytov came in, bearing a disintegrating cardboard box. He carried it hurriedly over to Porfiry's desk where he let it drop. 'We found these in Rostanev's room. Letters. Hundreds of them.'

Porfiry picked several out at random. 'They are very much in the style of the letter he sent to Dr Meyer. The handwriting matches exactly.' Sorting through the letters in his hand, he brandished one eagerly. 'Ah! The letter to Gorshkov. It seems that, in typical civil service style, he made a copy of each letter before he sent it. I am confident that we will find copies of the letters sent to Meyer and Vakhramev in this box.' Porfiry read the letter out loud. '"To my dear friend Mr Gorshkov, how I feel for you. To lose a child is painful enough. But to have your pain mocked by a miserable skinflint who is not fit to touch the hem of your dead baby's blanket. I am referring to the ogre Ferfichkin, who slanders you around the city as a madman and a debtor. I myself heard him say that he would dig your dear Anastasya out of the earth and boil her bones to make a poultice just to teach you a lesson. That is the kind of man Ferfichkin is. And to think he lives, and grows fat on pies and sweetmeats, while your poor baby lies rotting in a flimsy cardboard coffin. Yours in sympathy, a well-wisher."' Porfiry blinked thoughtfully. 'You will notice he signs himself "A well-wisher" every time. There is another, more significant pattern to them, however.' He looked at Virginsky enquiringly.

'He is, in every case, providing the recipient with a motive for murder.'

Porfiry nodded grimly.

'Goading them to it,' added Salytov darkly.

'Perhaps,' said Porfiry.

'The letters certainly are designed to touch a raw nerve,' said Virginsky.

'He pushes them and pushes them. But they actually commit the murders,' continued Salytov. 'The men you let go,' he added pointedly.

'And how is the investigation into the possibility of a revolutionary cell at Ballet's the confectioner's progressing, Ilya Petrovich?' asked Porfiry in retaliation. 'I understand Nikodim Fomich was to assign some men to it. Have any significant leads come to light that I ought to be informed of?'

'Nothing significant, so far,' answered Salytov resentfully. 'Perhaps the boy and his associates are not involved in these murders, as I first thought. However, I remain convinced that they are criminal and possibly dangerous individuals. Time may yet prove me right.'

'Nikodim Fomich will not be able to extend that operation indefinitely.'

'The same may be said of your investigation,' countered Salytov.

Porfiry took refuge in lighting a cigarette.

'Isn't it true though, Porfiry Petrovich,' put in Virginsky brightly, 'that you have never really explained how the letter Vakhramev took to Setochkin's was removed from Setochkin's study? Only Vakhramev was in there with him. He would seem to be the most likely suspect.'

'I detect a conspiracy against me,' said Porfiry, his face screwed up into a smile that seemed almost to pain him.

Virginsky and Salytov were evidently startled to find themselves on the same side. Virginsky was the first to try to put some distance between them. 'Even if what we seem to be saying is true, the writer of these letters is still the murderer, is he not? The recipients, Dr Meyer, Vakhramev, Gorshkov, are merely his weapons.'

'Nonsense,' said Salytov, who appeared to be just as eager to differentiate his views from those of the younger man. 'If Meyer contaminated the chocolates, he committed murder -- cold-blooded, premeditated murder -- which he has sought to cover up with this story of a mysterious other who bumped into him outside the confectioner's.'

'And Rostanev says he is not a bumper-into,' said Porfiry, with amusement. 'Did you discover anything else of interest about him, Ilya Petrovich?'

Salytov consulted a small notebook. 'I talked to some of his neighbours about his habits, which were described as regular. It is generally agreed that he keeps himself to himself. He rarely goes out, except to go to work, and has never been known to have visitors.'

'Never?'

'He is without a single friend in St Petersburg, it seems,' said Porfiry to Virginsky's incredulous question. 'That is dangerous.'

'And he has no servant,' Salytov informed them.

'A man without friends, without even the company of a cook, will inevitably spend too much time with only himself for company. He will get to brooding. He will live in a world shaped only by his own dreams. A world in which he will perhaps see himself as all-powerful -- with the power to correct the present and avenge the past.' Porfiry pursed his lips conclusively.

'But he is such a funny little man,' protested Virginsky.

'Appearances can be deceptive,' said Porfiry. 'I wonder, however, how it is possible for him to hold himself so completely aloof from all his neighbours. I can well enough imagine the kind of overcrowded dwelling he resides in. On Gorokhovaya Street, I have no doubt.'

'Gorokhovaya, 97,' confirmed Salytov.

'I expect he has little more than a cupboard under the stairs, or perhaps just the corner of some kitchen. It is when you have such a general promiscuity of lives that the instinct for isolation becomes greatest. But the opportunity is lacking.'

'He has a room to himself,' said Salytov. 'With a bed in it. There is not much space for anything else, I grant you. He keeps all his possessions in boxes under the bed. My God, you should see the number of quills we found. He is at the end of the corridor and the one room next to his is vacant. So I dare say he has all the solitude he desires.'

Porfiry looked at Salytov without speaking for several moments. 'That is good work, Ilya Petrovich,' he said at last, stubbing out his cigarette. 'Now, shall we see if our guests have arrived?'

*

Behind his wire-framed spectacles, Dr Martin Meyer's eyes flickered and latched on to Porfiry with a tensioned eagerness that became immediately abashed. His face was fuller than Porfiry remembered it and there was a ruddiness to his complexion that had not been there before. He rose hesitantly from his chair in the waiting area outside Porfiry's chambers.

'Dr Meyer,' said Porfiry, taking the proffered hand. 'You look .

. . well.' It seemed an inappropriate thing to say, as if there was something shameful in the man's evident good health. But it was the truth.

'I . . . I have been to hell and back,' said Meyer, glancing down then straightaway meeting Porfiry's gaze again. 'But I have found a way through.'

'Good.'

'The Lord came to me in my darkest hour. I sank so low, I was ready to take my own life. I had nothing left to live for, or so I thought. I was poised on the edge of the precipice. And then I heard the words of the Psalm calling me back.'

Porfiry smiled but said nothing.

'I know that Raisa and Grigory are in a better place.' The eagerness that had been noticeable in his eyes now seemed closer to fervour. 'Even the Lord Jesus did not eschew the company of prostitutes and sinners. Did he not allow His feet to be anointed by Mary Magdalene?'

'You have forgiven her? In your heart?'

'I had nothing to forgive her for.'

'If only it hadn't required such a terrible upheaval to bring you to this realisation.'

'There is nothing that you can say that I haven't already thought a thousand times over. It is I who needed her forgiveness. But it is too late for that now. Still, I console myself that we will meet again in that better place.'

'You have become a true believer, I see. And I took you for a thoroughgoing man of science, an atheist.'

'I was, and look at the good it did me.'

'Porfiry Petrovich.' Porfiry recognised the voice, clipped with the impatience of command, before he turned to face Prokuror Liputin. Next to him, hanging back a little, Ruslan Vladimirovich Vakhramev pulled at his lips contemplatively and avoided meeting anyone's eye. A change had taken place in him too. His face was just as florid as before, but whereas once this had seemed to be the effect of bluster, there was now a raw quality to the skin, as if shame had worked upon it like a corrosive agent. His silver whiskers, formerly perfectly groomed, had been allowed to go to seed, as it were, and hung limp and lacklustre. His glance had grown more complex, and was meek as well as evasive. In the space of days, he had aged immeasurably.

'Good day, Your Excellency,' said Porfiry. 'And Ruslan Vladimirovich, thank you for coming in.'

Vakhramev nodded minimally in acknowledgement. His eyes darted towards Porfiry, then away, scattering his gaze wildly about.

'As I understand from the officer you sent to arrest him, he had little if any choice in the matter,' said Liputin.

'It was not an arrest; it was a request. I have need of Ruslan Vladimirovich's assistance. I do not intend to detain you any longer than is necessary. We are just waiting for -- ah! And here she is!'

Lara Olsufevna held herself with her accustomed upright bearing as she swept into the bureau, leaving the young *politseisky* who had brought her trailing. She viewed the men around her with deep suspicion through the pince-nez that saddled her imperious nose.

Porfiry bowed deeply to her; her narrowed gaze made it clear that this cut no ice. 'Greetings to you, Lara Olsufevna,' he ventured. Her lips trembled and pursed, perhaps indicating the softening of her distrust. 'It is my belief that the three people here,' continued Porfiry, 'Dr Meyer, Ruslan Vladimirovich, and Lara Olsufevna, have each met, at various times, the individual responsible for the deaths of Raisa and Grigory Meyer, Colonel Setochkin and Yemelyan Antonovich Ferfichkin. Dr Meyer bumped into him outside Ballet's the confectioner's. Ruslan Vladimirovich enjoyed the pleasure of this man's company at a certain farewell celebration in an establishment on Sadovaya Street many years ago.' Understanding the allusion, Dr Meyer glared at Vakhramev, who looked down, his face flooding with colour. Meyer continued to look at the other man, his expression becoming agitated rather than fierce. A great emotional turmoil seemed to be raging within him. 'And this lady, Lara Olsufevna, spoke to him at the funeral of a child. I am talking about the Uninvited One. We might also call him Nikolai Nobody. But who exactly is he?'

Porfiry looked up and nodded a signal to Virginsky who was standing on the other side of the crowded police bureau. Virginsky opened a door and Lieutenant Salytov pushed in Rostanev, still plucking and tightening the points of his beard. Salytov propelled him roughly forward. Rostanev smirked and began to walk directly towards Porfiry.

Meyer, Vakhramev and Lara Olsufevna followed the investigator's eye-line.

'If any of you now see the man in question, please do not hesitate to point him out to me.'

They watched Rostanev approach but no one said a word. A final push from Salytov sent the little civil servant buffeting into Dr Meyer. Meyer looked down at him in bemusement and then peered over his head, to continue his search for the suspect.

'No no no! It was not him,' said Lara Olsufevna scowling in disapproval at Rostanev. 'The personage I spoke to was taller than this individual -- and a gentleman, of course.'

'Can you be sure it is not the same man?' asked Porfiry.

'I think I would have remembered meeting such an ill-favoured brute as this.'

'Ruslan Vladimirovich?' Profiry turned to Vakhramev.

'It was a long time ago,' said Vakhramev quietly. 'But this face, once seen, would never be forgotten. And I have to confess that I have never seen it before in my life.'

'He is not the one,' confirmed Dr Meyer.

'Thank you all so very much,' said Porfiry calmly. 'You have been a great help. You may go now.'

With an air of bewilderment, the group of three witnesses broke up. Vakhramev glanced at Liputin uncertainly, but reassured by the other man's nod moved hesitantly away. Liputin encouraged him further with a dismissive sweep of his hand. The *prokuror* himself did not move. Lara Olsufevna drew herself up stiffly, conveying a sense of insulted dignity. This provoked an even deeper bow from Porfiry.

'Gorshkov,' she said. 'Gorshkov killed Ferfichkin.'

With that, she turned and swept from the bureau, as if summoning an invisible retinue behind her.

Meyer seemed reluctant to leave. His gaze latched on to Porfiry. 'If I may help in any other way . . .'

'I will let you know.'

Meyer nodded as if he had expected this answer. After a moment, he began, 'That other man . . .'

'Ruslan Vladimirovich?'

'Yes.' Meyer shot Porfiry an exposed and suffering look. 'He knew Raisa before. In the days when . . .' Meyer broke off and rubbed the joint of a forefinger against his cheekbone.

Porfiry gave a wincing smile and nodded.

'Did he sleep with her, do you know?'

'I do not believe so.'

'It doesn't matter. Someone like him did. Many men like him, in all probability. Let him stand for them all. At any rate, he is a respectable gentleman now. No doubt he has put all that behind him.'

'It would seem so.'

'He has a wife and family?'

'Yes. A daughter.'

'A daughter?' Dr Meyer nodded as he considered this. 'I hope he loves his daughter. I hope he loves her enough to forgive her whatever she may do or become. Let him not cast her out.'

The doctor bowed slightly. He gave Porfiry a final imploring look before walking with diffident step towards the door.

'You too, Axenty Ivanovich,' said Porfiry to Rostanev. 'And let this be a lesson to you. No more letters.'

Rostanev's chuckle warbled brassily in his throat.

'Don't forget to pick up your things from Alexander Grigorevich on the way out. Though I think we will hold on to the knife.'

Rostanev's leer twitched into place. He dipped his head but didn't move, until a shove and an 'Away!' from Salytov sent him over to Zamyotov's counter.

'So, Porfiry Petrovich,' said Prokuror Liputin. 'Once again you have let everyone go and are left with nothing. Will you ever bring these cases to a conclusion, I wonder?'

'I hope so,' said Porfiry.

'I would expect a more definite reply at this stage of the investigation,' answered Liputin.

'I can't believe you let that madman go,' cut in Salytov. 'Surely there was something we could have charged him with? The letters, for instance. He admitted to the letters.'

'Of course, we could have put together a charge based on the malicious letters. However, in the meantime I have a murderer to catch.' Porfiry lit a cigarette and blew out smoke as Virginsky came over to join them. 'You know, I never really believed it was Rostanev.'

'You arrested him, didn't you?' said Virginsky.

'True, Pavel Pavlovich. But did it not strike you that there was something rather too convenient about the way we were led to him? All those coincidences? I mean to say, if Rostanev really did poison the chocolates, would he have been so foolish as to have his name entered in one of Ballet's order books?'

'I believe that is what I said at the time and you overruled my objection.'

'Of course. I wanted you to look through the books. It was good training for you in the more routine aspects of an investigator's job. Besides, you might have found something interesting.'

Virginsky was indignant. 'I found what you were looking for.'

'Exactly! And I am always suspicious when one finds what one is looking for.'

'And that is it?' said Salytov, equally as indignant as Virginsky.

'No, Ilya Petrovich, that most definitely is *not* it. Rostanev may not be the murderer, but I have a strong suspicion that he will lead us to him.' They watched Rostanev load his pockets with quills. 'And, incidentally, that is why I preferred not to charge him in connection with the letters.' Porfiry lit a cigarette. 'I have already arranged to have him watched, of course.'

Porfiry nodded to two men who were loitering near the entrance to the bureau, one grubby-faced in a tattered coat and top hat, the other dandyishly turned out in a light-coloured suit and with a moustache so large it made him seem top-heavy. As Rostanev left the bureau, the ragged man sauntered after him. A minute or two later, the smarter one followed.

Prokuror Liputin looked down at Porfiry with a half-sceptical, half-admiring gaze. 'Porfiry Petrovich, I am glad to hear that you have planned it out so thoroughly. If one did not know you so well, one could be forgiven for thinking that your approach was decidedly more haphazard -- improvisational even. I can see that it will not be long before you have your man.'

Porfiry held his smile as Liputin took his leave.

9: The diminished man

The following day, a sticky heat returned to St Petersburg. The humidity of the air mingled with the dust to create a cloying atmosphere; it sapped the energy just to breathe it.

Porfiry and Virginsky were walking north on the sunny side of Gorokhovaya Street. Momentarily blinded by the sunlight in the countless windows, Porfiry had a sense of the sky as an oppressive weight above his head. The sun's hostility seemed personal. The high, deep apartment buildings on both sides of the street seemed to lean over him, dark masses crowding in impatiently, each one containing a village-worth of souls and all their unknowable secrets.

They stopped outside a barber's, level with number 97 on the other side of the street.

'Ah,' said Porfiry. 'This would be a good place from which . . .' He squinted into the shop. 'I thought so!' The dandyish man from the bureau was sitting in the seat nearest the window. The barber bobbed and floated around him, his hands flicking out to snip and comb reverently at the seated man's plump moustache. It seemed that the barber's deference was directed wholly towards this magisterial and self-possessed specimen of facial hair, rather than its wearer. The man in the seat gave no indication of recognising Porfiry, except that his eye enlarged forbiddingly, as if this was an important business in which he could not be disturbed.

Porfiry turned away to watch the entrance to number 97. Every now and then, individuals, or groups of men, in civil service uniforms came out and headed off briskly in one direction or another, some with their lunches parcelled in brown paper under their elbows.

A few minutes later, they were joined by the freshly groomed police spy. He stroked his prized moustache jealously, completely in its thrall. Without looking at Porfiry, he gave his report: 'We followed him directly here yesterday. Akaky Akakevich took the first watch. I relieved him at midnight. I am expecting Akaky Akakevich at any moment to relieve me. The subject went straight inside yesterday and has not come out. The yardkeeper is watching the rear of the building for us. He has reported nothing.'

'I see.' Porfiry continued to watch the entrance opposite. The exodus of civil servants seemed to have tailed off. 'You have not seen him leave for his department then? He would come out by the front door for that, I think.'

'I have not seen him.' The man swayed unsteadily.

'Are you drunk?'

'No sir. I've been on my feet half the night. My legs have turned to jelly. I just went into the barber's for a bit of a sit-down.'

'Very well. As soon as Akaky Akakevich arrives you may go home.'

The man's head tipped forwards, under the weight of his gratitude.

*

According to their briefing from Salytov, Rostanev's room was on the fifth floor; that is to say, in the attic of the house.

'You will find, Pavel Pavlovich,' said Porfiry as they tramped the stairs, 'that as an investigating magistrate in St Petersburg one is always climbing one flight of stairs or another.' He paused, breathing heavily, to rest one hand on his knee as he stooped to look out of a low window. 'I wonder if Ilya Petrovich has this right. One would expect such a man to live underground.'

'Such a man?' said Virginsky.

'The solitary, brooding type. The modern kind of madman.'

'Perhaps he likes to look down on the city and its denizens?'

'You may have something there, Pavel Pavlovich.' Porfiry took out and lit a cigarette.

'You think that the murderer will have contacted Rostanev?' asked Virginsky.

'Certainly, it will be interesting to find out from Axenty Ivanovich if he has had any visitors overnight. That's my chief purpose in visiting him. It is not a social call. Of course, it is likely that Rostanev himself is unaware that the person in question is a murderer.' Porfiry drew deeply on his cigarette. His expression darkened. 'You know, Pavel Pavlovich, I am surprised and -- I confess -- more than a little concerned that he has not gone into the department this morning. I would have expected it. The department is his life.' Porfiry dropped the cigarette and ground it with his heel. He gave Virginsky an urgent look. 'We may be too late already.'

Porfiry took the steps two and three at a time. Virginsky was momentarily surprised by the older man's speed. He quickly recovered and gave chase.

As they reached the fifth-floor landing, Porfiry almost collided with a young man in civil service coat who was hurrying out, his bleary eyes fixed on the cap in his hands.

'Rostanev?' barked Porfiry, as he dodged the human obstacle.

The young civil servant gaped after him.

'Funny little man with a pronged beard? Last door on the left or right?'

'Right,' said the bewildered-looking young man.

They reached the end of the corridor. Porfiry gave Virginsky a significant look before pounding the door with the side of his fist. There was no answer. Porfiry knocked again and put his ear to the door.

'There's someone in there. I heard a sound.'

'What sound?'

'Not a good sound.'

Porfiry turned the handle of the door and found it locked.

'Axenty Ivanovich! Can you hear me? Open up now. It's Porfiry Petrovich. I wish to speak to you.'

He was answered by a long, croaking groan. There was a break, then a second groan sounded, higher and more urgent than the first, like a compressed force escaping. Finally, a low rumble faded gradually to nothing.

Porfiry rattled the door in the frame. 'I could send you downstairs to fetch the yardkeeper, or . . .' He looked down at the door handle regretfully. 'It is a pity we don't have Ilya Petrovich here with us. He has a way of getting through locked doors.'

Virginsky frowned resentfully. 'Stand back!' He puffed himself up and took a step back, possessing the corridor with his arms outstretched in readiness.

'My dear boy, what do you intend to do?' asked Porfiry, alarmed.

Before Virginsky could answer, they heard the hook lifted, followed by a protracted, gurgling moan. Virginsky lowered his arms slowly. The tendons in his neck flexed as a repulsive force twisted his head away from that sound.

The door opened outwards in Porfiry's hand. 'It is perhaps as well that you did not charge it,' said Porfiry dryly. But as the door reached its full extent, and they were able to see inside the room, all thought of drollery evaporated.

It was the blood they saw first. His hands were wet with it. And the sheets of the bed where he was lying were drenched in it, as was his nightshirt. The nightshirt was pulled up past his groin, revealing the ragged, red-glistening wound, a dark, incomprehensible void from which the blood was still pumping in rhythmic spurts. The blood was in his beard too, the tines of which had clearly been pulled and twisted by those sodden fingers.

His right hand, with which he had reached out to unlock the door, so small was his room, hung limp in the air. The left lay across his abdomen, weak and lifeless.

On the bed, next to him, pooled in blood, was a mess of something fleshy, a bundle of butchered tissue. Porfiry stared at it in horror, disbelieving, or rather not wanting to believe what he saw. But there could be no mistaking it: the tubular stub, wrinkled and retracted; and still attached to it, a loose, ravaged appendage sprawling open to reveal the compact globes of his testes, like secret eyes, peeping fearfully up at them.

A penknife, similar to the one that had been taken from him at the bureau, but with a blade that looked strangely, freshly, rusted, lay nearby.

Rostanev turned his face towards them, his eyes bulging, as though surprised by the absolutism of pain. Another creaking, rattling groan came from his throat. His legs stirred, the knees rising up slightly, and then falling apart, airing the gaping mutilation. The wound continued to haemorrhage copiously.

'My God,' said Virginsky.

'What happened here?' Porfiry asked the question in no real expectation of an answer, at least not from the diminished man upon the bed.

But a word came from him, a word that grew out of another visceral moan and faded into an empty gasp: 'Voices-s-s-s-s-s.' He closed his eyes on his pain.

A sharp spasm brought his legs together, the tension of which gripped his whole body. His hands contracted into fists and pummelled the mattress. His head shot back, mouth racked open. From it came a full-throated scream.

The moment the scream ended, his body relaxed. A profound change was visible in his face, a collapsed emptiness, his features rendered almost unrecognisable.

For an instant, Porfiry was overwhelmed by the horror of what he had just witnessed and by the grotesque aftermath of it displayed before him. This was all that there was in the world and all, even, that the world could promise. Every human hope and endeavour came to this. And even when this bleak sentiment faded, all that was left in its place was a reminder of every other scene of violence and destruction that he had been called upon to survey in his career.

It was this thought that caused him to remember Virginsky's presence.

The boy's face -- for in this moment Virginsky appeared to him as a lost and terrified boy -- was white. His head was shaking in a tremble of denial. His arms began to shake too, violently. Porfiry held him firmly by both forearms, feeling the vibrations of his distress pass into him.

'He's . . . d-d-d-dead.'

Porfiry nodded.

'This is bad,' said Virginsky. 'This is bad.' He repeated the phrase several more times, his eyes staring in wild distraction into Porfiry's.

'Yes,' said Porfiry calmly. 'But it will not always be as bad as this.'

'Who's done this to him?'

'I think he did it to himself.' Porfiry's voice sounded distant and weak, empty of everything apart from puzzlement.

'Why would he?'

Porfiry looked down at the wreckage of a man on the bed. He frowned, as if squeezing an emotion out through his brows. 'It's a renouncement. Is this not what members of the *skoptsy* sect do to themselves?'

'How can you?' cried Virginsky, accusingly.

Porfiry's frown thickened.

'Here you are, even now, thinking it over, puzzling it out, reducing it to a mystery to be solved. Can you not see?' Virginsky's face was appalled. 'The blood?'

'You have to learn to look beyond the blood,' said Porfiry, quietly. 'There will always be blood. If you cannot see beyond the blood, you will see nothing.'

'It's just an intellectual exercise to you, a game!'

'I cannot stop myself thinking. And I am not sure what purpose would be served if I did.'

'How can you be so cold?' said Virginsky.

'You are in shock,' answered Porfiry. 'You don't know what you're saying.' He released his hold on Virginsky's arms and took out his cigarette case. 'Here.'

Virginsky looked at the opened case with unexpected avidity. He grabbed a cigarette and took it shaking to his lips. Porfiry lit it for him, steadying the bobbing cigarette with one hand. Virginsky immediately began to cough. He held the cigarette away from his face, wincing out the smoke. He looked again at Rostanev. 'Are you sure he is dead? Should we not try to help him -- to a hospital?'

'He is dead,' said Porfiry. 'The severed artery has stopped pumping.' He lit a cigarette for himself.

A floorboard creaked in the next room. There were footsteps in the corridor. Porfiry shut the door on the faces of Rostanev's neighbours, catching inquisitiveness turn to horror in the closing sweep.

Virginsky attempted to smoke his cigarette once more. His face darkened to a hue that brought to mind the flesh of a pickled cucumber. Then he lurched forward and vomited, turning his face from Porfiry though he held on to him to stop himself falling over.

'It's all right,' said Porfiry. 'There is no shame in it. No shame in it at all.' It was out of tact that he avoided Virginsky's eye as he patted his shoulder gently.

Footsteps receded outside the room and everything was quiet. Porfiry listened to the air and smoke pass through his cigarette and the comforting crackle of burning tobacco.

10: Panic in Stolyarny Lane

It is strange, thought Porfiry in the *drozhki* back to Stolyarny Lane, *how such discoveries disrupt one's experience of time.*

How long they waited in Rostanev's room before the arrival of the yardkeeper, he could not have said. As long as it took to smoke a cigarette through was one answer. But on this occasion the cigarette in his hand had burnt with such exquisite, vegetal slowness that it had not been possible to conceive of its extinction. At the time, he had been conscious to a heightened degree of his presence in a moment of infinite elasticity and power. He looked back on it now with nostalgia and incredulity. And then it occurred to him that he was in another such moment now, and that what such upheavals as Rostanev's death brought about was a dislocation of every moment from its neighbour. Undoubtedly, it was the propinquity of death that caused the effect. Each moment's ending was like a tiny death in itself, an intimation, as well as a reminder, of mortality. Life became transformed into a series of segmented deaths.

Perhaps too the act of smoking, in which he was engaged now, contributed.

The lapping clatter of the horse's hooves imposed an alternative patterning of time and reminded Porfiry that, however much he might desire to, he could not postpone the headlong rush of the present away from itself. It was as if a spell had been broken. The flow of time returned, marked off now by the passing apartment buildings.

The *drozhki* came to a halt. They had reached their destination in no time at all. It seemed incumbent upon them to leap from the carriage as if propelled by the momentum of the tragedy.

Porfiry looked at Virginsky. The younger man gave every appearance of having recovered from his earlier slip. He drew himself up and breathed through his nostrils with eager, savage attack, as if to show he was ready for anything. His eyes flashed fiercely. Porfiry nodded grimly then looked up towards the block that housed the bureau.

*

'We must concentrate on the meaning of the act,' said Porfiry. It calmed him to be back in his chambers, positioned once again behind his desk. However chaotic and senseless events outside that room became, here was one place where he could order his thoughts and clarify his perception. He inhaled deeply from his cigarette; his eyelids fluttered half-closed. 'Rostanev excised his generative organs by his own hand. Perhaps it is a judgement on the act of generation itself? An expression of disgust at something he has fathered? Alternatively, we might imagine that he has found himself, a solitary man, to be tortured by his sexual drive, which he has no hope of requiting, except through self-administration or through visits to prostitutes -- a class of woman he despises. That brings us back to Raisa Meyer, does it not?'

'Perhaps it is simply the by-product of his madness,' said Virginsky, seated at his desk by the window. 'A random act, wholly without meaning.'

'Everything has meaning,' said Porfiry. 'This could be interpreted as an act of self-hate, or perhaps more accurately, a symbol of what we might call life-hate. We could even consider it to be an act of childish petulance directed against -- whom? women? or a particular woman? -- in return for what we may imagine to have been a lifetime of rejection. As if to say, "They will be sorry now!" Of course, we have already alluded to the *skoptsy* sect. With them, I believe, the removal of the genitalia is understood to be a spiritual act, a commitment to the spiritual life, chosen over a more worldly existence -- the life of the flesh we might say, which is utterly renounced.' Porfiry broke off to consider the swirls of smoke from his cigarette. 'He spoke of being defiled by women, I seem to remember.'

'But you are proceeding as if you believe Rostanev to be the murderer,' objected Virginsky.

'I have a strong sense that someone wants me to believe Rostanev the murderer. It would be convenient for this person were we now, with Rostanev dead, to consider these cases closed. If I want to get closer to this person, I must take a moment to follow the path he has laid out for me.'

'But now you're talking as if you believe this other person responsible for Rostanev's death. And yet I thought you were of the opinion that that came about as a result of self-mutilation? There is a contradiction, surely?' Virginsky seemed almost belligerent.

'My dear boy,' said Porfiry cheerfully, 'the two hypotheses you mention are not mutually exclusive. Yes, I am certain that Rostanev mutilated himself. Otherwise, I believe he would have named his assailant when he had the opportunity. And yet, instead, he struggled -- with his last breath, as it were -- to blame it on *voices.*' Porfiry whispered the last word with melodramatic emphasis.

'I confess that I am confused.' Virginsky's tone was pettish.

Porfiry smiled sympathetically. 'That's quite normal. One gets used to it. One must grope for the signposts in the mist.'

'But each of the signposts points in a different direction,' complained Virginsky.

'That's perhaps because someone has played a trick on us, and twisted them around. But who?' Porfiry drew from his cigarette. 'Nikolai Nobody -- that's who,' he murmured to himself.

'Porfiry Petrovich?' said Virginsky, sitting up so that Porfiry narrowed his eyes expectantly.

'Yes?'

'When we were in Rostanev's room, did you hear something in the next room?'

Porfiry nodded slowly. 'I believe I did.'

'And yet didn't Ilya Petrovich say that the room next to Rostanev's was vacant?'

'Nobody lives in it,' said Porfiry wonderingly. '*Nikolai* Nobody. Well done, Pavel Pavlovich. I think perhaps we should take a look at that vacant room.' Porfiry kept his cigarette at his lips as he drew deep from it. He showed no inclination to hurry.

'We let him go,' said Virginsky, with a dead tone.

He was answered by a deep boom that seemed to fill, and expand beyond, the confines of Porfiry's chambers. The windows rattled as it receded. It was not thunder. They had heard thunder only days ago. This was something different.

'An explosion,' said Porfiry, rising falteringly from his chair. 'And nearby.'

Virginsky was already on his feet, craning to look out of the window.

'Can you see anything?' asked Porfiry.

Virginsky shook his head. Porfiry crossed his chambers and

opened the door to the police bureau. Uniformed officers were rushing blindly in every direction, voices raised in panic. The faces of the men and women whose lives had brought them into the bureau at that particular moment were stricken with fear. Shocked into silence, they watched the disarray of the police in bewilderment.

Porfiry caught sight of Nikodim Fomich crossing the floor. They fell in together.

'It's very close, Porfiry Petrovich.'

'Yes.'

'I have a bad feeling about it.' Nikodim Fomich seemed about to say something more but shook his head. 'A very bad feeling indeed,' he added, as they exited the bureau.

'It feels like an attack,' said Porfiry. 'On us.'

'Yes.' Nikodim Fomich became tight-lipped as they descended the stairs.

Virginsky caught up with them as they reached the ground floor. 'What's happened? Does anyone know?'

He was not answered.

They stepped out into a sun-startled day and a pungent scent of burnt saltpetre.

'Black powder. Primitive,' said Porfiry and immediately regretted it. It wasn't clear that the others had heard him, however. Their gaze was transfixed. He had seen what they saw but it was almost as if by not referring to it, he sought to un-see it; more than that, to undo it; to remove from the record of things that had occurred the scattered ground of writhing, wailing bodies that Stolyarny Lane had become, the charred faces streaked with blood, some stretched with pain and some in awed repose, the frayed and flesh-stripped limbs, a burnt-meat smell. And in amongst the human bodies, there were the horses, flailing, thrashing, twisting their necks against the pain and the incomprehensible loss of footing, turning a blood-filled eye on the men who had brought them to this.

'These are our men,' said Nikodim Fomich, quietly. 'My men.' And indeed there were police caps strewn about like garlands. 'We need medical staff.'

'A surgeon has been sent for,' said a *politseisky* who was crouching uselessly over one of his wounded colleagues.

'A surgeon? We will need more than that. We will need doctors and medical support staff. We will need to get these men to a hospital. See to it, man.'

'Yes, sir.' The *politseisky* rose to his feet, clicked his heels and ran off.

A pistol was discharged as the first of the horses was shot. Porfiry caught the heavy, relinquishing fall of its head.

Nikodim Fomich was scanning the faces of the fallen men desperately.

'What is it?' said Porfiry.

Nikodim Fomich let out a stifled cry and rushed forwards. Porfiry followed the line of his trajectory. A reeling dizziness came over him. Fiery red hair matted with a darker red, a face accustomed to the colour of fury, now more furious than ever, eyes that often bulged, now almost bursting: Salytov lay unmoving on the ground. His mouth was open as if he was about to let rip with a torrent of abuse, but no sound came from it. His eyes stared straight up into the clear, unblooded sky.

Porfiry felt a heavy dread inside him, burdening his limbs and coarsening his muscles. It was hard to move against it.

A weighted roll of Salytov's eyes towards them released him.

'Give him air! Don't crowd him!' cried Nikodim Fomich, who was pressing in on Salytov. He crouched over him, surveying the mangled body with great emotion, revering it almost, unable to touch it, but covering it with his gaze, like a lover before his mistress's naked beauty for the first time, greedy for it, it seemed.

Salytov clenched his teeth. His head quivered with a tremendous effort.

'Don't try to move,' murmured Nikodim Fomich.

But Salytov lifted his head. 'Trap,' he got out, before his head fell back against the ground. Rust-smeared lids came down over his eyes.

Nikodim Fomich's gaze flinched away from him, as if he had been slapped. He curled a fist over his mouth.

'What is it?' demanded Porfiry.

Nikodim Fomich stood up and moved Porfiry away from Salytov. 'He came to me. Just before. He had a tip-off. Anonymous, of course. It purported to come from a member of the Ballet's revolutionary cell.'

'As far as we know, there is no Ballet's revolutionary cell,' protested Porfiry angrily.

'It was you!' Nikodim Fomich shouted in sudden indignation. 'You suggested he should continue his surveillance. What were your reasons for doing so if you did not believe in the cell? Was it one of your pranks, Porfiry Petrovich? Were you trying to make a fool of Salytov?'

'No, of course not. But I thought the surveillance had come to nothing.'

'It came to this!' Nikodim Fomich shook his head bitterly. 'The contact requested a meeting, promising information about a bomb-making factory. I authorised Salytov to go. With a contingent of men.' Nikodim Fomich looked over the carnage, away up Stolyarny Lane. 'They were waiting for him. Revenge, of course. For all the pressure he has been putting on their boy.'

'You do not know that,' said Porfiry.

'But it adds up, does it not, Porfiry Petrovich?' Nikodim Fomich's face was anguished.

'We must be very careful. It is not clear what has happened here, except that a number of men have been killed and some others very severely injured.'

'But you will now focus your investigation on the confectioner's?'

'It may be that that is precisely what someone wants me to do.'

Nikodim Fomich gave him a scathing glare.

'We will naturally talk to the boy from Ballet's, as well as his associates.' Porfiry looked down at Salytov. 'It will help if we are able to get any meaningful statements from the survivors here. Was anyone seen, I wonder?'

'That will come in due course. First we must see to their medical needs. In the meantime, would it not be wise to hasten to Ballet's to pick up the boy, if he is there, that is? It may be that he has already gone into hiding.'

'And if he is there, and has been there all day? If he denies any involvement, and has an alibi, and witnesses to corroborate it, what then?'

'*Talk to him!*' Nikodim Fomich yelled the command at Porfiry, as if he were giving a junior officer a severe dressing-down. He shook his head impatiently, then added, his voice only marginally softer: 'It cannot do any harm to talk to him, can it?'

*

The murmur of genteel conversation, teacups chinking, crises of decision over which pastry to choose; the starched, unsullied tablecloths, upon which the worst catastrophe that could be imagined was a spilled cup of hot chocolate: the whole confection was saturated in a cloying atmosphere of contentment that stirred a dangerous rage in Porfiry.

As he watched the self-satisfied clientele pick over their sweetmeats with a mannered fastidiousness, he felt revulsion grip him and a desire to overturn the tables. He imagined these people with their faces running in blood, their smart, fashionable clothes shredded over their twitching limbs. It was an after-effect of shock, a super-imposition of the scene he had come from, but he wondered if it were not also a visualised wish. He wanted to punish them, he realised. And yet they were blameless, at least in the matter of the bomb blast. He breathed in deeply and looked at Virginsky. The strain of the day showed in the rippling tension of the young man's face, which was white and drawn. Once again, he was puffing himself up and breathing heavily, battening on his emotional armour.

'Are you all right?' asked Porfiry quietly.

Virginsky's eyes flared antagonistically.

Porfiry winced in disappointment, bowed his head and approached the counter.

'Is Tolya here?' he asked.

A plump-faced man with a waxed moustache and very black hair treated Porfiry with haughty disregard. He directed a fawning smile towards a waiting customer, giving a precisely gauged bow. Porfiry noted with satisfaction that the elegant cut and superior tailoring of the fellow's frock coat came under considerable strain as he bowed.

'Monsieur,' Porfiry said, switching to French. 'Monsieur Ballet, is it? I have to tell you that I am an investigating magistrate, here on official business. I wish to speak to Anatoly Denisovich Masloboyev. He works here, does he not?'

The man continued to talk to the customer for a moment or two longer. When at last he turned to Porfiry, his eyes were lidded and his face looked as if he had just inhaled smelling salts. He too spoke in French. 'Will you people never be satisfied? This is a respectable establishment with connections at the imperial court. I, Ballet, have vouched for Tolya. I had thought that would be an end to the matter. I had been assured as much by a very high authority indeed.'

'Things have changed. Produce Tolya now and it will be better for him -- and you. If you cannot produce him I will have to assume that he was in some way involved in the atrocity perpetrated this morning on officers of the Haymarket District Police Bureau. If that is the case, you will find that your high-placed friends will have no hesitation in removing their protection, as well as their patronage -- if you persist in sheltering a wanted criminal, that is.'

'I know nothing of any atrocity. I . . . am sorry to hear of it. However, Tolya has been here all the time. Please believe me when I say he is a good boy, a hard worker. I have no complaints.'

'Let me speak to him.'

Ballet sucked in his cheeks and nodded to the stout female shop assistant who had followed their exchange apprehensively from the other end of the counter. At his signal, she disappeared through the door to the back of the shop. Ballet turned a sour face back to Porfiry.

'The officer against whom you made a complaint,' said Porfiry, blinking frantically at Ballet, 'was injured in the atrocity.'

The confectioner was startled. 'But that doesn't mean that Tolya did it.' He blanched under Porfiry's steady gaze. 'Or me! You surely do not suspect me?'

'Have you discussed Lieutenant Salytov's persecution of Tolya with anyone?'

'Well, yes. I have discussed it with many of my customers -- to universal outrage, may I say.'

'With whom in particular have you discussed it?'

'That is an impossible question to answer, monsieur.'

'Let me put it another way. Of all those you have discussed the matter with, is there any one person who seemed to you to take an inordinate interest in it? That is to say, a greater interest than most of the other people you discussed it with?'

Ballet angled his head as he looked at Porfiry with something that could have been amazement. 'Now that you come to mention it, there was one gentleman who asked very many questions.

Indeed, he came back . . . and asked more questions. I thought, perhaps, he was investigating the case, in some official capacity.'

'Did he give you his name?'

'I asked him for his name. He said people called him, in Russian, *Nikto. Nikolai Nikto.*'

'But *nikto* is not a name, monsieur. It simply means *nobody*.'

'Yes, that's what I thought, after he had gone. I thought it was a strange name. I thought perhaps he was a police spy. An officer of the Third Section. I never saw him again.'

'And had you ever seen him before? I mean, before he came here asking questions?'

'It's difficult to say. Possibly yes. He looked familiar. But then again, one sees a lot of people. Eventually everyone appears familiar.'

'I see.'

Tolya came through the door and hung back, watching the magistrate with a look of queasy trepidation. It was a moment before Porfiry recognised him, such was his preoccupation. He smiled reassuringly to the youth and switched to Russian: 'Ah, Tolya, there you are. There is nothing to be afraid of, if you tell the truth. Come forward; I wish to speak to you.' Tolya moved uncertainly along the counter, glancing at Ballet as though for approval or permission. 'There has been a very serious incident,' Porfiry continued. 'A bomb attack outside a police station on Stolyarny Lane. Do you know anything about it?'

The boy shook his head. There was fear in his eyes. His face was drained of colour, sickened.

'Your master tells me that you have been here all morning. Is that true?'

'Yes, sir.'

Porfiry smiled. 'Good. I'm glad to hear it.' Porfiry paused and looked at the boy as if considering him seriously for the first time. 'You've had a rough time of it recently, haven't you, Tolya?'

'I . . .' The boy's brows came together and he swallowed heavily.

'Lieutenant Salytov, the police officer with the red hair, he had been persecuting you, hadn't he?'

Tolya looked down. 'It wasn't fair,' he mumbled.

'That's exactly right. It wasn't fair.'

'I hadn't done anything. He just . . .'

'He just didn't like you, Tolya. It was as simple as that.' Porfiry paused, then added: 'It was unjust.'

Tolya flashed a questioning glance at Porfiry, torn between belief and distrust. 'He had no right,' he asserted, his belligerence fragile, almost false.

'It must have made you very angry, to be treated that way.'

'He broke my stilts.'

'But what could you do about it? He was an officer of the law. Who could you turn to?'

'I told Monsieur Ballet.'

'Of course. And did you discuss it with anyone else? With any of your associates?'

'What associates?'

'Come now, Tolya. Let us not play games. You have been very honest with me so far. That is good. The leaflets that were found in your room. They did not appear out of thin air. Who gave them to you?'

Tolya looked fearfully between Porfiry and Monsieur Ballet. 'A man.'

'Did he have a name, this man?'

'No. I mean, not really. He called himself . . .'

'Nikolai Nobody,' supplied Porfiry.

Tolya shrugged, seemingly unimpressed. Porfiry looked at him searchingly, forcing a nod of confirmation.

'He has planned this for a long time, and carefully,' murmured Porfiry. He turned sharply to Virginsky. 'Come, Pavel Pavlovich. I think the time has come to examine Mr Nobody's lodgings, don't you?'

11: The vacant rooms

As he took the key from the yardkeeper, a grizzled old soldier with a dour demeanour, a thought occurred to Porfiry: 'Why is it never let?'

The yardkeeper shrugged.

'But don't the owners want the rent from it?'

'You'll have to ask them.' After a long pause, he added: 'About that.'

'Don't worry, we will,' said Porfiry. The pronouncement seemed not to concern the veteran. 'Have you never seen anyone going into or coming out of the room? Surely you have been curious.'

The yardkeeper gave a deep, wheezy sigh. 'All sorts of people come and go here. I can't be expected to notice them all.'

Porfiry echoed the yardkeeper's sigh with one of his own. 'Very well. And we will also have the key to the room next to it, Rostanev's, if you please. I take it the room is still unlet?'

The yardkeeper nodded sharply. 'Not for long.' Again there was a break before he completed his thought: 'I shouldn't wonder.'

Porfiry took the key in two jerky moves, fixing the yardkeeper with a vindictive gaze.

*

Porfiry acknowledged, as he placed the key in the lock, a reluctance to confront the emptiness that lay beyond that door. He hesitated and even came close to suggesting that they should look in Rostanev's room first. It was the peculiar apprehension that comes on the threshold of attainment. The greater part of his dread was made up of the fear that they might, in fact, find nothing; that all his deductions, instincts and intimations, had been mistaken and had led him simply to an empty room. He recognised another fear too, wholly irrational but now more powerful: that of coming face-to-face with the man they were tracking down. He reasoned that there was no real possibility that the murderer would be inside the room now and yet he felt his sinister presence lying in wait for him. As he turned the key, he had the sense that he was about to unleash something formless and evil upon the world.

The first thing that he saw, upon opening the door, was a full length mirror in a wooden frame on a swivel stand. He moved towards it, noting the stifling heat and acrid chemical smell in the room. The mirror, awash with sunlight, reflected his image back to him, mockingly; the room presenting him with his own emptiness. Virginsky came into the frame, next to him, an eyebrow cocked wryly. The two men paused to consider their own reflections.

'What does this tell you, Pavel Pavlovich?'

'That he is vain?'

'Good. That is certainly one word for it. That he takes the trouble to furnish an otherwise empty room' -- Porfiry cast a glance around, confirming this designation -- 'with a mirror suggests a level of self-absorption that might justifiably be described as morbid. What else? There on the floor, for instance, what do you see?'

Virginsky directed a frown towards where Porfiry was pointing. 'Dust?'

'Describe it.'

'It is . . .' Virginsky crouched down to examine the dusty boards more closely. 'Black.'

Porfiry nodded encouragement.

'Like charcoal dust.'

'Indeed. Possibly it has come from the stove. Or possibly it is from the manufacture of black powder explosive. What else unusual do you notice, Pavel Pavlovich?'

Virginsky furrowed his brows further and scanned the room. 'Footprints. In the dust,' he asserted, more confident now.

'Yes. And?'

Virginsky's gaze latched on to a single gleaming strip in the grimy floor. 'One board has no dust on it at all and no footprints, either.'

'Suggesting?'

'Suggesting . . . suggesting it was not in place when the dust was deposited.'

Porfiry smiled and took out his cigarette case. He went so far as to place a cigarette in his mouth.

'Porfiry Petrovich, do you think it wise to light a cigarette in this room, given that it has likely served as a manufactory of explosive materiel?'

Porfiry replaced the cigarette hastily in its case. 'Quite so, dear boy. Now, as you are already down there, perhaps you would be good enough to see if the board in question is, as I suspect it might be . . .'

'Loose,' said Virginsky, lifting the board clear with an echoing clatter.

Porfiry crossed the room, his soles creaking in the dust, to look down on their discovery. Lying along the narrow uncovered space was a length of rubber hose, like a black snake feeding on the darkness below the boards. Virginsky lifted one end out and gently tugged it, to discover that the other end, out of sight beyond the extent of the exposed trench, was firmly attached to something. He looked at Porfiry quizzically and handed him the loose end as he continued to grub around in the floor space.

'There's an end of rope here too, tucked away. I can just reach it.' Virginsky eased his hand under the board.

Porfiry continued to puzzle over the pipe, though he kept a distracted eye on Virginsky too, especially when the young man produced, in the manner of a conjuror with his rabbit, the train of a rope ladder, the wooden rungs knocking against the open edge of the boards. Porfiry was torn between the two pieces of evidence. He laid down the pipe and turned his attention to the rope ladder. 'Here, look at this,' he said, showing Virginsky the frayed end beyond the knot that tied together the two sides of the ladder. Reddish brown flakes and particles were caught up in the fibres of the rope, marking a narrow band. 'What do you say that is?'

'Rust?'

'Yes. That's what it looks like to me too. We will take this back to the bureau. Now, what are we to make of this hose?'

Virginsky picked up the stiffly pliable pipe and ran his hands down its length as far as he could. He got on to his knees and peered into the hole, following its course into darkness. 'It seems to be going towards the room next door.'

Porfiry nodded.

'Rostanev's room,' said Virginsky, looking up at Porfiry. His voice was slightly breathless.

'Shall we see where it comes out?' Porfiry smiled and fluttered his eyelids, as if he had suggested a mildly diverting pastime.

*

The image of the room as they had last seen it superimposed itself on the negative stillness that met them now. The only residue of that grotesque tableau was the dark russet stain in the centre of the thin, comfortless mattress. The bed dominated the room, which seemed far smaller than its neighbour.

'Someone must be paying the rent for that room next door,' mused Porfiry. 'Why else would they allow it to remain empty? I dare say, however, that if we were to pursue the matter with the owners, our enquiries would lead to *Nobody*.'

'He must be a man of some standing,' ventured Virginsky. 'To be able to afford the rent on a vacant room, presumably in addition to his proper lodgings.'

'It may be that he has a private income as well as a salary. Even so, there are many nobles who manage to destitute themselves despite such double advantages. Perhaps he has found a way, uniquely in St Petersburg, to live so far within his means that he is able to meet the extra burden comfortably.'

The space beneath the bed was empty now, as all Rostanev's boxes of belongings, the quills, papers and jars of ink, had been removed to the police bureau. It was apparent that the deceased clerk had had little else to his name. The room resonated with a faintly metallic echo of despair, the tubular-constructed iron bedstead vibrating to their voices.

'The pipe was at the rear of the room. It would come out somewhere around there, I think,' said Porfiry pointing to the far corner of the room. 'Somewhat near that leg of the bed.'

Virginsky put a hand on the bed and gave it a testing push. It moved with a protesting wail and a slight tug of resistance. A curve of the black hose, which appeared to be rammed deep inside the end of the hollow leg, came snaking out of a knot hole in the floor. The bed settled unevenly, tipped up at one corner by the tough hose.

'What on earth?' cried Virginsky.

'The voices,' said Porfiry, startled by his own conclusion.

*

'Who? Who is he?' Back in his chambers, Porfiry lit a cigarette and stared wonderingly at Virginsky. 'We must have missed something, Pavel Pavlovich. I can feel him. I have the quite desperate sensation that I have encountered him. That I have stared him in the face and even spoken to him. That's how real he seems to me.'

There was a knock at the door. Zamyotov peered in. '*This* has come for you.' His tone was ironically excited; he waved a letter tantalisingly through the gap in the door. Porfiry nodded to Virginsky, who rose and snatched it from him. 'Temper!' chided Zamyotov, before disappearing.

'It's from the owners of Gorokhovaya 97, following our enquiry concerning the letting arrangements of the room next to Rostanev's.'

'Don't tell me -- Nikolai Nobody,' said Porfiry despondently.

'No. According to this, both rooms were let to Rostanev.'

'But that's impossible,' cried Porfiry. 'As well as insane. I mean, on his salary it's a miracle he could afford the rent on one room, let alone two. And if he did rent two, why would he choose to live in the smaller one? No, this is a screen.' Porfiry applied himself to smoking intently for several moments. 'Someone . . . paid his rent for him . . . and used the vacant room for his own purposes. Who would do such a thing?' Porfiry Petrovich took one final deep draw on his cigarette, so deep that he fell into a coughing fit. When at last it died down, his eyes running with tears, he was able to gasp: 'Pavel Pavlovich, give me that school list again.'

Virginsky crossed to Porfiry's desk with the paper. Porfiry scanned the names eagerly. 'We have him,' he said quietly, his voice hoarse from the recent paroxysm.

12: Philosophical ideas

'What is this concerning?'

Porfiry looked at the man who had just spoken -- a man of average height and nondescript appearance, possessing the kind of face, clean-shaven in the civil service style, that seemed instantly familiar and yet was difficult to remember, a kind of blankness -- and knew he had his murderer. He noted the control with which the other held his face, and therefore his emotions, in check. *He must be in turmoil beneath that blank mask*, thought Porfiry. He watched the corner of the man's mouth closely, waiting for it to pinch up in minuscule betrayal of what he must be feeling. But Collegiate Registrar Yefimov gave nothing away.

Behind Yefimov, the banks of copyists and clerks looked up, regarding Virginsky and Porfiry with evident trepidation. The jerry-built towers of files and papers had been reconstructed higher than ever. The men twitched protectively, bound to their stools by their duties, but desperate to throw themselves between the unwelcome visitors and their treasured documents. Only Yefimov seemed unconcerned at the magistrates' return.

'We wish to talk to you about Rostanev,' said Porfiry.

'Of course.' Yefimov bowed.

'His name came up in connection with a murder victim called Yemelyan Antonovich Ferfichkin.' Porfiry paused to study Yefimov's face at the mention of Ferfichkin's name. He noticed the man's eyes veer to the side and up, once, quickly. 'It was over a debt to do with the sewing of a fur collar on to an overcoat. He could afford the collar but not the cost of having it attached. Ironic, is it not?'

'A tragedy. It is such small, insignificant tragedies that make up the lives of men like Rostanev.'

'How could he afford the collar, I wonder?'

'I gave him an advance on his salary.'

'How very generous of you.'

'I know what it is like. I understand how important such a thing can be to a man.'

'A man who has been humiliated and insulted all his life?'

'To any man,' said Yefimov. 'But yes, particularly to the sort of man you describe, a man like Rostanev.'

'And you?'

'As I said, I understood what he was feeling. It was not just a question of a collar. The collar stood for something.'

'What did the collar stand for, I wonder?'

'Honour. Status.'

'Really? It was not just a collar then? Not just a collar to keep the wind from his neck?' Porfiry smiled. Yefimov did not. 'So the money was advanced?'

'Yes.'

'Was it ever repaid?'

'I am sure Axenty Ivanovich intended to repay the debt.'

'But didn't the department require that the money be repaid?'

'I advanced the money out of my own pocket.'

'You are a veritable benefactor. Of course, this placed Axenty Ivanovich in your debt.'

'It was not a question of that.'

Porfiry nodded absently, barely acknowledging Yefimov's comment. 'I wondered, the last time I met you, where we had met before. And now I remember. It was you, that time in the Haymarket District Police Bureau, it was you I encountered in the corridor. I asked you to stand aside and you would not. You demanded that I give way. I would not. There was nonsensical talk of honour then. Finally, you pretended to have an attack of vertigo and fell in a swoon against the wall. Do you remember what I said?'

'I do not remember the incident at all.'

'On the contrary, you remember every slight and insult that you have ever suffered. And you remember very well what I said, don't you?' As Porfiry said the words, he watched Yefimov's lips twitch as he shadowed them: '*It is always the same with you hypochondriacs.* Do you remember?'

'I do not.'

'But you were at the bureau that day. You came to investigate the noxious smell from the Ditch. I wonder, would I have been the next on your list?'

'I don't understand what you mean.'

'Of course you don't. However, humour me for a moment, if you would be so good. I have been trying to work out how you are connected to Ferfichkin, other than through Rostanev's fur collar. I'm sure it was you, anyhow, who recommended Ferfichkin's tailoring skills to your subordinate -- was it not? You don't have to answer that yet. It can wait. But something must have connected you directly to Ferfichkin. There had to be some reason why he was on your list. And then it came to me, the complaint Ferfichkin made against his former master. The nobleman who had his name expunged from the record. That was you, wasn't it?'

'This is *ridiculous*!'

'It is something we will be able to check. If Ferfichkin lived with you as your servant, he will have been listed at the same address as you at the Address Bureau. There is little point denying it, if it is true.'

'Very well. But it means nothing.'

'Oh, it means something. These things always mean something.'

'Besides, the whole thing was a joke.' A strange, high-pitched laugh came from Yefimov. His face for an instant distorted into the antithesis of the controlled mask it had presented until then: a leering gargoyle's features took him over. 'It was my idea. I *commanded* him to do it!'

'Indeed? I find that hard to believe. Besides, if it was a joke, it was one that wasted police time, and could have got you into a lot of trouble.'

'But the man was always tormenting me. You would never believe it! He was a torturer! He would never come when I called him. He behaved as though I was the servant and he the master. And when I happened to make a legitimate complaint about his behaviour, he became mortally offended. He accused me of slander, although there was only he and I there. How *ridiculous*, I think you'll agree. I believe he didn't really understand the law. So, as a joke, I made him go round to the police station and press charges against me. Of course, the police saw it was an absurd joke and sent him away with a flea in his ear.' Yefimov began to laugh again.

His laughter had the effect on Porfiry of cutlery scraped on a plate. 'Everything is a joke to you,' he said, in a dead, flat tone.

Yefimov shrugged and struggled to resume his former control.

'You have heard about Rostanev?' asked Porfiry.

'You arrested him. I have not heard a thing since then.'

'We released him without charge.'

'I see.' Yefimov gave every impression of being surprised by this. 'He has not presented himself at the department.'

'He is dead.' There was a stirring of the scribes behind Yefimov.

'I know nothing about it.' Yefimov was smiling as he said this.

'He died through loss of blood, caused by an act of self-mutilation.'

'Poor mad fellow.'

'Was he, do you know, an initiate of the *skoptsy* sect?'

'You will have to ask some of the others, some of those who knew him better than I did. I really cannot say.' Yefimov gestured towards towards the clerks, who had begun to put down their quills as the discussion held them.

'Who conducted the public health inspection of the apartment building opposite the Novo-Alexandrovsky Market on the nineteenth of June? It's on Izmailovsky Prospekt near Sadovaya Street.'

'I will have to consult the department diary.'

'Perhaps this will help to jog your memory. I am referring to Colonel Setochkin's building. The sanitation inspection in question took place on the day that Colonel Setochkin was murdered.'

'That really doesn't help, as I have no idea who Colonel Setochkin is.'

Porfiry raised both his eyebrows. 'I find that hard to believe. Of course, I can quite understand that Colonel Setochkin had little idea who you were -- you are after all a truly insignificant individual. If ever he came across you, he would surely have failed to notice you. You are the kind of man one looks straight through. Your face, I find, is not one that imposes itself upon the memory. Have you not found this to be the case?'

Yefimov did not reply.

'I take that as an affirmative. Yes, I look at you and I think: here is the eternally low-ranking civil servant, if not embittered by failure, then certainly inured to ineffectualness. A man no longer young, but who has not successfully passed beyond a certain moment in his youth, a moment before his dreams have soured, his ambitions become frustrated and his ideals smothered -- the moment, in other words, when he can believe himself still the commander of his own destiny. To hold on to that moment, despite a lifetime of clearly evidenced disappointment, requires a level of egotism and vanity that is almost admirable. And yet, my friend, you have to admit it: yours is the kind of face that is forgotten the instant you turn from it. In the past, when you were a young man wanting to make an impression on the world, no doubt this was deeply irksome to you. But now, given your recent activities, I am sure you have found it distinctly to your advantage.'

'I confess I have no idea to what you are referring.'

'You would disappoint me if you said that you did. However, let us agree that someone from this department carried out the inspections at Setochkin's building that day.'

'I really cannot agree that without checking.'

'There is no need to do that. Your eagerness to check the diary leads me to believe that there will be no record of the inspection. And yet there is the testimony of Setochkin's butler. He spoke of the visit of a public health inspector. Is it usual in such inspections for there to be a certain amount of going in and out of the apartments?'

'It may be necessary.'

'It must be inconvenient for the residents.'

'One endeavours to demonstrate a degree of consideration.'

'So you have carried out such inspections yourself?'

'On occasion.'

'You try to make yourself unobtrusive?'

'At this time of the year many apartments are vacated, those belonging to the better class of person at least. The inconvenience is minimised.'

'I can imagine. Most of the time, they do not know you are there. It would be possible for you to be admitted to an apartment and then forgotten about, especially if the tenant had become used to your comings and goings.'

Yefimov said nothing.

'You might, let us imagine, enter one apartment, go out on to the balcony -- this was a building with a certain number of balconies overlooking the courtyard -- and attach to a bar of the balcony a rope ladder that you had concealed about your person. Yes? So far at least it is theoretically possible? And so, when you have assured yourself that the yard is empty, you descend to the balcony below.

There you lie in wait until an opportunity presents itself. An opportunity to point the pistol that you had earlier purloined from this second apartment through a windowpane, also opened earlier, in order to fatally shoot the resident of that apartment. You could also reach your hand through the open pane to retrieve a letter that your victim had just placed on a desk by the window. That was a stroke of luck that you exploited to cast doubt on Vakhramev's story perhaps. To confuse the doltish police. Or simply you could not resist taking with you a small memento of your cleverness. Then it would be a simple matter for you to climb immediately back up the rope ladder, which you would pull up after you, and then go back into the first apartment. We will admit that it called for exceptional daring. Or perhaps, rather, it was simply that you were blinded to the danger by your arrogance -- by your own incredible belief in your superior intellect, which is in itself a limitation, a failure of the imagination. Did it not occur to you that you might have been seen? At any rate, you were lucky. But as you have said, many apartments are vacant at this time of year.'

'But why would I do it?'

'We will come to that in a moment. You were the one who bumped into Dr Meyer outside Ballet's, were you not? You substituted the chocolates he dropped with another box, which you had previously contaminated with poison. As an official of the Ministry of Public Health you would have access to aconite, as well as the medical understanding necessary. Were you trained as a doctor?'

'I did embark upon the study of medicine, although I did not complete the course.'

'A disappointment, no doubt, for you. One of many, I am sure. Are you aware that you killed Raisa's son Grigory as well as Raisa, your intended victim?'

'I have no idea what you are talking about.'

'You were the one at the brothel with Vakhramev, Golyadkin and Devushkin.'

'Those names mean nothing to me.'

'Come now, you were at school with Golyadkin, were you not? You will not deny that you attended the Chermak Private High School in Moscow? Your name is on the list of pupils, by the way. You were in Golyadkin's class.'

'I . . .' Yefimov did not deny it.

'Tell me, what happened between you and Raisa all those years ago? What did she do that was so terrible that you harboured your resentment, your vengeful longing, we might call it, for so long? You went to the brothel -- *uninvited*, what bitter pleasure it gave you to describe yourself in those terms. You saw yourself as better than the other men, no doubt, with whom you had already quarrelled. You had an appreciation of beauty to which they were blind. You had a soul. Were you overcome by some romantic notion -- a philosophical idea almost? You saw this girl, so young, so lost. You were young too, then. In a moment of romantic madness, you offered her a way out. Was that it? Or was it just a joke to you, all along? Anyhow, she came to you, to your apartment. We have the testimony of a former associate of hers that something like this happened, although the woman in question did not name you, of course. At any rate, Raisa saw you as you really are -- with Ferfichkin, your servant. The terrible, humiliating relationship you had with Ferfichkin -- the torturer. She saw how pathetic and squalid your life really was.'

'This has really gone on quite long enough. You have no right to come here and make these unfounded and quite obscene allegations.'

'She was just an inconvenience to you, then, wasn't she? A terrible mistake, an embarrassment -- and you had to be rid of her. What could be easier? She was a prostitute. So you offered her money -- and what? She threw it in your face? You could never forgive her for that. And you could never forgive Ferfichkin either, for witnessing the scene.'

Yefimov said nothing for a long time, but simply looked at Porfiry with an expression of studied disdain. However, Porfiry was not inclined to speak either. He had a sense that everything hung on the words that would come next from Yefimov; that the question of his guilt or innocence would be resolved in them. It was as he thought. 'But you have no proof,' said Yefimov at last. *The guilty always insist on proof*, thought Porfiry.

'The greatest and most compelling proof is your character.' Porfiry returned Yefimov's gaze steadily.

'You think you know my character!' Yefimov could not control his outrage.

'I believe so. You are a common enough type. Educated to a superfluous level, cynical to the point that you are capable of any cruelty, without feeling it to be such. Alienated, I might say, from yourself and your fellow men. At first sight you seem simply to be a minor official, a petty tsar, but there is more to it than that. You have nourished your resentments. They have festered underground over the years until they have burst forth as crimes. It is entirely in keeping with your personality, for instance, that you would adopt the name Nikolai Nobody, given to you contemptuously by your childhood enemies, from whom you could not tear yourself away. You wallow in that which you hate, and that which hates you. It is small wonder that you imagine yourself suffering from vertigo. Your hypochondria is the most clinching proof of all. You may deny it all, but it is all easy to prove. I have only to ask Vakhramev to look at you. And Dr Meyer will be able to confirm that you were the man who bumped into him outside Ballet's. You were also seen at the funeral of Gorshkov's child.'

Yefimov shook his head in mute denial.

'It is also in keeping with your character that you chose each method of murder carefully, matching it to the victim, and, I imagine, the insult that provoked each murder. Poison for Raisa, whose charms were tainted by her past as a prostitute. She had refused your gift of money, but you made her swallow the gift of death. And a needle for the tailor Ferfichkin, whose very existence tortured you for so long, like a thorn in your side. As for Setochkin, the military man, you chose the weapon of honour, the pistol. Did he perhaps dishonour you in some way?'

'Please be so good as to tell me,' said Yefimov. 'You are, after all, the man with all the answers.'

'I will tell you this. You arranged for two rooms to be rented in Rostanev's name. Did you pay the rent on both of them, I wonder? Or merely on the second room, the one which you kept vacant? You came and went, visiting your underling. Of course, you knew him from your schooldays too. He was the one creature in that dreadful place more miserable and misbegotten than you. The only one left for you to abuse. Is that what bound the two of you together? And is that why you found him a job at the department? Rostanev was no doubt flattered by the attention of a superior -- and one to whom he was in debt. At night, you would go into the empty room and speak down the rubber hose, which would transmit your voice to Rostanev's bed, where it would resonate, and he would hear it as the voices in his head, telling him what to do. It was in this vacant apartment that you created the bomb which was only today thrown at Lieutenant Salytov. By you, of course. Your position here at the department allows you to come and go more or less freely. The purpose of this attack was to throw suspicion away from you by incriminating the boy from Ballet's, whose case you had heard about by talking to the manager. And, of course, it was you who gave Tolya the radical pamphlets. All this was a secondary precaution in case your attempts to incriminate Rostanev failed. Rostanev, in whose name you bought the chocolates and whose death you engineered, as the final proof of his criminal madness.'

Yefimov smirked, involuntarily. It seemed to Porfiry that this part of the plan must have given him particular pleasure and satisfaction.

'Yes, you saw to that, putting the idea of self-mutilation into his head through the speaking tube. You merely took his ideas -- *If your hand offends you, cut it off!* -- and gave them back to him, twisted and exaggerated beyond recognition.' There was a murmur of disquiet from the clerks behind Yefimov. One or two of them rose from their stools. Porfiry continued: '*And* you made Rostanev send the letters. In fact, you made him send more than you needed him to, even putting yourself forward as a target for his malice. All this was merely a smokescreen for the ones that were truly necessary, by which I mean the ones to Meyer, Vakhramev and Gorshkov. You think that you have been wonderfully clever, but in fact you have been rather stupid, blinded by your overestimation of your intellect and abilities, which are really quite limited. Similarly, you underestimated your adversaries, the officers of the law who would pursue you. Your stupidity has manifested itself in a way that is typical of men of your sort. That is to say, in overelaboration. You constructed layers of incrimination, by which you hoped to confuse the hapless and, in your view, oafish police. And yet all you have succeeded in doing is revealing the patterns of your peculiarly Byzantine imagination. You hoped to conceal, but in fact you have revealed yourself, more patently than if you had carried a placard proclaiming your guilt.'

'But what of Setochkin?' shrieked Yefimov. 'Why did I kill Setochkin?'

'Do you wish to tell me?' answered Porfiry. 'Perhaps if you tell me, I will understand you better. I will appreciate your cleverness, after all. I have a feeling that your reason for killing Setochkin is sublime. It may even be exquisite, the evidence -- at last -- of a refined and superior sensibility. The proof, even, of your genius. A masterstroke. I will only fully understand you when I understand that. And isn't it important to you that I should understand you? That everyone should understand you? After all, you're not a madman, not like Rostanev, who could be manipulated by your superior will to do whatever you wanted him to.' Porfiry noticed more of the clerks get to their feet. They began to drift over, forming a wide arc behind Yefimov. Sullen, discontented glances passed along the line.

'I do not admit to any of this,' said Yefimov suddenly, his voice startled.

'You played him like a pipe organ. You pulled out his stops and he responded. But then again you believe that the great mass of humanity consists of such automatons, do you not? Only the select few, the super-beings, the men like you, are capable of original acts and thought, of true self-determination.'

'I am not the only one to hold such philosophical ideas. To think is not against the law, as far as I am aware.'

'Give me evidence of your superhumanity. Make me believe as I want to believe -- in you as more than an ordinary man, as a hero. Tell me why you killed Colonel Setochkin.'

'*Colonel* Setochkin! How diligent you are in giving the man his rank. Tell me, if you were walking down the street, Nevsky Prospekt, for example, and such a man, such a *colonel*, were coming in the opposite direction -- would you step aside? Or would you stand your ground, and insist that you were as much a man as he and every bit as entitled to walk on the pavement? Would you, in short, demand that he got out of your way? But what if he took no notice of you, what if he looked straight through you, what if he did not acknowledge your polite request -- not even your existence? In short, what if he brushed you aside as if you were no more than a fly? What if he shouldered you into the road, so that your clothes were mired with the splatter from a passing cart? And what if the worst of it was he hadn't even realised that he had done it! So insignificant were you in his eyes that he failed to see you as a man, or as an obstacle, as anything. What then? What would *you* do then?'

'Good God! Is that what this is about? A man has died because he would not get out of your way on the Nevsky Prospekt!'

'It is a question of honour. He failed to show me the respect that was due to me.'

'You will come with us now.'

'But I have confessed to nothing. And even if I had, I would get off. No jury would convict me. To have been so possessed by vengeance over such a trifle proves my insanity. Thank God and the Tsar for the new juries!'

Yefimov began to laugh. There was a strangled cry behind him. One of the clerks broke away from his companions, moving with great difficulty, as though running through soft sand. He held one hand out stiffly in front, clenched around a flicker of steel. This hand jerked forwards, into Yefimov's back, and came away empty. Yefimov's face lurched upwards, spasms of pain distorting it. And then he fell forwards, on to the floor. He lay twitching for several moments. Blood darkened the bottle-green frock coat of his civil service uniform around the projecting handle of a penknife.

The clerk backed away, awed by his own action. The phalanx of scribes closed around him. In a moment, he was lost to sight.

'Who was that man?' cried Porfiry, still clinging on to Yefimov. The fingers of one hand felt the dampness of the other man's blood. 'Surrender him now.'

The clerks stared back at him, blank-faced and silent. Before long, the memory of the assassin's face mingled with those of his colleagues.

'Which one of them was it, Pavel Pavlovich? Can you say?' The strain of his burden gave Porfiry's voice a desperate edge.

Virginsky shook his head, his face wide open with wonder. 'What about *him*?' He held a shaking finger towards Yefimov. Porfiry felt the civil servant writhe in his arms; his cheek brushed Yewfimov's grimace.

'I'll stay with him. You go and raise the alarm.'

Virginsky watched as Yefimov's groping hand closed its fingers around the handle of the penknife and pulled. The awkward yanking motion failed to bring the blade out cleanly. It pivoted the knife on its axis and churned the blade through the ruptured kidney. When the knife did come away, falling with a mocking clatter to the floor, the unstopped blood chased through the fabric of his coat.

'Quickly, Pavel Pavlovich! If there is to be any hope of saving him, you must go *now*!' It had not seemed possible, but the body in Porfiry's arms gew suddenly heavier.

But all Virginsky could do was cast a hesitating glance towards the knot of clerks. Something in their enlivened defiance held him.

*

They stood on the steps of the ministry, looking across Chernyshov Square, their thoughts clogged in the faltering traffic. A restive dray horse stamped and snorted between the shafts of an ambulance carriage, unable to proceed. It seemed to sense the urgency of the moment, perhaps scenting blood in the air. Its eye stood out with animal panic.

Porfiry looked down at his right hand and saw it stained with Yefimov's blood. He could not bring himself to light the cigarette between his lips.

'I am not cut out for this.'

Porfiry looked up sharply. 'Nonsense.'

'He may die because of me.' There seemed to be no great conviction to Virginsky's words.

Porfiry shrugged. 'You did not plunge the knife in.'

'I couldn't move!' It was as if Virginsky was pleading to be blamed.

'You're not the only one, it seems,' said Porfiry, frowning at the stationary ambulance. He added, more gently: 'Next time, you will move. You will be prepared.'

'There won't be a next time.'

'So what would you do instead? Go back to Riga with your father?' The sarcasm in Porfiry's voice was harsher than he intended.

Virginsky's response was quick with affront: 'There is work for me on the estate. I have ideas about more efficient methods of agricultural management. My father would be amenable, I'm sure.'

'You think you will escape the memory of what you have seen? Rostanev in his bed? It will go with you. It will haunt you and there will be nothing you can do about it. Something has been awoken in you, Pavel Pavlovich. You cannot leave it now. It will not leave you.'

'What are you talking about?'

Porfiry sighed heavily. He found he was clutching his cigarette case, which he offered to Virginsky. Virginsky declined. At last Porfiry lit his own cigarette. He gave Virginsky a long, assessing look. 'The appetite. There is only one way to appease it. And that is to give in to it. You will work here, not because it is a way for you to serve the Russian people, not because it will make you happy, or bring you honour, nor, indeed, for any reason that you can admit to. You will work here because you need to. We have spoilt you for anything else.'

'I cannot get the sight of that man out of my head.'

'Rostanev? You will see other things. Some may even be worse than that. I cannot promise you otherwise.' Porfiry emptied his lungs of smoke.

A slight smile played on his lips as he held Virginsky with his gaze. His nod released them.

They turned their backs guiltily on the ambulance, as its driver shouted at the three coaches blocking his way. They walked away from the frantic whinnying of his horse.

13: In the secret heart of the city

'For you.' The letter that Zamyotov handed him was battered and dusty, split along the folds. It was post-marked 'Terek'.

He felt a strange emptiness as he read the single line of the message.

'Bad news, Porfiry Petrovich?'

Porfiry could hear the insincerity of Zamyotov's smile without having to look up. His own words came out heavily: 'If only this had arrived two days ago. Rotanev would still be alive. As would Kheruvimov and Pestryakov. Indeed neither Ilya Petrovich nor any of our men would have been injured.'

'Good heavens. What on earth does it say?'

Porfiry handed the letter to Zamyotov.

'Ah, it is a reply to the telegram I sent to the Caucasus on your behalf. So it has come at last!' Zamyotov read the brief message out loud: '"Sir, the scoundrel you are referring to went by the name Yefimov. Your servant, Devushkin." Well, there you are, Porfiry Petrovich! Your case is solved. You should be pleased.'

*

Porfiry breathed in the cleansing scent of linseed oil. It came from the unmoving figure on the bed: he had to believe it was a man, given that it was a patient in the Obukhovsky Men's Hospital. However, the face was covered in bandages, holding in place the scented, liniment-soaked gauze. Through a slit in the bandages, Porfiry could see that the eyes were closed. The eyelids had a strangely naked appearance. It was a moment before Porfiry realised that the lashes were missing. There was another gap in the bandages for the mouth, and vents for nostrils.

The crisp white sheet folded over the man's chest seemed like an infinite weight pinning him down. His bandaged arms and hands lay stiffly on top of his covers.

'Ilya Petrovich?' Porfiry spoke gently, taking a seat next to the bed.

Salytov's eyes opened and sought Porfiry out. The slit of his mouth opened on to blackness, as he swallowed drily. 'Did you get the bastards?'

'It was not the boy from Ballet's who did this to you, Ilya

Petrovich, or any of his associates. The bomb was thrown by the civil servant Yefimov. It was not a revolutionary plot, merely a mask for his personal vendettas. It was intended to distract and confuse us.'

Salytov closed his eyes. 'Yefimov.' His mouth as he said the name appeared disembodied, giving its pronouncement a strangely oracular authority. It seemed that it was not Salytov speaking, but some unseen force, blind, yet all-knowing.

'He's dead . . . now,' said Porfiry, falteringly. 'He escaped justice in this life, but he will not in the next.'

'Your faith is touching, Porfiry Petrovich. I wish I shared it.' Salytov opened his eyes again. 'How did he die?'

'One of his subordinates killed him. In a fury of revenge, it seems, for the way Yefimov treated Rostanev. There are . . . complications surrounding the attack.'

'What complications?'

'The perpetrator is being protected by his colleagues. They will not give him up and we -- that is to say, Pavel Pavlovich and I -- cannot positively say which one of them it was. These civil servants tend to look alike, you know,' he added in an abashed aside.

'You witnessed it?'

'N-yes.'

The figure on the bed began to shake. The eyes gleamed with mirth. 'You witnessed the attack, but you cannot identify the attacker!'

'It happened very quickly and in great confusion. Yefimov did not die immediately. We had to... we had a responsibility to tend to him. It took some time to get help. He died on the way to hospital, it seems.'

Salytov's eyes became suddenly serious. 'How many of our men died in the blast?'

'Two. Kheruvimov and Pestryakov.'

'I led them into it.'

'You could not have known. And besides, the operation was approved by Nikodim Fomich.' After a moment Porfiry added: 'I too must bear some responsibility.'

Salytov did not answer. His eyes were closed again and he seemed to have drifted off into sleep.

*

Porfiry was in no hurry to get back to the bureau. He allowed himself to be led by the city, following an echoed shout, or the glimpse of something moving through an entry. He felt himself drawn into the secret heart of St Petersburg, passing through it by the chain of interlocking courtyards. He felt himself privileged. He found that he didn't mind the dust of construction, or the summer stench. He had been released from his hatred of his city. Every step took him away from one set of lives and towards another, lives overlooking lives, each one mingling with the next.

Occasionally he would emerge on to one of the city's broad thoroughfares, or the stone embankment of one of its waterways. He would follow that course for as long as the whim took him, until the enticement of another entrance beckoned.

He found himself, at last, on Nevsky Prospekt. It was late morning. The sun burned down from a clear sky. It seemed that, after being cloistered within a hidden city, he had now emerged into a public one. In some way, it seemed like he had rejoined his fellow citizens after a long, enforced separation. He welcomed his immersion in the cries of street vendors, the clatter of carriages, the snatches of conversation.

He stood in the middle of the pavement, forcing the streams of pedestrians coming in both directions to part around him. Now and then he was buffeted by a passing shoulder. His strange obduracy attracted puzzled backward glances and, from those who were coming straight at him, threatening glares. He was disdainfully ignored by cavalry officers and frowned upon by civil servants. Young ladies averted their gaze, something in their eyes suggesting a suspicion of madness. But Porfiry held his ground, the sole constant in the ceaseless cross-tides of unbound humanity. He let them flow away from him without regret.

He looked into faces, the healthy, the lean, the sallow, the consumptive, some beautiful, some haughty, faces distorted by suffering or set in determination, faces empty of everything apart from a simple enjoyment of the day's warmth; he searched these faces, recognising none, but feeling somehow that he knew them all. Was he also looking for some flicker of reciprocal recognition, some acknowledgement of how things stood between them?

At last he shook his head, as if trying to shake off his folly. A smile broke into his face as he turned his back on the vanity that had detained him.

It was time to get back to Stolyarny Lane.

Acknowledgements

I would like to thank Andrei Travinin for so generously showing me his city and his guidance over Russian names; Virginia Rounding for her adjudication on transliteration issues; Justin Zamora for help with Church Slavonic; and Yaroslav Tregubov of the St Petersburg Historical Society for the maps. Any mistakes I acknowledge as my own.

My greatest debt, of course, is to Fyodor Dostoevsky, in whose masterpiece *Crime and Punishment* the original Porfiry Petrovich made his appearance.

If you've enjoyed reading this book, please post a review on your favourite review site. I love hearing from readers, so if you'd like to get in touch, my email address is contact@rogermorris.co.uk or you can follow me on twitter, where I'm @rnmorris. You can find out about my other books on my website, www.rogermorris.co.uk.

child atypical
sewerage
Trial by jury
polite apologetic   Perjury
what / who makes a detective
Detective as Hero
Sewers